THE SHADOW ENFORCER

THE SHADOW ENFORCER SERIES: BOOK ONE

N. M. THORN

THE SHADOW ENFORCER

THE SHADOW ENFORCER SERIES BOOK 1

N.M. THORN

The Shadow Enforcer

By N.M. Thorn

Copyright © 2021 by N.M. Thorn. All rights reserved.

nmthornauthor@gmail.com

This is a work of fiction. Any resemblance to actual persons living or dead, businesses, events, or locales is purely coincidental. Reproduction in whole or part of this publication without express written consent is strictly prohibited.

Cover art design by www.originalbookcoverdesigns.com

Edited by Spirit Editorial

PROLOGUE

* * *

Thirty kilometers south of Kyiv, Kievan Rus.
August 6th, 996 A.D.

LIKE A SWARM OF LOCUSTS, PECHENEGS' horde invaded the land, killing people, burning towns and villages, leaving nothing but death and destruction in their wake. It wasn't the first time Pechenegs' tribes invaded Kievan Rus, but never had they been able to win a battle against the mighty Vladimir's army.

Never, until now...

Dark smoke curled over Dnepr, its dirty swirls obscuring the stars and the moon. The red flares of fires illuminated the horizon with their sinister glow, and the ancient river rolled blood-colored waves along its shores. Kievan Rus was burning, the smoldering flames devouring everything in their way like hungry beasts.

Just thirty kilometers south of Kyiv, a small group of Vladimir's warriors were fighting against the overwhelming forces of Pechenegs' horde. Pushed back to the side of the river, they stood no chance, and every man knew it. Yet they didn't lower their weapons and give in but stood their ground at the cost of their lives.

The Pechenegs' battle cry rose in the air, carried by the night breeze. The moans of the wounded and dying, the clang of metal on metal, the neighing of horses and screams of people turned into a raging storm of sounds, overwhelming in its ferocity. A sickening reek of blood and the stench of sweat and human excrement were overpowering as it was, but in combination with the acrid smell of smoke, it made the air nearly unbreathable.

The fear and desperation were almost palpable, and the expressions on people's faces reflected the hopelessness of the situation. Thrusting his sword forward, Dmitri ran it through the throat of the man attacking him. As he pulled the blade out, bright red blood spurted from the wound. He didn't wait and raised his sword again, parrying a giant battle ax of another foe.

From the corner of his eye, he caught sight of his younger brother fighting by his side. Despite the hopelessness of the situation, a soft smile was playing on his lips, and his blue eyes were lit up with wild excitement. Nikolai was fighting in his usual fast and aggressive manner, swinging his sword as if the word *exhaustion* didn't exist in his lexicon. He was drenched in sweat and blood from head to toe, and Dmitri could only hope that none of that blood was his.

The boy has no fear, he thought as he glanced at his little brother with affection shadowed by a never ceasing concern. Since their mother had passed away, Dmitri had taken on the role of a parent, taking care of his little brother, making sure they both survived long enough to see adulthood. Being too fast and too fearless for his own good, Nikolai didn't make it easy on him, always running toward danger as if he were invincible.

Noticing a Pecheneg approaching his brother from the other

side, Dmitri quickly changed his position, deflecting a powerful strike from the enemies' sword a second before it would've sliced Nikolai's shoulder. His younger brother flashed him a quick smile, but suddenly his eyes widened, and his lips parted, fear distorting his blood-splattered face.

"Dima," Nikolai roared, using his childhood nickname, raising his deep voice over the ruckus of the battle. He pointed with his sword to the left and then ran in the same direction without waiting for Dmitri to follow.

"Nikolai! Kolya!" shouted Dmitri warningly, his heart beating heavily in his throat. But when the young man didn't stop, Dmitri cursed colorfully and followed his brother, jumping over the dead bodies of his enemies as well as his comrades, deflecting attacks and destroying any Pecheneg that was unfortunate enough to get in his way.

Soon, he saw what had alerted his brother, planting the seeds of fear in his dauntless heart. On the opposite side of the battlefield, Prince Vladimir, blocked from all directions, was facing a group of Pechenegs. Outnumbered, he fought valiantly, crashing his sword down on his enemies from the height of his tall horse. One of the attackers threw a spear, and it flew through the air, piercing the horse's chest. Nikolai halted and cried out as if the weapon ran through his own heart. Ignoring everything else, he doubled his speed, making his way toward the Prince, fighting for his every step.

Time slowed down as the stallion neighed, rearing on its hind legs, and then started to fall. The Prince stayed in the saddle, his sword still in his hand. The horse collapsed, falling on top of Vladimir's leg. The Prince cried out in pain and struggled to free himself from the weight of the animal, but to no avail. There weren't many of Vladimir's warriors still standing, and once they saw their Prince fall, they halted for a brief moment and started to retreat, pushed back as their enemies doubled their efforts, motivated by their victory.

By the time the first Pecheneg approached the Prince of Kievan Rus, Nikolai's sword met his curved blade. Throwing the attacker back, the young man spun around, his chest rising and falling with ragged breaths.

Not as fast as his brother, when Dmitri reached them, they were surrounded by a large group of Pechenegs who were trying to get their hands on the Prince. Nikolai was fighting them tooth and nail, but Dmitri knew—it was only a matter of time before his brother would fall, and he couldn't allow that.

As anger fueled by fear spiked his adrenaline, he attacked silently and forcefully as he'd never fought before, quickly making his way to his brother. Just as he broke the tight circle of his adversaries, he saw his brother struggling to defend the Prince.

"Watch out!" Vladimir cried out as he was finally able to break free, but neither the Prince nor Dmitri was fast enough.

A curved blade pierced Nikolai's side, going through his armor and chainmail as if it were nothing more than paper. Like in a terrible nightmare, Dmitri watched his brother fall to his knee, his left hand clasping the horrid, bleeding gash on his side, dark blood spilling between his trembling fingers.

"Kolya! No!" A terrible howl filled with despair beyond any limits erupted from Dmitri's lips. He swung his sword, crashing it down onto anyone who tried to stop him without looking. The ground trembled beneath his feet, but he barely registered it.

"Dima, get Prince Vladimir out of here!" Nikolai yelled as Dmitri approached him. With visible effort, he got up to his feet, his sword in his hand. "I'll try to get you a few minutes..." He looked around, a feverish glimmer in his eyes.

"Nikolai, no..." Dmitri observed the battlefield. No more than ten of Vladimir's warriors still stood with the Prince, fighting forcefully to give Vladimir a chance for survival. "You're wounded. You will—"

Nikolai laughed, blood spilling from the corner of his mouth, coloring his white teeth a shade of scarlet. "Then I'll see you in Hell, *brat moi*."

"Brother mine..." exhaled Dmitri, echoing his brother's words. For a brief moment, he squeezed Nikolai in a tight embrace, his heart bleeding with despair. "If not here then in Nav, but I'll find you. I'll go to *Peklo* if I have to. May the mighty Perun give you strength."

Dmitry bent down and helped Vladimir to his feet, throwing his arm around his shoulders. Nikolai smiled and made the sign of the cross, blessing both his brother and his Prince.

"May God be with you," he said, his hand squeezing the grip of his sword. "Both of you." Without saying another word, Nikolai turned around and cut into the approaching forces of their adversaries.

Dmitry barely realized what he was doing as he started to fight his way toward the bridge. Vladimir was helping as much as he could, but all Dmitri could think about was his brother. As they reached the *Vasilevskiy* bridge, Dmitry looked around. The battle was over, and the Pechenegs were quickly closing the distance, heading toward them.

"Too late," whispered Vladimir, his eyes wide but not with fear. Regret reflected on his face as he glanced in the direction of the great city of Kyiv.

"No," growled Dmitri, pushing the Prince under the bridge. "My brother didn't give up his life to see you captured by these monsters. Go under the bridge and hide. I will hold them down."

"I'm indebted to you and your brother," said Vladimir, disappearing under the bridge. "I will never forget..."

Dmitri turned around and for a moment shorter than a heartbeat, he saw the lines of Pechenegs part. Even though he was far away, he could see his brother clearly. Nikolai lay on the ground, a tall man pinning him down with his arms. As the man leaned down, Nikolai didn't move and didn't react.

He's dead... The debilitating thought lingered in Dmitri's mind as he raised his sword to his shoulder, getting ready for his last fight.

Like a dark, disgusting wave, the enemies rushed toward him, their barking battle cries rising toward the sky. This was it. In his mind, he knew he wasn't going to walk away from this place alive, but he didn't care. Grief and fury the likes of which he'd never experienced before overwhelmed him. A powerful wave of heat rushed through him, originating in his feet, and a sharp pain throbbed behind his eyes, making them burn and water.

The earth trembled beneath him, and a deep fracture split the ground, separating him from his enemies. He looked over his shoulder, wishing with all his heart that there were more bushes and tall grass to conceal the area beneath the bridge. Just as he thought this, the earth shook again, and limber branches and roots broke through the ground.

In front of his eyes, they grew taller and thicker, reaching high and spreading wide. A curtain of green leaves and sharp thorns covered the newly developed shrubbery until the entire area under the bridge was completely veiled.

He laughed mirthlessly, not recognizing his voice in this terrifying, hollow sound. But as he turned around, a spear whistled through the air, piercing his heart. His fingers unlocked, and he dropped his sword. For a split second, he just stood there, his hand grasping at the spear protruding from his chest. As he collapsed to his knees, he felt absolutely nothing—no pain, no fear, no regret. It was over... He was done... No more fighting, struggling, suffering...

"Nikolai," he whispered, his eyes searching the battlefield soaked with blood and covered with dead bodies. For a moment, he thought he saw his brother lying sprawled on the ground, but he couldn't be sure. "I'll find you... no matter where you are... brother mine..."

The world spun around him as he fell, hitting the ground with his back. As the darkness wrapped its arms around him, welcoming him into its deadly embrace, he exhaled for the last time and let go.

CHAPTER 1

~ DAMIAN BLAKE ~

The rain hadn't stopped since he left Florida, following him all the way through the not-so-sunshiny state, then into Louisiana and finally into Texas. Now, it was beating heavily on the metal roof of a tiny diner located somewhere off highway ten just outside Houston. The steady drumming of the falling water mixed in with the monotonous chatter of a few visitors created a peaceful, relaxed atmosphere. The heavy odor of fried food and beer wafted through the room, adding to the already slow and sleepy surroundings.

Damian propped his elbows on the counter, rested his face in his hands and closed his eyes, enjoying the warmth and dryness. A gentle touch to his shoulder made him flinch and pull back. A young waitress stood in front of him, behind the bar. She smiled and placed a plate with a piece of apple pie before him.

"I didn't order—," he started, but she shook her head, interrupting him.

"Thank you," she said with a slight Texan drawl, moving the plate closer to him. She tucked a loose strand of her dark hair behind her ear and added, "For repairing that darn garbage disposal, that is. It's been broken for ages, making all those funny noises, but John is all hat, no cattle." She threw a defiant glance at a young man in a cook's attire, but he just smiled sheepishly and raised his arms.

"No problem, ma'am." Damian lowered his eyes, his hand rising to readjust his hair automatically. He raked his fingers through the longer strands on the front, covering the left side of his face where an old scar cut through his eyebrow down to the middle of his cheek and then shrugged. "But I'll take the pie. Thank you." He thought a moment and added, "And the bill, please."

She moved her hand to her pocket but then changed her mind. "On the house." She waved her hand dismissively as she walked away, disappearing behind the door into the kitchen.

Damian smirked, thinking about asking her for directions to the nearest motel but then changed his mind. It was only five in the evening, and he hoped to hitch a ride to the next town before nightfall. He finished his pie quickly and got up, reaching into his pocket for his wallet. He pulled out a twenty-dollar bill and placed it under his empty plate.

Glancing outside the window, Damian cursed under his breath at the never-ending rain and grabbed his backpack from the floor. As he approached the door, he pulled out his half-broken umbrella from the side pocket of his backpack and was ready to walk out when the waitress called him. He turned around and looked at her with curiosity, not sure what to expect. Standing a foot away, she gazed up at him, craning her neck as if he were the Empire State Building. Then she cleared her throat and smiled shyly.

"Forgive me for asking... but how far are you traveling, sir?" she asked, fidgeting with a large black umbrella in her hand.

"Phoenix," he replied, wondering what this was all about.

"On foot?" The arches of her dark brows rose slightly.

"I hope not." He chuckled. "That would be an awfully long trip."

She nodded, and a shy smile graced her pleasantly round face again. "Well, anyway," she continued, offering him the umbrella. "I saw you arriving here on foot, and with this nasty weather, I thought you could use a better one. Yours is good for nothing."

"Thank you, ma'am," he said, inclining his head slightly. He took the umbrella and threw his in the garbage can.

She smiled one more time and waved goodbye before heading back into the kitchen.

* * *

DAMIAN WALKED out of the parking lot, taking a street leading back toward highway ten. The rain almost stopped, but the net of small droplets hung in the air, amplifying the cool freshness of the evening air. Since the sky was overcast by low, gray clouds, he didn't doubt that the reprieve was temporary and hoped to find a ride before the next wave of a downpour would start.

The small street was empty, and for a while, he kept walking in complete silence, deep in thought. So, when he heard the sound of a horn, he flinched and spun around. A twelve-foot rental truck passed him and came to a stop a few yards ahead of him, pulling slightly to the side of the road. The passenger door opened, and an unfamiliar man in his sixties with a thick mop of graying hair stuck his head out and waved to him.

"Hey, son!" he yelled, his voice deep and raspy. "I heard you're looking for a ride to Phoenix?"

Damian froze for a moment, but as realization dawned on him, his lips quirked up at the corners, and he sped up toward the truck, switching to a light jog. The man gestured for him to get in and scooted back to the driver's seat. Damian threw his umbrella and his backpack on the floor of the truck, climbed inside and shut the door with a loud bang.

The man pulled the vehicle back on the empty road and cast him a sideway glance, a smile crossing his lips.

"Big fellow, aren't yah," he muttered, his open-hearted smile growing wider, and since Damian didn't reply, he added, "How tall are you, kid?"

Damian shrugged, feeling tiredness settling in his muscles. "Six-four."

The man nodded appreciatively and offered his hand. "I'm Sam. Well, Simeon Vetrov. But everyone calls me Sam."

Slightly turning in Sam's direction, Damian shook his hand. "Damian Blake. Thanks for the ride, sir."

"It's nothing." Sam waved his hand dismissively. "For some reason, Sophie took a fancy to you. She told me you were *walking*"—he stressed the word 'walking' and shook his head, twinkles of amusement dancing in his steel-gray eyes—"to Phoenix, and since I was traveling in the same direction, she asked me to give you a ride."

"Sophie?" Damian asked but put two and two together before Sam could answer and added, "She's very kind."

"Yeah, that she is. I've been traveling this road for a few years now, and every time, I make a point to stop at her diner. The best apple pie in the entire state." Sam leaned forward, reaching for a cigarette pack in the small tray between the seats, but then changed his mind and grunted, placing his hand back on the steering wheel. "I'm going to Blue Creek, Arizona to visit my daughter. It's not far from Phoenix. You can take a bus from there to wherever it is you're going. I think if we drive through the night, by tomorrow evening, we should be in Blue Creek."

"Perfect. Thank you," Damian mumbled, folding his arms on his lap as a wave of weakness spread through him.

He closed his eyes, his eyelids getting too heavy to keep them open. It had been a few days since he left Florida, and the trip had been nothing but trouble from day one, starting with the raw weather and finishing with a few unwanted encounters.

"Get some sleep, son. I'll wake you up when I stop to get gas and grab something to eat."

Damian heard Sam's voice and nodded faintly. He was asleep before he could reply, and when Sam shook him awake a few hours later, he found the truck parked at one of the gas pumps at a gas station that looked like it had been built during the time of the Great Depression.

Following his traveling companion, Damian opened the door and walked outside. As soon as his feet touched the steady ground, a powerful wave of energy surged through him, and he stretched his shoulders and arms, enjoying his quickly returning strength. He took a deep breath, relishing the freshness of the evening air and the absence of rain.

"Feeling better?" muttered Sam without taking his eyes off the questionably looking credit card machine embedded into the prehistoric gas pump, doubt written all over his face. "Use your credit card at your own peril." He scratched the back of his head and turned to Damian, a lopsided smirk curving his lips. "I guess I better pay inside." He waved toward a building at the other end of the plaza.

The building was designed in the old western style with a few large wagon wheels decorating the entrance. A sign stating "The Eternity House and Grill" hung above the saloon-style double door, squeaking slightly with each gust of wind. The windows were lit with a dim, yellow light that resembled flickering candlelight, and a few vehicles and bikes were parked on the parking lot in front of it.

Damian gave the building a quick once-over and stilled as shivers ran down his spine, setting his mind on high alert. He caught up with Sam and held him back, grabbing his arm.

"Have you ever been to this place before?" he asked, realizing how strained his voice sounded.

Sam halted, giving him a puzzled stare. "No, have you?" he replied with a half-shrug. "Why? It looks like any of those tiny mom-and-pop joints by the main highway."

"No, I haven't been here before," replied Damian, frowning. "Why don't you let me take care of the gas. That is the least I can do to repay your kindness."

Sam tilted his head and then slapped him on the shoulder slightly. "Listen, son. If you are traveling from God knows where to Arizona by hitchhiking your ride, obviously, you're short on cash. So, it's okay. You don't owe me anything, and you don't have to pay for anything. It's all good." He winked at him, his kindhearted smile bringing forth the net of wrinkles around his eyes.

As Sam opened the door, a small brass bell rang, its melodious sound seeming too loud for Damian's stretched nerves. He walked inside first and halted by the entrance, quickly observing the area, taking in even the smallest details. The lobby of the restaurant wasn't large, and since it was stuffed to the brim with shelves full of merchandise, it appeared even smaller than it was. Despite it being a restaurant, the air was cold, and the only smell present was the barely noticeable odor of dust.

A low counter was located by the wall on the left next to the entrance into the seating area, and a young woman dressed in a black T-shirt with the restaurant's logo on it sat behind it, flipping the pages of a magazine lazily. Even though she looked absolutely normal, unmistakable vampiric energy permeated the air around her. Damian exhaled with a quiet groan of aggravation and stopped shielding his magical energy.

Slowly, she lifted her head, threw the magazine on the counter and got up, a welcoming smile stretching her lips. But as soon as her eyes moved from Sam to Damian, her smile disappeared. Her lips parted a little, forming the letter 'O', and a faint red glow lit up her eyes for a heartbeat, disappearing almost immediately.

Dammit, that's what I thought. Damian seized Sam's elbow, and Sam glanced at him, his eyebrows rising in shock.

"Sam, I need you to go back to the truck," Damian said, speaking urgently, his eyes never leaving the woman standing behind the counter. "Don't argue with me. Go back to your truck and lock the doors. Keep it running. I'll be back soon."

"Damian, what in the world—"

"Go," hissed Damian as he opened the entrance door and pushed him out.

The bell rang again. Damian winced, wishing to rip the bell off the wall. Instead, he headed toward the woman. Leaning forward a little, she braced her fists against the countertop, and a carnivorous sneer stretched her lips, exposing her long, sharp fangs.

"Would yah look at that?" she purred, the well-manicured nails of her small hands elongating, turning into sharp claws. "A meal on wheels. Supersized, too."

"I've heard supersizing meals is bad for your health." Damian chuckled frostily. "Trust me, you're trying to bite off a lot more than you can chew, vamp."

The vampire hissed and hopped atop the counter, crouching there like a predator ready to pounce. Damian stilled, gathering his magic in his hands as he watched the vampire leap off the counter toward him, aiming to sink her fangs into his jugular.

Before she reached him, he took a tiny step back, and two long daggers shining with the silvery light of his magic materialized in his hands. With speed rivaling that of a vamp, he moved his arms in a cross-motion, cutting the vampire's head clear off her shoulders. For a moment, he stood, staring down as her body disintegrated into a pile of ash. Then he turned on his heels and headed toward the entrance into the seating area.

"One down…" he muttered under his breath, crossing the

threshold with the bloodied daggers in his hands.

The seating area was a large, single room with a tall ceiling and windows covered with thick wooden shutters. Tables were spread evenly throughout the floor, and a group of men sat around a large table, discussing something in hushed tones. They weren't eating, but each of them had a glass filled with dark red liquid in their hands. The heavy, metallic odor of blood hung in the air, leaving no questions about the contents of their drinks.

As soon as Damian walked inside, they turned around and got up slowly. Their eyes lit up with a sinister red glow, and their lips pulled back in feral snarls.

Only six of them. No big deal. Damian turned his hands with the daggers slightly forward to expose the shiny blades and said with a frosty smirk, "Yeah, I know. Meal on wheels. Supersized."

"Aw, look what the cat dragged in," one of them grumbled, sarcasm dripping out of his every pore. "A wizard who decided to play a hunter. How refreshing." His scarlet eyes slid down to the daggers in Damian's hands, and he jerked his thumb at them. "Where did you buy those? Local flee market?"

"Wanna check them out closer?" Damian raised his left hand, taking a step forward.

The vampire hissed and was suddenly gone. He didn't disappear or teleport, but he was moving with such speed that he became nothing more than a blur. Expecting it, Damian stepped aside and swung his arm, meeting the approaching monster with a deadly strike of his dagger. The blade cut through the vampire's neck like it was nothing but a piece of paper but didn't take his head off completely.

The vamp fell to the floor, clutching his throat with his hands, dark blood gushing between his hooked fingers. The scarlet glow slowly vanished from his eyes as he stared at Damian in shock.

There were only a few known ways to kill a vampire—

decapitation, a wooden stake through the heart, and fire. Silver through their hearts was also effective, and in general, any contact with silver made them weaker. However, garlic, crosses and sunlight—all these were just urban legends the vampires spread around to deceive humans who didn't know any better.

Damian didn't wait for the vampire to recover and thrust his dagger through the monster's chest.

"*Illucious*," he whispered, and the blade ignited with a brilliant white light, turning the large vampire into a pile of ashes in a heartbeat.

The rest of the vampires stared at the blazing daggers in his hands with shock.

"The Light of Creation," offered Damian calmly. "Anyone else care to try?"

The vampires howled, anger making their glowing eyes brighter, their hands turning into claws. They charged him all at once, knocking the tables over as they approached at full speed. He spun around, the daggers in his hands cutting through the air with a soft whistle. A moment later, all five vampires lay on the floor in heaps of ashes.

"I hate vamps..." Damian straightened and took a deep breath, lowering his arms. But he had no time to relax as, all of a sudden, the presence of vampiric energy in the room tripled. He sharpened his vision, staring into the dark hallway leading toward the kitchen. He didn't see them moving. He sensed their ominous presence with his every cell. Soundless and deadly like any nocturnal predators, they weren't in a rush. Hiding in the shadows, they were observing him, making an effort to conceal their presence and intentions for as long as possible.

Even though Damian couldn't say how many vampires were quietly creeping up at him, he knew there were enough of them to make it dangerous. He threw a quick glance over his shoulder and noticed that the door into the lobby was closed and most likely locked.

He hissed a quick spell and touched his belt. The daggers disappeared and were replaced by a long whip that looked almost like a stockwhip. It was made out of a flexible metal-like material, and three sharp, silver blades with long silver chains were attached to the end of it. Hoping that the whip would help him keep the mass of monsters at a distance for a while, he assumed a fighting stance, ready to spring into action. The vampires growled and charged him, coming from the shady hallway like an ominous avalanche. There were so many of them, he had no time to count.

Damian took a step back, giving himself a bit more space, and his whip split the air with a soft hiss. The silver blades cut into the vampires' bodies, slicing and dicing them. Infused with the energy of his magic, the whip left behind piles of steaming ash. The screams of anger and curses in different languages filled the air. Despite his efforts, the circle of enemies grew tighter around him, pushing him toward the wall and away from the exit.

So far, the whip was doing its job, but he knew it was a matter of time before at least one of them would manage to slice him with their claws or sink their teeth into his body, weakening him. Besides, the constant use of his magic was taking a toll on him, too, draining his energy and physical strength.

As his back finally hit the wall, Damian swung his whip one more time, destroying a few more of his attackers. But the vampires kept coming, replacing the fallen, and in such close combat, his whip became obsolete. He cursed quietly, dropped the whip, and his daggers materialized in his hands again.

He growled and took a defensive position, ready to fight. But as his blades went up with the blinding white light, the entrance door exploded inward with a loud bang, showering all of them with splinters of wood.

The vampires gasped, and for a moment, they shifted their

attention away from Damian. He didn't care to find out what it was and used the opportunity to regroup. Fighting his way through, he attacked the vampires with all he had. Another loud bang of a gunshot bounced through the room. And then one more.

As Damian cut through the monsters, he saw Sam standing on the threshold, a shotgun in his hands. To his shock, every shot of his weapon reached a target, leaving a pile of ash at the old man's feet as he slowly progressed forward. A few minutes later, the vampires were gone—most of them dead, but a few of them retreated before either Damian or Sam could get to them.

Damian glanced at Sam in shock, his chest rising and falling with heavy breaths. The old man looked angry but not shocked, so Damian had no doubt he wasn't new to the World of Magic.

"How can you kill a vampire with a shotgun?" he asked, lowering his arms as the daggers vanished from his hands.

"Argentum NO_3," growled Sam, struggling to equalize his breathing. "Silver Nitrate and a big enough caliber bullet can vanquish any monster."

Damian nodded and lowered to one knee, moving his hand through a thick layer of ash as he tried to find his whip. He found it almost right away and raised his head, ready to get up. To his shock, he found Sam's shotgun trained on his face.

"Sam, wait—," started Damian. He dropped his whip and raised his hands in a peaceful gesture.

"Stay where you are, kid, and don't move if you know what's good for you," muttered Sam, placing the hot barrel against Damian's forehead.

"Sam, listen—"

"You're not human. What kind of monster are you?" the old man demanded, his eyes sparkling with anger, sweat running down his face.

CHAPTER 2

~ DAMIAN BLAKE ~

Damian shook his head, suppressing the bitter resentment rising within him like a tidal wave. "Lower your weapon, Sam," he said quietly, attempting to get up, but Sam pressed the barrel of his shotgun tighter to his forehead, forcing his head back.

"Stay down, kid," he growled, his unwavering gaze burning with anger. "Trust me. I won't hesitate to pull this trigger should you make a wrong move. You won't be the first monster I sent six feet under."

"Monster I am not—"

"*Human* you are not!" shouted Sam. "Your eyes are glowing friggin' orange!" A few drops of sweat slid down his forehead, making their way over his gray eyebrows into his eyes, but he didn't even blink.

"I'm just..." Damian's voice faded, and he bit his lip, throwing his hands up. "I'm a Child of Earth. I swear I'm not evil."

"Aren't we all children of Earth?" Sam narrowed his eyes, a dry chuckle escaping his tightly pressed lips.

"Something tells me you know what that means." In one fluid move, Damian grabbed the shotgun, ripping it out of Sam's hands effortlessly, and then rose to his feet, towering at least half a foot over him. The older man staggered back, and for a brief moment, his eyes widened. But he quickly got his emotions under control, glaring at Damian without so much as a shadow of fear.

Damian sighed and returned his weapon to him. Then he bent down and picked up his whip. As soon as he touched it, it vanished from his hands and wrapped around his waist, turning into his belt. "We should get going, Sam. Some vamps escaped, and they might come back with reinforcements at any moment."

"Are you an Elemental of Earth?" asked Sam, his tensed shoulders relaxing a little as his fingers wrapped tighter around the shotgun. He gave him a demonstrative once-over and smirked sarcastically. "You sure don't look like a dwarf to me."

"I'm not an Elemental," grumbled Damian, heading toward the exit door. "There is only one Elemental of each element, and the Elemental of Earth resides outside of this realm as far as I know. I'm just a wizard who can wield the elemental energy of Earth."

Damian stopped by the counter and leaned forward, taking a pot with a wilted, half-dead orchid in it. He touched the plant, channeling some of his energy through it. Like in a time-lapse video, the thick green leaves sprung up to life, a long stem sprouted from under the dirt, and within a heartbeat, beautiful white flowers opened up, turning their tender petals toward him.

Sam touched a fresh green leaf and smirked. "I'm sure you'd make the world's greatest gardener, son, but something tells me you're not a landscape architect." His eyes slid up and down Damian's massive frame, and his smirk brightened up.

"No, sir. I'm not." A tiny smile touched Damian's lips, the orange glow slowly leaving his eyes as he got his elemental power under control.

They walked out of the restaurant, heading toward the

truck. Sam unlocked the vehicle and put his shotgun inside a duffel bag, throwing it to the floor between the seats. Damian climbed in and settled in the passenger seat, closing his eyes for a brief moment. As the truck pulled out of the gas station and onto the evening street, Sam threw a glance at him.

"I think now I'm starting to understand why you didn't take a flight to Arizona," he murmured, switching his attention to the dark road. "The lack of money has nothing to do with it."

"Planes are not an option for me. Being so high above the ground weakens me. And cars..." Damian shuddered. "I don't own one, and I don't wish to change that. I travel from town to town, hitchhiking my way when I have to."

Sam nodded. "Got to be hard living like this nowadays?"

Damian shrugged indifferently, staring out the side window, hoping that Sam would stop his interrogation. He didn't like talking. Even more so, he didn't like talking about himself. Over the years, he got used to solitude, and the company of others—mundane or supernatural—felt like a burden to him. Needless to say, being in the confines of the metal box humans called a vehicle didn't help his mood. Feeling drained after the fight with the vampires, all he wanted was a few minutes of silence and privacy.

"So, how old are you, Damian?"

Sam's voice cut through his train of thoughts, and he winced, turning back to his travel companion.

"Thirty-five," he replied, suppressing the desire to jump out of the truck and lie down flat on the side of the road.

"Thirty-five plus how many centuries?"

"Let's leave it at thirty-five, sir," he said peacefully, stifling a sigh.

"Fine, fine." Sam raised his hands, but then quickly lowered them to the steering wheel. "You don't look a day over a hundred, anyway. And that extra piece of décor..." He moved his finger across the left side of his face. "Don't tell me you slipped in the shower."

Damian threw a reproachful glance at him, his fingers raking through his hair of their own accord. "A shower is a dangerous place, you know?" he growled without hiding his annoyance. "I think they should stop including them in modern architectural plans."

"Okay, okay, relax," muttered Sam, sounding amused. "I got the point—you don't want to talk."

"What gave you that idea?" murmured Damian. He leaned back in his seat and closed his eyes.

One minute later.

"Just one more question and that's it."

Dammit!

Damian threw a scorching gaze at him.

"What's in Phoenix? Family? Friends? A lover?" asked Sam, ignoring Damian's grunt of displeasure.

"Clean slate," replied Damian. "I have no one."

"A man like you doesn't have a love life?" Sam turned to him, his eyebrows rising, but then lifted his hand with two fingers extended and added. "No more questions. Scout's honor. But I do have a proposition for you, though."

For a moment, Damian considered his options, but since hearing Sam out would mean at least temporary silence after —*hopefully*—he made a split-moment decision and flicked his wrist, motioning for Sam to continue. "Listening."

Sam sighed, suddenly serious. "I told you I was going to visit my daughter in Blue Creek." Damian nodded. "Well, there is a little more to the story."

Looking troubled, Sam scratched the back of his head, and his hand reached for the cigarette pack. He picked it up, ready to grab a cigarette, but then threw it back and exhaled, pressing his lips into a tight, straight line. Damian observed his moves with curiosity, noticing that the pack was still almost full, only one cigarette missing, but didn't ask about it.

"My daughter's husband passed away recently. Three months ago, to be precise. Not long before his death, he had started reconstruction of his family estate. Now that he's gone, the construction stopped, and my daughter is not in the right state of mind to do anything except..." Sam's voice wavered, and he glanced at Damian, sorrow shadowing his features. "Anyway, if you're not set on Phoenix, I wondered if you would mind sticking around Blue Creek for a while. It's a nice little town, you know. The nature is beautiful, and the folks are friendly. I own a small hardware store there and offer handyman services. Since you know how to fix a garbage disposal, I assume you don't shy away from hard physical labor and don't mind getting your hands dirty. I could give you a job and a place to stay. What do you say?"

Damian frowned, staring at Sam, thousands of thoughts crowding his mind. "Sam," he said calmly. "I don't mind staying in Blue Creek to help you with the construction, but I must ask you—and please be honest with me."

"What do you want to know?"

"You're a hunter, aren't you?" asked Damian, turning slightly to face him.

Sam smirked, rolling his eyes. "Yes, Mr. Obvious. A retired one. So what?"

"Once a hunter always a hunter," objected Damian dryly. "There is no such thing as a retired hunter. There are only active hunters and dead ones. If you are touched by the World of Magic, there is no way back, and you know it."

"Yes, so what?"

"Is there anything I need to know?" Damian continued, ignoring the light layer of sarcasm in Sam's voice. "Do you want me there as a handyman or as a man who can hold his own against the supernatural?"

Sam sighed and stared straight forward, his hands squeezing the steering wheel so tight his knuckles turned white. For a while, he remained silent, and Damian didn't insist on the answers, giving him a moment to think.

"Both?" he said at length without taking his eyes off the midnight road, and there was no assurance in his voice. Then he slammed his hand on the wheel and shook his head. "To be honest, kid, I have no idea. I've lived in Blue Creek for years. My daughter was born there, and I swear, I'd never seen anything remotely close to the supernatural. Not even a random ghost." He fell silent again, a pensive expression suffusing his features. "It's just a gut feeling, you know?" He pressed his hand over his chest, making a circular motion. "Maybe I'm totally wrong, but I could use your help with the shop and the construction, anyway. So what do you say?"

"I'll go with you, but I have two conditions."

"Which are..."

"I value my privacy. So, you can help me find an apartment to rent or a motel, but I live on my own," said Damian firmly. "And you leave my past in the past. No more questions."

"Deal," Sam agreed, offering him his hand.

"You got yourself a supernatural handyman," said Damian, squeezing his hand in a tight handshake.

CHAPTER 3

~ DAMIAN BLAKE ~

Blue Creek was a tiny town in the middle of the Sonoran Desert just outside Phoenix. The sign on the border stated, "*Welcome to Blue Creek, Arizona, population twenty-four thousand*", but some joker—no doubt a future guest of the local correctional system—had crossed out three zeros with white paint, leaving only the number twenty-four.

Following the bumpy two-lane road for another ten miles—rising, falling and curving among the tall Saguaro cacti and other spiky representatives of the desert flora—the truck finally rolled into the town. The place had been built in the mid-eighteen-hundreds by some adventurous but not very bright gold miners. Impacted hard by the second wave of the Spanish influenza pandemic, the mines closed in late 1918. Since there was no evidence that any gold had ever been found in this area, it was a miracle the place survived without turning into one of the famous Arizona Ghost towns.

However, the locals, proud of their history, restored some buildings to their original glory. Now, downtown looked like something from a Western movie, including an old church, small shops, a saloon-looking restaurant and even a brothel, which wasn't active, of course, and was used as a tourist attraction.

By the time Sam drove the truck through downtown toward the other end of town, it was late evening. The deep-ultramarine sky was spangled with millions of bright stars, and the air was fresh with that particular cool crispness of a late evening in the desert. He parked in front of a small, two-story hotel with a flickering neon sign stating, "*Night Owl Inn*" and pointed at it.

"This hotel is about a five-minute walk from my daughter's house and about fifteen minutes from my shop," he said, waving back toward downtown. Reaching into his pocket, he brought up his wallet and pulled out a credit card, offering it to Damian. "Here you go. You can pay for a month ahead and get yourself something to eat. There are a few diners and fast-food joints in the area." He shrugged with his kindhearted smile. "The town is small. Almost everything is within walking distance."

Damian smiled uncomfortably but didn't take the card, shoving his hands into his pockets. "Thank you, sir. I have money."

Sam gave him a look full of doubt but put the credit card away. "As you wish, son. Get some rest tonight, though. God knows you look like you need it. I'll pick you up tomorrow at seven in the morning so we can get started."

DAMIAN GRABBED his backpack and umbrella and walked toward the motel door while taking in every detail of the building and the surrounding areas. It looked like it had seen better days, its paint peeling in places, and a thin web of tiny fractures ran from the main entrance all the way to the red roof. He pulled the door open and walked inside.

The small lobby was dimly illuminated by a table light standing on the counter. A young woman, no older than sixteen, sat behind the counter with a focused expression on her round, freckled face. Her eyes were glued to the cellphone she held in her hands, and large headphones wrapped tightly around her head.

Damian approached the counter, and when she didn't react, he rapped his knuckles on the scratched wooden counter. "I need a room, please."

Without taking her eyes off the screen of her phone, she mumbled, "I have two rooms available on the second floor." She reached into a drawer with her left hand and shuffled through the contents without looking.

Sometimes, I hate the power of Earth... Damian sighed. "I'm sorry, ma'am, but do you have anything on the ground level?"

"I don't think so." She put away her phone and finally looked up at him, taking her headphones off. "We have a group of—" As she met his eyes, she cut herself off and froze, staring with her mouth open. Then she turned toward the back door and yelled, "Mom! We have a visitor here who needs a room on the first floor."

An older woman walked into the room almost immediately, wiping her hands on a small towel. She glanced at Damian, her deep brown eyes alight with interest, but quickly looked away, staring at the computer screen over her daughter's shoulder.

"I have two rooms on the second floor," she confirmed, shaking her head. "We have a big group of tourists who pre-registered almost every room on the first floor." She typed in something, and a winning smile lit up her face. "It's your lucky day, sir. I found one for you. It was reserved for someone else, but I know this person won't mind taking a room on the second floor." She straightened up and asked, "How many nights?"

"Let's start with one week," he replied. "But I may need to extend my stay."

"Sounds good." She reached into the drawer and pulled out a

key with a red plastic disk attached to it, placing it next to the computer. "Your ID, please."

Damian reached for his wallet and produced his driver's license. As he passed it to the woman, she glanced at him with a renewed interest. Typing quickly, she entered all the information.

"That would be four hundred fifty-five dollars," she announced, picking up the key from the counter.

He paid for his stay, and the woman offered him the key. "Room One-thirteen A," she said, pointing to the exit door. "Through this door and all the way to the left. It'll be the corner room on this side of the building."

Thanking the woman and her daughter, Damian walked out of the lobby and headed toward the other end of the hotel. He found the room easily and put a do-not-disturb sign on the door handle before walking in. Inside, the room was a little bit bigger than he expected it to be. A large, queen-size bed took most of the real estate, but there was still enough space left for a bedstand and a table with a small TV on it.

He threw his backpack and the umbrella on the floor by the bed and approached the window. Sliding the heavy curtains open, he was pleasantly surprised to find that the window wasn't sealed. He turned the lock and pushed the window open, enjoying the freshness of the night air barging into the room. He loved sleeping under the open sky with the earth beneath his back, energizing him and recharging his magic. Nowadays, more often than not, it wasn't an option, so sleeping with the window open was his best choice.

Damian walked into the washroom and quickly undressed, wincing as his every muscle responded with soreness. Fighting a few vampires had never been a problem for him. However, it was a first for him to get into a confrontation with such a large group of undead, and he couldn't help but wonder why so many of them had gathered in a tiny hole-in-the-wall restaurant.

Where was the King of Texas, anyway, and did he even know about it?

Most of the vampires, lycanthropes, demons and other common supernatural beings were regulated by the Demonic rulers of the state where they resided. The Demonic Kings and Queens preferred to lie low, keeping the supernatural world away from humans. Exposing the World of Magic to mundanes was considered one of the greatest offenses, and none of the supernatural sovereigns wanted to deal with the consequences.

However, there were always rogue groups of vampires or packs of werewolves who didn't care about staying within the boundaries of the law, hunting and killing like they used to from the time of creation. This is where the human hunters came into play. There weren't enough of them to take care of all the supernatural violence occurrences, and they operated outside of human law, which presented a serious problem for them, making their job so much harder and more dangerous.

I've never seen so many rogue vamps in one place... Why?

Damian rubbed his forehead with a low groan. All these unanswered questions were giving him a headache. Or maybe he was just tired. He glanced in the mirror and cringed inwardly at the thick, black stubble covering his cheeks and the gray circles under his eyes. He tucked his hair behind his ear and sighed, running his fingers over the old scar that disfigured the left side of his face. He hated this scar. Not because it ruined his looks—he didn't care about that. He hated it because it was a constant reminder of the fight he had lost centuries ago, and the terrible price he had paid for his failure.

"I'll shave in the morning," he promised himself and hopped into the shower without waiting for the cold streams of water to warm up.

* * *

He woke up with a start fifteen minutes before the alarm went off and sat up, staring around the dark room. Something wasn't right. While he wasn't new to night terrors, he was sure it hadn't been a nightmare that woke him up this morning. Channeling his power toward his eyes, he looked around but found nothing suspicious on the inside.

"Dammit. Sometimes, I really wish I still had my other sight," he muttered under his breath, lowering his feet to the cold floor. He got up, headed toward the door and carefully opened it, soundlessly stepping outside barefooted. The cold morning air enveloped him, and he inhaled deeply, reveling in the close presence of his element.

Quickly surveying the surroundings, Damian made sure there were no humans anywhere in close proximity. When he channeled his power, his eyes always lit up with a bright, orange light, and he didn't need any attention from either human or the supernatural members of this community.

Even through the prism of his power, he didn't notice anything unusual. He closed his eyes and relaxed his mind, allowing the energy of Earth to flow freely through him, gently directing it toward his hands. Intertwining it with his magic, he moved his hand in a wide arch and whispered a short spell, *"Latentius revelare."*

The world around him shimmered, and now, he could see the flow of magical energy. His vision wasn't as clear as it would have been if he could use the second sight, but it was enough for him to register slight fluctuations and spikes of dark magical energy in the distance. The small hairs on the back of his neck stood on end with the expectation of trouble, and he frowned.

So much for a peaceful little town where there isn't even a random ghost, he thought, considering his next step, but the loud ring of the alarm clock in his room made the decision for him. He waved his hand again, releasing his magic, and then returned to his room. He had less than an hour to get ready before Sam would come to pick him up.

* * *

HE MADE it to the main entrance of the hotel five minutes before seven, but Sam was already there, waiting for him, leaning his shoulder against an old, black Ford F-150 pickup truck. As soon as Sam noticed him, he pushed away from the truck and opened the passenger door, gesturing for him to get in.

"Good morning," said Sam, starting the truck. "Did you get some rest? I hope it's okay to ask you this question."

Damian slammed his door shut and smirked. "I'm fine. Thanks." He relaxed in his seat, folding his arms on his lap. "Where to?"

"Nowhere until you put your seatbelt on," said Sam, giving him a pointed stare.

"I'm a Child of Earth. Something as trivial as a car crash can't kill me," murmured Damian with a half-shrug.

"Isn't that swell," muttered Sam, driving the truck out of the hotel's parking lot. "But a very trivial cop can give me a not so trivial ticket for you not wearing a seatbelt. My truck, my rules. Besides, I'm your boss anyway, so buckle up, kid." He winked, making a right turn onto the main road. "I mean it."

Sam wasn't kidding when he said his daughter's house was within five minutes' walk from the hotel. What Damian didn't expect was the way her house looked. He expected a standard three bedrooms, two baths single-family home with a few cacti planted in the front yard and a pathway paved with small, reddish pebbles. Instead, Sam drove his truck through a wrought iron dual swing gate with an old-style sign above it stating *"Paradise Manor"* and parked it in the circular driveway in front of a large mansion.

Built in the adobe style, the house had two large wings, and there was no doubt the building was as old as this town. The original look and feel had been well preserved, while some modern adjustments had been made to ensure the structural integrity and comfort of this large home. The front yard was designed in a traditional desert landscape style, but it felt as if no one had been maintaining it for a while.

A bunch of construction materials covered by a large, blue tarp were piled up on the left side of the driveway. A layer of sand and dust lying over the tarp suggested that the construction had stopped a while ago, and no one had bothered to continue with the work. All in all, the house gave out a strange vibe of despondency and abandonment.

Sam pressed the button of a doorbell next to the main entrance but then pushed the door open without waiting for the owners of the house to let him in. Noticing Damian's hesitation, he waved for him to follow and walked in.

Feeling the touch of the cool air to his skin, Damian halted in the middle of a spacious foyer, looking around with curiosity. From the lobby, two hallways ran in separate directions. The hallway on the left was blocked by plywood, and Damian assumed it was the part of the house under construction.

The interior of the house mirrored the overall style of the exterior. The ten-foot ceiling was supported by beautifully crafted stained-wood beams, and the doors—natural solid oak—stood out against the traditional mud adobe-style walls. The floor was made of polished concrete. However, a thin layer of dust covered it, and it lost its former shine.

A large mirror in an antique frame hung on the opposite wall, surrounded by a few wall candle sconces. The candles were untouched, and it was obvious they were nothing but a part of the overall décor. Damian observed the mirror with interest. Its surface appeared to be tarnished a little, and he wondered if it was one of those old silver pieces.

A small foyer table with an opened newspaper and a set of keys on top was positioned under the mirror. One of the pages unfolded, and Damian could clearly see the title of an article printed in large, bold letters: *"An eccentric serial entrepreneur, investor and philanthropist, Cole Adams is still missing."*

"River!" shouted Sam, turning toward the right hallway. His voice bounced against the ceiling, echoing loudly through the building. "I hate this house with its weird echoes and sound effects. River Rose! Don't make me come and get you, girl!"

The loud clinking of heels sounded in the hallway on the right, and a young woman in her late twenties or early thirties emerged from the shadows, halting in front of them. A large, furry feline followed her every step, its round, green eyes shining brightly against the darkness of its fur.

River was relatively tall for a woman, and her pantsuit couldn't hide the athletic build of her body. A fair-skinned ginger with light-blue eyes, she could have been called beautiful, if not for the bitter set of her full lips, and the dark shadows surrounding her eyes and underlying her high cheekbones. A slight bulge of the jacket over her hip suggested she was packing, and a police detective's badge on her belt explained the presence of firearms.

"Dad, I'm so glad you're back," she said, her melodious voice sounding a little raspy as if she'd been crying for a while. She hugged Sam, kissing him on the cheek, and as she pulled away, her gaze stopped on Damian.

"This is Damian Blake," introduced Sam, waving in Damian's direction. "He'll be helping me with the construction and in the shop."

"Nice to meet you, ma'am." Damian extended his hand, and she stepped forward, taking it.

Her cold fingers wrapped tightly around his hand, squeezing it a little stronger than he expected. The cat followed her every move. It circled his legs a few times, sniffing and rubbing against his jeans. Once satisfied, it halted by his side, and he could swear the feline was appraising him.

"River Evans," the woman introduced herself, her attentive eyes drilling through him as if she were trying to read his soul. "So, where did you serve and how long ago, Mr. Blake?"

"Well, helloooo ther-r-r-eeeee," purred the feline, tilting its head, its large ears with long, furry brushes perking up. *"Just look at this specimen! Mmm mmm mmm."* The cat rolled its green eyes and lay down at his feet, sounding almost as if it were snickering. *"Hopeless underachiever-r-r."*

Damian grunted, and for a moment, his attention switched from River to her cat. As a Child of Earth, he had always known he could hear the voices of animals and even communicate with them, but usually their voices sounded like a soft whisper in the back of his mind, unobtrusive and easy to block. Never had he heard such a loud and clear voice.

That's going to be... um... uncomfortable, a thought flashed through his mind as he switched his attention back to River.

"I never said I served, ma'am," started Damian, but she wagged her finger at him, a tired smirk ghosting her lips.

"I'm a detective, Mr. Blake. So, where and when? Easy questions," she repeated calmly with a half-shrug, the vibe of authority unmistakable in her voice.

Damian thought for a moment, wondering how to answer these so-called easy questions, but then he made a split-second decision to stick to the truth as much as he could.

"You're right," he agreed. "I did serve under a special law enforcement agency, the name and location of which I cannot disclose. Sorry, ma'am, but this information is classified."

"Special law enforcement agency my ass," murmured the cat, stretching its paw, its claws exposed. *"Fr-r-eak of nature."*

Goddammit, all I need—a smart-ass cat. Damian sighed, focusing on blocking the voice of the animal.

"So, Dad," said River, turning to Sam. "You managed to hire

some secret agent to work as a handyman?" She chuckled mirthlessly, shaking her head.

"You should see him with flowers," retorted Sam snidely.

River opened her mouth to reply, but the loud shrill of the doorbell interrupted her. She snapped her mouth shut and moved toward the entrance. The door opened before she reached it, and a tall man dressed in a perfectly fitted business suit walked inside. His brown eyes halted on River, and for a moment, they lit up with affection, but as his gaze darted to Sam, the light got extinguished and was replaced by wintry frost.

"Mr. Vetrov," he said dryly instead of a greeting, and Damian was positive whoever this man was, there was no love lost between Sam and him.

"Jesse," replied Sam in kind.

As Jesse's gaze landed on Damian, a shadow of displeasure crossed his otherwise handsome features, but he quickly composed himself and didn't say anything to him.

"River, we're going to be late," he said, his voice unexpectedly deep for his slender build. He placed his arm around her shoulder, ushering her toward the exit, but she took his arm off and walked back to her father.

"Dad, you know where everything is," she said, waving toward the blocked part of the house. "Do whatever you need to do."

She squatted and petted the cat, running her hands through its thick, dark fur. Looking up at Damian, she tilted her head, the corner of her lips lifting just a touch.

"It's amazing," she muttered mostly to herself, "but Gypsy actually likes you. It never happened before. She hates strangers. Especially men." She glanced at Jesse and jerked her chin toward him. "Jesse, my partner, has been around forever, and she never comes close to him. Not without hissing and scratching, at least." She straightened and gave Damian a curt nod. "I'm sure we'll have the opportunity to talk again." She thought for a moment and added, "Assuming my father is not going to fire you in an hour."

She chuckled, the sadness never leaving her light eyes. Then she turned and left the house with Jesse on her heels.

"Don't wor-r-ry, sweetie," purred Gypsy, following her owner with her round, green eyes. *"I'll check him out for you. Let's see if there is any presence of intelligent life in that pretty head of his."*

"Oh, brother," muttered Damian under his breath, rolling his eyes at the cat.

"I heard that!" hissed Gypsy, her claws making an appearance.

CHAPTER 4

~ DAMIAN BLAKE ~

As soon as River and her partner left, Sam turned to Damian, a crooked smirk on his face.

"Well, son," he said, jerking his thumb at the plywood, "let's get started then. Let's see if size and strength are directly proportional." He opened his tool bag and produced a heavy-duty crescent nail puller, offering it to him.

Damian chuckled, shaking his head. "I don't need it." He approached the plywood and found a nail that stuck out slightly. Wrapping his fingers around the head of the nail, he pulled it out easily. A few minutes later, most of the nails were out, lying on the floor in a tiny heap of metal.

"Whoa," mumbled Sam, applying the nail puller to remove the last few. "You *are* as strong as you look."

"*Show off,*" murmured Gypsy, rolling her green eyes.

"Shut up," Damian grumbled at the cat, glowering down at her.

"What did you say?" asked Sam, throwing a curious glance at him.

It's going to be a long day. Damian sighed. Carefully shifting the plywood down, he moved it to the side. "Nothing. Let's see what we need to do." He motioned at the long, dark hallway.

As soon as Damian took his first step, Gypsy sped forward with her bushy tail up, passing him to lead the way.

"Gypsy, shoo. Go back," he hissed. "All I need is to hurt this stubborn cat while working."

"You're not the boss of me, peasant," huffed the cat, trotting ahead of him. *"As far as I know, you're working for my mistress. So, down, boy. Roll over."*

Damian stilled for a brief moment, wondering if River would shoot him point-blank if he killed her favorite kitty, but then gritted his teeth and proceeded forward.

As they walked along the hallway, Damian noticed all the doors stood ajar, but as far as he could tell, everything was in flawless condition. The floors were perfectly polished, and even though everything was covered in a thick layer of dust, this part of the house seemed to be cleaner than the right wing. Even the family portraits were hung and aligned as if someone had inspected their position with a ruler. There wasn't even a sign of incomplete construction.

Sam halted at the end of the hallway in front of a large double door. That was the only door that remained shut in the entire left wing.

"I don't understand," he muttered, scratching the back of his head. "River said her late husband started the construction in the left wing of the house and never got a chance to finish it." He shrugged, his eyebrows rising in confusion. "I don't get it. Do you see anything out of order here?"

He put his hand on the handle, ready to push it down, when Gypsy hissed and arched her back, her tail tripling in size. A light wave of magical energy brushed Damian's senses. He couldn't see it, but he was sure the moment Sam touched that door handle, something had changed. In one motion, he grabbed Sam's shoulders and yanked him back, stepping between him and the door.

"Procedia Amnia," he shouted a protection spell, and the yellowish glow of his magic enveloped them.

"Damian, what's going on?" yelled Sam, staring around wildly.

"Silence," hissed Damian. Closing his eyes, he channeled the energy of Earth, increasing his sensitivity to the magical energy field.

"Open your eyes, Sasquatch!" squealed the cat, spitting and hissing at the locked door. *"You're a Child of Earth. Use your magical sight! Don't you see what's going on here?"*

"No, I don't see!" shouted Damian, throwing his hands up, desperation making his voice deeper. "Shut up, Gypsy, I need to focus."

"Are you talking to the cat? Are you out of your fucking mind?" yelled Sam. His face, covered in cold perspiration, paled, and he punched the wall of the protective spell. "I need to get out of here." He was taking short breaths, sweat running down his face, his eyes wide with uncontrollable fear. "Let me out! I need to be away from here!" Suddenly, he stopped talking, pressing his hand over his heart, his fingers locking and unlocking spasmodically.

"Sam!" Damian seized his shoulders and shook him once. "Look at me, Sam! Remember who you are! You are a hunter! Behave like one." He let go of the older man's shoulders, staring down at him heavily. "What you feel is a powerful turn-away spell. Nothing more!" He threw his hands up, slamming them down to his hips. "Fight it, goddammit! Fight it, so I can focus and figure out what's going on."

Ignoring the burning need to be as far from this place as possible, Damian channeled his elemental energy, carefully entwining it with his magic. He opened his eyes, glowing with the bright orange light of his power, but still couldn't see anything that would explain the situation.

"Gypsy," he said through gritted teeth, "please tell me what you see."

The cat turned around and threw a furious glance at him. *"You really don't have the second sight?"* she asked, swiping her tail angrily from side to side.

"No, I don't," he replied in a quick whisper. "Tell me what you see, or so help me—"

"He's talking to the cat," mumbled Sam, bewildered, wiping the sweat off his brow with a shaking hand.

"Runes and sigils," hissed Gypsy, turning to face the door, fur standing along her back. *"They are everywhere."*

"Latentius revelare," Damian whispered the second spell and brushed his fingers over the surface of his protective shield. It shimmered slightly, revealing an entirely different picture to his eyes. Even through the prism of his spell his vision was blurry, but he could see a set of runes and sigils glowing with a soft white light written all over the door and the wall around it. Some of them he recognized right away, but some he had never seen before.

He wasn't sure if it was his fight with the turn-away spell, or his use of magic, or maybe it was the realization of what these runes meant to do, but cold sweat dripped down his back, soaking his shirt through, and every muscle in his body tensed. He staggered a step back and froze. Quickly settling on a plan of action, he made the only decision possible in this situation.

"Sam," he said as calmly as he could muster, "I need you to pull yourself together, man."

The older man grunted and exhaled with a soft hiss, lowering his head for a brief moment. "Tell me what you need me to do, son," he said quietly, but his voice was firm and strong again, even though his face was still strained.

"I need you to run," said Damian, an expectation of trouble

clawing at his heart. "As soon as I remove my protection spell, I need you to run back like you've never run before. Can you do it, old hunter?"

Sam nodded, swallowing hard.

"Remember, run and don't look back. I'll be right behind you," said Damian, his jaw clenched. "Ready?"

Sam nodded again.

"Incanto Comlium," whispered Damian, removing his spell, and then shouted, "Run!"

In a heartbeat, an ear-splitting pandemonium unfolded around them. Amplified by the strange acoustics of the house, the terrible noise seemed to be coming from every direction at once. Bouncing off the ceiling, every screech, every hiss and howl seemed to be repeated infinitely, merging into a continuous ruckus. The air became darker than it had been before, rendering Damian's vision useless.

He didn't wait to find out what would happen next. Bending down, he grabbed the cat, pivoted on his heels and ran after Sam as fast as he could. The floor trembled with every step he took as the power of Earth responded to his emotional state.

As soon as he was out in the foyer, he waved his arm and shouted, *"Procedia Amnia!"* The yellow glow of his spell blocked the exit out of the hallway, and with horror, he saw a dark, shapeless mass slam into his shield. He heard Sam's breathless gasp but ignored him.

Dropping the cat to the floor, he grabbed the piece of plywood and a handful of nails. Placing the plywood back over the threshold into the hallway, he held it in place with his shoulder and drove the nails in with the heel of his right hand, securing it back the way it was. Once done, he halted, breathing laboriously with his mouth open as he tried to catch his breath.

"Gypsy," he panted, pointing at the blocked entrance into the hallway. "Tell me... Is there a rune that looks almost like an eye on this piece of plywood?"

The cat stared at it intently and nodded. *"Yes, there is one, and it's huge and glowing. I've never noticed it before."*

"Oh, God damn it all!" he yelled, slamming his hand against the wall by the plywood, leaving a red splatter on its surface, and the entire house trembled.

Damian turned around. Pressing his back against the wall, he slid down to the floor and raised his aching hand closer to his face. Noticing that the heel of his palm was bleeding, he shook his head and chuckled bitterly, dropping his arm atop his bent leg. Gypsy approached him and rubbed her head against his side, purring.

"Hey, you, why aren't you healing?" she asked, stretching up to give a nudge to his fingers. *"Don't you know? All Children of Earth have healing powers."*

"I can't self-heal, Gypsy," he said, exhaustion settling in his tense muscles. "I can't heal others either. Only if I die, the energy of Earth takes over, healing or restoring my body. I'm immortal, but my existence is not pain-free."

"You're the worst Child of Earth I've ever met," murmured Gypsy, settling in his lap. *"But you're okay, I guess... for a peasant, that is. I think I'll let you pet me now..."*

"You're immortal," echoed Sam. It wasn't a question. He just stated the fact as if he were trying to talk himself into believing it. He stood by the foyer table, sweat still trickling down his pale face. "And you can talk to cats."

Damian raised his eyes at him, and anger bubbled up in him, ready to spill. He swallowed, clenching his teeth as he fought to get it under control.

"Is there anything you want to tell me, Sam?" he asked, his jaw set.

"I had no idea, Damian," replied the old hunter quietly, squeezing the edge of the table with his hands until his knuckles turned white. "I swear on my daughter's life, I had no idea there was something other than incomplete construction behind this door."

"There is something behind this door, alright," muttered Damian. He rubbed his face tiredly and exhaled. "I wonder if your daughter knows what it is. You should ask her, I think. If she doesn't know, she should be aware of the situation."

"Do you think she is in danger now that we kicked that hornets' nest?" Sam approached the piece of plywood blocking the entrance into the left wing and moved his fingers over it as if trying to feel something on its surface.

Damian didn't reply right away, his mind presenting the images of everything that had transpired from the moment Sam touched that door handle.

"No, I don't think so," he said at length. "What you saw back there was the response of some powerful protection magic. Wards and spells, you know? Even the rune inscribed on this piece of plywood is a part of the protective spell work." He shrugged, brushing Gypsy's fur absentmindedly. "There is something hidden behind that last door—something that could be extremely powerful, or dangerous, or both. And someone has gone the extra mile to make sure no one will find it." He frowned, a deep crease appearing between his eyebrows. "Over the years, I've seen a lot of different protection spells in action, but never have I seen anything as powerful as this."

"Over the years?" Sam chuckled humorlessly. "All thirty-five years of your immortal life?"

"Give or take a few centuries," growled Damian, unimpressed with Sam's persistent need to know more about him. "We should ask your daughter, Sam. Maybe she can shed some light on all this."

"River is not touched by the World of Magic." With a strenuous grunt, Sam lowered himself down next to Damian and stretched his legs, massaging his knee. "Even if there is some kind of terrible magical secret hidden within these walls, she won't know." He glanced at Damian and shrugged apologetically. "Besides, you know how people are. You can throw the strange and unexplainable into their faces, trying to prove the existence of magic, but all you'd get is a one-way ticket to the local psych ward." He chuckled and leaned his head against the wall, closing his eyes for a moment. "People prefer to look high and low for a so-called *reasonable explanation* than admit the existence of the supernatural."

"How is it possible that the daughter of a hunter is not exposed to the World of Magic?"

Sam shrugged. "I made sure of it," he replied. "After her mother passed away, I did everything I could to keep her... you know... normal? To give her a normal childhood."

"Was that how you became a hunter?" asked Damian. "Your wife's death was not..." His voice trailed off as he realized how intrusive his question was. He cleared his throat and added quietly, "I'm sorry, sir. I shouldn't have asked that..."

"Don't worry, kid. Unlike you, I don't mind answering your questions," replied Sam, tones of sarcasm coloring his voice. "Rosa died in childbirth, leaving me alone with a baby." He stopped talking, and his gaze became distant and foggy, as if he were reliving his wife's last moments. "Rosa was touched by the World of Magic. She was a witch who could wield winds. A good witch." A soft smile appeared on his face, and his eyes lit up with the love and affection he'd kept through the years, even after his wife was gone. "She exposed me to the supernatural. Well, you know how it is"—he tapped Damian on his knee —"once you're exposed, there is no way back. I didn't want it for River. So, I kept her safe, away from all this magic-bullshit."

"Rosa Vetrov... It means *a wind rose* in Russian, doesn't it? How appropriate... She was a Child of Air?" asked Damian, his eyebrows rising. "You know how extremely rare that is?"

"All Children of the Elements are rare as far as I know," objected Sam quietly. "But, no, she wasn't. She was a powerful witch, and the air magic was her strength. And you're right about the name." Twinkles of humor appeared in his eyes. "She used to joke that my last name put her true nature on display." He turned his head, observing Damian with curiosity. "I didn't know you spoke Russian."

"I speak a few languages," replied Damian and switched the subject. "So, if River knows nothing about magic and this house's secrets, who would know then? Her late husband's family, perhaps?"

"They're all dead," said Sam, staring at the silver mirror. "Nick was the last of his family. Now, he is dead, too, so we have no one to ask."

"I'm sorry," said Damian, feeling Gypsy shifting in his lap to get closer to him, the heat of her body touching his skin through the thin shirt. He scratched her head between her ears, listening to her loud, even purr.

"Slightly lower, please," purred Gypsy, stretching her paws. *"Yes, that's right... Who's a good boy?"*

"Is there any documentation left about his family and their estate?" asked Damian, ignoring the cat. "Anything that could help us learn what's going on here? I think it would be a good idea to know what it is since River lives here alone."

"Yeah, I agree," replied Sam. "I'll dig around. River may know some of their family's history, so I'll try to ask her, too. Myself, I didn't like Nick's parents much. They didn't appreciate the idea of their precious son marrying into a simple family and considered their marriage a *misalliance*. Rich, arrogant assholes—" He grunted, cutting himself off, and then added, "I shouldn't be speaking ill of the dead." He rolled his eyes. "Anyway, after Nick and River got married, his parents moved to their other home in Fountain Hills, and then shortly after, they both died. On the same day."

"On the same day?" Damian repeated in disbelief. "And you as a hunter didn't find it suspicious?"

Sam smirked, regarding him with reproach. "Of course, I

did. But just like the local authorities, I didn't discover anything suspicious. A car accident—tragic but absolutely normal. Some drunk asshole driving an industrial van ran the red light and smashed into their sedan. Their car was totaled, compressed into a ball of metal. They had to use a blowtorch to cut through it just to get the bodies out."

"Uh-huh," murmured Damian, but after his run-in with the wards in this house, he wasn't convinced that this accident wasn't staged by something or someone supernatural. "And Nick? How did he die?"

"Suicide." Sam got up with a strained groan and brushed his hands over his pants, shaking off some dust. "Right here, in this house." He fell silent, staring at his feet. "River found him... She's still..." His voice shook, and bitter wrinkles materialized around his tightly pressed mouth. He swallowed, rubbing his forehead. "She doesn't believe Nick took his own life, even though the investigation and the autopsy report confirmed the suicide, she's still searching..."

Damian nodded and got up, too. Everything Sam had told him about Nick's family didn't feel right. "Sam, is there a library in this town?"

"Of course. Downtown," replied Sam, but this time refrained from questions. "You can walk there, if you don't want to rent a car, that is." He rubbed the back of his neck, a vibe of discomfort lingering over him. "Listen, Damian, can I ask you a favor?"

"What can I do for you, sir?" He lowered the cat to the floor, and she waved her tail, showing her utter displeasure.

"I don't want River to know about all this"—he pointed at the left wing of the house—"magical stuff. I'll come up with some kind of excuse why we can't finish the reconstruction right now. However, I'm worried about leaving her alone in this house. During the day, she's at work, coming home late, but at night she's here absolutely alone. Do you mind taking a few night shifts, guarding the house? Inconspicuously? I would do it myself, but I'm afraid it's above my pay grade..." He chuckled mirthlessly.

"I can do it," replied Damian. "But just like any human, I need food and sleep. So, I won't be able to help you in the shop during the day if I'm awake the entire night."

"I understand, son. I didn't expect you to work twenty-four-seven." Sam patted him on his shoulder, looking up at him, humorous twinkles back in his eyes. "Just for the first—um, let's say—five days to begin with? If everything is fine after that, we can return to our original agreement. And I will pay you for this week, of course. Just make sure she doesn't see you hanging around the property."

"No problem, sir," replied Damian, wondering if he could spend five nights awake and then still have enough energy to hit the library.

Before leaving, Damian bent down and petted Gypsy, eliciting a long stretch and a loud purr out of her.

"You take care of your mommy, Gypsy," he said to the cat with a wink.

"He is talking to that damn cat again," muttered Sam, bewildered.

"Not the sharpest tool in the shed, are you? She's not my mother, you Sasquatch. She's a human, and I'm a cat—a superior species. Besides, it's a physical impossibility," announced Gypsy, narrowing her green eyes. *"But for whatever reason, I still like you. I think I'll ask my mistress to adopt you."*

CHAPTER 5

~ DAMIAN BLAKE ~

The same evening, Damian returned to Paradise Manor. First, he circled around the fence to make sure he could get in unnoticed. As expected, the house was stuffed with state-of-the-art security equipment, so getting onto the property without triggering an alarm was practically impossible.

So much for me not using any magic. Cursing under his breath, he cast a cloaking spell over himself, praying to all the gods he knew that the security equipment didn't include heat detectors. While even the simplest cloaking spell could hide him from cameras, they were absolutely ineffective against heat detectors and pressure sensors of modern security systems.

Damian vaulted over the fence and landed soundlessly on the other side. Stepping softly on the paved driveway, he moved toward the house. However, as he came closer, he halted and stepped away from the driveway into the shadow of the building.

River and her partner Jesse stood by the entrance, discussing something animatedly. Even though Damian kept his cloaking spell, which made him invisible to the human eye, he didn't want to take any chance of something going wrong. Remaining in the shadow of the house, he came closer to the entrance. As a few words of their conversation reached his ears, his initial reaction was to step away, not willing to eavesdrop. However, something Jesse said caught his attention, and he stilled, listening.

"...I'm worried, River," her partner said, leaning toward her slightly. "With Nick gone, you're all alone in this giant, empty house."

River smiled, a tired but friendly smile lighting up her face. "Thank you, Jesse, but I'll be all right on my own." She glanced at the house over her shoulder, and sadness settled back in her light eyes. "Nick left this house to me, and I'm not going anywhere."

Jesse threw his hands up. There was something so desperate in this gesture that it set a few red flags in Damian's mind. A shadow of fear crossed Jesse's features but disappeared almost immediately. He took a deep breath and reached forward, brushing River's shoulder gently.

"Nick was my best friend and my partner of many years. Of course, I understand," he said softly, his deep voice calm and sympathetic. "Listen, if you don't want to move out, maybe I can move in instead. There are so many empty rooms in this house, we can live there for weeks without crossing each other's path." He smiled, his straight, white teeth prominent against his almond skin. "I promise, I'll stay out of your way. I just want to make sure you're safe."

Jesse's voice wavered, modulating slightly higher, and that small change in the way he sounded sent chills down Damian's spine. Something wasn't right, but he couldn't put his finger on what it was.

River took a step closer and hugged him, giving him a quick peck on his cheek. He hugged her and closed his eyes, visibly enjoying the moment, and as she drew back, he held her hand in his.

"Thank you, Jesse. You're the best partner and friend I could wish for." She pulled her hand out of his grip and shrugged, taking another step back. "I'm a big girl. I'll be fine. And if I need your help, I have you on speed dial. Go home, Jesse. I'm tired, and we have a lot of work to do tomorrow. Apparently, that crazy entrepreneur is not going to find himself."

She smirked and waved goodbye. Without waiting for his response, River turned around and walked inside the house, the metallic click announcing that she locked the door.

For a few seconds, Jesse stood, staring at the locked door, but then threw his hands up and headed back to the gates, muttering something incoherent under this breath. Damian waited until he was gone and walked out onto the driveway. Still keeping his cloaking spell up, he circled the property, carefully surveying every corner, but since he didn't find anything suspicious of either the mundane or supernatural variety, he returned to the main entrance.

Carefully checking the positions of the security cameras, he found a blind spot by the left wing of the house and settled there in the shadow of the building, releasing his magic. The rest of the night, Damian spent listening to the sounds of night birds screeching over the desert and crickets leading their never-ending concert. He didn't notice any disturbances in the magical energy field around the house, and once the first pink rays of the rising sun touched the purple rock formation in the distance, he got up and cast the cloaking spell over himself again.

Throwing one more glance at the house, he headed toward the gates. While the night had passed uneventfully, the conversation between Jesse and River left him with an unpleasant feeling. It could have been something as simple as a man trying to get in the good graces of the woman he liked. But Damian knew better. When the World of Magic was involved, nothing was ever simple, and things were never what they appeared to be.

River was the widow of Jesse's late partner and according to him—his best friend. Even if he had feelings for her while her husband had still been alive, most likely he had enough decency not to act upon those feelings.

What had changed now? If he was a decent man before, he wouldn't make a move at his friend's grieving widow only three months after his death? Or would he?

Another item to add to the growing list of mysteries surrounding River Rose Evans and Paradise Manor. Damian sighed and vaulted over the fence, noticing that this time it took a lot more effort.

* * *

As soon as he returned to his hotel room, he set up an alarm clock for ten in the morning. Since it was five-thirty, he hoped that four and a half hours of uninterrupted sleep would be enough for him to get some rest. He collapsed on his bed without taking the cover off and was asleep as soon as his head touched the pillow.

When the alarm rang, he sat up and rubbed his chin with his hand, wondering if he should forget about going to the library today. Nevertheless, the events of the last twenty-four hours left him with a sense of unease. Despite Sam's nosiness, he liked the old hunter and didn't want to leave him to deal with something he was obviously not equipped to handle.

He took a quick shower and grabbed breakfast in the small restaurant across the road from the hotel. An hour later, he approached the Blue Creek City Library. It was small, but to his surprise, the building was as modern as they come, and since it was located at the very edge of downtown, it didn't stand out as much as it would if it were in the middle of the "Old West" district.

The sun was blasting mercilessly from the unblemished blue

sky, and the temperature outside topped a hundred degrees. Even though his connection with the elemental energy of Earth protected him from sunburns, a half-hour of a brisk walk in the Arizona dry heat had taken its toll. His shirt was soaked with sweat, and his dark hair plastered over his forehead. Damian crossed the parking lot and stopped in front of the door, enjoying the touch of the fine mist coming out of the misting system to his overheated skin.

As he walked through the wide glass doors into the building, the difference in temperature was jarring. He took a deep breath and headed toward the counter. A young man sat behind it, immersed in a book he was reading. When Damian knocked on the counter to attract his attention, he gave a start and dropped the book. His large blue eyes traveled up, his lips parting a little.

"How can I help you, sir?" he asked, raking his fingers through the mop of his dark hair awkwardly.

While he wasn't male-model material, his friendly and slightly shy smile lit up his face, turning his eyes into two narrow arches, setting off his high cheekbones.

Damian couldn't help but smile back. "I'm new to Blue Creek, and I wanted to learn a little about the town's history," he said.

"Are you a member of our library?" asked the young man, but then chuckled apologetically. "Sorry, you just said you're new here." He grabbed a blank form and a pen and placed them on the counter. "Please fill out the application, and I'll need your picture ID."

Damian gave him his driver's license and quickly filled out the form. A few minutes later, he received a brand-new plastic library card and his ID.

"Well, Mr. Blake," said the man, his shy smile gracing his face again, "what kind of historical information are you looking for?"

"I haven't rented an apartment yet," started Damian from afar. "In the meantime, I am staying in the Night Owl Hotel. A few minutes of walk north, there is a beautiful old house. Paradise Manor, I believe. I was wondering if you have any information about the history of this building and the family who owns it."

"Oh, Paradise Manor," mused the young man, his face lighting up with excitement. "Good choice, Mr. Blake. This is the oldest and most mysterious building in the entire town." He glanced around and leaned forward slightly. "Rumor has it—it's haunted."

"Haunted? Really?" Damian's lips lifted at one corner into a lopsided smirk.

The young man narrowed his eyes, looking as if he were suppressing his laughter. "Aw, Mr. Blake, I see you don't believe in the supernatural."

Damian just shrugged without either objecting or confirming the statement. "Fascinating... What can you tell me about Paradise Manor, Mister—" He paused, giving the young man an arched stare.

The man offered his hand. "Jamie," he introduced himself. "James Coldwell."

"Damian." As soon as Damian touched his hand, a soft ping of magical energy rushed through him. It was so weak that he barely registered it, and he had to wonder if the young man knew he had magic.

"Why don't you sit down right there." Jamie pointed at a table with a computer monitor atop at the far end of the room. "I'll bring you some reading materials, and if there are no other visitors, we'll chat."

Damian headed toward the empty table and sat down, quickly observing the library. Besides him, there was no one in the room. It was softly illuminated by the fluorescent lights, and the slightly musty scent associated with most libraries hung in the air.

Jamie returned a few minutes later, sporting a few books. He sat down in front of the computer next to Damian, put the books on the table and logged into the library system. After a few seconds of searching, he turned the monitor toward Damian.

"Here is everything we have about Paradise Manor and the history of this town's founding families." He placed his hands on the books and then pointed at the computer. "These are the scanned newspaper articles from that time. You may find a lot of interesting information there, too."

"Founding families?" repeated Damian, frowning.

Jamie nodded. "Oh yeah. The three original families who started it all." He waved his hand around. "Evans, Anderson, and Brown. Three families—three tragic stories."

"You seem to know a lot about this place. A history buff?" asked Damian. "If you have time and don't mind spending it with me, I would love to hear the story from you."

"Well..." Jamie stared down at the books, heat creeping up his cheeks. "I'm not a history buff. My father was, though. He was the one who did all the research and assembled a huge collection of materials about the founding families and the history of Paradise Manor. I know only what he told me when I was still in high school." Sadness shadowed his features, and he stifled a sigh. "I wish..." His voice trailed away, but he raised his eyes, forcing a smile. "Anyway, I'll be happy to share with you everything I know, which is not much."

"Thank you." Damian leaned back in his chair, ready to listen.

"It all started in 1847 when the three original families arrived... well... here," started Jamie, shifting slightly in his chair to get into a comfortable position. "At the time, there was nothing here except cacti, rattlesnakes and scorpions. The quality of the land wasn't the best either, but they were positive there was gold. So, they started by building underground mines and hiring workers to do all the manual labor."

Jamie fell silent for a moment, his fingers fidgeting with the cover of the book.

"I don't know all the details," he continued at length, sounding slightly apologetic. "Myself, I always found it strange that even though they never found even the tiniest hint of gold in this land, they never stopped digging all the way until 1918 when the Spanish flu killed most of their workers, forcing them to close the mines." He shrugged, pointing at the computer screen. "You can read all the reports—old and modern. There is no gold here. So why did these three powerful and obscenely rich families spend their entire lives—for a few generations, too—trying to find something that wasn't there?"

He took a pause, giving Damian a quizzical look.

"The mines were opened for seventy-one years," murmured Damian. "What did they do after the mines were shut down?"

"They built the city of Blue Creek and stuck around here," said Jamie, spreading his arms. "I can't explain that either. All of them had money and could live anywhere in the world, but they chose to stay here until the last of their kin was gone."

"Nick Evans was the last?" guessed Damian.

"Yes, Nicolas Lee Evans. He was the last surviving descendent of the founding families," confirmed Jamie. He glanced at Damian with curiosity but didn't ask anything. "His ancestors built Paradise Manor at a time when the mining had just started, and for a while, all three families lived there." He thought for a moment, a shadow of doubt crossing his face. "I think they all lived there until the pandemic was over. Don't quote me on that. I don't remember the exact date."

He opened one of the books, quickly shuffling through the pages, but after a few seconds put it away with a guilty smile.

"It should be somewhere in this book," he continued. "You

can look it up later. From what I recall, after the pandemic, the Browns and the Andersons also built houses for themselves next to the Evans' mansion. Their homes weren't as magnificent as Paradise Manor but large and beautiful, nonetheless. You can find pictures in the books and the archives.

"Unfortunately, their houses weren't preserved—rebuilt a few times, first by their descendants and then by those who bought the property. They were sold many times over, and the last owners leveled the houses to the ground, building modern homes from scratch. Since the size of the lot was large, they moved their homes as far away from Paradise Manor as was possible."

"How did they die? Age? Sickness?" asked Damian, thousands of thoughts crowding his mind.

"Not at all," replied Jamie, a twinkle of excitement igniting in his eyes. "This is where it gets interesting." He moved his chair closer to Damian and leaned forward just a little, lowering his voice to a whisper. "Every single person in all three families—direct descendants and related by marriage—died an unnatural death under mysterious circumstances. Freak accidents, strange disappearances, murders, suicides. You name it—it happened to the members of these families."

He glanced around as if worried that someone could overhear them.

"Some say these families were cursed, but when and by whom—no one knows. And this is where the story about the ghost of Paradise Manor comes from, I guess." Jamie shrugged and chuckled. "I know you don't believe in curses and ghosts, so I'm not gonna go there."

"Maybe I do. Maybe I don't," said Damian, propping his elbow on the table as he leaned to the side slightly. "Humor me."

"Rumor has it that every time someone was going to die in the Evans family, the Lady of the Mirror appeared to them," he said with a shrug. "It could be just an urban legend. I don't know. But a few days before his death, Nick came to the library and spent an entire day going through anything he could find in our archives about the founding families and Paradise Manor. Just like what you're doing now." He tapped his finger on the books.

The door into the library opened, and a woman with a little boy walked inside. Jamie got up, telling them that he'd be right with them.

"He was also searching for information about the curse and the infamous Lady of the Mirror. Found nothing," said Jamie, throwing a pointed stare at Damian as he walked away.

"Ghosts, monsters, curses," muttered Damian, opening the first book. "What the hell did I get myself into?"

He spent the next few hours going through the books and articles in the digital archive. He found quite a bit of information on the founding families and even architectural plans of Paradise Manor, but there was nothing there that could point him in the right direction. If anything, now he had even more unanswered questions than before.

It was almost five o'clock when he shut down the computer and got up, gathering the books to return them. As he approached the counter, Jamie put away the novel he was reading and lifted his face.

"Thank you, Jamie," Damian said, placing the books on the counter. "Most likely I will come back tomorrow to continue my research. But I must admit, you gave me more information than all these books put together."

"Really?" The face of the young man lit up with his bright smile. "In that case, I have one more interesting fact you're not going to find in any book in this library."

"Oh?" Damian straightened, staring down at Jamie with interest.

"All the members of the founding families had arranged marriages. Some say that all their marriages were within their families, like cousins and such, but I doubt that. They were way too smart for inbreeding. Anyway, within families or not, all marriages were arranged. All except for one," said Jamie, holding one finger up.

"Nick Evans," whispered Damian, his heart thudding heavily in his chest. "He married River Vetrov against his parents' wishes."

"Exactly." Jamie cocked his eyebrow. "How did you know? You said you were new here."

"I work for Sam Vetrov," explained Damian, trying to sound as nonchalant as he could muster. "He mentioned a few things about his daughter and her late husband."

"Oh yeah, that explains it." Jamie shrugged apologetically. "Sorry, my previous job wasn't as peaceful as this one, and I got used to being suspicious of everything and everyone."

"If I may ask—," started Damian, but then changed his mind and fell silent.

"Not a secret." Jamie shrugged indifferently. "I used to work in Chicago for a large... eh... military institution... sort of... I was a guard, and the job was too dangerous and stressful for my taste. So, about a year ago, I quit and returned to Blue Creek."

"Sort of?" A wild thought flashed through Damian's mind. *A military institution in Chicago. Sort of?* He could think of only one military-like institution in Chicago that belonged to the World of Magic—the Guardians Order, an ancient secret organization of highly gifted witches and wizards, who acted upon direct orders of the Destiny Council.

"Sorry, I always have a hard time explaining this part, because of their crazy NDA, you know?"

"I do know," murmured Damian, giving him a short nod. *After all, this boy knows what he is... Good. We have a Wizard in town.*

He thanked Jamie for his help once more, said his goodbyes, and walked out the door.

CHAPTER 6

~ DAMIAN BLAKE ~

The next five days went by uneventfully. Damian spent most of his time between patrolling Paradise Manor during the nights and searching for anything he could find on the founding families in the local library during the day. The nights passed by quietly—no supernatural activities of any kind—and he allowed himself to hope that whatever was locked in the left wing of the house wasn't putting River's life in danger.

Sam, on the other hand, believed that his daughter was safe, and even though Damian didn't completely share his optimism, he decided not to argue. Grateful for Damian's help, Sam gave him a few days off to take a rest after all the sleepless nights, expecting him to start working in the shop early next Monday.

However, the more Damian learned about the history of the town, the more he believed that something wasn't right here. He copied the architectural blueprints of Paradise Manor, planning to ask Sam to take one more trip to the left wing of the mansion when River was at work.

* * *

It was past seven in the evening, and the sun was slowly moving toward the horizon when Damian grabbed a small running backpack and placed inside a few new candles he had bought in a local store earlier today. He got dressed quickly, putting on a black tank top and track pants. After quick consideration, he pulled the belt out of his jeans and wrapped it around his forearm. As soon as the belt touched his skin, it turned into a leather bracelet, hugging his wrist tightly.

During the last few days, his schedule had shifted into a strange semi-nocturnal lifestyle where he was awake all night and most of the day, getting no more than four to five hours of sleep, which wasn't peaceful either. Now that his night shifts were finally over, he felt like he needed to do something to unwind and relax his mind. For him, spending time alone with nature was the best way to ease up and get a much-needed rest.

As soon as he walked out of his hotel room, he put the backpack on, locked the straps over his chest and took off running toward a purple rock formation a few miles north of Paradise Manor. As he passed the mansion, he slowed down and channeled his magic. Whispering a spell, he checked the surrounding area for fluctuations in the magical energy field and any kind of supernatural presence. Since he detected nothing abnormal, he kept running, enjoying the touch of the cooler evening air to his skin.

By the time he reached the purple mountain, the sun was replaced by a large moon hanging low over the horizon. Staring at the bright, orange disk, Damian just now realized that it was the time of the full moon. While the three nights of the full moon were always more prone to supernatural activities, he still loved it. Perhaps it was his connection with the energy of Earth, but the full moon energized him, reinforcing his strength.

Damian slowed down to a walk and then came to a stop at the foot of the purple mountain. He unlocked his backpack and shrugged it to the ground. Connecting with the energy of Earth, he moved a few rocks lying around into the position he needed, creating a small amphitheater. Then he pulled out the candles and positioned them on top of the rocks.

"*Ignius,*" he whispered, and tiny flames ignited on the wicks, dancing in the windless air.

Once all the candles were lit and securely placed around the amphitheater he had created, he touched his bracelet, and the silvery whip materialized in his hand. He stopped in the middle of the makeshift arena and took a deep breath, exhaling slowly as he allowed the power of Earth to consume him.

Enjoying the surge of energy through his body, he laughed quietly and spun around, the whip cutting through the air with a high-pitched whistle. The weapon in his hand lit up with a brilliant light, and with every move he made, one of the candles was extinguished. Stepping softly on the rocky ground, he continued his dance, light on his feet and fluid like a night predator.

A few seconds later, it was over, and he stopped, breathing evenly as if he hadn't just run a few miles or danced with a whip. The ground trembled under his feet, responding to the dangerous power he was wielding. A blissful smile played on his face as he spread his arms, inhaling the scent of the night desert. Here, he was at home. He was calm and happy, and nothing bad could ever happen.

Damian touched his whip, and it wrapped around his wrist, turning into a bracelet. Halting in the center of the arena, he assumed a ready stance. Taking a deep breath, he brought his hands to his chest, palms up and then exhaled, lowering his hands. Turning ninety degrees, he began a martial art pattern, exchanging powerful punches with sharp kicks and palm strikes.

After completing a few patterns, he went around the arena, collected the candles and checked them. "I need to work on precision," he muttered under his breath, noticing that his whip had cut one of the candles in half instead of breaking the wick.

As he threw the last candle in his backpack and put it on, he noticed a shadow moving across the night desert, visible in the bright light of the full moon. He stilled, carefully surveying the area. A light fluctuation of magical energy touched his senses, and he channeled his power toward his eyes, staring intently into the darkness. Something dark, small and round rolled away quickly, and he chuckled, silently cursing his overly stretched nerves.

"Friggin' jackalope," he mumbled, shaking his head. But as he turned around, he held his breath. Standing in a half-circle, a small pack of desert coyotes blocked his path. Low growls rumbled in their chests, their hackles raised. He listened to the animals, realizing he couldn't hear their voices.

Not coyotes, are you? He took a step back and connected with the power of Earth again, his eyes lighting up with a bright orange light. Two daggers materialized in his hands, and he bent his knees slightly, ready to spring into action.

The coyotes exchanged a look in a very un-coyote like manner, and the air around them shimmered, a dark mist surrounding them like a thick veil.

Shifters... A thought flashed through Damian's mind, setting his nerves on edge. *In a pack?*

Unlike werewolves, shifters didn't like gathering in large groups. They liked being subservient to an alpha even less. In most cases, they led a solitary and quiet existence, trying to stay under the radar of both human and supernatural authorities. However, every now and then, there were a few shifters who didn't mind working for someone else, doing their bidding for a handsome compensation. Strong, fast, and ferocious, they were perfect guns or swords for hire. Besides, their unique magic allowed them to keep all their clothes and weapons on them while shifting, and that made them even more dangerous.

As the mist disappeared, he saw six men standing before him, armed with automatic firearms as well as knives and swords. Dressed in army fatigues, all six of them were tall and muscular, and Damian had no doubt they knew how to use their weapons well. One of them—the oldest by the looks of him—stepped forward, raising his hand in what appeared to be a peaceful gesture.

"Hey, man," he said, an uneven smirk playing on his thin lips. "We don't want to fight with you."

"Smart choice," replied Damian icily, his attention on the group of shifters behind their leader.

The man's smirk grew wider as he shook his head. "You look like a nice fellow, so we'll give you two options. Option A—come with us willingly and live. Option B—fight us and die a slow and miserable death."

Without any rush, Damian lifted his right hand, and still holding the dagger, extended the middle finger, a dark smirk playing on his lips.

"I was hoping you'd say that," growled the leader, a predatory light igniting in his yellow eyes. Stepping aside, he waved at his team, uttering a single word, "Fire."

"Procedia Amnia," hissed Damian at the same time, wrapping a protective shield around himself just in time, too, as the silence of the night was shattered by the barking sound of automatic weapons. The bullets hit his shield and fell to the ground, doing him no harm. A few seconds later, they emptied their magazines and lowered their weapons to reload.

My turn. I choose Earth... Releasing the protective magic, he spread his arms wide, bending the energy of Earth to his will. The daggers in his hands shone brighter, and the muscles of his arms and chest tensed. The land trembled, and a deep, wide fracture ran through the hard desert land, surrounding the attackers and blocking their way out. The shifters screamed, falling as the earth kept quaking.

Damian took a step closer to them. With a low growl rumbling in his throat, he turned his arms, his fingers squeezing the grips of his daggers so hard his joints cracked. Dark roots broke through the surface, wrapping around the shifters' legs and arms, immobilizing them and lifting them off the ground. The men screamed in horror, struggling to free themselves, but to no avail.

With one wave of his hand, Damian created a bridge over the trench. He crossed over and halted in front of the leader, disgust curving his lips into a snarl. Seizing his hair, he pulled his head back and pressed his dagger under his chin. The man jerked, struggling against the restraints. Damian snapped his fingers, and long thorns erupted from the roots, penetrating the shifter's skin, drawing blood.

The man yelped and stilled, staring at Damian, his eyes filled with terror. "Who are you, man?" he croaked, half-strangled by the roots. "What are you?"

"I'm no one," growled Damian, anger coiling within him. "All I want is for people to leave me the fuck alone!" He pressed his dagger deeper under the man's jaw, a thin rivulet of blood trickling from under the shining blade. "Who sent you after me and why?"

"Please, man..." His voice died out as he met Damian's glowing eyes. "I swear, I don't know. I'm just a sword for hire. We all are. I received the assignment through some phone app. That's all I know."

"Where were you supposed to take me if I gave in to your demands?" asked Damian, releasing the pressure on the dagger slightly.

"Just some abandoned house in Las Vegas," replied the shifter. "They wanted you out of the state. I have no idea why. I swear, man, I told you everything I know. Please let—"

"Out of the state or out of the way?" murmured Damian, talking to himself, ignoring the shifter.

He was about to ask the shifter another question when a tiny fluctuation of the magical energy touched his senses. He lowered the daggers, and they vanished from his hands. Straightening up, he narrowed his eyes, staring in the direction of the magical disturbance, and his stomach twisted with dread. A first wave, dark and sinister, rushed through the desert, enveloping him with its poisonous energy.

"Did you sense it?" whispered the shifter, his voice hoarse with fear. "Man, let us go or we are all gonna die... Something is coming."

"Nothing is coming," muttered Damian as the second wave of dark magical energy spread around. Lowering down to the shifter, he continued in a quick whisper, "You got lucky, dumbass. I have no time to deal with you." He closed his eyes, connecting with the power of Earth once again, and the trench in the ground closed up as if it were never there in the first place. "I'm leaving. In about an hour, the roots will disappear. Leave and, for your sake, I hope our paths never cross again."

Without waiting for the shifter's response, Damian took off running. Bathed in the silvery light of the moon, the path was clearly visible. Also, he could sense the flow of the dark magical energy, and the closer he got to Paradise Manor, the stronger and more potent the waves became.

He stopped in front of the gates into the property, his chest rising and falling with laborious breaths, sweat running down his flushed face. The accumulation of the dark energy was so thick here, he could practically see it without the use of his magic. A black mist that looked like a swarm of angry hornets rotated above the building. Glancing up at the cameras, he didn't see the tiny red lights around the lens and assumed that the security system was down.

Without wasting more time, he vaulted over the fence and ran toward the house, but as he reached the main entrance, he came to a screeching halt. The door was locked and even though he couldn't see the barrier blocking it, somehow, he knew it was there. He had no idea what would happen if he tried to open the door, or just touch the door handle. He reached for it, his fingers trembling slightly, but his hand ran into an invisible, solid wall.

At the same time, a blood-curdling scream—the cry for help of a woman, scared and desperate—broke through the thick walls of the mansion, raising the small hairs on the back of his neck.

"*Exitius!*" roared Damian, placing all the magic he could gather into a single strike.

The invisible wall exploded, and the dark mist appeared in its place, quickly dissipating. The door blew up with a thunderous bang, showering him with wooden splinters.

CHAPTER 7

~ DAMIAN BLAKE ~

Damian approached the threshold and quickly surveyed the room. The foyer was dark as the weak, silvery glimmer of the moonlight coming through the doorway couldn't illuminate its every corner. As soon as he stepped inside, freezing air enveloped him, sending shivers down his back. A stream of dark magical energy rushed through the house, making him stop and hold his breath, sharpening his already stretched senses.

Soft whispers filled the room, but because of the strange acoustics of this house, he couldn't figure out where they were coming from. It seemed like the hissing sound was coming from every direction at once, flowing above and below him, wrapping around his body, invading his mind with its malignant presence.

He groaned and bent forward, wrapping his arms around his head. The whispers became louder, more invasive, commanding him to leave and never come back. A short cry filled with dread and hopelessness sounded somewhere in front of him, breaking through the haze in his feverish mind. With sheer effort of will, he straightened and looked around, searching for River.

"Detective Evans?" he breathed out, a white cloud forming in front of his lips. "River... are you here?" His soft voice carried through, bouncing from the ceiling and walls in a weird, hollow echo.

The whispers got agitated, fusing into a loud, continuous noise. He could no longer distinguish separate words. It seemed like the terrifying meaning was projected directly into his mind. The darkness became thicker and heavier, and he could feel its cold and sinister touch on his skin. The flow of evil energy rose to the next level, wrapping tightly around his arms and chest, suffocating and immobilizing him, draining his strength and magic.

"No..." he growled. Resisting the hold of the malignant energy, he reached for the power of Earth, barely detecting its flow through the surrounding darkness. As his eyes lit up a bright orange, two daggers materialized in his hands. Gathering every scrap of magic and elemental energy he had within, he channeled it through the blades. The rays of undiluted energy of Creation erupted from them, cutting through the dark energy as if it were something tangible.

As he moved forward, fighting for his every step, the darkness retreated and slowly dissipated, falling to the floor in shreds of gray ash. The flow of dark energy subsided, and the whispers quieted down, melting into a heavy silence. The air warmed up slightly, but it was still too chilly for comfort. A heartbeat later, he stood in the middle of the empty foyer, breathing laboriously, his shirt soaked with sweat despite the cold temperature.

Cowering in the corner between the foyer table and the wall, River sat on the floor with her legs bent, her head bowed down to her chest. He approached her and squatted, noticing that she was holding Gypsy tightly in her arms. She squeezed the poor cat so hard that he had to wonder if Gypsy was still alive.

"Detective Evans," Damian called her, softly touching her shoulder. "River? Are you okay?"

She raised her head and looked at him, recognition lighting up her face. She dropped Gypsy to the floor, and the cat meowed, sounding relieved. To his shock, she wrapped her arms around his neck, pressing her trembling body to his.

"Nick," she said, threading her fingers through his sweat-soaked hair. "I knew it was you. I knew you'd come back to me."

He cringed, realizing she was talking to her late husband, thinking he was Nicolas Evans.

"River, I'm not Nick." He unlocked her arms gently and pulled away. She met his eyes, smiling through tears, and Damian noticed a barely visible purple glow in her dilated pupils.

"Nick, I love you," she said, pulling him closer again.

"Dammit," murmured Damian to himself, making his daggers disappear. "She's infected with some demonic energy."

Quietly cursing under his breath, he lifted her and straightened, holding her in his arms. "Okay, Detective, tell me where your bedroom is," he murmured into her ear. "Time to go beddy-bye. Let's see if I can get rid of this demonic infection with my limited abilities, otherwise we'll be in a world of trouble."

She chuckled, pressing her wet cheek to his. "I don't remember you being so tall, Nick. But I don't care." Her hand caressed the back of his head and neck as she continued in a happy whisper, "I don't care about anything. You're here, with me. That's all I need."

He sighed and took the first step toward the right wing of the house, but she stopped him.

"Pick up Gypsy, too," she murmured into his ear. "We shouldn't leave her alone, right?"

Stifling a sigh, he looked down at the cat, jerking his chin toward his shoulder. "Gypsy, up," he said, hoping that in the given situation, the smart-ass feline would do as she was told. He wasn't that lucky.

"*Gypsy, up.*" The cat mimicked his voice, rolling her green eyes. "*Who do you think I am? A friggin' dog? Kneel before me, peasant, and I'll decide if you're worthy of carrying me.*"

"Goddammit!" hissed Damian, and despite his effort to contain his energy, the floor trembled a little. "Not now, Gypsy. I need to help River, don't you see?"

"*Fine, I'm doing it for my mistress. Not for you,*" the cat agreed mercifully. She crouched and jumped up, pushing off his bare arm with her claws extended before landing on his shoulder.

He hissed in pain and glanced down at four bleeding scratches on his bicep. "You did that on purpose," he muttered through clenched teeth.

"*Yah think?*" the feline's voice filled with sarcasm sounded in his mind, and he grunted, fighting the desire to grab the cat by the scruff of her neck and propel her across the room.

"Are you talking to my cat, Nick?" River giggled like a little girl, kissing him on his cheek. "You're so cute when you do that."

Damian froze in place at the touch of her hot lips to his skin and swallowed hard, shivers running down his back. Just to make sure his appearance wasn't modified by some crazy spell, he turned slightly and looked at his reflection in the antique mirror. The edges of the mirror were covered in frosty swirls that were quickly melting as the air became warmer. A dark shadow moved behind him, but it was so fast that he wasn't sure it wasn't his imagination. He frowned, observing the room as it reflected in the silver, but could see nothing except his usual self with the cat on his shoulder and a young woman in his arms.

Pressing River tightly to his chest, he walked through the foyer and into the dark hallway. Family portraits and antique paintings lined the wall, and a thick, burgundy carpet covered the floor, dimming the sound of his steps. A light scent of vanilla lingered in the air, and everything around looked so peaceful and normal, as if nothing out of the ordinary had happened in this house just a few minutes ago.

"Take the second corridor on your right. Her bedroom is the only door at the end of it," directed Gypsy. "Even you can't miss it."

"Thanks," murmured Damian, walking briskly through the hallway.

He found her bedroom and pushed the door open with his foot. Gently lowering River on the wide, king-size bed, he sat down on the edge next to her. The cat hopped off his shoulder and settled by her side, purring loudly.

River looked up at him, her eyes alight with love. He knew she didn't see him—she saw her dead husband, but he couldn't take his eyes away. Reaching up, she gently brushed his hair off his face. He flinched as she exposed his scar, pulling away.

"Nick, what did you do with your hair? It looks terrible," she said softly. "Did you cut it with our kitchen knife or something?"

Damian frowned, wondering why she could see his hair while hallucinating her late husband. "Yeah, something like that," he replied, taking her hand and lowering it down. Then he moved his hair over the left side of his face to cover his scar and added, "With a dagger, actually."

"You have a dagger?" she asked, staring at him in awe. "Since when?"

"Two of them, ma'am," murmured Damian absentmindedly, observing her with interest. She was dressed in silk pajamas. It was pale blue with black tuxedo kitties printed on it, reminding him of Gypsy. His lips quirked up in a mirthless smile. "A bad-ass detective, alright... Let's see if I can cleanse you."

No purifying energy... no healing power... Goddammit, I'm useless...

For the best effect, he was supposed to position his hands over her forehead and heart, but he quickly decided against it. Pressing his palm against her forehead, he took her hand with his other hand and channeled the energy of Earth, circulating it through her gently. Her eyes opened wider, and she gasped, staring at him with her full lips parted.

Little by little, as he kept moving the elemental energy through her body, the purple glow in her eyes vanished. Her fogged gaze cleared, and the expression of love on her face was replaced first with shock and then with anger. Damian let go of her, and she jolted into a sitting position. He was about to get up, but before he could make another move, he was staring at the barrel of her gun.

"Damian Blake," she hissed, cocking her weapon. "On your knees, hands behind your head."

"Ma'am, I was—"

"On your knees, Blake, or so help me, I will shoot you where you stand!"

"Like father, like daughter," muttered Damian as he lowered to his knees, locking his hands behind his head.

"Mrrr... I like your position... Satisfying," purred Gypsy snidely.

"What are you doing in my bedroom, Blake?" River got up, holding her gun trained at him.

"I swear, ma'am, I mean no harm," started Damian as peacefully as he could muster. "I was doing my evening run, passing by Paradise Manor, and I noticed that your front door was gone, and the security system was down. I thought someone broke into your house and wanted to make sure you were safe—"

An expression of confusion fogged her eyes. Her hand trembled, and she lowered her gun but kept it level at his chest.

"What do you remember?" he asked quietly. Still keeping his hands locked behind his head, he sat back on his heels.

"I don't remember... No, I do remember..." Her voice faded, and she finally lowered her weapon. "I don't know how to explain it." She sat down on her bed and placed her gun next to her, rubbing her forehead. A strained expression crossed her features as she traveled back in memory, trying to make sense of what had happened. "If I tell you, you'll think I'm crazy."

He smirked, cocking his head a little. "And why do you care what the man you're holding at gunpoint thinks?" She gaped at him as if she had a hard time comprehending his statement. He looked heavenwards and added, "Just tell me what you remember. I promise I'm not going to judge or think you're crazy. I've seen more *'crazy'* in my life than I care to admit."

She took a deep breath, ready to continue, but then exhaled as if deflated. "Why don't you get off the floor and sit down, Damian."

She pointed at a chair next to a small vanity table. Damian got up, pulled the chair a little closer to the bed, lowering himself down.

"You're right about the gunpoint, though." She chuckled apologetically. "I hope you understand how I felt when I found a man whom I'd seen only once before sitting on my bed."

"I understand, ma'am, and I don't blame you," replied Damian, rubbing his arm where the scratches left by Gypsy's sharp claws prickled painfully. "Please continue. What do you remember?"

She nodded. "I woke up because I heard someone calling my name," she started. "The voice sounded familiar, but maybe I was still partially asleep because I didn't recognize it right away." She bit her lip, and bitter wrinkles materialized around her mouth. "I can't believe I didn't recognize Nick's voice right away. It's only been three months..."

Her voice shook, and she pressed the heels of her hands to her eyes, fighting tears. Damian didn't say anything, allowing her to continue when she was ready.

"I remember getting off the bed and walking to the foyer," she continued at length, dropping her hands on her lap. "As I walked, I could hear him calling me." Tears spilled from her eyes, but she didn't bother wiping them. "This house and its stupid acoustics. I couldn't understand where his voice was coming from. It sounded as though it was coming from every direction at once."

She fell silent for a moment, thinking. Then she raised her eyes at Damian, looking like a lost little girl.

"This is where the real crazy started," she said with a half-shrug. He nodded, encouraging her to proceed. "I don't know why, but I walked up to the mirror. When I looked in it, I didn't find my reflection there. At first, I saw Nick. He was saying something, but I couldn't make out his words. His face was strained as if he were screaming, but I couldn't hear anything. Then the whispers began... Louder and louder, until I could hear nothing but these strange, hissing voices. And then came darkness..." Her voice trailed off, and she looked out the bedroom window, sadness and fear reflected in her light, blue eyes. "After that, I don't remember anything until the moment you woke me up here."

Damian got up tiredly, straightening his pants. "If I may ask, ma'am," he started, but she threw her hands up, interrupting him.

"Can you drop that ma'am-thing already?" she asked, sounding slightly unnerved. "A moment ago, you were practically in my bed. I think that would permit the use of first names."

"Yes, ma'am... um... River." He chuckled at his own awkwardness. "Sorry, old habits die hard."

"So, what did you want to ask?"

"It's the middle of the night," he said, glancing out the dark window. "Your door is broken, and the security system is down. I think I should stay with you for the rest of the night." Her eyebrows climbed up, and he quickly corrected himself. "I mean not with you in your bedroom, but with you inside the house." He rubbed the back of his neck, realizing how awkward he sounded. "I just don't want you to be alone, and you need to get some sleep. Tomorrow is a workday."

Partly, he was expecting her to turn his suggestion down, just as she had when her partner had offered the same thing. Since she didn't reply right away, he nodded and took a step, heading toward the exit.

"Damian," she called him, and he halted, turning to face her. "Thank you. Yes, please stay here. I know it sounds childish, but... I don't want to be alone tonight..." She dropped her head, fidgeting with her wedding band. "There are quite a few empty bedrooms here. There's one right next to mine." She pointed to the left. "Take any one of them."

"I'm not planning on sleeping, ma'am," he objected slowly. "I'll survey the house one more time and then stay guard while you're asleep. Won't be the first time for me." He reached the door and pushed it open. Then he half-turned and offered her a tiny smile. "Good night, River."

CHAPTER 8

~ DAMIAN BLAKE ~

Damian walked through the house, getting familiar with the plan of the right wing. The location of the rooms was similar to what he had seen when he and Sam visited the left wing. However, when he reached the very end of the hallway, something seemed to be different. Maybe he was too tired, but at this point, he couldn't put his finger on what it was. Since he had copied the architectural plans of the house, he could compare the blueprints to the actual layout of Paradise Manor, and he decided to do that as soon as he was back at the hotel.

As he walked into the foyer, he approached the mirror and stopped, staring at it for a few seconds. Besides his own reflection, he didn't notice anything else. Just to be sure, he cast a spell and checked the walls of the house and the plywood barrier blocking the entrance into the left wing, but except for the protective rune on the plywood, he didn't detect anything supernatural.

After a while, he returned to River's bedroom and lowered himself to the floor outside her door. He spent all night staring into the darkness, fighting the exhaustion, but he couldn't allow himself to close his eyes even for a moment.

The hallway had no windows, and the doors of the other rooms were shut, so when the first ray of the rising sun touched the house, he couldn't see it. His wristwatch beeped at seven in the morning, and he stared at it in shock, realizing that the night was over.

Damian doubted that whatever had attacked River would dare try again during daylight, but he didn't want to leave her sleeping in a house without a front door. The events of the last night took their toll on him, and he felt drained magically and exhausted physically. He groaned and closed his eyes, leaning his head backward against the wall.

Come on, River, he thought, fighting the fog in his mind. *Don't you have to go to work? Wake up... wake... up...*

Exhaustion took over, and he blacked out for just a few short minutes—at least he thought only a few minutes had passed. Feeling a rough kick in his side, he jolted to his feet to find a standard issue police pistol pointed at his face.

"What are you doing here, asshole? Lost your way?" hissed Jesse, his deep-brown eyes dark with scorn.

Damian glowered at River's partner, anger rising to a dangerous level within him. He didn't think. Instinct and years of training did all the thinking for him. In one swift motion, he ducked to the side slightly, grabbed the gun with his left hand and slammed Jesse's arm with his right hand, disarming him. Squeezing the gun in his hands, Damian stepped back, pointing the weapon at Jesse who gaped at him, dumbstruck.

Before Damian could say anything, he felt the barrel of another gun pressed against the back of his head.

"Damian, you're assaulting a police officer." River's cold voice sounded behind him. "Turn around slowly and give me your gun."

"It's not my gun," started Damian but didn't move, his attention on Jesse.

"I don't give a damn. I said, stand down!" she barked,

thrusting her gun against the back of his head with some force. "It's an order!"

"Yes, ma'am..." Even though everything inside him was boiling, he couldn't allow for the situation to escalate where River would shoot him in the head and see him rising as if nothing happened. Damian turned around, his jaw pressed so tightly, his teeth squeaked.

River lowered her weapon, her face flushed with anger. She ripped Jesse's gun out of Damian's hand and pointed at the floor next to the door into her bedroom.

"Sit!" she yelled, her voice ringing on high notes. Then she turned to Jesse and gave him his Glock back, a sarcastic smirk curving her full lips. "I didn't think I'd see the day when a handyman would disarm the almighty Jesse Williams."

"River, I found him sitting by your door and assumed the worst. What did you expect me to—," Jesse attempted to explain, but she interrupted him just like she'd interrupted Damian a few minutes ago.

"He was here with my invitation," she growled, pushing her long copper hair out of her face, anger still shining in her eyes. Then she took a deep breath to calm down and added, "Let's go. I'll walk you out, Jesse." River pushed him in the direction of the exit, and even though she looked calmer, the tone of her voice promised nothing good to her partner. Then she switched her attention to Damian, pointing at him. "You sit here and don't make a move until I come back. I need to have a word with you. Am I clear, Mr. Blake?"

"Crystal," grumbled Damian. He lowered to the floor and bent his legs, resting his arms atop his knees.

"Down, boy. Stay," purred Gypsy snidely as she passed him, waving her bushy tail in his face. *"What a good boy you are."*

I swear... I'll kill this cat... Damian lowered his head atop his folded arms and closed his eyes, his mind drifting on and off.

River came back a few minutes later and touched his shoulder. He flinched and raised his face, looking up at her. She didn't smile, her face void of emotions.

"Follow me," she said, and he knew that even though her voice sounded soft now, it wasn't an invitation but an order.

She led him into a light, spacious kitchen and motioned for him to sit down. He didn't object. Feeling too tired to argue about anything, he pulled one of the chairs out and sat down heavily, stretching his long legs. She measured coffee into a coffeemaker and added some water. Then she turned the machine on and placed two empty cups on the counter.

A few minutes later, the warm, bitter aroma wafted through the air, and he inhaled deeply. He loved the smell of coffee in the morning even more than he liked the taste of the actual drink. River turned around and narrowed her eyes, observing him with unconcealed interest. He averted his gaze under her steady stare, and his hand went up automatically, brushing his hair over his face.

"You don't need to do that," she murmured, waving her hand in his direction. "At least not on my account."

"Do what?" He raised his eyes at her and leaned forward, resting his elbows on the edge of the table.

"This." She smirked and pulled a long strand of her hair over her face. "You don't need to hide your scar, and you definitely shouldn't feel self-conscious about it. First, it doesn't spoil your appearance. Second, it is part of who you are. Our scars tell the story of our lives. Some of them we can see in a mirror, but some of them, we can only feel. And those are the worst type." She sighed, frowning, sadness shadowing her features. As the coffee machine beeped, she turned away from him and poured the drink. "Milk and sugar?"

"No, thank you," replied Damian, now feeling more self-conscious about his scar than ever before. "I take my coffee black."

She chuckled, shaking her head as she added creamer and

two spoons of sugar in her drink. "I don't think I can drink it without milk and sugar."

River placed a cup in front of him and sat down across the table to face him. Gypsy hopped on her lap, and she threaded her fingers through her long fur absentmindedly. He took a sip of his coffee, carefully observing her over the rim of his cup.

She had a pleasant oval face and the kind of pearl-white, almost translucent, complexion only true redheads had. Her long, copper hair wasn't pulled back into a ponytail, and it fell down her shoulders, reaching the middle of her back. Dressed in sweatpants and a simple T-shirt, she looked slim, but her well-toned muscles—maybe a touch too bulky for a woman—suggested she was a regular at the local gym.

Noticing his attention, the corners of her lips quirked up just a little, but she didn't shy away from his gaze. Lifting her cup, she took a sip and then placed the cup back, visibly enjoying the taste.

"Let's talk," she said at length.

"About?"

"You."

"No."

"Excuse me?"

"I said no," he repeated calmly. Taking one more sip of his coffee, he placed it back on the table and got up. "I need to have an hour of sleep and then I'll come back with your father to fix your front door and check your security system. Thank you for the coffee." He turned around, ready to leave.

"I didn't say you can go," she called after him, tones of authority in her voice. "Sit your ass back down, Damian Blake."

"I don't need your permission." He turned around to face her, trying to stay as calm as he could. "Don't assume for one moment that you can boss me around like you do your partner, and that I will obey your every command."

"I assume nothing." She slammed her palm against the table.

"But until I understand what's going on here, you're going nowhere."

"Goodbye now." Damian pivoted on his heels and headed toward the exit.

"Damian, stop!" she yelled after him, tones of desperation ringing in her voice.

He winced inwardly but didn't slow down. She ran after him, halting him by the door. Grabbing his arm, she forced him to turn around. Damian looked down at her, exhaustion adding to his aggravation.

"Damian, please," she said quickly. "If you have some criminal record, I don't care. I'm a cop. You know that if I wanted to check your background, you wouldn't be able to hide anything from me. But I don't care about that."

He smirked, taking her hand off his arms gently. "Good luck with checking my background, my lady." He inclined his head in a slight bow, sarcasm in his every move.

"My lady?" she repeated, looking confused, but then shook her head as if trying to chase some unwanted thoughts away. "I don't care about your past, Damian. Whatever it is you don't want to speak of, I'm not going to force the subject. I promise... If I ask something you don't want to discuss, just tell me to shut up." She stopped talking, her eyes pleading with him. "But I have to understand, and to do that, I will have to ask a few questions. Please, Damian." She threw her hands up and sighed. "I need help. As a detective, I got used to trusting my gut, and right now, it tells me you're the person I need."

He didn't reply, staring silently at her.

"The way I talked to you..." She looked to the side, into the darkness of the hallway. "You're right. It was uncalled for. I guess it's because of my job. I have to speak with people a certain—"

"Bullying someone into submission is not a good way to ask

for help, ma'am," he interrupted her dryly, but his aggravation started to simmer down.

"River?" A guilty smile crossed her face as hope lit up her eyes. "We used to be on a first-name basis just a few hours ago?"

He rubbed the bridge of his nose, frowning. "I know I'm going to regret it, but let's do it..." He walked back into the kitchen and sat down, wrapping his hands around the still-hot cup of coffee.

"Yes," she whispered, but his sensitive hearing caught it, and he smirked, thinking that the bad-ass detective wore pajamas with kittens and could get excited like a little girl.

River sat down at the table across from him and for a few seconds remained silent, staring out the window. Then she sighed and looked at him.

"Let's proceed with caution, Damian," she said softly. "I'll ask you a question, and if you don't feel like answering, just ignore it. I promise that I have a reason to ask all these questions. It's not my curiosity. Okay?"

He nodded, still unsure he made the right decision by coming back to this light, clean kitchen stuffed with modern tech to the brim.

"Damian, I just witnessed you disarm a trained police detective, who happened to be ex-special forces," started River, her eyes boring into his. "You did it without thinking. It was pure instinct. Where did you get trained?"

"It's classified, I already told you," replied Damian, sounding flat, almost bored. "But I can tell you that the agency where I served took my training seriously. So, yes, it's embedded in me." He smirked bitterly and added in his mind, *Literally.*

"When I told you that I had seen a reflection of my late husband in the mirror and that I had heard his voice, you didn't blink an eye," she proceeded with her next question. "It wasn't your first encounter with something... um... supernatural, was it?"

"I'm an open-minded person." Her question set his mind on high alert. Remembering all the effort Sam had put in to keep his only daughter away from the World of Magic, he didn't like where all this was going.

"Do you believe in the supernatural?" she asked. Her eyes widened in the expectation of his answer, and he noticed that she held her breath.

Dammit... I can't tell her the truth, he thought, cringing inwardly, and then added out loud, "My personal beliefs are irrelevant."

"I see," she mused, regaining her calm. Her eyes stared into his without blinking, and he felt as if he was submitted to a lie detector test. "Have you heard the story about the ghost of Paradise Manor?"

"Yes."

"Do you believe it has factual bases?"

"My beliefs are irrelevant," he said again, avoiding the answer. "Do *you* believe it to be the truth?" He leaned forward just a little, arching his eyebrow at her.

"I do," she replied quietly. "Before Nick passed away, he told me he saw her reflection in the mirror."

"The antique one? In the foyer?"

"Yes." She nodded, biting her lip. "A few days later, Nick committed suicide." She frowned. "I don't believe he took his own life, Damian. He wasn't depressed. We were so happy... He would never..."

Her voice trembled, tears gathering in her eyes. She averted her gaze, pressing her fingers to her eyes, and for a few long seconds, heavy silence enveloped the room. Damian shifted slightly, not sure what he should do in this situation. On one hand, he wanted to comfort her, ease her pain somehow. On the other hand, he didn't think it was appropriate for him to do that.

"Anyway." She cleared her throat, composing herself. "I

believe in the supernatural. I believe the Lady of the Mirror killed my husband. I don't know how, but something tells me you may know more about this stuff. Am I right?"

He remained silent.

"I'll take your silence as a yes," she continued. "When we spoke earlier, you said staying guard while I was sleeping wasn't the first time for you. What did you mean?"

He stifled a sigh. "I used to work as a personal security guard for a while," he replied without going into any details.

"A bodyguard?"

He nodded. "Something like that."

"Do you lie, Damian?"

"What kind of goddamn question is that?" he asked, wondering where she was going with all this. "We all lie. Do I lie? Yes, I do when I have no other choice. Am I lying to you now? No, I am not. But if you push me any further, I will—just to make you stop." He got up, moving his chair back with a loud screech. Then he leaned across the table, towering over her. "What do you want from me, River? Speak plainly, or I swear I'll turn around and leave, and you won't be able to stop me this time."

"Fine," she said through clenched teeth, rising. "I'll tell you straight, and you can think whatever you want after that." She stood with her arms crossed, angry twinkles dancing in her eyes. "I believe my husband and the rest of his family were murdered by a ghost—the Lady of the Mirror. I've seen her a few times after his death, and I believe she is after me now. I need your protection. I want to hire you as my personal bodyguard." She stopped talking, her chest rising and falling with angry breaths. "Was that plain enough for you?"

Damian froze in place, cold perspiration covering his forehead. A chain of memories flashed in his mind, images replacing each other faster than he could capture the meaning. The eyes of another woman gazing at him with love as she took her last breath surfaced in his memory—the woman who had trusted him with his life, and he let her down.

Before he knew it, he shook his head no. River circled the table and stopped in front of him, taking his hand into hers. The touch of her soft skin to his ripped him out of his stupor, and he shied away from her. Swallowing hard, he gathered his thoughts.

"River," he said, his voice hoarse, "I don't think it's a good idea... Besides, I don't think your father would—"

"My father wants his daughter alive, and something tells me he's just as open-minded as you are," she objected, filling the word *'open-minded'* with enough sarcasm for him to feel it. "He would be happy if he knew I wasn't alone here. The house has plenty of empty bedrooms, a gym, and an inground lap pool. Everything here is at your disposal if you agree to help me."

"It's also a little uncomfortable, you know?" he objected gently, discomfort lingering around him. "You're a young lady, and I'm a single man. I'm not sure it would be appropriate for me to live in the same house with you. It would ruin your reputation."

Her jaw dropped as she stared at him, her eyebrows climbing up. "You're kidding me, right?" she muttered, blinking furiously at him. "My reputation? When were you born exactly?"

Damian's lips curved into a smile. "I was born in the year nine hundred sixty-two of our Lord Jesus Christ, my lady." He touched his chest over his heart with his hand and gave her a ceremonial bow filled with mockery.

For a moment, she gaped at him, unable to form words, but then she clapped her hands and burst out laughing, tears of laughter glistening in her eyes.

"At least you have a sense of humor," she managed to say, wiping her eyes. "So, what do you say, Damian? Do we have a deal?"

"*That's what you get for speaking the truth, Sasquatch,*" purred Gypsy, amusement in her round eyes. "*You'll fit well in her antique collection.*"

"River, before I make my decision, just one question... What if I kill your kitty? Accidentally, of course?" asked Damian, giving Gypsy a menacing stare. The cat hissed, arching her back.

"No problem," replied River with a dismissive wave of her hand, an evil grin on her face. "I'll just cut your balls off and shove them... well, you know where."

Damian laughed, noticing Gypsy showing him a paw with a middle claw extended. He sobered up quickly, his fingers tracing the shape of the leather bracelet on his wrist.

"Okay, Detective," he said quietly. "If your father agrees with this arrangement, I'll move in to your house and keep an eye on things here. But if you try to boss me around again, I'll be gone faster than you can pull your gun out. If you want to run a background check, go for it, but don't ask me any personal questions." He thought for a moment, his memory returning to that other woman who had died in his arms centuries ago. He couldn't make the same mistake. Never again. He forced the painful memory to the back of his mind and added, "And if at some point, I tell you to do something, you do it. No questions, no objections. I will never ask you for anything unless your safety is at stake. You understand?"

"Yes, my lord." She curtsied awkwardly, humorous twinkles in her eyes, and for the first time since he met her, he saw her face relaxed and the shadow of sadness gone from her gaze. "You know I'm almost thirty—a mature adult, so to speak? Does my father's consent to this arrangement really make any difference?"

"It does for me," replied Damian dryly. "I'm going to go back to my hotel, get at least a few hours of sleep, and then come back here to install a new door for you. What time do you come home from work usually?"

"I'm a detective." She smirked. "My day doesn't always start and end on schedule. But I'll try to get home early today and help you settle in. Give me your phone number. If you're not here by the time I'm home, I'll call you."

"I don't have a phone."

"Sometimes I don't know when you're serious and when you're joking, Damian," she muttered, staring at him with wide eyes.

"I'm serious. I don't have a phone," he repeated calmly.

"My father said you also don't own a car," she said, exploring his face with curiosity. "What cave did you crawl out from?" He threw a warning gaze at her, and she raised her hand in a peaceful gesture. "Never mind. No more questions. Your cave is your business."

"Good," he murmured under his breath and nodded to her. "I'll see you later tonight."

He turned around and walked out the door before she could stop him with more questions.

CHAPTER 9

~ DAMIAN BLAKE ~

Once back in his hotel room, Damian dropped on the bed and pressed his hands to his face. He lay still for a moment, processing everything that had happened in the last twenty-four hours. Then he sat up sharply, a deep vertical wrinkle showing between his eyebrows.

"Dammit," he mumbled, staring out the window. "I shouldn't have done it."

He got up and stood in the middle of the room, feeling lost. Then he stripped his dirty clothes, put them inside a plastic bag and headed into the shower. He yanked the shower curtain closed and opened the faucet. Without waiting for it to warm up, he stepped into the bathtub under the cool jets and closed his eyes, bracing himself against the wall with his hands.

I couldn't protect the woman I loved from the supernatural. She was a powerful witch, and I was in my full power, too, at the time... and I still failed, he thought as streams of water ran down the long strands of his hair on the front, washing over his shoulders and back. *What the hell is wrong with me! What in the world made me think I can save this child—human without magic! I have no more than a quarter of my former power left. Goddamn idiot!*

He slammed his hand against the wall and straightened, his chest rising and falling with angry breaths. He dropped his head, staring at the rivulets of water running down the drain in front of his feet, slowly getting his anger and desperation under control.

But if you refuse her your protection, whatever killed her husband and his family will kill her for sure, whispered a tiny voice in the back of his mind. *She's better off with you than on her own.*

"I need to figure out what's killing the members of the founding families and why." He reached for a bar of soap and a bath sponge. "And I need to do it fast, before it's too late for River."

Making up his mind, he finished the shower quickly and dried himself with a towel before stepping out of the bathtub. He decided to skip sleep entirely and go back to the library, hoping to find Jamie there. He needed more information about the founding families and everything about their untimely demise. There was just too much mystery surrounding Paradise Manor and its inhabitants—weird deaths, a ghost, the strange obsession with gold which wasn't there, and of course, the warded left wing of the house.

Whoever placed the wards and protection spells there made them extremely powerful. There had to be a reason for that. Perhaps, if he could learn what was hidden behind the last door, he would figure out what kind of mighty power is after her. The memory of River's eyes glowing with the sinister light of demonic infection surfaced in his mind, and he frowned, running his fingers over his chin. Whatever was haunting Paradise Manor wasn't a joking matter, and he was positive the secret of the old mansion and the evil haunting it were connected someway, somehow.

And then there were Jesse and the group of shifters that attacked him last night. It was on a level of intuition, but Damian was positive River's partner was somehow involved in all this mess. He just needed to figure out how and what his motives were.

As far as the shifters, he had no idea where to start. He had been in Blue Creek less than a week. Despite Sam's words about the town being supernatural-free—he rolled his eyes at the thought—he had taken all the precautions to keep his supernatural identity hidden and had made sure to suppress his magical energy signature completely at all times except for when he needed to use his magic. So, why would anyone want him out of the state and how did they know he was there in the first place? Things just didn't add up.

He glanced at his watch. It was ten past eight, and the library wouldn't be open until nine. He had enough time to grab something to eat and be there at the opening. If Jamie was working today, he could spend a full hour with him before meeting with Sam at his shop to replace River's front door. Deep in thoughts, Damian got dressed, putting his blue jeans and a simple black T-shirt on. He glanced at his bracelet, considering if it stood out attracting too much attention, but then decided to keep it as is.

A loud knock made him flinch and spin around. Wondering who that could be, he headed toward the door and opened it. The teenage daughter of the hotel owner stood in front of him. Her face was flushed, and her round eyes stared up at him without blinking as she tried to catch her breath.

"Is everything okay?" he asked, wondering why she looked like she had just run a mile. "I thought I just paid for one more full week ahead."

She shook her head and swallowed. "You're fine, Mr. Blake," she managed to say, panting. "My mom sent me to ask you for help." She took another deep breath and exhaled through her mouth, the air coming out in a soft gasp. "She called Mr. Vetrov first, but he wasn't going to be in his shop for another hour, so he said to see if you were in your room. My mom said if you don't have tools, you can use whatever she has. Can you come with me, please?"

"One moment, please."

He walked back into the room, grabbed the key and walked back out. Locking the door, he put the key in his pocket and followed the girl to the other side of the building. She led him to a staircase and ran up to the second floor, skipping a step.

"Dammit," he muttered, pursing his lips. "This day is just getting better and better."

With a deep sigh, he headed upstairs, feeling how with each step he took, his connection with the elemental energy of Earth grew a tiny bit weaker. It was just the second floor, so it wasn't bad, but he could still feel the distance between him and his element.

The hotel owner, Mrs. Davidson, waited for him by the very last door, a small tool bag standing next to her feet. As soon as she saw Damian, relief reflected on her tense face, and she smiled.

"Mr. Blake, thank you so much for coming," she said, picking up the tool bag.

"What can I do for you, ma'am?" he asked, throwing a quick glance at the closed door with two joined hearts painted under the room number. The do-not-disturb sign hung on the handle, and even though the door was locked, he could hear the TV playing on the inside.

"This is our honeymoon suite. A young couple rented it a few days before you arrived. Very nice people and all. Paid for their stay in full," she continued, picking up her bag from the floor. "Anyway, I haven't heard from them since they moved in, but the people in the next room complained that their TV plays day and night. I came here yesterday and knocked on the door, but no one answered. So, I checked in the morning again with the same result. Now, I'm truly worried about them, and I was wondering if you could help me unlock this door, please."

"Don't you have something like a skeleton key?" asked Damian. He pushed on the door handle just to make sure, but just as Mrs. Davidson said—it was locked.

"I used to have a second set of keys for every room in the hotel, but I searched everywhere, and I couldn't find the one for the honeymoon suite." She shrugged apologetically.

Damian took the tool bag from her hands and quickly explored its contents. He didn't really care what tools she had since he wasn't planning to use them to open the lock, but he had to make it look legit. To his surprise, he found a hook and pick toolset and grabbed it, returning her the bag.

"Let's give it a try," he muttered. Taking a position so neither Mrs. Davidson nor her daughter could see what he was doing, he channeled a little bit of his magic, touched the lock and whispered, *"Recludius."*

The lock clicked, and the door cracked open, but when Damian pushed it, it didn't budge. A wave of sweet, sickening odor assailed his senses, and he pressed his hand over his nose and mouth, staggering back. Together with the reek of decay, he detected the slight smell of sulfur and the presence of vampiric essence.

Slowly, he turned toward Mrs. Davidson, thinking of what to do next. If the situation was normal, he would just call the police and let them handle it. But when vampires and demons were involved, the situation was nowhere near normal, and sending human police against even a single demon would be equivalent to killing them.

"Mrs. Davidson," he said, trying to sound as kind and calm as he could muster, "the door is blocked from the inside, and..." He fell silent, trying to find better words to explain.

"Are they all right?" she asked, and the way she sounded told him she already knew the answer to this question.

"I don't know, but I don't think so," he replied, throwing a quick glance at the teenage girl who stood a few feet away, her face drained of all color. "I'll have to break the door to get in. Why don't you take your daughter downstairs? She shouldn't be here, ma'am."

He waited until they left and turned back to the door. "I hope the few minutes before the police arrive will be enough to deal with whatever supernatural assholes are hiding inside," he muttered as he struck the door with a powerful push kick. With a loud bang, the door cracked and flew off its hinges. The nauseating reek of decay assailed his senses, and he grunted, hiding his face in the crook of his elbow. However, time was of the essence, so he stepped inside, ignoring the stench.

The room looked like a disaster area. The windows were tightly covered with shutters and the only light illuminating the area was coming through the doorway. All furniture except for a large king-size bed was destroyed, lying on the floor in heaps of broken wood. The TV was on the floor, playing loud enough to conceal any other sounds in the room. Two young people—a man and a woman—lay on the bed, tied up to it with thick ropes and gagged, their bodies malformed by decomposition.

There was no doubt they had been dead for at least twenty-four hours. However, there was something about the corpses that drew Damian's attention. Fighting nausea, he approached the couple and quickly explored their bodies. From the outside, he didn't notice any injuries that could have caused death. Their clothes were torn but relatively clean. He noticed a few bruises and scratches on the exposed skin of their arms and faces, but none of it could have killed them.

However, both young people had hypodermic needles inserted into their veins. Despite it, Damian was positive they hadn't been using drugs. Glancing around the room, he noticed a few small glass jars coated with brown stains of dried out blood on the inside. Whoever killed this couple drained their blood all the way to the last drop.

He approached the jars and squatted next to them, making

sure not to touch or move anything. A very slight presence of vampiric energy signature brushed his stretched senses again. If vampires were involved, the drained blood would make sense. But why would they use needles instead of just sinking their fangs into the necks of their victims?

He straightened, ready to leave, when he heard a constrained moan. It was so feeble that if not for his sharp hearing, he wouldn't have noticed it. Damian froze in place, listening intently. Someone moaned again, the sound coming from behind the closed bathroom door. Moving soundlessly across the floor, he approached the door and pushed it carefully with his hand.

It opened up easily with a soft squeak. He stepped inside and stilled with his mouth open. At the other end of the spacious bathroom, a large metal cross was nailed to the wall. A man was strung up on the cross, his arms stretched wide apart as if someone had been trying to crucify him. But instead of nails, his arms and body were attached to the cross by thick silver chains.

He was completely naked, and in every place where silver touched his bare skin, it left angry red spots and bleeding welts. His head was bowed low to his chest, the dirty mop of his light, wavy hair obscuring his face. A weak presence of vampiric energy lingered around him, but even if Damian couldn't feel it, the effect silver had on him left no doubt—the man on the cross was a vampire or some kind of representative of the undead supernatural community.

"What the hell," mumbled Damian, heading toward him. *Why would vampires torture one of their own?*

The man moaned again and lifted his head slightly, which caused him visible effort. His eyes weren't glowing scarlet as Damian expected from a thirsty vamp. Instead, they were pure, crystal-blue, a haunted expression slowly vanishing as his gaze lingered on Damian's face. His full lips parted, a few drops of dark blood slipping from the cut on his lower lip. A weak, tortured smile lifted the corners of his mouth, exposing his straight, white teeth. But just like there was no scarlet glow in his eyes, his fangs weren't expanded.

Damian froze, barely able to breathe as he recognized the man on the cross.

A single thick, red drop escaped the vampire's eyes, leaving a shining path on his dirty cheek, and relief suffused his features.

"Hello, brother," he whispered. His eyes rolled back, and he fainted, hanging limply in his restraints.

CHAPTER 10

~ DAMIAN BLAKE ~

A strangled scream escaped Damian's tightly pressed lips as he closed the distance between himself and the vampire in two long-legged strides. With shaking hands, he unraveled the silver chains, careful not to inflict more pain and damage on him. With a loud clatter, the chains dropped to the ceramic tiles one by one.

Holding the vampire in his arms, Damian lowered him gently to the floor. He placed his head on his lap and grabbed a towel lying next to him, wrapping it around the man's hips.

"Nikolai," he whispered, throwing the man's matted hair off his face. "Kolya, *malish*... please open your eyes, my boy... please..."

Damian stared down at the motionless face of his brother, unable to believe his eyes, gathering tears making his image a shapeless blur. All these centuries, he had been sure his brother was dead. He had seen him fall in battle. He'd been told that he didn't make it. Every day, he wished Nikolai was alive, and every day, he mourned his death. Every day, until today.

Gently caressing his brother's cold cheek with his thumb, Damian smiled, an explosive concoction of emotions—happiness, pain, disbelief—brewing within him. He looked just the way he remembered him—the image of his brother the way he'd seen him the last time forever engraved in his memory. The same strong face with angled features framed by soft blond curls. The same bright blue eyes and full lips. A few centuries later, he still looked like the twenty-eight year old man he was then.

Damian slapped him slightly on his cheek, but the vampire remained motionless. *Dammit, they tortured and starved him.* A thought flashed in his mind, and he looked around, searching for something sharp. Noticing a few empty glass jars on the floor next to the cross, he grabbed one of them and smashed it against the floor.

Holding a sharp piece of glass, he raised it over his forearm, ready to slice it, when the door into the bathroom opened up with a loud bang.

Damian flinched and leaned forward, instinctively shielding his brother with his own body. But before he could turn around, a loud voice behind him commanded, "Slowly, put down the glass and put your hands behind your head." Damian made a move to turn around, but the voice stopped him in his tracks. "Do it now! Hands behind your head!"

With shivers running down his back, Damian lowered the piece of glass to the floor and placed his hands behind his head, interlocking his fingers. "Whatever you think I did, I didn't do it, sir," he said, holding his position.

Two pairs of hands seized his arms, twisting his hands behind his back. As the metal of the handcuffs bit into his skin, Damian grunted, clenching his teeth. They hauled him to his feet, forcing him to step back. Two policemen approached his brother, checking his vitals, and Damian cringed inwardly, realizing that to them he appeared to be dead—no pulse, icy-cold skin, no breath. And if that wasn't enough, there were two dead people in the other room.

Triple homicide... Dammit, where is Mrs. Davidson?

"He's alive," he said to the policemen who were checking the vampire. "And I didn't do any of this. Please, ask the owner of the hotel. She can confirm that I just opened the door into the room a few minutes ago and found everything the way you see it."

"We'll figure it out," said another deep male voice behind him. "In the meantime, read him his rights and take him away."

Damian winced and turned around as he recognized the voice. "Jesse... um... Detective Williams, please, let me—," started Damian but cut himself off, realizing that with River's partner running the show, he was doomed to spend at least twenty-four hours in jail.

A crooked smirk distorted Jesse's lips, and he huffed, shoving his hands into the pockets of his suit pants. "Not so high and mighty now, are you?" Then he jerked his chin at Damian and commanded, "Get this ogre out of here."

Throwing a glance at his brother, Damian noticed that he moved, slowly regaining consciousness. If only he could wait another few minutes, Nikolai could confirm his innocence.

"You have the right to remain silent. Anything you say can and will be used against you in a court of law. You have the right..." The voice of a policeman melted into the disarray of thoughts in his mind as they led him through the room and out the door.

* * *

DAMIAN WENT through the booking procedure barely realizing what he was doing, answering all the questions like on autopilot. A stampede of wild thoughts swirled in his mind, and he couldn't focus on anything. Recording his information, taking mugshot and fingerprints weren't a problem for him. But when the time came to take his clothes off for the strip search procedure, he stiffened, realizing what the examiner would see as soon as he checked him.

"What on earth...?" exhaled an older man in police uniform, staring at his back. "I've never seen anything..." He walked around and halted in front of Damian, staring up at him, his eyes widened with horror. "All this scar tissue on your back and legs... How did you receive all these injuries? Who did this to you?"

"Is this question a part of the booking procedure, sir?" Feeling exposed and vulnerable, Damian averted his gaze, his voice a strained whisper as he put all his effort into keeping his power under control.

The officer looked up at him and shook his head. "No," he replied, tones of sympathy and remorse in his voice, "sorry, I couldn't help it. You can get dressed now."

Damian barely registered the rest of the booking process. When he was escorted to the holding cell, he stopped in the middle of the room and turned around, observing the tiny space he was confined to. With his wide shoulders and his height, he felt like the walls were closing in on him. A deep shudder ran through him, and he staggered backward until his back hit the wall. He slid down to the floor and pulled his legs to his chest, wrapping his arms around his head.

He wasn't sure if it was just him being uncomfortable with small spaces or if it was his connection with the element of Earth that gave him this semblance of claustrophobia. Even riding in modern cars alone made him anxious, and right now, he could barely control his nerves and his power that was connected to his emotions.

* * *

A GUST of cold air rushed through the cell, and Damian lifted his head, wondering if it was an air conditioner or something entirely different. As he looked around, his vision blurred, cold wrapping around him, freezing him from the inside. He blinked a few times, pressing the heels of his hands to his eyes, shivering violently. When he could see again, his surroundings had changed.

He sat on the rough floor of a tiny cell, completely immobilized by the size of it. The room was so small he could only sit in the same position with his legs bent and his head bowed low. Even with his head down, he was still touching the ceiling, and his shoulders touched the walls on either side. The cell was semi-dark and smelled musty. A narrow ray of light broke through the little window covered by iron lattice, reflecting from wide metallic cuffs on his bound hands.

Damian stared at the cuffs and shuddered, his heart beating heavily against his ribcage. "No," he hissed, cold sweat running down his face. "It can't be... I'm done with all that. I paid—"

He wasn't sure how long he spent in this tiny, dark hole. His limbs had gone numb by the time the door into his cell opened and someone grabbed his arm, pulling him out. With his mind on fire, he resisted, but to no avail. A moment later, he found himself on all fours in a long, well-lit hallway. Right before his face, there was a pair of well-polished white shoes. Slowly, he lifted his face and saw a tall man dressed all in white standing in front of him.

"No," moaned Damian. "It can't be. It's some kind of illusion. I'm done with all of you. We had an agreement."

The man chuckled gently. "What are you talking about, child?" he asked, leaning forward a little. "Don't you remember what happened to you? You died defending Prince Vladimir. An honorable death of a warrior, I must say. Just a moment ago." He thought for a moment and added with a half-shrug. "Well, technically, you didn't die. Your power makes you immortal. So, yes, we had no choice but to remove you from the battlefield and bring you here."

Damian gaped at him just now realizing it wasn't an illusion. It was a memory. He was reliving one of the most painful memories of his life, and he remembered everything as if it happened just yesterday.

"Sorry about the cuffs." The man sighed, helping him to his feet. "Just before you were killed, your power activated. Unfortunately, these cuffs are the only thing that keeps your power from running wild, destroying this wonderful building." He waved his hand around, leading him through the long, white hallway. "I'm too fond of this place. It has a sentimental value, you know? So, let's keep it intact, shall we?"

He stopped in front of a tall white door and opened it, allowing Damian to walk in first. At that time, everything he saw in this place looked strange to him—the unusual furniture, the way this man was dressed and the way he spoke. The man crossed the room and sat down in one of the large, soft armchairs, gesturing for Damian to take a seat.

"I'm prepared to make you an offer, and something tells me, you won't refuse it, my child," said the man, watching as Damian took a seat.

I'm not a child... I wasn't then, and I am definitely not now. I should have told him to take this offer and shove it...

"You have a remarkable power, boy. You don't know it yet, but the elemental beings of Earth are quite rare. So, we are the only people who can teach you how to control and use your element and your magic," continued the man, his unyielding glowing eyes drilling through Damian's chest. "Once you're ready, you'll join our team, fighting on the side of Light to keep the realm of humans safe and to protect the World of Magic from exposure. Should you accept my offer, we won't just teach you how to use your power, we'll enhance and magnify it tenfold making you one of the most powerful beings of magic. So, what do you say, boy?"

A cold shiver ran down Damian's spine as he recalled how

this man had made him feel at the time. Lost and confused, he could barely understand what he was saying. Magic? Elemental powers? All that made no sense to him, but he remembered what he asked next.

"How about my brother? Is he here too?"

"I'm truly sorry, child," replied the man, a shadow of sadness darkening his glowing eyes. "Unfortunately, we were too late to save Nikolai. He was lost to us."

The pain of loss constricted his chest, and he struggled to breathe, gasping in short, uneven breaths. His little brother was his world. Except for Nikolai, he had no one in his life, and he had sworn to his mother on her deathbed that he would die before he would let anything happen to him. Now, his brother was dead... He failed...

"Say yes, child," continued the man, his voice kind and insinuating. "Say yes, and I swear, we will help you avenge your brother."

Damian raised his bloodshot eyes at him. He knew it was just a memory and there was nothing he could do to change it.

"Yes..." A soft whisper escaped his lips, setting his destiny in motion forever.

A loud banging sound invaded his ears, and the room spun around him, disappearing into a sickening swirling blizzard. He closed his eyes and allowed the rotating darkness to swallow him.

* * *

WHEN HE OPENED HIS EYES, he was back in the holding cell, lying flat on the icy concrete floor. The banging didn't stop, and someone's voice was screaming something, but he couldn't understand the meaning, his mind still trapped somewhere between his past and present. He pushed himself up with a low groan, scrambling into a sitting position.

Nikolai is alive. That was his first thought as he stared at the jail guard banging at the bars of his cell with his baton. The second thought was more troubling. *What if they took him to a hospital? A thirsty vampire who was tortured for God knows how long? Heaven and Earth, I hope not... I need to get out of here...*

"Blake. Damian Blake!" shouted the guard.

"Yes, sir," Damian managed to say. Still feeling unsteady, he got up to his feet and approached the bars, wondering what could have triggered this old memory in such a vivid detail.

"Turn around, hands behind your back," the guard ordered, a pair of handcuffs dangling from his finger.

Damian turned around and crossed his hands behind his back, allowing the guard to restrain him.

"Let's go," said the guard unlocking the cell. "Detective Williams wants to have a word with you." His eyes moved up and down, taking in Damian's height, and he smirked. "I see why he said to take special care while handling you."

Damian shrugged indifferently and followed the guard into an interrogation room. He walked inside a small room with a table, three chairs and a one-way mirror that took most of the space on one of the walls. Sitting down on a bolted chair, he patiently waited while the guard removed his restraints just to secure his right arm to a cuff bar. As soon as the guard was gone, he folded his arms on the table and rested his forehead atop his folded arms.

Even with all the security camera and handcuffs, he could easily escape using his magic. However, since exposing the World of Magic to humans wasn't a good idea and living his life as a fugitive wasn't in his plans either, he decided against it. Besides, he wanted to wait and see what Detective Williams had in mind, still believing Jesse had some kind of hidden role in everything that was going on in Blue Creek and in the mystery surrounding Paradise Manor.

Detective Williams wasn't in a rush, and Damian wasn't sure

how long he spent in the freezing interrogation room alone. From the moment the guard brought him in, he didn't move and didn't change his position. He felt exhausted, and his mind was drifting on and off, lingering on the border between a dream state and the strange reality he lived in. When the door into the room opened up and Jesse walked in, he felt almost relieved, hoping to get at least some answers to all the questions swirling in his head.

Jesse didn't sit down, but instead, walked to the security camera and turned it off manually. Damian stifled a sigh, knowing perfectly well that this meant nothing good to him.

"Damian Blake," said Jesse, his lips distorting into a snarl as he made his way to the table and sat down. "Your records are so clean, it's almost unreal for a man like you. Not so much as a parking ticket came up."

"You can't get a parking ticket if you don't own a car," muttered Damian with a half-shrug.

Ignoring him, Jesse threw a folder on the table and opened it, pulling a piece of paper out of it. He put the paper on the table and took a pen out of his inside pocket as if ready to write something, but then changed his mind and placed the pen back down. "Who are you, Blake, and what are you doing in my town?"

Damian raised his eyes, meeting the dark gaze of the detective without blinking. "I'm no one," he replied calmly. "I'm in *your* town"—he stressed the word 'your' unable to hide his sarcasm—"because I work for Sam Vetrov. He can confirm my statement."

"So, what you're saying is that you're some kind of trained killing machine who works as a handyman?" Jesse laughed coldly. "This makes total sense. Who do you think I am, asshole?"

Damian's lips curled up in an uneven smirk before he could stop it, eliciting a growl of anger out of Jesse. The detective jumped to his feet and walked around the table. Seizing the longer strand of his hair on the front, he yanked Damian's head backward exposing his face.

"Don't presume for one second that you can lie to me, Blake," he growled, fury contorting his face. "I remember the way you disarmed me. You didn't even blink. Your body functioned on its own. Call it instinct, muscle memory, natural reaction. Call it whatever the hell you want. I know one thing, though—it takes years of vigorous training to achieve this level of expertise in any style of martial arts. So, let me repeat my question, douchebag. Who are you?"

"No one," repeated Damian, doing his best to stay calm. "I'm also not the person who killed the young couple in the hotel. You're wasting your time with me instead of searching for the real killer."

A low growl sounded in Jesse's throat as he pulled Damian's head farther back and ran his thumb over the scar on his face, cutting into his skin with his fingernail.

"I will get the truth out of you, or so help me God, I will make your ugly face look symmetrical," he growled through gritted teeth, anger permeating the air around him.

Damian jerked his head, ignoring the pain as he left a strand of his hair in Jesse's hand. Squeezing his fists, he pulled against his restraints, doing all he could to keep his power under control as fury boiled up in him. Despite his efforts, the floor quaked a little, and the pen rolled off the table, falling to the floor with a soft thud.

Jesse seized Damian's neck, forcing his head up, and then raised his right hand, his fingers clenched into a tight fist. Damian dropped his left arm and remained still, taking deep breaths as he stared straight up at the infuriated detective. He couldn't allow himself to react. He couldn't lose control of his power.

"Well, hello, Detective," a deep but soft voice filled with

mockery sounded on his left. "I do admire your interrogation technique."

Jesse let go of Damian and staggered back, looking in the direction of the entrance. Damian turned his head and held his breath. Accompanied by detective River Evans, his brother stood in the doorway. He looked absolutely normal as if he hadn't been tied up with silver to a cross just a few hours ago. Dressed in an immaculate business suit and tie, he stood tall with his left hand in the pocket of his pants, his blue eyes blazing with silent anger. Damian's mouth opened, but his brother frowned giving him a barely visible shake of his head, and he snapped his mouth shut.

Nikolai took a step forward, offering his hand to Jesse with a perfect smile that left his eyes icy-cold.

"Allow me to introduce myself, Detective," he said, his voice perfectly leveled and calm. "Cole Adams." His fingers wrapped around Jesse's hand, and the detective paled as the vampire squeezed it a little stronger than etiquette required. "I'm here to testify on behalf of the man who saved my life." His frosty smile grew wider as he finally let go of Jesse's hand and pointed at Damian.

River approached Damian and unlocked the handcuffs, setting him free. "Mr. Blake, please accept my apologies. You're free to go." She threw an angry glance at Jesse and switched her attention back to Damian. "I hope our agreement still stands?"

He got up, rubbing his wrist where the handcuff bit into it, skinning it to blood. "Of course, ma'am. It's not your fault that your partner is a self-important asshole," he replied with surprise noticing how hoarse his voice was. "I have to go back to the hotel room and take care of a few things. I'll see you tonight just as we agreed."

Keeping his eyes down, he headed toward the exit, barely able to take a breath. All he wanted was to spend a few minutes with his brother, to speak with him, to make sure it was really him, his mind still refusing to process the reality. But Nikolai, or Cole Adams rather, made it clear—he didn't want to disclose the fact that they knew each other. At least not yet.

As he reached the exit, Cole seized his elbow, stopping him.

"Detective Williams," the vampire said, his voice coming out like a dangerous purr of a large feline. "Is there anything I need to sign?"

Jesse shook his head, his eyes darting from Damian to River and then back. Cole smirked darkly and opened the door for Damian.

"Mr. Blake," he said, warmth suffusing his hard features, "please allow me to give you a ride to wherever you need to go. This is the least I can do at the moment to express my gratitude."

Unable to say a word, Damian nodded and walked out the door.

CHAPTER 11

~ DAMIAN BLAKE ~

A little while later, Damian walked out of the police building accompanied by his brother. He halted and turned to face him, but Cole shook his head, a warning in his cerulean eyes.

"Keep walking. Don't say a word until we get inside my car," he said so softly that Damian had to strain his hearing.

Cole crossed the parking lot and stopped in front of a silver sports car. Damian stared at the luxury vehicle that cost more than some people's houses and raised his hands, backing away from it.

"I can't..." he mumbled, throwing a guilty look at his brother. "I don't think I can even fit in into this car."

Cole chuckled, gazing heavenwards. "I forgot about your dislike of small spaces," he said, throwing his hands up. "I can't believe you still didn't get over it. Anyway, this is my fastest car, and I wanted to get here as fast as I could. Besides, I'm only two inches shorter than you, and I fit inside without any problems. So, man up, big bro, and get in."

Still chuckling, he walked around the car and slid into the driver's seat. Gritting his teeth, Damian folded his massive frame into the passenger seat and locked the seat belt. Cole started the engine and drove the car out of the parking lot and onto the main street.

"Just fair warning, brother. This town thrives on gossip," he said, pushing down the accelerator pedal, ignoring the speed limit signs. "Everyone knows everyone, and everyone has their noses in their neighbor's business. There are no walls thick enough that could stop the wagging tongues." He wrinkled his nose, and Damian's heart skipped a beat. His brother had never gotten rid of this little childhood habit. "So, let's keep up appearances. Damian Blake? Is that the name you go by?"

Damian nodded, not sure he was capable of coherent speech at the moment. Cole smiled, throwing a sideways glance at him as he pulled his car into the parking lot of the hotel, stopping it in front of the main entrance.

"What a dump," he murmured, shutting down the engine.

Only too happy, Damian got out of the car and headed toward the hotel. He unlocked the door and let his brother in first. Cole halted in the middle of the room and looked around, shaking his head.

"Jeez, man, how do you live like this?" he asked, turning to face Damian. "I don't care what you say, put your shit together. I'm getting you out of here."

Damian stood by the door, unable to move or say a word, silently gazing at his brother whom he had buried centuries ago. Cole met his eyes, and the expression on his face changed, perfectly reflecting everything Damian felt at the moment. His lips parted a little, and a deep vertical wrinkle crossed his forehead.

"I thought you were dead," they both said at the same time.

"Technically, I am dead." Cole shrugged, opening his arms.

"I don't care," replied Damian, his voice coming out in a raspy, strangled growl.

He covered the distance between them and pulled his

brother into a tight embrace. Closing his eyes, he swallowed the tears burning behind his tightly pressed eyelids, feeling Cole's arms locking around his shoulders. His fingers found their ways into his brother's mass of unruly blond curls, and he stilled, barely able to believe it wasn't a dream.

"Your body was never found, but I never believed that you died that day under the bridge... I have been searching for you." Cole pulled away, the pained, vulnerable expression on his face making him look younger. "All these centuries... As soon as my maker allowed me to live on my own, I started looking for you all over the human realm. Where were you?" He stopped talking, and his lips opened up, his fangs slightly elongating, betraying his vampiric nature for the first time since Damian met him in this strange town. "What are you? You can't be human... Who are you, Dima?"

"I'm no one," whispered Damian, averting his eyes. "I'm a Child of Earth whose powers were partially stripped. The energy of Earth in combination with magic makes me immortal, but I am... less than no one..." His voice broke, and he pinched the bridge of his nose with his fingers, biting his lip.

"I think I've heard of you," whispered Cole, his pale face losing whatever color he had. "The Queen of Arizona warned every vampire in the state that you were moving here. You're some hunter or slayer who moves from state to state, destroying everything undead in his way. She was forced to cooperate with the Demonic rulers of other states to send a few teams to intercept you along the way from Florida. Are you a slayer, Dima? *The Shadow Slayer?*"

"Is that what they call me? The Shadow Slayer? Cute..." Damian shook his head, barely meeting his brother's widened eyes. "But no. I'm not a slayer, brother. Slayers kill vampires. The proper name would be the Shadow Hunter, I guess, since I don't discriminate against *any* supernatural monsters. If they kill humans, I kill them. As simple as that."

"Simple? Nothing is simple." Cole staggered back a few steps and dropped to the bed, looking up at him, a haunted expression in his glowing scarlet eyes. "Are you going to kill me, Dima? I'm an ancient vampire. I'm fast, strong, deadly. I have killed hundreds of humans over the centuries. Am I one of the monsters you're going to slay?"

"Never," whispered Damian, chills running down his spine at the thought. He approached his brother and sat down on the floor, crossing his legs. "I swear, I'd rather die than lose you again. I don't care what you are."

Cole smirked, sadness shadowing his features. "We're both old enough to know it doesn't work like this, brother," he objected, his fingers digging into the bedspread, tearing holes through it. "In the World of Magic, there is always someone who yanks your leash. In my case, it's my maker and the Queen of Arizona. Who are you bowing to, big bro? Who pulls your strings?"

"No one," replied Damian. A blur of memories, painful and unwanted, flushed through his mind, his lips curving into a bitter smirk of their own accord. "I stand alone. No one yanks my leash. Not anymore."

"Impossible..."

With a suppressed sigh, Damian scrambled to his feet. Grabbing the collar of his T-shirt, he pulled it off and turned his back toward Cole, his moves painfully slow.

"I have the scars to prove it," he said quietly. "I refused to obey. I got tired of being a mindless pawn in someone else's game." The bed squeaked as Cole got up, and Damian winced, feeling the gentle touch of his brother's cold fingers on his back. "I got my freedom, but at a terrible price." He turned around, putting his shirt back on. "Do you believe me now?"

"I've seen a fair share of shit in my life," said Cole, his voice deep, his eyes glowing brighter. "But I've never seen anything like this. Who was your master, brother? What did they do to you?"

"I swear, I will never lie to you," replied Damian, his fingers tracing the edge of his leather bracelet, "but this is the only thing I can't tell you." He looked out the window, the dull ache in his heart expanding, constricting his throat. "I can't tell you who they were. It was one part of my agreement with them—I must keep their identity a secret. But I can tell you some of what they've done to me. They partially stripped my power and left me on my own in the realm of humans—a broken and helpless mess at the mercy of any supernatural freak who had a grudge against me. Trust me, there were plenty of those..."

He smirked bitterly, his mind traveling back in time. For a few long moments, complete silence engulfed the room. Like all vampires, Cole could keep motionless for a long time, and right now, he was absolutely still and quiet, his glowing, wide eyes filled with murderous intent. His look sent shivers down Damian's back, and he swallowed hard.

"So, yeah," he continued at length. "For years, I moved from place to place, trying not to attract attention to myself from either the human or supernatural community. I don't age, and I gain enemies very fast, as you have probably noticed. So, I never stay more than a few years in the same city. Like I said, I'm no one. And this is the best I can do."

"Oh... God damn them all," hissed Cole, pain and anger making his voice shake. "You're not alone, Dima. Not anymore." He looked away, frowning, but then smirked and waved his hand around. "We'll start by leaving this shithole. Get your stuff. I'm taking you home."

Damian chuckled, shaking his head. "Wait, Cole. I'm leaving this hotel today, but I can't go with you. There is something I must do first." In so many words, he told his brother everything that had happened since he left Florida and followed Sam Vetrov to Blue Creek, Arizona.

Cole listened to him without interrupting, and when he finished, he just smirked, throwing his hands up.

"You're a real magnet, aren't you? How did you manage to get neck-deep into supernatural shit in a matter of a few days?" he murmured. "Ghosts, demons, shifters-for-hire, vampires, warded secret chambers." He whistled. "And that not counting the local human authorities. Wow! Sounds fascinating. I wouldn't miss this fun for the world." Cole laughed, his laughter youthful and contagious, making Damian smile, too. "Count me in." He sobered up and headed toward the exit. "I believe you need to check out, and I wanted to ask the hotel owner a few questions, anyway."

He kicked the door open and gestured for Damian to follow him. Taking the narrow path by the wall, they headed to the hotel main entrance and walked inside. The lobby was blissfully empty, and the hotel owner's daughter sat behind the counter, as always deeply engaged with her cellphone.

Damian approached the counter and knocked on it, throwing a veiled glanced at his brother. The girl sighed and put away her phone with a disgruntled look. As her gaze darted from Damian to Cole, her eyes widened, and she held her breath for a brief moment. Then she jolted to her feet, clasping her hands in front of her, her eyes lighting up in awe.

"You are..." she breathed out, pressing her hands over her mouth. Then she squealed and added in one breath, "You are Cole Adams. Please tell me you really are Cole Adams." She fell silent, looking pleadingly at him.

Cole smiled, humorous twinkles dancing in his eyes. "What if I am?" He leaned forward, cocking his eyebrow at the girl.

"Ohmigod... ohmigod... ohmigod..." she kept repeating breathlessly, hopping in one place. "No one will believe me..."

Damian threw a puzzled glance at his brother, but he gave him a tiny shake no and reached into his jacket pocket, producing a business card. Grabbing a pen from the counter, he wrote something on the back of it and gave it to the girl.

"When you go shopping at the Blue Creek game shop, show this card to the owner," he said, straightening. "He'll give you my newest game free of charge." He thought for a moment and added, "Can I have your cellphone, please?"

"Of course... Anything," she whispered, offering it to him.

Cole took the phone out of the girl's trembling hand and switched it to the camera. Pulling her closer, he snapped a selfie and gave it back to her. "Now, everyone will believe you."

"Ohmigod... Thank you so much, Mr. Adams," she squealed, staring at the screen of her phone.

"You're very welcome, sweetheart," he replied with a sunshiny smile. "Now, Mr. Blake and I need to speak with your mom. Can you please fetch her for us?"

"Mr. Blake?" She raised her eyes, looking as if she just remembered Damian was here too. "You and Mr. Blake—"

"Are like this." Cole winked at her, showing her two crossed fingers. "BFFs. So, would you get your mom for us, please?"

She nodded and rushed out the backdoor. A few minutes later, she came back, accompanied by Mrs. Davidson. As soon as the hotel owner saw Damian, she blanched and froze in place, her eyes wide.

"Hello, Mrs. Davidson," said Damian, reaching into the back pocket of his pants. "I would like to check out. What do I owe you?"

She shifted her terrified gaze to the computer screen and then shook her head without lifting her eyes. "You owe me nothing, Mr. Blake. Please bring your keys to the front desk once you're ready to leave."

Damian put away his wallet, ready to go, but Cole seized his arm, stopping him. He leaned forward ever so slightly. "Hello, Mrs. Davidson," he said, his voice soft and sweet. "My name is

Cole Adams. Would you be so kind as to answer just one question for me?"

She raised her head, locking her eyes with Cole's. "Cole Adams?" she asked, a sheepish smile stretching her lips. "As in the Cole Adams, that rich entrepreneur who disappeared in Blue Creek a short while ago? It was all over the newspapers..."

"Yes, ma'am. As you can see, I re-appeared. Newspapers like to exaggerate things," he replied, leaning forward a little more. A soft scarlet glow ignited in his eyes, but neither Mrs. Davidson nor her daughter seemed to notice it. "Mrs. Davidson, can you please tell me why you didn't tell the police that Mr. Blake didn't kill that couple or abduct me for that matter?"

She blanched and perspiration covered her forehead, but she didn't say anything, her fingers squeezing a pen until it broke in her hands.

Cole's smile grew wider, and his eyes shone brighter as he leaned closer to her and whispered, his voice sounding like an insinuating purr, "Please, answer my question."

Damian stilled, realizing what his brother was doing. The vampiric energy spiked around Cole as he turned on his "charm", invading her mind with his glamor.

"I don't know..." The woman's lips trembled, tears gathering in her eyes, but she couldn't break the trance on her own, and Cole wouldn't let go. "I don't even remember why I sent my daughter to bring him over... I remember calling Sam, and after that everything is blank..."

Cole took her hands into his gently and pulled her closer. "Look into my eyes, darling," he murmured, his vampiric energy rising even higher. "Who asked you to summon Damian and leave him there? Look back... it's all in your brain... somewhere..."

He pulled her closer, whispering something into her ear. The woman's transfixed eyes became foggy, and she moaned, her fingers caressing Cole's hand.

"A woman... tall and beautiful... long black hair and large brown eyes," she moaned. "I remember... she told me to summon Mr. Blake and then call the police once he was inside the room."

A dark smirk crossed Cole's face, and he let go, pushing away from the counter. The woman stared around, dazed and confused, as if she had just woken up. Her eyes settled on the vampire, and her eyebrows rose.

"I'm sorry," she mumbled. "Did you ask something?"

"No, ma'am," replied Damian. "We'll be on our way now. I'll drop the keys off in a few minutes."

He grabbed Cole's arm, ushering him out the door. They made it to the room without talking. Once inside, Cole shut the door behind them and shoved his hands into the pockets of his pants.

"Wow," he muttered, rocking back and forth on his feet slightly. "Your life is like a friggin' fairy tale. The farther you go, the scarier it becomes."

"What are you talking about?" asked Damian, quickly stuffing whatever little belongings he had in his travel backpack.

"The woman who ordered Mrs. Davidson to feed you to the local hounds," said Cole, observing his backpack with interest. "Do you know who she was?"

"I can count the people I know here on the fingers of one hand," replied Damian, checking the room and the bathroom to make sure he didn't forget anything. "Who is she, anyway? Do you know?"

"I have a suspicion." Cole smirked, his eyebrows rising as he watched his brother approach him with a single backpack in his hand. "That's all you have?"

"I travel light." Damian swung the backpack over his shoulder and opened the door, allowing Cole out first. "So, who was she?"

"If I'm not mistaken, she's the Queen of Arizona's Vampire Court," murmured Cole, making his way through the parking lot. "Congrats, big bro. You made her blacklist, and it means nothing good for you." He rubbed the back of his neck and added with a soft chuckle, "And to me by association."

CHAPTER 12

~ DAMIAN BLAKE ~

The sun was gone, and night had fallen over the town when Cole drove his car through the gates of Paradise Manor. He parked it on the driveway in front of the entrance and leaned back in his seat, leaving the engine running. Damian noticed that the house entrance door was back in place and assumed that Sam had taken care of it while he was imprisoned.

"You know, I live maybe a mile away at the most," said Cole, pointing to the west of the property. "A while ago, I purchased the old Brown's estate as my vacation home."

"A vacation home?" repeated Damian absentmindedly, but then looked at his brother and smirked. "Who are you, Cole Adams? Teenage girls recognize you, panting after you as if you're a movie star. Where did you get all the money?"

"Not a movie star but one of Arizona's most eligible bachelors." With an indifferent shrug, Cole reached into his inside pocket and gave him a folded newspaper clipping. Damian took it and unfolded the paper, reading the already familiar headline —*An eccentric serial entrepreneur, investor and philanthropist, Cole Adams is still missing.*

"Eccentric serial entrepreneur," Damian read out loud. "Serial, alright. It's just a word other than the entrepreneur that comes to mind."

"Hey, take it easy, Shadow Slayer." Cole laughed, giving him a slight punch on the shoulder. "It's been centuries since I fed on a human without their consent or killed for that matter. I promise I don't glamor them to get their blood donation either. Everything I do is legit. As far as money—I work hard to earn it. I own a large tech company in Phoenix, and I built it from the ground up," explained Cole with a half-shrug. "Pays the bills, you know?"

"How do you do it, Cole?" asked Damian quietly. "You don't age either. And how do you manage to control your nature, being around humans all day long?"

"Haven't you heard? I am eccentric." He laughed, throwing a strand of his hair off his face. "People think I do plastic surgeries to keep my youthful appearance. And once in a while"—he twirled his wrist, a mischievous grin on his face—"I use magic to modify some records and memories. The almighty dollar can buy some serious wizard-power." He fell silent, thinking, humor slowly dying down in his bright eyes. "As far as my nature. I'm a thousand-year-old vampire, Dima. I know how to control my urges."

Damian nodded and opened the car door, stepping onto the warm asphalt of the driveway. Cole shut down the engine and followed him. As Damian pressed the button of the doorbell, Cole touched his shoulder, a guilty grin on his face.

"I'm going to need an invitation," he said quietly. "You know, vampire and all."

"I know," replied Damian, feeling torn inside. He still wasn't sure how he felt about his brother being an ancient vampire with hundreds, if not thousands of kills, under his belt. Could he trust him the way he used to, or was he loyal to his kind now? After all, they had been separated for over a thousand years. But one thing he was positive about—vampire or not, he still loved his little brother as much as he had when they were kids, and he wasn't lying when he told him he would die before he would let anything happen to him.

The entrance door opened softly, ripping him out of his thoughts. Still dressed in her business suit, River stood in the doorway. As her eyes halted on Damian, a barely visible smile touched her lips.

"Damian," she said. Her arm rose to touch his hand, but she changed her mind half-way through and lowered it. "I'm glad to see you. Are you okay after everything that happened this morning? I'm so sorry I couldn't be there earlier. I would never have let Jesse treat you like that."

"I'm fine. Thank you, ma'am," he replied but didn't move. "I see your father took care of the door. Have you had a chance to discuss our arrangement with him yet?"

"Yes, we discussed it alright." Sam's voice sounded from inside the foyer, and a moment later, he appeared next to River. Giving Damian a quick once-over, he smirked. "Before I sign off on your little arrangement, I would like to have a word with you, kid."

"No problem," replied Damian, "I expected that."

River huffed and threw her hands up. "I feel like I'm back in the fifteenth century, and my father's discussing my dowry with my future hubs." She rolled her eyes, eliciting a snort out of Cole. "Hello! Macho-men!" She waved her hand in front of her father's face. "I'm standing right here—a modern, independent woman, by the way."

Damian lowered his eyes, suppressing laughter.

"Hello, Detective," said Cole, offering her his hand for a handshake. "It's nice to see you again."

River shook his hand, her eyes narrowing for a heartbeat as her gaze darted from Cole to Damian and back. "I'm glad you're here, Mr. Adams. I would still like to discuss with you a few matters associated with your own case."

"Call me Cole, please." He smiled, his smooth elegance shining through a touch too strong, and Damian wondered if his brother turned on his vampire *'charm'* or if it was his natural demeanor. "There is no need for formalities."

"And who are you?" asked Sam, frowning, before River could say anything.

"Cole Adams," replied Cole, his smile growing wider as he offered his hand to Sam.

The old hunter squeezed his fingers in a handshake but held it a little longer than was necessary by accepted standards. "You have icy-cold hands, Mr. Adams," he said through gritted teeth, suspicion reflected in his eyes.

"It's a cool evening," replied Cole with an easy smile.

"Uh-huh, I guess you're right," muttered Sam. "Seventy-five degrees for Arizona is close to freezing temperature. Should I offer you a fur coat to warm up?"

"Father," hissed River, switching her attention to Cole. "Mr. Adams, please come in. Ignore my father."

As soon as they walked into the foyer, Cole stiffened, grabbing Damian's arm, but before he could say anything, River invited them to follow her through the hallways into the living area. Despite its size, the room was well illuminated with LED lights. A black leather sectional stood by the wall with a small glass coffee table in front of it. A couple of leather armchairs matching the couch were positioned on either side of it. A big-screen TV mounted on the opposite wall was tuned to the local news channel, and a few folders with the police department logo lay on the table.

"Mr. Adams," said River, throwing a reproachful glance at her father, "would you mind accompanying me to the kitchen while these two... antiquated jackasses discuss whatever they need to discuss."

She gestured toward the door, motioning for Cole to follow

her. Sam frowned, ready to object, but then changed his mind. As Cole and River left the room, he turned to Damian.

"What happened here last night?" he asked, a muscle twitching in his jaw. "River told me some of it, but her explanation was more than confusing."

In a few words, Damian described the events of the night before without holding any information back. When he was done, Sam exhaled, dropping his head into his hands. For a few moments, he remained silent and then raised his face, looking as if he had aged ten years in one moment.

"Can you protect her, son?" he asked quietly. "Do you know what is after her and why?"

"I have no idea." Damian sat down next to Sam, leaning forward slightly. "But I'm going to find out. In the meantime, it would be best if I moved here. I think this is the safest option for River since she doesn't want to hear about moving out."

Sam pressed his fingers to his eyes, exhaling, and then raked his hand through his gray hair. "Goddammit. I wish she had never gotten involved with the Evans-boy. That family is cursed, I swear."

"They weren't cursed, Sam," objected Damian, leaning back on the couch. "At least I don't think so. But some powerful supernatural creep is definitely after whatever is hidden in the left wing, and as long as River is here, she's in their way. I copied the architectural plans of the house, and I intend to visit the warded area again while she's at work."

"Fine. Maybe you're right," said Sam, turning a little to face Damian. "Here is what I was going to say, kid. River, even though she's some big shot police detective, for me she is always going to be my little girl. Do you understand that?"

Damian nodded.

"So, if by some strange coincidence," continued Sam, drilling him with his eyes, "while staying in this house, you lose your way around and find yourself in her bedroom at night, especially without a—"

Damian snorted as wild laughter bubbled up in his chest, and he struggled to suppress it. Sam threw a scorching gaze at him, and Damian raised his hands in a peaceful gesture, his eyes watering with laughter.

"Sam," he managed to say finally, "remember when we were driving here, you asked me how old I was?"

"So?"

"I'm over a thousand years old, man," said Damian, regaining his composure. "I was born in the year nine hundred sixty-two. Were you seriously going to give me the birds and the bees speech?"

"Jesus Christ almighty," breathed Sam, slapping his hand over his mouth. "Are you seriously that old? You look like a thirty-year-old boy."

"Who are you calling a boy? He is practically falling apart from age... A shitkicker... Your daughter is safe with him, Sam. I'm not sure all his body parts are still functioning..."

Damian winced at the sound of Gypsy's voice in his mind and threw a warning gaze at her. The cat strolled into the living room and hopped onto his lap, rubbing her head against his stomach.

"Hey, Sasquatch, did you know you brought a vamp into this house?" The cat stretched luxuriously, offering him her back to scratch.

"What is it with you and this cat?" asked Sam, his eyebrows rising. "She can't have enough of you. I hate cats. Give me a dog any day, but cats?"

"And the cats hate you too, Sam. It's mutual." Gypsy yawned, displaying a set of sharp fangs, and turned on her side under Damian's fingers.

The old hunter got up and leaned forward, massaging his knee. Then he halted in front of Damian, staring down at him intently. "Save my little girl, kid." His voice shook, and he frowned. "I wish I knew how, but it seems you're my only hope." He extended his hand to him.

"We're doomed." Gypsy snickered.

"I'll do everything I can," promised Damian, trying to muster as much confidence to his voice as he could, but doubt tore at his heart. He moved the cat to the couch and got up, shaking Sam's hand.

"Oh, awesome. I think they finally came to an agreement, and my future has been arranged." River's voice filled with sarcasm beyond limit sounded behind him, and Damian turned around. Both she and Cole walked into the living room, wild twinkles of laughter dancing in the vampire's eyes.

"Damian, I have to go," said Cole, suddenly serious. "My... um... banker summoned me." He lifted his hand with his cell phone. "Give me your number. I'll call you tomorrow before coming here."

"He doesn't have a phone. Can you believe it?" said River before Damian could answer, rolling her eyes. "But I'll force one on him tomorrow. I'll text you his new phone number as soon as I have it."

Cole's eyebrows climbed up, but he just thanked River and turned to Damian. "Would you mind walking me to my car?" he asked, giving him a pointed stare.

*   *   *

THEY WALKED BRISKLY through the hallway, and Cole stopped in the foyer in front of the silver mirror.

"Damian, the Lady of the Mirror," he whispered. "I don't think we're dealing with a ghost."

"How do you know?"

"I don't know. Just a guess." Cole grabbed Damian's arm and

pulled him closer to the antique mirror. "Look. What do you see?"

Damian stared into the mirror and then glanced at his brother. He could see his own reflection and the reflection of the surroundings, but the vampire wasn't there even though he stood right next to him.

"You don't have a reflection," muttered Damian, thousands of thoughts speeding through his mind. "You're a vampire—"

"Yes, I'm a vampire," Cole interrupted him snidely. "But I do have a reflection, and I don't sparkle under the sunlight. Doofus." He chuckled, pulling him out of the house. "Reading too many fantasy books lately?"

He led him toward his car and bent down, staring into the side mirror. Damian glanced over his shoulder and smirked. Of course, Cole had a reflection, and he knew it. Fighting with the undead for centuries, he was familiar with all their strengths, weaknesses and sneaky tactics. The no-reflection-story was just another urban legend the vampires had been spreading around for centuries to mislead humans.

"The mirror in the foyer is made of silver," said Damian. "Do you think this is the reason you don't reflect there."

Cole shook his head, a thoughtful expression suffusing his features. "Doubt that. Not the first silver mirror I've seen." He sighed, shoving his left hand into his pocket. "This is the reason I think the Lady of the Mirror is a spirit, but not a ghost."

Damian rubbed his chin, staring at Cole's reflection in the car window. "You're probably right," he said after a moment. "There are quite a few spirits that inhabit mirrors. I think if we find out which one we're dealing with, it'll help."

"If it would help, this particular spirit doesn't want to reflect evil," said Cole quietly, fidgeting with the car remote.

"You're not evil..."

Cole smirked, looking into the darkness of the night sky over Damian's shoulder. "I'm a vamp, Dima. I'm not proud of my past, but I've learned to live with it and everything I've done. I killed many people. Especially when I was new to all that." He dropped his head, frowning. "I'm positive that in the eyes of this spirit, it makes me evil."

"I think I know who it is," muttered Damian. "I'll have to do some research to confirm my suspicion, but if I'm right, it's good news."

"That's good." Cole raised his face, a haunted expression settling in the ocean depths of his eyes. "Here is the bad news. The phone call I received earlier wasn't from a banker."

"I figured," murmured Damian, unease spreading through him. "What's going on?"

"The Queen is summoning me in the middle of the night. It won't be the first time she summoned me at night, but—" He looked down at the small remote in his hand. "I have no choice. She's the Queen, and she's a lot older and stronger than I am. With my maker MIA, she is the only one who holds my leash, and she's not afraid to yank it. I have to comply with her demands, no matter what they are. Unless I want to rebel and become one of the rogues, that is. But that would mean the end of my peaceful co-existence with humans." He raised his eyes at Damian, and his lips parted. For a moment, he looked like a little child begging his big brother to protect him. "You have no idea how much I don't want to go. Especially not today..." His voice trailed off, and he smirked, his features becoming hard again. "We all have our bane, right? You have your scars. I have my leash."

"Cole, watch your back."

"I always do. Otherwise, I wouldn't have made it to this age." The car locks clicked as he pressed a button on his remote. Opening the door, he slipped inside and glanced up at Damian. "For God's sake, brother, get yourself a cellphone, would yah?" He chuckled, his natural cheerfulness returning to him. "No phone, no car. You live like a caveman, dude. Come on." He thought for a moment and added, "Unless you want me to create a blood bond with you instead." Cole winked, displaying the full length of his dangerous fangs.

Damian shuddered and rolled his eyes exaggeratedly. "Jeez, man, hide those blades. You look like a friggin' walrus."

Cole laughed, his fangs retracting, and started the car. "I'll see you tomorrow. Be careful."

The car took off and disappeared into the darkness.

CHAPTER 13

~ COLE ADAMS ~

A small sports car zoomed over the freeway, raising clouds of dust in its wake. Cole barely paid attention to anything around him, driving at the maximum speed he could squeeze out of his vehicle. Luckily, it was close to midnight, and the freeway was nearly empty. He wasn't worried about getting into an accident since his sharp vampiric senses and speed allowed him to react instantly to the changing situation on the road.

Even though he could move a lot faster than any vehicle, he enjoyed the power and the speed of a good sports car, and every time he sat behind the wheel, his heart sang in tune with the roaring engine. But today, he didn't feel his usual elation and excitement. The last call he received from the Queen set his nerves on edge, even though she hadn't said anything unusual or out of character.

It'd been close to two weeks since someone poisoned him with Silver Nitrate and abducted him from his vacation home in Blue Creek. He had no idea who it was or why they had done it. He also couldn't understand how they had managed to pass by his high-tech security system without triggering it. However, with all the events of the last day, he had no time to look into it.

What bothered him even more was that during this time the Queen of Arizona hadn't made an attempt to find him—or at least he didn't think she had. However, she showed up at the hotel to glamor the owner, and now, she wanted to see him in the middle of the night. Cole slammed his hand on the steering wheel, pressing down on the accelerator pedal.

More than anything, he was worried that the Queen had somehow learned he was the only brother of the so-called Shadow Slayer. He wasn't worried about himself. Through the centuries, Cole had survived more intrigues, backstabbing and betrayal of vampire royal courts than he cared to admit. He knew how to hold his own. He was worried about his brother. Damian was different. He had always been strong but too honest and straightforward to swim with the sharks and live to tell the tale.

On the other hand, the Queen of Arizona—an ancient vampire born somewhere in Persia during the rule of Alexander the Great—was as clever as she was deceiving and merciless. On the surface, she ruled in favor of keeping peace with the human population of the state, staying under the radar of the Destiny Council and any magical authorities. Nevertheless, Cole knew better. Well aware of all the shadow dealings and corruption of the Arizona Court, he didn't want any part of it. Instead, he spent years building his tech-company, running a legit business from both human and supernatural perspectives.

It seemed that Queen Roxana had decided to move against Damian, declaring open war on the Shadow Slayer to protect her shady enterprise from possible destruction. If that was the case, Cole would have to make a tough choice—support his Queen and stick with his kind or lose everything he worked so hard for and stand by his brother who killed anything without a heartbeat. For Cole, it wasn't really a choice. Now that he had his brother back in his life, he would do anything to keep him safe.

"*I'm no one...*"

Damian's words sounded in his mind, and he frowned, pressing his lips in a straight line. That didn't sound like the man he had admired since he could remember. While Damian had always been shy and awkward around people, he had never sounded so despondent and drained of life.

"Dima, what happened to you?" he whispered, pain gripping at his soul. He didn't like the chain of events associated with Paradise Manor in the slightest. Even more than that, he didn't like that his brother was in the middle of this unexplainable supernatural mayhem.

* * *

Cole passed through Phoenix, taking the road toward Paradise Valley. He had driven this path so many times, he could find his final destination with his eyes closed. Weaving through the narrow private road surrounded by tall Saguaro cacti, he approached the large wrought iron gates and stopped next to the security monitor, rolling down his window. He pressed the intercom button and upturned his face, showing who he was to the security cameras.

"The Queen summoned me," he said, pressing the communication button again.

The gates unlocked with a loud click and moved apart slowly. He pressed the button to roll up his window and drove his car across the property. Located between two mountains, the Queen's villa presented an astounding view. A large modern house—glass, stone, wood and copper—stood surrounded by a perfectly manicured desert landscape. He circled a large fountain with multicolored streams of water bursting around a roman style statue of a naked man and woman in a tight embrace.

Parking on the driveway in front of the main entrance, he squeezed the steering wheel, gathering his power of will before shutting down the engine. He got out of the car and headed toward the brightly lit entrance. The tall glass door opened before he had a chance to ring the bell, and the Queen's butler inclined his head, inviting him in with a sugary smile that showed the pointy tips of his fangs.

"Queen Roxana is awaiting you in her private chambers, my lord," he said, gesturing toward the dark hallway on the right of the dimly lit lobby. His lips stretched wider, and for some reason that sent shivers down Cole's back.

He thanked the butler and headed into the wide hallway. The sweet odor of pumpkin spice enveloped him, and he grunted, annoyance flaring through him. He had always hated this smell, but the Queen loved it, and her house was stuffed with scent diffusers, candles, and other types of expensive air fresheners permeating the air with their sickening-sweet fragrance.

The hallway was pitch-black, but that didn't slow him down. Cole had walked this hallway so many times, he didn't need light to find his way around. Besides, his sharp vision allowed him to see in the darkness relatively well. A feeling of being watched coiled within him, and he picked up the pace, his feet stepping soundlessly on the thick carpet.

He didn't see it coming. He detected the movement on his right with his heightened vampiric senses. His reaction was immediate yet belated. Someone's hand seized his shoulders. He spun around, leaving the jacket of his business suit in the hands of the assailant. The vampire growled, annoyance lingering around him as he threw the jacket to the floor.

"Baby-vamp." Cole laughed. "Too slow... too weak." He threw a punch that was too fast and powerful for the other vampire to block. Cole's fist crashed the attacker's jaw, and he crumpled to the floor, a cry of pain escaping his lips.

Knowing the Queen, and the way she loved to play her games, Cole didn't expect the baby-vamp to be alone. He ripped his tie off and threw it to the floor next to his jacket. If the Queen wanted to see him fight, he didn't need a noose around his neck. He rushed through the hallway at full speed and slowed down only when he stepped into a spacious lobby illuminated by the light of the moon coming through the tall, arched window.

The next attack came almost right away. The vampires moved fast and absolutely soundlessly, skillfully hiding their presence in the shadowy corners and behind the furniture. A rush of cold air infused with the vampiric energy alerted him, and he ducked to the side, anticipating the punch. He was right. A fist sailed past his face as a brawny vamp appeared in his vision for a brief moment and sped up, disappearing into a blur of motion again.

Cole picked up speed. He didn't need to see to know there were three vampires moving stealthily around him, getting closer and closer. They were fast and strong. It meant they were old, but maybe not as old as he was.

"Come and get me, assholes," he whispered and laughed, a dark and ominous sound that reverberated against the tall, vaulted ceiling.

Something moved next to him, but he didn't react. Instead, he stepped to the side and threw a punch, calculating the trajectory of the approaching attacker. His calculations were perfect as his fist connected with a vampire's nose. A sickening crunch and a howl of pain followed his move. Cole didn't stop to check on the man who was lying at his feet with his hands clenched to his face as dark blood gashed between his shaking fingers.

Stepping back into the empty space, he spun around just in time to avoid a powerful roundhouse kick directed at his head.

Even though his attacker missed his target, he didn't spin out of control. Quickly regrouping, the tall man stepped back, putting a few feet between them. Without waiting for his next move, Cole took a step forward, estimating the distance between him and his opponent. Then he pushed off the ground, brought his knee up and extended his leg into a powerful flying side kick.

His foot connected with the vampire's solar plexus before he could do anything to react. The force of the impact sent the large man flying across the room, and he hit the opposite wall with his back, sliding down to the floor. With his hands pressed to his chest, he stirred slightly, struggling to get up, but that wasn't in Cole's plans.

He crossed the lobby, seized the man's shirt, lifting him off the floor slightly, and then punched him in the face with full strength. The man gasped and hung limply in Cole's hand. Cole dropped him, but as he was ready to get up in search of the last vampire, someone jumped on his back.

The attack was silent and unexpected. The force propelled Cole forward, and he hit his forehand against the wall. For a heartbeat, he felt disoriented, which gave his assailant just enough time to rip his shirt off his shoulder and sink their fangs into his flesh. With a terrible roar, Cole reached back and seized the vampire, flipping them over his shoulder just to realize it was a woman. Uncontrollable anger swirled within him, about to explode. He raised his arm, ready to knock her out when someone's hands squeezed his head tightly, applying more and more pressure, eliciting a scream of pain out of him.

He reached back once more, but his hands found nothing. The pressure lifted abruptly, leaving him with a dull headache. He jumped to his feet and spun around just to receive a mighty blow between his eyes. The bright flare of light exploded in his vision as he collapsed to the floor and blacked out.

* * *

FEELING a few gentle slaps to his cheek, Cole groaned and cracked his eyelids open. The soft, flickering light of multiple candles and a delicate scent of smoke mixed in with the fragrance of pumpkin spice touched his senses. He made a move to get up just to realize he couldn't. He pulled against the metal restraints attaching his wrists and ankles to the enormous four-poster bed.

"Welcome back, my warrior..." A voice, soft and gentle like the purr of a cat, sounded on his left.

He turned his head, knowing ahead of time what he was going to see. A young, slim woman stood by the bedside. Candlelight reflected against her light, golden-brown skin, giving her a mysterious, exotic look, and her large brown eyes fogged with desire as she stared down at him without blinking. Her fingers brushed over her rich black hair styled into a single thick braid, and a slow, seductive smile stretched her sensual coral lips.

The light traveled through the sheer fabric of her wide pants and short top practically unobstructed, leaving almost nothing to the imagination. She looked delicate, seductive and enchanting, but Cole knew better. As far as ancient vampires go, she was one of the most dangerous of them all.

Cole sighed and turned away, closing his eyes.

"Your Majesty," he said flatly. "You summoned me because you wanted to see me fight or because you felt the need to knock me unconscious?"

She laughed softly, her laughter sounding like a gentle silver bell.

"Aw, Cole, don't be such a Debby Downer... What did you say to my baby-vamp earlier? Too weak? Too slow? I just wanted to show you that no matter how good you are, there is always someone who's older, faster, stronger..." She lowered herself down on the edge of the bed, her every move slow and graceful. "But I must admit, I do love watching you fight, my

Russian warrior. You have no idea how arousing you look when you feel cornered. The best foreplay ever." She ran her long, beautifully manicured fingernail over his cheek. "Almost as arousing as you look right now, tied up to my bed... helpless... completely in my power."

She leaned forward and kissed him, her tongue forcing his lips apart. Cole didn't resist but didn't answer her kiss either, patiently tolerating her advances. She didn't seem to care. Pulling away a few seconds later, she touched her lips with the tips of her fingers and smiled, candlelight reflecting in tiny crystals embedded in each of her nails.

"I missed you, lover," she said quietly. "You were gone too long—"

"And you didn't bother looking for me," he interrupted her icily.

"What makes you say that?" She smirked, arrogance shining in her dark eyes adorned by a generous layer of eyeliner and mascara. Cole didn't reply, turning his face away. She seized his chin, forcing him to look back at her.

"Please tell me why you summoned me, my lady," said Cole with a deep sigh. "I'm tired, and the thirst is driving me insane. I've spent almost two weeks attached to a cross and wrapped with silver, barely receiving any blood. I need a few days of peace so I can fully recover, and I still have a business to attend to..."

She moved her fingers over his lips, silencing him. Pressing deeper with her sharp fingernail, she cut his lower lip, letting a few drops of blood slide down his chin. With a soft moan, she leaned down. Her tongue swept over his chin and moved up over his lips. He wrinkled his nose, his upper lip curling into a snarl, exposing his fangs as he fought the desire to be as far away from this room and her possessive hands as he could. Turning his head to the side, a feral growl vibrated in his chest.

She gasped at his reaction, obviously reading it in her favor.

Straightening, she ripped his torn, bloodied shirt off, her hungry eyes traveling over his unobstructed torso. Her fingers fumbled with the button on the waistband of his pants as she slipped her hand inside, gently stroking him.

"Roxana, please, let me go," he moaned, his muscles tense as he pulled against the restraints. "Please, not now. I am drained, and the fight you made me go through didn't help. I don't think I'm capable of—"

"Your body suggests otherwise," replied Roxana dryly, giving a not-so-gentle squeeze to his crotch.

He hissed and jerked away from her, but then stilled, staring furiously at her.

"And if I let you leave, where are you going to go, Cole?" She pulled her hand out and got up, staring down at him with narrowed eyes, her arms crossed over her chest. "Home? Or to spend quality time with the Shadow Slayer?"

"What are you talking about?" asked Cole through clenched teeth.

"Don't play me for a fool," she hissed, her glowing eyes suddenly only inches away from his. "You should've known better by now. There is nothing you can hide from my eyes. The Shadow Slayer freed you from whoever held you captive, and then you testified to his innocence and gave him a ride back to the hotel."

Her hands squeezed his arm, her long fingernails digging into his bicep, drawing blood.

"What did you expect me to do? The man saved my life," growled Cole. "I owed him this much. Now we're even."

"Please tell me how you are still alive, imbecile! I bet you anything, he knew what you were the moment he touched your silver adornments!" She pulled away and backhanded him. His head jerked to the side, red spots dancing in his vision.

"Of course, he knew what I was, just like I knew who he was.

But I don't think he cared!" barked Cole, blood dripping from his split lips.

"I don't give a damn about what you think! You destroyed my plans, you fuckin idiot!" she shouted, her fangs expanding to their full length.

Cole tensed. Queen Roxana didn't like to use modern-day profanities, and hearing her say it, made his blood run cold. Even if he wasn't playing a part of her bed décor at the moment, he stood no chance fighting her. Besides, being the Queen of Arizona, she had a lot of supporters, mostly in the underground layers of the supernatural community, and killing her would mean certain death for him.

"I personally made sure that the hotel owner didn't testify in his favor. I *wanted* the Shadow Slayer in jail and under investigation by the human authorities," she continued in an angry hiss. Her lips curled up into a sneer, and her fingers hooked as her nails elongated into claws, digging deeper into his flesh. "That ogre made a mistake by showing up on my territory, and I'll make sure he's not going to leave it. At least not alive."

"How did you know?" asked Cole, touching his bleeding lips with the tip of his tongue. Icy fear coiled within him, poisoning him, sending his mind into a wild frenzy, but he made an effort to appear calm.

"Know what?" she asked, looking confused.

"That the Shadow Slayer would be there in the first place. And that there were two dead humans in that room?" he answered her question quietly, a terrible suspicion forming in his mind. "Did you put out the order to abduct and torture me, keeping me in that shithole hotel for all this time?"

"How dare you throw such ugly accusations at me!" she shouted. "I'm your Queen! If I wanted to torture you, I could have done it without playing any games. You're nothing but dirt under my feet." She stomped her foot, but Cole could sense some fluctuations in her voice through the righteous display of her fake anger.

Dammit! She is the one... but why? Does she know that the Shadow Slayer is my...? But I was taken before Damian even arrived here... What the hell is going on? Who is she after? Me or my brother? Or both? Thousands of crazy thoughts originated in his mind at once, and he couldn't find any answers that would make sense.

Making a split-second decision, he changed his tactics. "Of course, my lady," he mumbled, hoping that he looked believably horrified. "Oh, God..." He closed his eyes, praying his Academy Awards worthy performance was enough to convince her. "What was I thinking? I swear, once I tell you everything, you won't be as angry with me anymore. All I want is to beg for your forgiveness. Please untie me..."

"Oh, really." She rolled her eyes, tapping her fingers on the elbows of her folded arms.

"You are my Queen. I'm yours to do with as you please. But please, give me a chance to explain first," he pleaded, strangling the burning anger within him. "I believe I deserve this much."

"Let me be the judge of what you deserve." She glowered down at him for a moment, but then sighed and unlocked his restraints. "Go ahead, beg." She flicked her wrist with a dark smirk on her face. "If anything, that should be entertaining."

Okay, brother, you owe me big time... Groveling is not my style...

Cole sat down on the bed, massaging his sore wrists. Stifling a sigh, he lowered to his knees and wrapped his arms around her legs, everything inside him burning with the need to get up and tear her apart with his bare hands.

"My lady. My Queen, I'm yours," he whispered, pressing his forehead to her knees. "Please forgive whatever I've done to upset you. All I ever wanted was to please you."

He flinched as her cold fingers brushed the skin of his back, tracing the shape of his muscles. She seized his hair and pulled on it, forcing him to sit back on his heels.

"So, what moved you to go against me and testify in favor of the Shadow Slayer?" she asked, gazing deep into his eyes. Her anger noticeably dwindled down, replaced by curiosity in her brown eyes.

"My Queen." He reached for her, and she placed her hand into his. He brought it closer to his lips and planted a soft kiss on her knuckles, the familiar sweet scent of her hand lotion invading his nostrils. "When the Shadow Slayer didn't kill me, I decided to help him. Like I said earlier—it was the least I could do to repay him. But also, I wanted to know why he was in our state. And the only way to find out was to create a bond with him."

"A blood bond?" asked Roxana, staring at him in disbelief. "I didn't realize you—"

"No, my lady." Cole chuckled. "First of all, you don't have to have a sexual relationship to create a blood bond with a human."

"I know that, dumbass." The Queen rolled her eyes reproachfully, her anger gone by now. "But where is the fun in exchanging blood with a human if you don't get to have a little"—she wagged her thin eyebrows at him suggestively—"you know. Besides, I wouldn't mind watching you two deadly giants in each other's embrace. Yum..."

Suppressing nausea at the thought of touching his brother that way, Cole smirked. "No, my lady, I was thinking about the bond of friendship, if you know what that is. Male bonding, sort of."

"And how did it go for you?" she asked snidely.

"Actually, it was going well. Until you summoned me, that is," he said with a half-shrug. "So, you have a choice to make, my Queen. You can let me continue what I've started, or..." His voice trailed off as she narrowed her eyes at him, disbelief imprinted on her face. But he spread his arms wide, a dark, alluring smirk playing on his lips. "Or you can keep me here, tied up to your bed—your willing sex-accomplice."

She stared at him for no longer than a few seconds, but to him, it felt like an eternity.

"Tempting," she murmured, her half-closed dark eyes fogging up with lust. "But I think you have a point. From what I hear, no vampire has ever been able to get close to the Shadow Slayer. No one even knows if he's just an incredibly skilled human hunter or if he has magic." She shrugged then, and added not without a hefty share of sarcasm, "But who knows. He could be nothing but a stupid bed-time story—a boogeyman the vampire-parents came up with to keep their vampire-kids at bay."

"We have a unique opportunity to find out, my lady," Cole murmured, his fingers caressing the smooth skin of her legs.

"Fine," she said faintly as his hand progressed up her thigh. "But before I let you go, I want to explore how willing of a sex-accomplice you truly are." She smiled and waved her hand at him. "Rise."

Cole got up and rolled his shoulders, flexing his well-defined muscles. A soft hiss escaped her lips as her eyes traveled up and down his tall, lean body.

"Your pants," she said quietly, but even her whisper sounded like a harsh order, "off."

Cole pulled down the zipper and let his pants slide down his narrow hips slowly. She leaned back a little and flicked her wrist.

"Everything—off..."

He smiled coldly but complied with her demand. Straightening, he gazed down at her as she observed him as if he was one of the statues decorating her gardens.

"You reminded me of him," she murmured wistfully, rising. "Just as proud... just as perfect." She moved her hands along his sides, down to his hips, slipping to his behind. "If not for that resemblance, by now, I would've probably killed you many times over for your disobedience and insolent behavior. Would be a shame though... You know how to please me better than anyone..."

"Remind you of whom?" he asked, closing his eyes for a moment as she proceeded exploring his body shamelessly.

"I prefer you silent," she replied and closed his mouth with her kiss.

CHAPTER 14

~ DAMIAN BLAKE ~

It was well past midnight when Damian finally settled in his new room. Over the years, he had gotten used to a life on the road with fleabag motels, flimsy beds that nearly broke under his weight, and questionably looking showers. So, to him, the spacious master bedroom River had set up for him seemed better than any luxury suite of a five-star hotel. It had a direct entrance into the pool area which led to the home gym and exercise center. The pool deck had a backdoor, leading to the outside of the Paradise Manor property into the desert, and he could take a midnight run toward the purple mountain any time he wished without the need to cross the entire right wing of the house.

Damian put his black tank top and sports pants on, ready to go out to check the house, but a careful knock on the door stopped him in his tracks.

"Come in," he said, heading toward the door.

River walked inside, almost running into him, and chuckled. "I was hoping I would catch you here before you leave for"—a guilty smile crossed her face—"whatever it is you do here at night."

"What can I do for you, ma'am?" he asked, gazing down at her with curiosity.

"It's River. Please call me by my name," she said quietly. "I thought we passed that official, military-like form of communication." She glanced to the side, a vibe of discomfort around her getting heavier. "Listen, Day... Damian... Why don't you take a break from your guard's duty tonight? From what I understand, you didn't sleep for twenty-four hours straight already. Because of me."

"Thank you, but I can't," he objected softly. "At least, I shouldn't."

"As my personal bodyguard, you're no good to me if you're falling off your feet because of sleep deprivation." She sighed, and her expression closed up. "I promised I was not going to boss you around, but this one time... As your employer, I am giving you this night off. You'll start your work tomorrow." She tapped his arm and smirked. "Nothing is going to happen in those few hours. Get some sleep, soldier. You look like you're at the end of your rope."

Before he could object, she pivoted on her heels and left the room. For a moment, he stared at the closed door. Then he turned around and headed back to the bed where he collapsed without taking his clothes off. He knew he was tired, but until he assumed a horizontal position, he had no idea how truly worn out he was. His every muscle was sore, and his legs buzzed with exhaustion. He kicked his sneakers off, took the socks off and grabbed one of the pillows, wrapping his arms around it as he turned on his stomach.

* * *

A NOISE COMING from behind his door woke him up with a start. Damian jolted to his feet, his pillows and blanket falling to the floor in his wake. The door was shaking as something scratched and tore at it. Still dazed, he rubbed his face, shaking off the last shreds of sleep.

"Wake up! Waaaakeee uuuup!"

The words sounded in his mind, and it took him a moment to realize it was Gypsy scratching at the door vigorously, trying to wake him up.

"What the hell?" he muttered, heading toward the exit as he noticed a furry paw reaching through the narrow space between the door and the floor. He opened it and saw the cat, her fur standing on her back, her tail tripled in size.

"Finally!" she squealed furiously, the sound of her voice in his mind giving him a throbbing headache.

"Gypsy," he hissed. "Don't you know how to meow anymore? Why are you waking me up, screeching in my head like nails on a chalkboard!"

The cat hopped in place, swinging at his bare feet with her paw, her claws extended. *"You're the worst Child of Earth I've ever met! I understand you don't have the second sight, but do you have your other senses! Or brain, for that matter?"*

"Shut up!" snapped Damian and closed his eyes, sharpening his other senses as he channeled his magic.

The fluctuation in the magical energy field was so insignificant that he could barely detect it. From the moment his powers had been partially stripped, he had never been able to trust his senses completely, so he had learned to trust his intuition. And since right now it was throwing one red flag after the other, he wasn't going to take any chances.

Without saying another word, he walked out into the hallway and ran toward River's room, his bare feet stepping softly on the carpet. Her room was only a few yards away, but the spikes in the energy field noticeably increased, becoming more and more prominent the closer he got there.

Damian halted in front of her door and closed his eyes, placing his palms against it. He checked the area inside her room for dark energy, but since he didn't detect anything troubling, he removed his hands and channeled more of his magic.

"*Praecidio Amnia*," he whispered, placing the protection spell over River's room. He thought for a moment and channeled the energy of Earth, entwining it with his magic. Quickly, he drew four glowing orange runes at each corner of the door and whispered the second spell, reinforcing the protection. For a heartbeat, the runes lit up brighter and then disappeared.

The spikes in the magical energy became faster and stronger, and a wave of cold air rushed through the hallway, coming from the main foyer. Gypsy hissed, pressing her side to his leg.

"That can't be good," he muttered and took off running toward the epicenter of magical disturbance.

The closer he got to the foyer, the colder it became. Now, he could feel the dark magical energy flowing through the walls, floor and ceiling, wrapping around him, burning his skin with its icy touch. He stopped a few feet away from the foyer and channeled as much of the elemental energy as he could safely hold in his body. Taking a step forward, the floor trembled under his feet, but at this point, he didn't care if someone would detect a seismic disturbance in the Arizona desert.

Like in some gut-wrenching nightmare, the walls of the house flexed and shuddered soundlessly. A strange wave moved through the drywall, making them sway, gathering closer around him. He swallowed hard, feeling the small hairs on the back of his neck rise. The darkness grew heavier, becoming almost tangible, and the temperature dropped lower, making him shiver.

The dark magical energy invaded all his senses at once, suffocating and immobilizing him with its powerful presence. He groaned, pressed the back of his hand over his mouth, and moved forward, fighting the resistance of dark energy. The ground shook, responding to his every move. The walls and the ceiling kept moving and grinding as the dark magical presence intensified further.

As soon as he crossed into the foyer, the frosty winter blizzard hit him with full force. He leaned forward against the overwhelming wind and raised his arm to shield his eyes but could see nothing through the rotating particles of ice. Taking another step forward, he slipped on the ice covering the floor and almost fell, barely able to maintain his balance. Something sharp bit into the bare soles of his feet, but he had no time to check what it was.

Loud whispers filled the foyer, coming from every direction at once. Someone called his name, laughing and mocking him. Someone who wasn't supposed to be here ordered him to leave, and with shock, he realized that he wanted nothing more than to obey this nagging voice.

His eyes closed of their own volition, and he felt something cold and hard squeezing his head, wrapping tightly around his forehead like a heavy, metal hoop. The surroundings shimmered and changed. He was no longer in Paradise Manor. Down on his knees, he found himself in the middle of a dark forest, a woman lying on his lap. Her pale face relaxed as her wide-open eyes stared into eternity, blood seeping from the corner of her mouth.

No, not again... I don't want—

As an unbearable pain squeezed his heart, Damian struggled to get up, but he couldn't make a move. Nothing was holding him, yet his body refused to obey him.

"Damian..." A soft whisper echoed through the dark woods, painfully reverberating in his head. It swirled within him, enthralling his mind and controlling his weakened body. "I know you want to know who killed her. You want vengeance. I can help you. I have what you want. All you need to do is leave Paradise Manor and never come back. Say yes, Child of Earth, and I'll give you the information you've been seeking for centuries. Just say, yesssss..."

Damian lowered his head, struggling against the hold of the dark magic. "No," he growled through clenched teeth, and the surroundings swirled around him, changing again. He was back in Paradise Manor.

The wind howled, and a powerful impact in his chest sent him flying across the foyer. He hit the wall with his back. Ignoring the pain, he scrambled to his feet, pressing his back against the wall. Feeling his way around with his hand, he realized he was standing by the mirror. A new presence, cold but somehow friendly, touched his stretched senses, calling to him.

Supporting himself against the foyer table, he turned around. A dim light emanating from the silver mirror illuminated a tiny area in front of him. Even though the surface of the mirror was covered in frost, instead of his own reflection, he could see the dark shape of a woman with long, flowing hair behind the glass. She was screaming something, but he couldn't hear anything through the earsplitting hiss of the whispers. The woman threw her hands up and then pointed toward the left wing of the house.

Fighting the effects of the dark spell, he raised his arm and one of his daggers materialized in his hand.

"*Illucious*," he shouted, but his voice came out in a hoarse whisper, his teeth chattering. A bright ray of light erupted from the blade. It cut through the darkness, illuminating the room and pushing the blizzard away from him.

Now, he could see the wall with the piece of plywood blocking the entrance into the left wing. The entire surface of the wall was covered in ice and snow, the blizzard beating mercilessly against it.

"*Latentius revelare*," whispered Damian, fighting the wind as he made his way to the plywood. Through the prism of his spell, he could see the protective rune blazing with the bright light of its magic, but the frost was creeping up closer and closer. The plywood cracked under the assault of the freezing temperature, and with horror, Damian watched the fracture growing longer, moving closer to the rune.

"No," he roared. His dagger vanished, leaving him in darkness once more. He placed both hands against the icy surface of the barrier and leaned against it, the muscles on his arms and back bulging with the strain. The cold slithered through him, making his joints ache, but he ignored the pain. Gathering all the magic, elemental power and physical strength he had in his half-frozen body, he shouted, *"Calidarius."*

A wave of heat spread around his hands, quickly de-icing the plywood. Once the frost was gone, he turned around, pressing his back against the barrier, and both daggers materialized in his hands. Calling to his magic, the blades in his hands lit up with the unbearable brightness of the energy of Creation. The darkness hissed and retreated, shattering into dirty gray flakes that dissipated before touching the ground.

He groaned and slid to the floor, which no longer was covered in ice. The temperature started to rise slowly, but he couldn't stop shivering, his teeth chattering. He let go of his magic, and his daggers vanished, but his stiff fingers kept shaking uncontrollably. The light of the moon reached into the foyer, and he noticed that his feet were bleeding, most likely cut by ice. He could feel no pain, but at this moment, he was too drained and cold to worry about it. All he wanted was to close his eyes and sleep.

"Child of Earth, open your eyes!" An unwelcome high-pitched voice sounded in his frazzled mind. Damian opened his eyes and saw Gypsy pushing him in his side. *"Get up! You'll die if you sit here! You need to warm up. Start moving. Get your blood flowing."* She seized the bottom of his pants with her teeth, her entire tiny body leaning back in an effort to pull him up.

He scrambled to his feet, the room around him spinning.

River... As the thought rushed through his fogged mind, he forced himself to move forward, barely dragging his feet. He remembered reaching the door to River's room, but he had no idea how long it took for him to get there.

"*Incanto Comlium,*" he muttered, removing the protection spell he had placed over her room. He cracked the door open. With relief, he saw her sleeping peacefully in her bed and closed the door quietly. This little effort took too much of his strength, and he leaned forward, bracing himself against the wall. His hands resonated with pain, and he pulled back.

Still feeling drowsy, he made his way to the kitchen and opened a small wine cabinet he'd noticed there earlier. Grabbing the first cup he could find, he filled it with whisky and drank it in a few large gulps, his teeth knocking against the glass. Then he placed the cup on the countertop and leaned against it, dropping his head low.

"Wow! I'm sure it's five o'clock somewhere."

Like through a fog, he heard River's sarcastic voice and slowly turned around, almost losing his balance.

"I... am... s-s-orry," he stuttered, his speech slurred.

Her eyes widened, and her jaw dropped as she took in his appearance. "Oh, my God, Damian," she gasped, closing the distance between them. She placed her hand on his arm and jerked it back. "You're freezing. I don't understand... Did you take a quick trip to Alaska?" Her eyes traveled down to his bleeding feet, and she gasped again. "What the hell is going on?"

"Quest-tions... can't... answer..."

"No more questions. Sorry." River wrapped her arm around his waist, gently directing him out of the kitchen. She walked him into the living room and helped him down on the couch. "I'll be right back."

She came back a few seconds later, carrying a large fleece blanket and a first-aid kit. She wrapped him into the blanket and lowered to her knees before him, placing the kit on the floor next to her. Lifting his bleeding foot onto her lap, she disinfected the wounds and placed a bandage over them. Then she repeated the procedure with his other foot. Her moves were quick and habitual, and he was sure it wasn't the first time she had done something like this.

Once done, she lifted the corner of the blanket and slipped under it, encircling Damian's torso with her arms. He stiffened and held his breath as she pressed her entire body to his, placing her head on his chest.

"What... are you... d-d-oing?" he managed to say.

"Sharing my body heat with you, dumbass." She chuckled, but there was no humor in her voice. "You are hypothermic. I don't understand how it's possible." She glanced up at his face and smirked. "I know, in your medieval standards, my behavior is unacceptable for a lady. But I sorta don't give a damn about what you think at this moment."

"I can get used to that..." Realizing what he just said, Damian groaned and leaned back on the couch, working hard to convince himself it was the whisky talking. However, it'd been centuries since someone took care of him, and he had no strength to say no to that. Gypsy snuck under the blanket and settled on his lap, her hot body warming up his stomach. He closed his eyes, enjoying the moment of peace.

Once he stopped shivering, River let go and got up, wrapping the blanket tighter around his shoulders. She left and came back a few minutes later with a cup of hot tea, a bitter, earthy scent of herbs spreading through the air. He took the cup from her hands, wrapping his fingers around it.

"Drink it," she ordered in a no-nonsense tone of voice. "Drink it, and I'm taking you to bed." He raised his eyes at her, and she pursed her lips, gazing at him with reproach. "To *your* bed where you're going to lie down and sleep for the rest of this crazy night. Alone." She thought for a moment and laughed softly. "Well, maybe with Gypsy. This traitorous cat seems to like you more than me now."

"*As if.*" Gypsy jumped down from his lap and walked around River, wrapping her bushy tail around her legs.

Damian finished his tea, and she took the cup from him, putting it on the glass table. He got up and swayed a little. He was no longer cold, but the extreme use of his magic had drained him, making him weaker. Trying not to lean too heavily on her shoulder, he made it to his bed and lay down. She pulled the blanket over him all the way to his chin, tucking him in as if he were a ten-year-old boy. Gazing down at him, she shook her head slightly, frowning.

"I would really like to know how a giant man like you could get hypothermia inside of a locked house in the middle of the Arizona summer," she whispered. He opened his mouth, but she raised her hands, stopping him. "I know, I know. That was a rhetorical question. Good night, Day."

Damian didn't remember her leaving the room. His exhausted body took over his racing mind, and he was asleep before she walked out the door.

When he woke up, the sun was blasting through the window, and the clock on the bed stand was showing past three o'clock. He pulled the blanket down and sat up, rubbing his chin. His eyes fell on a white box next to the clock, and he frowned, trying to recall if it had been there last night. A folded paper lay on top of the box, his name written on it.

He took the paper and unfolded it.

"*Hi, Day.*"

He read the first sentence and smirked at the nickname River had given him, shaking his head.

"*As promised, inside this box, you'll find your new cellphone. I picked it up earlier this morning for you. Don't argue with me, soldier.*

I can almost hear you saying, 'I don't need it, ma'am.'

Yes, you do. Since you're my bodyguard, I should have a way to get hold of you if I need your help, so please keep it with you at all times. I've completed most of the setup, so it's fully functional. If you need my help with the security settings, I'll help you tonight when I get back from work.

I took the liberty of adding three phone numbers to your contact list—mine, my father's, and Cole Adams'. He's going to call you later on today.

See you later,
River.

P.S. I know you're not going to tell me what happened here last night. But whatever it was, I have a feeling it was about me and my safety... So, thank you."

Chuckling, he put the letter on the bedstand and opened the box. Inside, there was a smartphone in a black protective case. He pulled it out and almost dropped it as it started to ring and vibrate in his hand.

As the screen lit up, he read the name on the caller ID.

Cole Adams.

CHAPTER 15

~ COLE ADAMS ~

With a digital tablet in his hand, Cole walked into a conference room and closed the door. As soon as he appeared, the chatter died down, and all five employees turned around, looking at him with expectation in their eyes. He smiled easily, greeting them with a wave of his hand, and then headed toward the leather chair at the head of the table.

"Okay, Dennis, let's do it." Cole sat down and raised his eyebrows, looking at a young man at the other end of the table.

Dennis smiled and got up, holding a remote control in his hand. Pressing a button, he lowered the shutters over the outside windows and the glass walls of the room. Now, the only light in the room was emitted by a large projector positioned in the center of the conference table.

"Cole," started the young man, "we finally processed all the feedback we've received from our beta-testers in the last two weeks. We had a few different test groups, but surprisingly, the feedback we received was very similar."

"What did they say?" asked Cole, opening his tablet and getting ready to type. "Let's start with the overall impression. Interface, graphics, rules, settings."

"They loved it!" A proud grin split Dennis' face, making him look like a happy young boy. "All age groups said the game is captivating, and the story is interesting. They had no problem navigating it or understanding the options. While they found the higher levels quite challenging, they enjoyed the game, nonetheless. The graphics, movements and action scenes were described as incredibly realistic, movie-like..."

Cole listened to the young programmer's report, processing only every other word, his mind elsewhere. For so many years he had been searching for his brother just to find him here, in Blue Creek, Arizona. It had flipped his life upside down in more ways than one, making it increasingly dangerous, but he didn't care. He couldn't wait for the workday to be over so he could see him again.

Being an old vampire, he knew that there were no coincidences in the World of Magic, and if Damian showed up in his life now, there had to be a good reason for that. He just didn't know what it was. Not yet. There were too many unanswered questions between them, and more than a thousand years of lost memories to be filled in. They had to sit down and have an uninterrupted talk. But most of all, he had to figure out how to handle the situation with the Queen.

Normally, Cole loved spending time taking care of his company, despite the fact that all his employees were human, and he constantly had to keep his true nature under control. But not today. Detective Evans texted Damian's phone number earlier, asking him not to call him until later to give him a chance to rest. Now, the cellphone was burning a hole in his pocket, and Cole couldn't wait for this endless meeting to be over so he could call his brother, feeling eager like a little boy.

"...it's interesting that most of the players pointed out the same small issue with the story." Dennis' voice cut through his train of thoughts, and Cole focused on his lead developer.

"What issue?" he asked, twirling a pen between his fingers.

"Ace, show it, please." Dennis nodded to a slim young woman with long black hair tied in a high ponytail on the back of her head. She pressed a button on the projector, and a video-clip of the game started playing, displayed on the white wall. In a large room filled with mirrors, two men were engaged in a deadly sword fight. She pressed another button, freezing the frame.

"Right here," said Dennis, pointing at the picture. "You can see Arigel's reflection in all the mirrors?"

"Yes, so?" Cole leaned forward, observing the image.

"He's a vampire." Dennis threw his hands up. "Almost every beta-tester pointed it out, stating that it would never happen like this in real life. Vampires have no reflection."

"I see." Cole smirked, recalling a very similar conversation he had with his brother just a few hours ago. "And since when are vampires real? In real life, how many vampires do you know?" He shook his head, laughter bubbling up in his chest. "Who's to say that if vampires truly existed, they wouldn't have a nice, clean reflection?"

"Be that as it may, sir." Dennis sighed wistfully, the expression on his face suggesting that in real life, he would much rather deal with angry vampires than with his teenage beta-testers. "Should we change this? You know how it is. In all popular fantasy books and movies, vampires don't have a reflection. Market expectations." He rolled his eyes.

"Let's do the change. After all, unlike real life, fantasy must make sense, right? Let's make people happy, Dennis," said Cole with a dismissive wave of his hand. "Anything else I need to know?"

"Just one more thing," continued Dennis, sitting down in his chair. "If you remember the maze level?" Cole nodded with a light flick of his hand, and the lead developer continued, "In the maze level, the player must escape the underground mines.

Originally, the maze was supposed to have only one exit—the one that leads to the forest. But when we started to design, we created a second door. It was a happy accident, you know? But then we liked it, and the product managers agreed with us. So, we decided to keep it to see how it would work during the usability testing. Interestingly, the alpha-testers—most of them —chose to use the small backdoor that leads into the vampire's castle at the edge of the forest, and so did the beta-testers." He shrugged. "It makes no sense. Why would they want to exit into a castle full of evil vampires? But they said it was more fun."

"Wait... what?" Cole rose, leaning forward slightly, his mind on high alert. "What did you say about the second door?"

The programmers exchanged a puzzled look.

"I said that the mines in the maze level have two doors," repeated Dennis. "The tiny backdoor we created by mistake exits into the castle at the edge of the forest. Should we keep it? The users like it."

I'll be damned...

Noticing troubled looks, he smiled. "Of course, keep it. Thank you, guys. You're the best," he said, heading toward the door. "In the next sprint, let's fix the last reported bugs with high and medium priority status and finish whatever user stories we have left in the product backlog. Hopefully, we can start getting ready for the last phase of beta testing soon. The faster we get this game to the market, the better."

He walked out the door and rushed through the narrow corridor between the cubicles, struggling to maintain an appropriate pace for a company owner. Walking into his office, he slammed the door shut and ran toward his computer.

"What if..." He opened a browser and typed in search criteria into the window. Clicking enter, he stared into the screen without blinking while the search results were loading—too slow for the eyes of a vampire.

He spent a few hours trying to find anything about the history of mines in Blue Creek. Since there wasn't much on the web, he started to search the history of the town and the background of the three founding families. Except for what he had already known, he didn't find anything new. Leaning back in his executive leather chair, he rubbed his chin, thinking. Then he got up and lifted the stationary phone receiver, dialing an extension.

"Ace?" he said softly. "Can you please come to my office?" He waited a moment and added, "Yes, now, please."

A few seconds later, Ace knocked on the door and cracked it open, peeking inside, her dark eyes wide.

"Please come in." Cole smiled, hoping his smile was friendly enough to get her in a relaxed state of mind.

The young woman came inside and halted by the door, her fingers fumbling with a leather string wrapped around her wrist. She was slender and short as it was, but her black jeans and shirt made her look even smaller. Standing by the entrance, shifting from foot to foot, she gave off a vibe of fear and discomfort.

"Cole... um... Mr. Adams?" she mumbled, her large brown eyes getting wider as her face became paler.

"Ace, relax," he said with a sigh. "I called you because I need your help."

"You're not firing me?" she whispered, hope lighting up her heart-shaped face.

"Not today, Ace. Unless you want me to, of course."

She hopped in place and pressed her hand to her mouth. "Dennis was saying something about that backdoor," she spoke in one breath, walking closer to his desk. "I'm sorry, sir, I was the one who added it. I thought you were going to fire me for doing that, and I was—"

"Ace, stop. Have I ever fired anyone for coloring outside the lines? Or for trying something new?" asked Cole, raising his hand to stop her. "I need your help, and it has nothing to do with our work. It's personal."

"Anything, Mr. Adams," she replied breathlessly, gazing up at him with googly eyes.

"I have my friend of many years visiting Blue Creek," started Cole. "He asked me a few questions about the local gold mines, which I couldn't answer. He wanted to know where the door into the mines is, but I can't find anything on the internet. Can you help me with that?"

For a brief moment, Ace stood, blinking at him with her mouth open. "You want to go underground?"

Cole nodded.

"You?" Her eyebrows climbed up.

He chuckled. "Why not?"

"You're so... um... clean..." she mumbled, and pressed her hand over her mouth, her eyes widening. "I'm sorry, I wasn't trying to be rude. I just had no idea you were the type."

"What type?" Cole all but snorted.

"The type to take a hike across Apache trail or climb the Superstition mountains," she replied with a half-shrug. "You don't strike me as one of those people who take midnight runs into the desert to search for rattlesnakes and scorpions. I don't know about your friend, of course."

Cole laughed, leaning forward a little. "So, can you find any information about these mines for me?"

She approached him and jerked her chin toward his computer, a lopsided smirk playing on her lips. "Can I use your PC, please?"

"Be my guest." He stepped away, gesturing for her to sit down. Folding his arms, he watched over her shoulders as she was typing something vigorously, her fingers hitting the buttons as if they were her worst enemies. A few minutes later, she looked up at him, a winning smile tugging at her lips. She pointed at the screen, inviting him to take a look.

"Voila. This is the map of the area from the Arizona Department of Mines and Mineral Resources," she explained and then shook her head, her eyes gleaming with excitement. "Don't ask any questions. Plausible deniability."

"Wasn't going to..."

"Most of it is accessible to anyone, and you can view it on their public website. But this particular map was behind their... Anyway," she continued as if she didn't just hack some state database. "The old entrance into the mines was right here." She tapped the screen lightly with her finger. "The owners closed the mines sometime in the early nineteen hundreds, but the door wasn't sealed until later on. Something about being unsafe and structurally unsound. Anyway, kids used to go there all the time, and after a few accidents, the entrance was destroyed. They leveled it to the ground. You won't be able to get inside, sir. Sorry to disappoint."

Cole stared at the map of the area, nibbling on his lip. "I wonder if there are any maps or at least original drawings of the layout of the actual mines."

"I doubt it," she replied. "These mines are surrounded by so much mystery, it's ridiculous if you ask me."

"How so?"

"Well, they were built to mine gold, supposedly, but nothing ever pointed out that there was any gold in this area. The way the underground passages were built wasn't common either. From the main entrance right here"—she pointed at the screen —"the workers dug into three separate directions. They say one of them leads directly toward Paradise Manor, by the way."

"Fascinating," murmured Cole, wondering if his original suspicion triggered by the programming *'happy accident'* was true. "Do you know if there was more than one entrance into the mines? Maybe some clever worker decided to build a tiny backdoor straight into the vampire's castle?"

A boyish grin split his face as he gazed down at her, and Ace giggled, a blush coloring her cheeks tender pink.

"If you want to believe local urban legends, there were three entrances into the mines," she said. "The main entrance that had been sealed by the state authorities and two tiny backdoors. As a matter of fact, one of them led into the vampire's castle."

"You don't say," murmured Cole, his voice becoming a soft purr as he leaned closer to her. "Please tell me you know where they are."

She looked up, her eyes just inches away from his, and her breath hitched. "I don't believe that the door leading into the castle exists... um, I mean into Paradise Manor. It makes no sense, and I don't think it's possible. The mansion is too far away from the mines," she croaked. As Cole straightened and broke their eye contacted, she averted her gaze and cleared her throat uncomfortably. "But I know for sure that a second door exists in the desert." She searched the screen for a few seconds and then pointed at a seemingly random location on the map. "It's somewhere here. I can't show it precisely on the screen, but if you and your friend want, I can take you there."

"Perfect." Cole rubbed his hands and reached into his pocket for his cellphone. "Let's take a trip there now."

"Now?" she mumbled, gaping at him, blinking. "It's only three and my workday is not over until five—"

"Then maybe we should ask the owner of the company if he'd let you leave early today?" Cole winked at her and picked up the receiver of the company phone, dialing his executive assistant's extension. "Mackenzie, please reschedule all my appointments and meetings for the rest of the day." He waited a moment, listening to his assistant and added, "It's personal. Just do it, please."

He hung up the phone and reached into his pocket for his cellphone. Quickly scrolling through the contact list, he found Damian's number and dialed it.

"Damian," he said, warmth filling his chest at the sound of his brother's voice. "Get dressed. I'm going to pick you up in a few. We're taking a guided tour into the Sonoran Desert." He listened to Damian's next question and laughed. "No, I'm not driving my sports car into the desert. You'll be fine. See you soon."

CHAPTER 16

~ DAMIAN BLAKE ~

Damian hung up the phone, staring at the dark screen in disbelief. Over the centuries, his brother hadn't changed a bit. No matter what the task was, Cole was going from zero to sixty in a heartbeat. He had just learned about the maze of problems Damian was facing with Paradise Manor, and he dove straight in, no questions asked.

A trip to the desert? It had to be something to do with the mines. At least Damian couldn't see any other explanation, and he didn't like it in the slightest. Over the years, he got used to working alone. No strings attached. Win or lose, it was only his safety at stake, and he didn't put anyone else in harm's way—especially not his brother.

After taking a quick shower, he opened the closet door and stifled a sigh. The closet was larger than the room he used to stay in at the Night Owl Inn, and with the amount of clothes he had, it looked terrifyingly empty. He was sure if he said something, his voice would echo from wall to wall. Getting dressed quickly, he put his jeans and a plain T-shirt on. The bracelet was still on his wrist, and he decided to keep it that way, at least for now.

Damian had enough time to walk to the kitchen and grab a cup of coffee and toast before his new phone rang, announcing Cole's arrival. Checking the house one more time, he walked outside and locked the front door with the key River had left for him.

A large white Mercedes G-Class SUV was parked in front of the house, and Damian felt something close to instant relief, realizing that he didn't have to tolerate the limited space of a sports car again.

Before he reached the vehicle, Cole walked around it and opened the front passenger door, offering his hand to a young woman. She barely touched his palm as she jumped to the ground. With her height of no more than five-foot-four, the vehicle seemed to be too high for her to just stepped out.

Even though Cole opened the back door for her, she halted and tilted her head slightly, gaping at Damian with unconcealed curiosity in her dark eyes. Turning to Cole, she gave him a tiny shake of her head, making her high ponytail bounce, and for some reason, she reminded Damian of a little, energetic bird.

"Wow, Mr. Adams, now I see why you said your friend would be better off in the front seat," she chirped, a wide grin splitting her face.

"You have no idea," murmured Cole, turning to his brother. "Damian, this is Ace Rogers, and she will be our tour guide today."

"Nice to meet you, ma'am," said Damian, offering her his hand.

She took it, her tiny hand disappearing in his wide palm. "No one has called me ma'am yet." Standing next to him, she barely reached his chest. As her eyes glided up and down his body, she exhaled, "You are ginormous." Then she gasped, pressing her hand to her mouth, and her eyes flickered to Cole and then back to Damian. "I'm sorry, I was trying to say, you're very big... No, tall! Oh jeez, I'm going to shut up now."

Damian exchanged a quick look with Cole, and the vampire bit his lip to stop himself from laughing.

"He's not as tall as you think, Ace," he said, gesturing for her to get in the back seat. "Only two inches taller than me."

"Yes, but unlike you, he looks like a—" She cut herself off, climbing to the back. "Can we just drive before I say something I will get fired for?"

Damian got into the passenger seat and closed the door, working hard not to burst out laughing. Her awkwardness and bubbly personality seemed to make the day a little brighter, and he didn't mind some blissful normality around for a change. Cole started the car, directing it around Paradise Manor and into the desert. For a while, they drove in silence with Ace giving occasional directions.

"Damian, did you have another sleepless night?" Cole asked carefully after a while, and added, catching Damian's puzzled gaze, "River said you needed to get some sleep."

"Just another night terror. A trip to a winter wonderland," muttered Damian, staring out the window.

Cole nodded and didn't press the issue. After a while, they left the road and turned into the open desert. As the monotonous landscape stretched around them, Damian wondered how Ace knew her way around. There were no visible landmarks, and all the cacti looked the same to him.

It was past four o'clock when Ace asked Cole to stop the car. They walked out, and she directed them toward a large, old pit in the ground. The time and elements had made the edges of the pit less defined, and dry grass and desert plants inhabited its walls. Moving carefully, the young woman made her way down the slope to the bottom of the pit and headed toward the opposite wall.

She stopped there, an expression of shock making her dark eyes look like two round plates. "It was here," she said, pointing at a wall of yellow-brown sand. "I swear, I know my way around, and I was here less than a year ago. There was a door right there."

Ace dug into the wall with her hand, removing handfuls of sand, throwing it next to her feet, but there was nothing there except for more sand. As the cloud of reddish dust settled down, she turned around, throwing a desperate glance at Cole.

"It's okay," he said softly. "We believe you. Let me check it out. Can you show me the exact location where the door used to be?"

She drew a rectangle with her finger, pointing at the wall. Cole approached it and placed his hands against it, closing his eyes. Damian detected the spike of the vampiric energy around him as his eyes lit up with the scarlet glow beneath his dark sunglasses.

"It's here, alright," murmured Cole so quietly that Damian could barely make out his words, positive that Ace couldn't hear him at all.

Turning his back to Ace, he channeled his magic and reached forward, whispering, *"Latentius revelare."* The air between him and the wall of the pit shimmered, and the dim outline of a door revealed itself, glowing with a barely detectible white light. Cole stepped behind him, his fingers squeezing his elbow.

"Check out the corners," he breathed out.

"Concealment magic and some wards," murmured Damian so quietly that only the vampire's sharp hearing could catch his words. He let go of his magic, turning to his brother half-way. "Powerful. But not as powerful as those in the house."

"Can you break them?" whispered Cole.

Damian nodded. "I think this spell work was built more to hide it than to lock it." He threw a quick glance at Ace and added, "But I can't take the chance of exposing the World of Magic."

"Okay, you two!" Ace's voice sounded behind him, ringing

with irritation. "Why are you whispering like two secret lovers in a corner?"

Both Damian and Cole turned around at once. She stood with her hands folded over her chest, fuming like a little girl who was about to throw a temper tantrum to her parents.

"You could hear what we were saying?" asked Damian, flabbergasted.

"Well..." She dropped her arms, and a guilty smile crossed her face. "I could hear you whispering, but I couldn't quite make out the words." She scratched the back of her head, which made her look even guiltier. "Too bad, you know?"

"Secret lovers? That would be more than awkward. Don't you think, Dima?"

Cole whispered even quieter than before, but Ace threw her hands in the air. "That's what I mean." She narrowed her eyes at Cole, placing her hands on her hips. "I always had sharp hearing. I can hear you whispering, Mr. Adams. I just can't hear your exact words."

"Fascinating," Cole murmured under this breath. He approached her, staring down into her wide-open eyes. For a moment, his vampiric energy spiked around him, but then he stepped back and gave her an arched stare. "Anything else we need to know about you, Ms. Rogers?"

"I could also see..." Her voice wavered as she pointed at the wall where the door was supposed to be.

"What did you see?" asked Damian softly.

"Nothing at the moment." Moving around Cole, she approached the wall and traced the invisible door with her finger, drawing its shape in the sand. "I saw the glowing outline of the door and some strange symbols," she said, gazing up at Damian. "I've never seen anything like this." She touched Damian's hand gently. "What was it? You can trust me. I won't tell anyone. Pinky promise." She lifted her fist with her pinky up, a prankish grin on her face.

Damian pressed his hand over his eyes and ran it down his face, staring at Cole over the young woman's head. She had magic, there was no doubt about that. Without his second sight, he couldn't tell how powerful she was or what type of magic she had, but that wasn't the problem. What troubled him the most was that obviously, Ace hadn't been exposed to the World of Magic yet, and he wasn't sure he wanted to send another innocent soul down that painful and dangerous path. There were hundreds of people who possessed some magical or elemental energy, but since it was never developed, they lived their entire life, leading an absolutely normal human existence none the wiser about what goes bump in the night.

Meeting Damian's eyes, Cole touched his sunglasses and gave him a sharp nod. Damian swallowed hard, clearly reading his brother's message. Cole wanted him to tell Ace the truth, promising to glamor her later, making her forget everything. He frowned, his fingers rubbing the rough surface of his leather bracelet as he hesitated, not sure he was okay with Cole messing around with Ace's memories.

"Damian," asked Ace, breaking his train of thoughts. "Can you open this glowing door?" Since Damian didn't reply, she continued, "Let's say—purely hypothetical—you or Mr. Adams can open the door into the mines. What are you going to do after? Do you know where to go? Where the main entrance is? There are so many passages there, you'll get lost in no time without me."

She tilted her head, a wicked grin on her face. Damian glanced at Cole, frowning. She was right. He had no idea in which direction to go once inside. Ace squatted and drew two circles on the sand, connecting them with a straight line.

"It's kind of like this," she said, craning her head back, her eyes moving from Damian to Cole. "This is where we are, and this line is the main corridor." She pointed at the circle she drew on the left. "This is the main entrance, or rather the place it had been before it got leveled down."

She drew a few more lines pointing in a few directions from the second circle, creating something that resembled a sun drawn by a five-year-old child.

"Let's look at it logically. There are many corridors and passages going in every direction from the main entrance. Some of them lead somewhere and some are dead ends. Many of them are dangerously unstable. If you don't know where you're going, you can wander in there forever. I grew up exploring these mines. I can get you in, out and to any place you want to explore." She drew a smiley face inside her 'sun' and got up, shaking the sand off her pants. "So, what is it going to be, guys?"

"Cold logic, alright." Cole smirked, shaking his head. "No wonder you are one of my best programmers." Switching his attention to Damian, he gave him a short nod. "Do it, Damian. Let's see what's behind this door."

"Stay back," muttered Damian, focusing on the task at hand.

He waited until his brother pulled Ace a few feet back, stepping in front of her, and connected with the energy of Earth. The ground quaked as he spread his arms wide, gathering the energy from his surroundings. Then he moved his arms forward, redirecting his attention to the mass of sand concealing the hidden door. His muscles tensed and a low growl vibrated in his throat as he wielded his power, bending the elemental energy to his will.

A large block of sand separated from the wall of the pit, lingering in the air. Damian waved his hand and moved it out of the way, dumping it to the side. He whispered a spell and touched the four points where he'd seen the runes, sending some of his energy through them. A bright, white light erupted from under his fingers, and for a few long seconds, he could see the energy of the concealment spell work. It disappeared in white, swirling wisps, and an outline of the actual door appeared under a thin layer of dirt and a web of entwined roots.

Damian released the elemental energy and exhaled, breathing laboriously. Before his powers had been stripped, something like this wouldn't have made him break a sweat. Now, any use of his magical or elemental energy came at a price. Wiping the perspiration off his forehead, he approached the door and brushed his fingers over it.

"Latentius revelare," he whispered and checked the entrance through the shimmering layer of the revealing spell. As he expected, the original spell work wasn't performed to stop someone from entering, but rather to conceal the door. Removing his spell, he turned around and caught a soft smile on Cole's face. He waved at the entrance over his shoulder. "The coast is clear. Would you like to give it a try?"

The door was pressed tightly into the pit, its edges fused seamlessly with the ground around, and he didn't want to exhaust more of his physical strength. Erring on the side of caution, he wanted to preserve his strength, physical and magical, in case he needed to use his power while they were inside. His brother, on the other hand, was an ancient vampire—super strength and high velocity came with the territory. Besides, it was practically impossible to get a vampire tired.

Cole stepped in front of the door and tilted his head slightly. "Break it or remove it... Hmmm... Always a dilemma." He flicked his eyebrow, and a bright grin appeared on his face. "Breaking is always a lot more fun."

Taking a half-step back, he hit it with his foot, the old wood exploding into a fountain of splinters under his powerful push kick. A cloud of dust puffed from the inside of the old mine, engulfing them with the smell of dirt and gravel.

"Whoa... that's just so awesome," Ace exhaled, staring at Cole in awe, her large eyes alight with excitement. "You two are something else." She pointed at Damian. "You're probably a wizard, right, Damian?" Without waiting for his response, she turned to Cole. "And what are you, Mr. Adams? Super strength. Just so-o-o cool!"

"I'm the owner of the company you work for," Cole grumbled, plastering a fake frown on his face, but couldn't keep it long and burst out laughing.

Damian glanced at her over his shoulder, thinking that for a person who wasn't touched by the World of Magic she sure accepted all his hocus-pocus easily, as if she had always known magic and the supernatural were real.

Once the dust settled, Damian peeked inside. A single passage ran from the entrance, disappearing into the darkness. He conjured a few light orbs and threw them inside, illuminating the path with their shimmering blue light.

"Ace," he said, turning toward the young woman, "I'll go first, and I want you to stay close to me. Cole will be behind you."

Damian stepped inside, with surprise realizing that the passage was tall enough for him to walk without bending down. The path was clean and unobstructed as if the workers had left the mines just yesterday. He didn't know much about mines, but the supporting wooden beams seemed to be sturdy enough, and the walls didn't look like they were ready to cave in. He shuddered, thinking about going farther through these confined corridors, but surrounded by his element, he didn't feel as bad about it.

For a while, they walked quietly, following the main pathway. A few smaller passages separated from it, going left and right, but Ace told them to keep moving straight, sounding confident. After a while, the corridor became slightly wider, merging inside a large opening. Most of it looked just as sturdy as everything they'd seen so far, but on the right, a large pile of rocks and debris concealed the wall.

"This is where the main entrance used to be," said Ace, pointing to the right. "So, where do you want to go from here?

There are a few corridors that lead from here and some of them are stable enough to explore."

"Earlier, you mentioned that possibly one of these corridors lead toward Paradise Manor," said Cole, throwing a heavy glance at Damian. "Do you know which one?"

"Hmm." Ace turned around slowly and stopped, facing one of the smaller openings. "I told you, Mr. Adams, I don't believe it to be the truth. I think it's just another urban legend to hype up the mystery around that building."

"Humor me," murmured Cole.

"As you wish." She pointed at the corridor she was facing. "If it existed—and I don't believe it does—it would be this one."

"Let's see if we can bust this myth." Giving an arched stare to Damian, he headed toward the doorway, but as soon as he reached it, he halted and turned around, his eye glowing with a scarlet light. "Damian, do you sense it?"

Damian shook his head and raised his arm, ready to cast a spell, but Cole stopped him.

"Preserve your energy," he said softly. "I can sense it clear enough. There is some kind of magical presence, but it's not strong. This is why you can't detect it. So, let's proceed with caution. I'll guide you."

They crossed the threshold and kept moving along the narrow passage. The ceiling became lower, and Damian had to bend down. Soon, he detected a strange energy signature, but just like Cole before, he couldn't say what it was. However, the farther they moved, the stronger it became. After a while, a layer of rocks and debris blocked their way, completely obscuring the passage.

"I told you." Ace lifted her shoulders in an apologetical shrug. "Some corridors were unstable. I guess this one collapsed. Sorry, I think this is the end of the road."

Damian placed his hands on the wall, closed his eyes and connected with his power. The wall didn't seem to be thick, and he was positive he could easily break through it. Pulling back a little, he struck it with his fist, channeling the elemental energy into his strike. With a loud bang, the wall of rocks blew up, bursting forward.

He stood in front of an opening large enough for them to go through. Damian stepped over the pile of rocks and found himself in a giant underground cave. It was shaped like a long rectangle, and the light of his magical orbs wasn't enough to illuminate every corner, leaving the left and the right sides of it obscured by thick shadows. However, at the opposite wall, he noticed a large double door reinforced with iron strips. Even without casting the revealing spell, he could see the runes and sigils inscribed on its surface.

The magical energy signature Cole had detected earlier became stronger, and now he had no problem sensing it. The problem was, it wasn't a single presence that he sensed. At least two different magical signatures were interlaced tightly—one of them was some kind of protection spell, but the other one he couldn't place. Nevertheless, it was so powerful that it made his hair stand on end.

"Cole," he whispered, turning to his brother while carefully gathering as much elemental energy in his hands as he could. "We need to go back. Do you feel it? I don't think we're ready to face whatever is hidden here."

Cole looked around, the vampiric energy around him almost palpable. "Too late for that, I think," he hissed, his fangs expending, his nails elongating into terrifying claws.

Heavy breathing sounded behind him, making Damian snap around.

"Holy cow," Ace yelped, her fingers clasping Damian's arm desperately. "I mean... holy bull."

CHAPTER 17

~ DAMIAN BLAKE ~

An enormous monster with the body of a bull and the head of a horse with a thick horn on its muzzle like that of a rhino stood a few yards in front of them, its eyes burning with a deep red light. It hit the floor with its hoof, and the ground quaked from the sheer force of the impact. It was so massive, Damian had to tilt his head backward to see it. Puffs of light gray smoke burst out of its nostrils as it lowered its terrifying head, pointing its sharp horn at them.

Damian stepped forward, spreading his arms wide to shield Ace and his brother, his heart thudding in his chest as he desperately searched his memory for anything he could use against the monster.

"Cole, take Ace and get out," he said quietly so only his brother with his vampiric hearing could hear him.

'What the hell is that?" whispered Ace, her voice shaking, her cold fingers digging deeper into his arm.

"Cole, go now," repeated Damian. "I have no time for explanations. I need—"

"I'm not leaving you to fight this thing alone!" hissed Cole, stepping next to him. "I'm not leaving you alone ever again!" His voice rose, ringing with defiance.

A low growl echoed through the area, rumbling like thunder, and the ground shook again as the beast took a step forward.

Damian grabbed Ace and pushed her into Cole's arms. Without giving Cole a chance to think, he turned and shouted, *"Ventius."* A blast of wind erupted from his hands, forcing both the vampire and the young woman out of the cave. Damian cast the second spell, erecting a large power shield blocking the entrance, leaving his brother outside.

In a heartbeat, Cole was at the see-through barrier Damian erected. With his full speed and strength, he punched the shield, but to no avail. Damian grunted but withheld the attack.

"Dima, no!" his brother yelled, his face ashen.

"Nikolai, listen to me," said Damian urgently, throwing a quick glance over his shoulder at the monster. "I need you to take Ace to safety. We can't kill this beast. The best I can do is seal him in this cave. But to do it, I need you to leave, and I need you to be fast—your kind of fast. Because I'll be right behind you, and trust me, you don't want to be underground when I'm wielding my element."

"I'm not burying you a second time, brother!" growled Cole. "If you die, I'll find you behind the veil and kill you myself." He lifted Ace into his arms and vanished.

Taking a deep breath, Damian turned around and raised his arms in what he hoped was a placating manner.

"Father of All Beasts," he said, carefully gathering as much of the elemental energy as he could in his body, "Mighty Indrik-Beast—"

The beast roared, digging the ground with its hoof. The walls of the cave shook, and clouds of dust and debris fell from the ceiling. The runes and sigils on the door across the room ignited brighter. Damian staggered back until his back hit his own shield.

Dammit...

"I came in peace?" he muttered without taking his eyes off the fuming monster while carefully removing the shield blocking his way out.

Indrik-Beast roared again, rearing on its hind legs before he charged Damian.

Dammit! This is why I always work alone... I hope you are out of the mines by now, brother...

Damian darted outside the cave and spread his arms, in one move connecting with the elemental Earth and channeling the energy from within. His muscles bulged with unimaginable strain, and his entire body lit up with a bright orange light. The walls trembled as he ripped out a large mass of dirt and rock and propelled it forward, blocking the entrance. The beast hit the barrier he created, partially demolishing it.

Damian kept backing away as he repeated the procedure, raising one barrier after another until he was sure that if the beast decided to follow him, it would take him at least a few minutes to break through the massive barricade he had constructed. The wall he created shook, and he knew he wasn't that lucky after all—the monster didn't want to give up.

He let go of all control of his power and allowed his element to consume him. The ground shook, responding to his mental command, and the grinding, rumbling noise of moving rocks filled the narrow passage. Damian turned around and ran, making the ceiling collapse and walls come down in his wake. He had no idea how he knew which corridor and passage to take, but he trusted his intuition and didn't stop to check for directions. All hell broke loose behind him as he raced through the corridor, passing the main entrance.

When he saw the rectangle of the exit door, he didn't slow down and practically flew through it. Spinning around, he manifested a huge block of solid rock and hurled it at the doorway, sealing it forever. Slowly, he turned around and got his power under control, his chest shuddering with heavy breaths.

Ace lay on the ground face down, and Cole was on top of her, covering her with his body, his arms folded over her head. As soon as he saw Damian, he was on his feet by his side.

"Cole," Damian whispered and dropped to his knees as his legs gave in. "It's over."

Cole lowered down next to him, crossing his legs. "Are you okay?" he asked casually, but his hoarse voice was beyond strained.

"I'll be fine," replied Damian, wiping the sweat off his forehead, just now realizing that he was covered in dust and dirt from head to toe. "Drained a little."

Ace approached them and sat down on the other side of Damian, her gaze darting from him to Cole and back, a strange discomfort lingering around her. Cole just took a quick glance at her and rolled his eyes.

"We're brothers, silly." He chuckled softly. "You have just witnessed some serious magic, a beast worthy of any Hollywood horror flick, and the only thing you want to ask us about is our relationship?"

"I didn't ask that," she said indignantly, folding her arms.

"You didn't have to," objected Cole, snidely. "The question was written all over your face. Now, come here, please." The vampiric energy spiked around him, and his eyes lit up a bright red.

Ace shook her head and didn't move. "Mr. Adams, you are a vampire, aren't you?" she whispered, inching her way closer to Damian. "Please don't make me forget all this..." She grabbed Damian's arm, gazing up at him pleadingly. "I swear I'm not going to say anything to anybody. I want to remember."

Damian smirked faintly, meeting her pleading dark eyes. "Ace, you have no idea what you're getting yourself into." He covered her hand with his and squeezed it gently. "Once you are exposed to the World of Magic, there is no way out. The ways of this world are complicated, filled with pain and loss. Are you sure this is what you want? Cole can set you free from all of this."

"Yes, I'm sure," she replied without giving it a second thought. "Being normal is highly overrated. I want to remember every little detail. Especially the real you, Mr. Adams." She glanced at him and sighed. "You both are amazing."

Cole relaxed his tensed shoulders, and his eyes returned to their normal blue color. "Remember, you can't talk to anyone about it. Exposing the World of Magic to humans is a serious offense. I'm sure Damian and I will pay for getting you into this mess." He frowned, shaking his head.

"I understand." She shrugged, all but rolling her eyes. "Who's going to believe me, anyway? Cole Adams, the owner of one of the biggest tech companies in Arizona and most eligible bachelor, is a vampire. Ri-i-ight." She giggled, pressing her hand to her mouth. "I don't need to get a one-way ticket to the local psych ward, thank you very much."

Damian threw a quick glance at his brother. "She has a point."

Carefully making sure that Ace couldn't see his back, he pulled his shirt off and lay down flat on the ground. With all the barriers between him and the Earth gone, he felt its energy flowing through his body, energizing him and partially restoring his strength. With a soft groan, he relaxed and closed his eyes.

"You're a vampire, Cole, I understand that." He heard Ace's voice above him but didn't bother opening his eyes. "But what is Damian? A wizard?"

"I'm no one," muttered Damian flatly.

"He's a lot more than a wizard, Ace. He's a Child of Earth." His brother's voice modulated slightly, and Damian cracked his eyelids open, observing him through his eyelashes.

"I'm sorry," Ace mumbled, sending a curious glance at Damian, "but I have no idea what that means."

"It means he is directly connected with the elemental energy of Earth. He doesn't need to use spells like wizards would to use its power. He can bend it to his will, do things you and I can't even comprehend," explained Cole patiently. "He's also a wizard. It means he can cast spells as you witnessed earlier." He sighed, meeting Damian's warning gaze.

"Whoa..." she whispered breathlessly. "Are there others like him?"

"As far as I know, besides the Earth Elemental, there is only one more Child of Earth," replied Damian. "He's not here."

"Have you heard about Antaeus?" asked Cole, rising, brushing the dust and sand off his pants and shirt.

"Greek mythology?" Ace's eyebrows shot up. "He was a son of two gods, as far as I remember."

"He was also the most well-known Child of Earth." Damian scrambled into a sitting position and put his shirt back on. Switching his attention to his brother, he held out his hand, and Cole grabbed it, pulling him to his feet. "Cole, we should get going. It's getting late, and I want to get some shuteye before my night shift starts."

I'm exhausted... How am I supposed to protect River when I can barely move? He rubbed the back of his neck, feeling soreness settling in his muscles at the thought of a sleepless night ahead.

"Wait, guys, just one more question?" Ace hopped to her feet.

"What?" Damian and Cole asked at the same time.

She giggled, her bubbly personality taking over again. "What was that beast in the mines? And how did it get there in the first place?"

"It was the Indrik-Beast," explained Damian, starting on his way to the other side of the pit where they had left the car. "If you're familiar with Slavic mythology, he's the Father of All Beasts."

"Slavic mythology," she repeated in disbelief, catching up with him "No, I know nothing about that. You're saying all that with such conviction, as if mythological beasts are real."

"Everything is real," muttered Damian without slowing down. "Cole is a vampire. Real enough for you?"

"Yeah, and this is the coolest thing ever," she whispered, winking at Damian as if he was her best buddy. "My boss is a vamp!"

Damian frowned. As he approached the car and opened the back door for her, he leaned down a little and whispered, "Be careful, Ace. Real vampires are not like what they show in the movies. They are deadly and brutal. Cole is not a common representative of his kind."

At least, I hope he is not... An unwelcome thought crossed his mind, but he forced it away. It was his past speaking—The Shadow Hunter-slash-Slayer in him. Through his long life, he had killed more vampires than he could count, and all of them were cold-blooded predators. Cole was his brother, and unlike those rogue vamps, he was trying to coexist with humans peacefully.

* * *

THE REST of the trip back to Paradise Manor, they drove in silence. Cole looked like he was deep in his thoughts, a frown making his features appear harder than usual. Damian was too tired to talk. Feeling slightly lightheaded from the excessive use of his magic, he closed his eyes and folded his arms in his lap, relaxing in his seat. Ace was slowly coming down from all the excitement, and by the time Cole parked his SUV in front of the mansion, she was fast asleep in the back.

Damian opened the door, but before walking out, he turned to his brother. "Cole, step out with me," he whispered and closed the door softly so he wouldn't wake Ace up. He walked around the vehicle and halted in front of Cole by the driver's door. "We need to talk when there is no one around. I was hoping you could help me with some research. Can you come by tomorrow morning?"

Cole nodded. "How about seven? I need to be at the office by nine. I hope two hours is enough?"

"Perfect." Damian glanced at the house, noticing the light in the windows of the right wing. River was home already. "Finding the Indrik-Beast in the mines gave me some unexpected insights into the mystery of Paradise Manor. I have a few ideas. I'll tell you everything when I see you tomorrow."

"Try to get some rest," said Cole, shaking his head. "You're drained more than a Child of Earth should be after a single encounter."

"I know," replied Damian, a dull ache settling in his chest, but he shrugged and added indifferently, "It is what it is. I'll be fine."

Cole's frown deepened, but he got back into his car and looked up through the window. "I'll see you tomorrow."

Damian followed Cole's SUV until it disappeared behind the gates and headed toward the house.

CHAPTER 18

~ DAMIAN BLAKE ~

Damian unlocked the door and cracked it open, sharpening his senses. Since he didn't detect anything out of the ordinary, he walked into the house and headed toward the mirror. He brushed his fingers over its surface, staring intently into its depths, but couldn't see anything except his own reflection.

"You didn't kill Nick Evans, did you?" he muttered under his breath. "You were trying to save him. Just like you helped me last night. Cole was right. You're not a ghost. You're something entirely different, and I'll find a way to communicate with you. I promise..." He ran his fingers over the mirror again, but since the spirit didn't respond, he sighed and headed toward his room.

Even before he approached the living room, he heard Jesse's voice coming from the inside and shuddered inwardly. He halted, but then resumed walking, stepping as soft as he could on the carpet.

I'd rather face the Indrik-Beast again than spend one minute talking to this self-important asshole...

Cursing his bad luck, he walked through the hallway, hoping

to avoid crossing paths with River's partner. He felt too tired to tolerate his arrogance and insolence right now, and at the mere thought of it, his patience was running dangerously thin.

"Are you kidding me?" Damian heard Jesse's voice and grunted, annoyance flaring in him to the next level. "River, what is this ogre doing in your house at night?"

Jesse walked out of the living room and seized Damian's arm, stopping him. Jesse's eyes swept up and down as though sizing him up, and his lips curved in disdain. Damian's knee-jerk reaction was to yank his arm out of this man's grip and send him flying across the floor, but instead, he clenched his teeth and did nothing, staring down at him frostily.

"What were you doing, asshole? Digging graves? You're covered in dirt like the homeless mongrel you are." He let go of Damian's arm and rubbed his hands together, cleaning the dust off his palms.

"I told you, Jesse," replied River. She made her way out of the room and stepped between her partner and Damian. "He's here because I want him to be here. You were always a great friend to me and Nick, and I appreciate that you care about my wellbeing so deeply. I truly do, but right now, I need you to respect my choices and back the hell off." She sounded calm and even, but the iron tones were clear in her voice as she moved closer to her partner, placing her hands on her hips.

"You want him to be here," parroted Jesse, his eyebrows climbing up, a layer of bitterness underlying his words. "So, let me get this straight. You rejected my offer to keep you safe, but you trust this drifter? Come on, River... You know nothing about him. He could be a—"

He stopped talking mid-sentence and threw his hands in the air, a pained expression crossing his face. As Damian observed his behavior, the same questions surfaced in his mind. Was Jesse a man in love and was it jealousy talking, or was there some other reason for his attitude?

River glanced up at Damian, a faint smile touching her lips for a heartbeat. "Damian, I'm sorry. Please ignore him."

"It's okay, River," he replied without taking his eyes off Jesse. "I need to clean up and then get a couple of hours of sleep before I start working. If you need me earlier, just wake me up."

He turned around and walked away, blocking the sound of Jesse's voice as he was trying to reason with River.

* * *

THE NIGHT WENT BY UNEVENTFULLY, and Damian managed to get another hour of sleep before Cole called him to let him know that he'd be at Paradise Manor in ten minutes. Cole rang the bell precisely at seven, meeting River on her way out to work. Dressed in a stylish gray suit with a digital tablet in his hand, he looked just like any businessman. Except for the dark sunglasses he wore at such an early hour, there was nothing about him that would point out his true nature.

"Do you eat normal food?" asked Damian, watching Cole settling at the kitchen table.

"Define normal," replied Cole with a shrug and then added, "If I have to. It doesn't do anything for me, but living in the world of humans, I have to pretend to be one."

"How about coffee?"

"I take mine with one spoon of sugar and an infusion of A-negative." Humorous twinkles lit up in his eyes as he cocked an eyebrow at his brother.

"Dream on, Dracula Junior. I'm not bleeding to make your coffee taste better," murmured Damian. Turning to the counter, he noticed Gypsy lying next to the coffee machine, licking her paw with a nonchalant look.

"Your vamp is cute," she purred between licks and raised her head, her emerald eyes drilling into Cole.

Damian smirked. "Hey, Cole, Gypsy thinks you're cute," he

murmured, filling two cups with coffee. "I think she needs to raise her standards."

"I'm flattered, my lady." Cole bowed ceremoniously to Gypsy, eliciting a groan out of Damian. Cole's lips curved up at the corners, making him look like a sly cat himself.

Hearing a soft thud, Damian turned around and noticed a small plastic creamer cup lying on the floor. He picked it up and placed it back on the counter.

"Now, be serious for one second. How do you take your coffee?" he asked, looking back at his brother.

"Black," replied Cole, but for some reason, his blue eyes crinkled at the corners as if he was stifling laughter.

Damian heard another soft thud and saw one more creamer cup lying on the floor. He picked it up, wondering what was going on, but as he straightened, he saw Gypsy gently pushing the next cup off the table with an innocent expression in her round eyes.

"Gypsy, what the hell?" he yelled, throwing his hands up.

"What?" Gypsy's mouth stretched into a feline grin, the tip of her pink tongue showing between her fangs. *"You have the world's best backside, and I'm sure if I ask you to bend down, you wouldn't do it for me. Anyway, can't a girl have a little fun?"*

"I'm going to kill this cat," moaned Damian, placing two cups of steaming coffee on the table.

"I'm not going to ask," murmured Cole, pulling a cup closer, but his shoulders shook in silent laugher. He took a sip of his coffee and put it down, sobering up. "So, what did you want to talk about?"

"About our little underground adventure," replied Damian, tracing the shape of the cup with his finger. "Based on what we discovered in the mines, I believe we should go back to our roots, and I was wondering if you could help me with some research. You're better with all this modern computer stuff."

Cole leaned back, staring at him quizzically. "Which roots do you have in mind and why?"

"Slavic roots, Nikolai. What do you know about the Indrik-Beast?"

"Not much." The vampire shrugged. "I've heard the name, but that's about it. Are you sure that was the Indrik-Beast?"

"How many magical creatures the size of a mammoth with a horn on their head do you know? I'm sure. Hundred percent," replied Damian. He bit his lip and stared out the window, gathering his thoughts. "So, here is the deal. According to Slavic lore, the Indrik-Beast is not a monster. It's neither good nor evil. It dwells underground, guarding wells, rivers, lakes—any body of water that has magical properties to it."

"Then what is it guarding in the Arizona desert?" murmured Cole, staring at Damian over the rim of his cup.

"That's the million-dollar question," replied Damian, a heavy knot twisting in the pit of his stomach. "But since the Indrik-Beast belongs to the Slavic world, I'm not going to be surprised if the monster haunting Paradise Manor belongs to the same realm."

"Slavic pantheon?"

"I hope not," muttered Damian. "All I need is to face Morena, the goddess of Winter and Death, when I barely have enough energy to kill a run-of-the-mill demon."

"I don't know about demons, but from what I've heard, you kill vampires just fine, despite your power-impotency," murmured Cole reproachfully, but then raised his arms, stopping Damian from answering. "Why do you think it's Morena?"

"The cold, the winter blizzard, the ice," replied Damian, his mind flashing back to the weird trip down memory lane he took during his incarceration in the city jail. He recalled how cold he had felt, and a deep shudder ran down his back. "Since I moved to Blue Creek, I witnessed a few supernatural occurrences, and all of them had just one thing in common—freezing temperatures."

"It can't be Morena," objected Cole after a moment. "Rumor has it she'll be out of the picture for a while. After her latest indiscretions, Veles keeps her under control."

Damian nodded, thinking that Cole was most likely right. Veles, the god of the Three Realms, was one of the most powerful deities of the Slavic pantheon, and if he kept the goddess of Winter and Death imprisoned, there was no way she could escape to play in the realm of humans. But who else could create a winter storm in the middle of Arizona's heat?

"I can almost hear your brain clicking," said Cole, smirking. "So, we don't know who it is, but we do have a few facts we can start with." He got up and started pacing between the table and the counter. "Firstly, we know we have to dive into Slavic lore. That narrows things down significantly."

"Yes and no." Damian followed his brother with his eyes, his fingers rubbing the bracelet on his wrist absentmindedly. "Any god or powerful being of magic from any pantheon could have summoned the Indrik-Beast. But you're right. We can start the research with Slavic lore."

"Good." Cole halted, turning to face Damian.

"There is also something I want to check out today after you leave."

Damian grabbed a large folder with the architectural blueprints of Paradise Manor and placed it on the table. He took the cups and put them on the counter next to Gypsy, giving her a killer stare. Then he unfolded the general plan, smoothing the creases down.

"Here is what I noticed," Damian said, pointing at the plan. "According to this blueprint, the location of rooms and hallways on the left and the right sides of the house is absolutely identical. But when I visited the left wing, the main hallway dead-ended into a locked door. In the right wing, in this place, there is another hallway that's positioned at ninety degrees to the main one. It leads to River's bedroom and the bedroom she gave me on the opposite side of it."

He circled the small hallway with two rooms on the plan and glanced at Cole, but he just nodded, encouraging him to proceed.

"In the left wing, however, this entire area was converted into a large, single space," Damian continued, "most likely by Nick Evans since he was the one who started the so-called 'reconstruction'. So, the question is, what is in this area"—he circled the left edge of the building on the blueprint—"and why is it warded so heavily?"

"Let's go and check it out now," offered Cole with a slight shrug. "River is away. Perfect time. Why should we wait?"

Damian folded the blueprint and shook his head. "No offense, but I work alone. I didn't feel comfortable when you went with me into the mines and brought a little human girl with you. I nearly killed both of you. I'm not making the same mistake again."

Cole tilted his head, narrowing his eyes. "You know that I'm a vampire with a thousand years of experience with the supernatural, right?" he said quietly and leaned forward slightly, bracing himself against the table. "I'm not easy to kill."

Damian froze in place, feeling cold perspiration covering his forehead.

"I know that. You don't need to remind me what you are every chance you get," he replied, everything inside him stretched like a tightly wound string. "The left wing of the house is heavily warded against anything that moves—good, evil, and in between. The first time I went there, I had River's father with me, and I almost lost him there." He wiped his face with his hand, his moves sharp and jerky. "I can't do it, Cole. Sorry." He exhaled and looked away. "I've been working alone for centuries, and I'm not going to change the way I do things now. I'm happy you're here, and if you want to help me with some research, I'd appreciate it. But I won't do anything to put you in danger."

"Your presence here has already put me in danger... My true nature puts me in danger. Life is hazardous to your health, don't you know?"

"Then I'll be gone from Blue Creek as soon as I finish helping River."

Cole sighed and sat down. "What happened to you, Dima?" he asked softly. "Why are you so... guarded and... abrupt? You told me your power was stripped, but why and how? You're a Child of Earth—a powerful one from what I can see. But you can't selfheal, you don't have the second sight, and you're getting drained from minimal use of your magic. I'm here... I can help you... Let's talk like we used to."

Damian smirked bitterly. "What do you want me to tell you? A lot has happened." He raked his hand through his hair, pulling it down over the left side of his face. "I'm okay."

"Fine. You don't want to talk about your past, I'm not going to force you," said Cole, raising his hands. "But look around, Damian. You have people who actually like you and care about you despite your attempts to push them away. And I am not talking about myself only. Are you going to keep an arm's-length relationship with everyone?"

"What are you talking about?" Damian scowled, his hand gripping the edge of the table tightly.

"River and Sam, of course." Cole rolled his eyes. "Are you really that blind? I've been around them for a few short hours, but I could see it. And you—"

"Okay, I'm done," Damian growled, rising, towering over his brother. "Aren't you late for work?"

"Good talk, big bro." Cole rolled his eyes. "Was that your attempt to intimidate me?" He laughed, throwing his blond curls off his face, but quickly sobered up and frowned. "You know that sooner or later, you will end up in a situation you can't handle on your own, Mr. I-work-alone? What are you going to do then?"

"Hasn't happened yet," objected Damian dryly. "I'll cross that bridge when I get to it."

"Consider yourself at that proverbial bridge." Cole got up, staring straight into his eyes without blinking in that unnerving vampire's way. "Get moving. We're going together."

Damian threw his hands up but decided not to argue. Cole had always been stubborn and fighting him was pointless. It seemed like becoming a vampire had amplified this part of his personality.

"Fine," Damian growled and turned to the cat. "Gypsy, are you coming with us?"

"Take the entire zoo, why don't you?" murmured Cole, his eyebrows rising.

"As you're well aware, I don't have the other sight, and you're a vampire. You don't have it either," replied Damian. "A cat's natural sight is more powerful than any revealing spell I can cast. She can warn me if something is wrong long before I detect it."

"Finally, you admit to the superiority of my species," said Gypsy. She got up, stretching lazily, leaning forward and then back. *"Kneel before me, peasant. We, Queens, don't walk. We ride with a flourish."*

Damian sighed but took one knee, allowing the cat to hop on his shoulder. "Tell me everything you see," he muttered, heading out of the kitchen, but then halted by the door, throwing a frosty glance at his brother. "And you're going to do what I say, when I say it. Am I clear?"

"We'll see how you behave." Cole grinned and slapped Damian on his shoulder as he maneuvered his way around him out the door.

Dammit!

CHAPTER 19

~ DAMIAN BLAKE ~

Damian removed the plywood carefully and placed it next to the doorway. After the last attack of the frost-monster, it was cracked, and he did everything he could not to damage it further in fear of deactivating the protective rune. He stared into the darkness of the hallway, and unease spread through him, sending shivers down his back.

"I know there is nothing I can say to change your mind," he said to his brother with a tentative smile. "But can I ask you to keep a few paces back? At least until I make sure it's safe?" He met Cole's eyes and sighed. "Please?"

Cole peeked around the corner, and his eyes lit up with a bright scarlet light as the vampiric energy spiked around him. Turning to face Damian, he said, "If it makes you feel better, I will give you a couple of yards head start." He tittered, the tips of his fangs showing slightly. "The Shadow Slayer is protecting a vampire."

"Keep rubbing it in, little bloodsucker," murmured Damian. "Jokes aside... if I tell you to run, you run at your full speed."

"You're pushing it—"

"Cole!"

"Fine, my lord and master." He bowed, his every move dripping with sarcasm. "I shall do as you command."

Damian grunted but didn't add anything and headed into the hallway. Stepping softly on the carpet, he sharpened his senses to the maximum, but just like the last time, he could detect nothing. Gypsy remained calm and silent, sitting on his shoulder. He halted a few steps away from the door at the end of the hallway and raised his hand, stopping Cole.

"Cole," he whispered, but despite his attempt at being quiet, his voice carried through the house, amplified by the weird acoustics of this place. He swallowed, feeling the hair rising on his arms. "Please do me a favor and don't play games. Stay where you are. I'm going to check out the wards and let you know when you can come closer."

"I don't see or sense anything," said Cole, wincing at the sound of his voice, echoing through the dark hallway.

"Neither do I," murmured Damian. "But the protective magic is all around us. Trust me. Stay back."

"Damian, I can see the runes and sigils," Gypsy's voice sounded in Damian's mind. *"But they are not glowing like the last time."*

"Thanks, Gypsy. Let me know if you detect any changes." Damian took a careful step forward and glanced over his shoulder to make sure his brother didn't move. To his relief, he saw Cole leaning his shoulder against the wall, his arms folded over his chest. "Well, let's see what's hidden behind this door."

Keeping in mind what happened last time when Sam tried to open the door, he sharpened his already stretched senses and carefully put his fingers on the handle. Nothing happened.

"Gypsy, did anything change?" he asked.

"No, keep going," the cat replied, but her claws dug into his shoulder through the thin fabric of his shirt.

Throwing one more warning gaze at his brother for good measure, Damian pushed down on the door handle. It vibrated under his fingers, and the soft ping of magical energy traveled through his arm, making him suck in a sharp breath. The door opened with a light squeak, and a wave of magic enveloped him. It wasn't the energy of protective magic. It was soft and calming, but he didn't recognize its origin or purpose.

"Here goes nothing..." Damian murmured and carefully slipped into the room.

As soon as he crossed the threshold, the amount of magical energy stored there engulfed him. He gasped for air, struggling to breathe, and the room around him spun as he started to fall. Or at least it felt like he was falling. There was no floor, walls or ceiling. He was suspended in midair, surrounded by slowly rotating waves of the same magical energy he had detected earlier. It wasn't black but rather ultramarine, bright blue sparkles coming closer to him and disappearing back into the spinning mass.

"What the hell?" he whispered, endeavoring to get in control of his body. For a moment, a rash of panic spiked through his mind, making his heart beat desperately in his chest, but he made an effort to suppress the panic and relax as much as he could in this situation.

He felt Gypsy move on his shoulder, pressing her soft side to his cheek, and this tiny patch of warmth gave him an unexpected boost of energy. For the first time in many years, he was glad he wasn't alone.

"Gypsy, what is this void?" he asked in a hoarse whisper.

"Void?" Gypsy shifted again, her long tail wrapping around his neck. *"What void? You're standing on the hard, tiled floor of a giant room."* She rubbed against his cheek gently. *"Can you get your second sight back, Child of Earth? I love my mistress and without your full power, you're a helpless kitten. You can't save her..."*

Dammit...

"*Veritatius revelare*," he whispered, moving his hand in a wide arch. The constant rotation ceased, and through the layer of the powerful illusion, he could see a giant room with a tall ceiling and a tiled floor. He moved his arm again, casting the second spell. *"Latentius revelare."*

The entire surface of the room—the walls, the floor, and even the ceiling—lit up with a multitude of runes and sigils. Long chains of hieroglyphs in a language he didn't recognize appeared on the ceiling, and on the opposite wall, he saw a door. It didn't look like a physical entity, but rather like glowing outlines, surrounded by hundreds of tiny runes.

"What is this place?" whispered Damian, staring around in awe.

He took a step forward and halted, feeling a sudden change in the magical energy flowing around him. The blue sparkles became agitated, shining brighter and moving faster. The wall started to vibrate, and the light buzzing noise of wards filled the air. Damian spun around and found Cole standing by the door. He hadn't touched it yet, remaining about a foot away.

"Cole," said Damian, his jaw set with fear, "back away carefully. Don't touch anything. The wards are reacting to you."

Cole's eyes widened, his fangs expanding, but he lifted his hands and stepped back softly. As soon as he was away, the wards stopped buzzing.

"Time to leave," muttered Damian. He walked out to the hallway and waved his hand, removing his spells. Then he closed the door and turned around. "Come closer, Cole. Slowly... Don't touch anything."

As soon as the vampire approached him, the wards and the protection spells reacted, buzzing furiously.

"That's strange," murmured Damian, heading toward the foyer. "The wards reacted to you, but completely ignored me. Last time I was here with Sam, the protective magic reacted to both of us. I could feel its resistance."

They walked out into the foyer, and Damian lowered Gypsy to the floor softly, petting her thick fur. He restored the plywood and halted, staring to the side at the silver mirror.

"Another mystery to add to my list," he muttered, shaking his head. Then he sighed and turned to face his brother. "Do you have a few more minutes?"

Cole glanced at his wristwatch and shrugged. "I'll be a little late, but no big deal. What did you see there?"

They moved back to the kitchen and sat down. As briefly as he could, Damian described everything he'd seen in the strange room. Cole frowned, unease lingering around him.

"I've never heard of anything like that," he said, fumbling with the case of his tablet. "Have you?"

"No." Damian rubbed his face, propping his elbows on the table. "I can't believe it." He lifted his head, staring somewhere above Cole's head into space. "After all the training I received, I didn't recognize most of those runes and sigils. There was some kind of inscription on the wall too, and I couldn't read it. I didn't know the language." He slammed his hand on the table, anger and distress clawing their way through him. "Gypsy is right. Without my full power, I'm nothing. I can't protect River."

"Training?" asked Cole, his glowing eyes drilling through Damian. "What kind of training?"

"Irrelevant." Damian cursed inwardly for letting it slip. "Forget about it, Cole. There is something I must do, and I need your help."

"Oh?" Cole gave him an arched stare, the corner of his lips curving up. "What happened to Mr. I-work-alone?"

"Ha-ha. The circus left, but the clown is still here," growled Damian, eliciting a chuckle out of the vampire. "Can you get serious for two minutes?"

"No, why?" Cole shrugged lightheartedly but then raised his hands and added, "Okay-okay... I'm serious. What can I do to help?"

"Out of all the magical graffiti in that room, there was one rune I recognized," said Damian. "It wasn't really a rune or a sigil, but rather a signature. Possibly, this signature belongs to the people who placed all this protective magic."

"Whose signature was that?"

"Guardians," replied Damian, leaning back in his chair.

"Guardians?" repeated Cole, his pale skin becoming parchment-like yellow. "As in the Guardians Order? The Order of highly powerful witches and wizards regulated by the Destiny Council? Please tell me it wasn't *them* you had in mind."

Damian dropped his head, dread settling in the pit of his stomach. More than anything, he didn't want to have anything to do with the Destiny Council or their representatives in this world.

Regulating the supernatural affairs in all realms, human and magical, the Destiny Council was one of the most powerful organizations. Yet, the way they ran their business wasn't always transparent, even for those who served them. Working in mysterious ways, they kept all the supernatural beings under their strict supervision, making sure that the World of Magic wouldn't get exposed, and that the Board of Destiny would run its course, uninterrupted and unaffected by outside forces.

"Yes, Cole, unfortunately, it was their signature," replied Damian quietly.

"How can you be so sure?"

Damian folded the sleeve of his T-shirt up to expose his upper arm. He channeled some of his magic and brushed his fingers over it. A rune glowing with bright white light materialized on his skin. It lingered there for a moment and then dissipated.

"This is how I can be sure," said Damian, avoiding Cole's horrified eyes. "I can never forget their signature, even if I wanted. It's branded into me."

"Dima—"

"Don't ask me any questions I can't answer," growled

Damian, and Cole snapped his mouth shut, a muscle twitching in his jaw.

"What are you going to do?"

"I'm going take a trip to Chicago to visit the Guardians HQ," replied Damian, lowering himself on the chair.

"How are you going to get in or get an audience with the Archmage for that matter?" asked Cole. "They don't let anyone even close to their property without a personal invitation as far as I remember."

"I know." Damian lowered his face into his hands and stilled, dealing with the disarray of thoughts racing through his mind. When he moved from Florida to Arizona, the plan was to start clean—no old acquaintances or old enemies. Showing up at the Guardians Order uninvited was never in his plans. "Do you know Jamie Coldwell?" He lifted his face, meeting Cole's troubled gaze.

"The young librarian?" he asked, unable to hide his surprise. "What about him?"

Damian smirked. "That young librarian is a Guardian wizard." He leaned back, folding his arms. "After you leave, I'm going to talk to him and see if he agrees to help me. I'll have to trust him with some information, of course, but he's my only hope to see the Archmage in a civilized and peaceful manner. Besides, something tells me he can be trusted."

Cole nodded, but the tensed set of his shoulders betrayed his true feelings. "What do you want me to do?" he asked quietly.

"Couple of things. First, I need you to do some research for me while I'm gone," replied Damian. "The Lady of the Mirror is not evil. She's never killed anyone. I believe, every time when she made an appearance to the members of the founding families, she was trying to warn them of some kind of danger. I need a way to communicate with her."

Cole rubbed the back of his neck. "I think I can do it," he

replied after a moment. "I already have some ideas on who she is, but I need confirmation. What else?"

Damian got up. His eyes fell on the cat, curled up on the counter. He caressed her back, listening to her purr.

"I don't know how long I'm going to be gone," he said, turning back to Cole. "Unless Jamie can open a portal, I can't teleport, and flying to Chicago is not an option for me. So, we'll have to drive, and it's about a twenty-six-hour trip in one direction. If everything goes well, I should be back within three days."

"You need me to keep an eye on Paradise Manor?" asked Cole.

"Yes, from the inside," confirmed Damian. "Before I leave, we should talk to River and Sam. You'll have to take my place and guard her. I trust you can keep your urges under control?"

"What kind of urges do you have in mind?" Cole rolled his eyes, and an uneven smirk appeared on his face. Damian sighed, shaking his head reproachfully, and Cole's smirk grew wider. "Relax, big bro. I'm a big boy. I can control my thirst and all other *'urges'*." He got up, all humor gone from his eyes. "Don't worry, I'll be a real gentleman, and I'll do everything I can to keep her safe while you're away." Glancing at his watch, he picked up his tablet. "I have to go now, but if you want, I can give you a ride to the library."

A FEW MINUTES LATER, Cole parked his car in front of the main entrance into the library and shut down the engine. "Call me as soon as you get to Chicago?" he said softly without looking at Damian.

"I'll be all right. Don't worry." Damian smiled, feeling the tension and unease in his brother's voice. "Besides, I'll see you tonight before I leave. Relax, Cole."

"I'm as relaxed as I can be." Cole turned slightly to face him. "There is too much you're not telling me. And I understand that for whatever reason your past cannot be disclosed, but when it comes to the Destiny Council and their representatives in this realm, I just..." His voice trailed, and he frowned, his fingers pulling down on his tie. "I wish you could tell me the truth."

"One day... I promise."

"There is something else, too," Cole continued, dropping his hand onto his lap. "The Queen is keeping close tabs on me. I'm positive I was abducted on her orders, but I have no idea what her true agenda is." Cole glanced at Damian, his eyes shadowed by concern. He wasn't scared, but he was asking for help without actually saying the words.

"Do you think she knows you're my brother?" asked Damian.

"I don't know, but the thought crossed my mind. Not once." The vampire sighed and averted his gaze. "Even if she does, you know I would never do anything that could hurt you, right?"

Damian smiled at him, and for a moment, an image of a small boy with platinum curls replaced the man sitting next to him.

"I'll kill her if she touches a hair on your head," Cole growled, his eyes shining scarlet under his dark sunglasses. "But there is a chance I won't have to do anything."

"What do you mean?"

"Problems in paradise." Cole shrugged. "The Queen's opposition is growing stronger by the day, and Roxana has a hard time keeping them at bay. To be honest, if I move my loyalty to the other side of the royal throne room, she's not going to enjoy it. I have money, and you know how it is—money talks, bullshit walks." He chuckled bitterly. "That could also be the reason for her strange behavior. She's trying to dominate me any which way she can."

"Including—?"

"Yes, including that," replied Cole. His face turned ashen, and he raised his hand to stop all other questions. "I'm fine. Remember our earlier discussion? There is always someone who yanks your leash. If it's not her, then it's my maker. If it's not him, then someone else will show up. A sacred space is never empty."

"If she treats you like this, why don't you support the opposition?" asked Damian, the words barely breaking through his constricted throat.

"Not so easy," replied Cole, shaking his head. "The political games and intrigues of the Vampire Courts are complicated, and things are always not what they appear to be. She's old. A lot older than me, and she still has a lot of supporters in the underground circles. As much as I want to see her dead, I must be careful. One wrong move, and it's ashes to ashes for me." He fell silent, thinking of something. "Especially now that you're back with me. I hate to say it, but since the Shadow Slayer moved to Blue Creek, the blood games became a lot more dangerous and complicated."

"Dammit," muttered Damian. "I had no idea that by moving here I would—"

"Stop. What are you talking about?" Cole interrupted him, looking heavenward. "Every day, I thank all the gods for bringing you back in my life. Forget about everything else. I'll be fine. I know how to navigate the Royal Courts. Not the first time for me."

"Watch your back?"

"Always."

Damian opened the door and walked out of the car, bending down slightly to see his brother.

"I'll see you later on at Paradise Manor." Cole waved his hand and started the engine.

CHAPTER 20

~ DAMIAN BLAKE ~

Damian followed the speedy sports car until it turned the corner and disappeared from view. Rubbing the back of his neck, he headed toward the library, a heavy feeling of dread twitching in his chest. Everything Cole had told him left a bad taste in his mouth, and his scalp was prickling at the thought that his move to Blue Creek had put his brother in a dangerous situation. He sighed. There was absolutely nothing he could do about it, except for being there for Cole whenever he needed him.

He approached the library entrance and pulled on the door handle. It was still closed. Glancing at his wristwatch, he realized that it wouldn't be open for another ten minutes and was about to walk away to sit down on the bench when the lock clicked, and the door opened up. Jamie Coldwell stood on the other side, a wide, friendly smile on his face.

"Damian," he said, gesturing for Damian to come in, "you're a little early today, but I thought I would open for you, anyway. It's too hot to hang around outside."

"Thank you," said Damian, slipping into the cool, air-conditioned room.

Jamie walked toward the front desk but didn't sit down. Instead, he propped his elbow on the counter, leaning slightly on it.

"Are you still researching the history of the founding families?" he asked, looking at him with curiosity.

"I am," replied Damian, "but this is not the reason I'm here today. I was hoping to have a private conversation with you, Jamie."

Jamie straightened, his shoulders as tense as his face. "About?"

"I'm about to ask you for a huge favor and something tells me you're not going to like it in the slightest," said Damian calmly. "But I need help, and you're the only person I know who can help me."

"Wow," exhaled Jamie, his dark eyebrows lowering over his eyes. "That's not a good preambular." He pointed at an empty desk. "Why don't we sit down, and you start by telling me what's going on."

Damian headed toward the desk and pulled a chair out, positioning it to face the young man.

"Jamie, I'm going to be as honest with you as I can be, and I hope you understand that everything I tell you must be kept in strict confidence. The lives of good people depend on it," said Damian.

"Now, I like it even less," murmured Jamie, but waved his hand for Damian to continue. "Don't worry, what happens in the library, stays in the library. Go on."

Damian shook his head, an uneven smirk curving his lips. "Jamie, I know what you are, and I'm sure you understand what I mean when I say, I need more than your verbal promise."

Jamie went white, and his hands clenched together so tightly, something cracked in his joints. "How could you... You are... You have..."

"Yes, I have magic, and yes, I can sense yours," replied

Damian, putting an effort into sounding friendly. "Between us, you're not very good at concealing it. Besides, when you told me about your previous job, you said you worked for a military-like institution. I assume you worked as a guard for the Guardians Order at their headquarters in Chicago."

Jamie opened his mouth, ready to say something, but Damian raised his hand interrupting him.

"Don't worry," he said softly. "Your secret is safe with me." He snapped his fingers, and one of his daggers materialized in his hand. He placed its tip against the desk, folding both his hands atop the pommel. "I swear, you're safe with me." Taking the dagger carefully by the blade, he offered it to Jamie.

"You want me to swear an oath," mumbled the young man, his eyes growing wider. Damian nodded, and Jamie took the dagger. Placing it in the same way Damian had done a moment ago, he continued, "I swear, anything you're going to say to me is never going to be repeated to anyone." As Damian took his dagger back, making it vanish, Jamie folded his arms on the top of the desk. "Why don't you start by telling me who you are, Damian? It's kind of unfair you know what I am, but I know nothing about you."

Damian chuckled, thinking how truly young Jamie was. "I'm no one, Jamie," he said softly. "As far as the World of Magic, I'm a wizard and a Child of Earth with some serious limitations to my powers."

"Child of Earth," repeated Jamie in disbelief. "But there's only one registered Child of Earth, and he's not in our realm." He shook his head, leaning forward a little. "It's not possible."

Damian raised his arms and connected with his element, making the floor tremble. "It's possible, Jamie." He lowered his arms, folding them on his lap. "This is why I've said, I'm no one."

For the next thirty minutes, he told him everything that had happened since he arrived at Blue Creek, only leaving out his personal connection with Cole Adams. When he finished, Jamie sat quiet for a few long minutes, staring at his hands. Damian didn't bother him, allowing him to process the information.

"The founding families and Paradise Manor have always been surrounded by a veil of mystery as well as endless gossip and speculation," he muttered mostly to himself. "My father spent years trying to break this veil and wound up with nothing."

"So, what is it going to be, Jamie?" asked Damian. "Are you in?"

The young man raised his eyes at Damian, and a soft smile lit up his face, turning his eyes into two narrow arches. "Hell, yeah! I'm in. I'll help you get an audience with Archmage Allerton. I have to finish what my father started." He thought for a moment, his expression losing its cheerfulness. "Besides, River Evans is a nice person. She doesn't deserve to die... Neither did Nick..." His voice shook, and he swallowed hard. "I'll do what I can to help you, Damian."

"Thank you," exhaled Damian and leaned back in his chair, just now realizing that all this time he had held his breath, expecting Jamie's answer. "Can we leave tonight? Let's say at eight?"

Jamie thought for a brief moment and nodded. "Yes, it gives me enough time to do everything I need to do."

"You understand that as a Child of Earth, I can't fly. I can drive, but I don't own a car." Damian threw a guilty glance at him. "What are you driving?"

"Honda Civic," replied Jamie, but as understanding dawned on his face, he added, "Never mind that. I'll rent something bigger and pick you up at Paradise Manor at eight."

Thanking Jamie one more time, Damian left the library and headed straight to the hardware shop, hoping to catch Sam there. Even though the shop was about a ten minutes walk from the library, by the time he reached it, sweat was running down his face and back, plastering his shirt to his body.

Damian opened the door and walked inside a small shop overloaded with assortments of home-improvement merchandise and tools. The odor of different paints and lacquers mixed in with the scent of wood hung in the air, and the sunlight made its way in through a large window upfront, reflecting in glass jars and plastic cases. A wave of cold air caressed Damian's overheated skin, and he took a deep breath, enjoying the absence of the blistering heat, even if it was just a temporary reprieve.

Sam sat behind the counter, reading the local newspaper. As soon as Damian walked in, the old hunter lifted his head and folded the newspaper, putting it away. His kindhearted smile graced his face for a brief moment but was quickly replaced by an expression of concern.

"Damian," he said, rising, his face beyond pale. "Is everything okay?"

"As okay as it can be." Damian made his way to the counter and halted there, his eyes traveling over the wall with a variety of tools, starting with hammers and screwdrivers and finishing with drills and blades for electric saws. He switched his attention to Sam and continued, "You know that I would never do anything related to River's safety without getting your approval first?"

"I know," replied Sam, waving his hand impatiently. "What's going on, kid? Spill it."

"Well, the good news," started Damian, "I was able to open that door at the end of the hallway in the left wing. The bad news, I now have another mystery on my hands, and this time, I know I can't solve it on my own. I need to get information, and the only place I can get it is in Chicago."

"In Chicago," muttered Sam, pursing his lips. "Are you planning to hitchhike your way there, too?"

"No, sir." Damian smirked. "This time I'm driving. I'll try to be back as fast as possible, but I know I'll be away for three days minimum."

"Is River going to be safe on her own?" Sam's voice shook, and he frowned, nibbling on his lip.

"This is what I wanted to talk to you about," said Damian. "I don't want River to be alone at night in Paradise Manor. Also, I don't think she should move out. Don't ask me why, I just know it. Call it intuition." He glanced at Sam with a half-shrug. "Besides, she won't do it, anyway. So, while I'm gone, I want Cole Adams to take my place."

"Cole Adams?" asked Sam incredulously. "What can this rich boy do that I can't?"

This is going to be harder than I thought... Damian rubbed his forehead. "Sam, I am about to disclose a secret that doesn't belong to me. I expect you to keep your mouth shut."

"Fine, what is it?"

"Cole Adams is an ancient vampire," said Damian quietly. "He can do many things you can't even fathom. I trust him—"

"I knew it!" Sam slammed his hand on the counter. "I knew he was a vamp as soon as I touched his hand." Then he pulled back, frowning. "You brought a vampire into my daughter's house, and let her invite him in? I'm not okay with that. Not in the slightest. I will move in and protect my daughter the best I can while you are gone. I'm not gonna let her spend a night with a bloodsucker under her roof! Are you out of your friggin' mind?"

Damian sighed, throwing his hands up. "Sam, I trust Cole. River is going to be a lot safer with him by her side than with you."

"How can you trust him, Damian?" Sam yelled, leaning forward over the counter. "He's a fucking leach. He has no soul, no sense of good and bad. He's a vampire for God's sake!"

"I trust him because he is my brother!" Damian shouted and

the glass in the window jingled drearily. "He would never—you hear me—never betray my trust or harm River!"

Sam fell silent, gaping at Damian in shock. "Biological brother," he managed to say after a moment.

"Yes!" yelled Damian, but then took a deep breath, getting in control of his emotions. "Cole is my kid brother, and I trust him with my life, no matter what his true nature is. I swear to you—River is going to be safe with him."

"I'll be damned," mumbled Sam, staring at Damian without blinking. "You told me you had no family."

"I didn't lie," replied Damian quietly. "All this time, I thought Cole was dead."

"So, after centuries apart, you believe you know him?" asked Sam, suspicion rising in his voice. "People change within a short span of a human life. You must consider that you and your brother have hundreds of years between you two. He's not the same man you remember. He can't be! He's not even a man anymore. You don't know him. How can you trust him?"

"Because I know I can." Damian pressed his hand over his eyes and exhaled heavily, shaking his head. "Don't trust him, Sam. I'm asking you to trust me. Cole is the only one in this town who stands a chance to protect River in case of a supernatural attack."

For a while, silence enveloped the shop. Sam didn't speak, staring out the window, his eyes filled with dread.

"Fine," he said at length. "If River doesn't mind Cole staying with her for these three days, I'm fine with it, too."

"Thank you, sir." Damian nodded and headed toward the door.

"And Damian," Sam called after him, making him halt and turn around. "If your little brother so much as looks at her the wrong way, I swear, I will silver him to death."

"I'm sure it won't come to that," replied Damian coldly.

He inclined his head and walked out the door.

CHAPTER 21

~ COLE ADAMS ~

The *InvictusGame Studio Corp.* was positioned in one of the multiple business centers of Phoenix. With a public golf course on one side and a small two-lane road on the other, the building stood alone, isolated from numerous business units located on the other plazas of the center.

Cole liked the privacy of this building, and from the first moment he laid his eyes on it, he stopped searching, even though his real estate agent was against it, suggesting checking out other options before making the final decision. He had made the offer the same day and had never regretted his choice.

His software company occupied the entire building, and he loved that all his teams were located on the same floor, allowing for better collaboration between the groups and individual team members. Being a creative and artistic person by nature, he enjoyed participating in product development and design meetings, inspiring and encouraging the productive atmosphere and freedom of creativity.

All his employees were human, but he had never had a problem controlling his thirst. Being over a thousand years old, he no longer needed as much blood as a younger vampire would need to sustain the appropriate energy level and keep the thirst from overwhelming his mind. The employees of the company loved him and finding the right workforce was never an issue for him as he kept them happy with a generous pay and the best benefits package a private business could offer.

The source of his problems lay on the other side of his complicated existence—the one he led in the shadows, doing everything he could to keep it from spilling into his nearly normal day-life. He knew the Queen of Arizona would love to have a lion's share of his corporation—if not all of it—and he was doing everything in his power to keep his business as far away from her grabby hands as possible.

Ancient, money-hungry, and insidious, Roxana was a true threat to the lifestyle he had worked so hard to build in Arizona. The Queen loved the thrill of the *hunt*, the sound of screams and the smell of fear, and using the blood banks and willing humans wasn't her style. While she didn't stop Cole from his business endeavors on either the human or vampire side of his life, she kept close tabs on him, making sure to remind him any chance she had that he was nothing but her servant and she had the power to destroy him at any time.

The Queen's opposition quietly supported Cole's attempts at finding easier and legal ways to satisfy the need for blood without killing humans or exposing the World of Magic. Nevertheless, Cole had no illusions—the only reason Roxana hadn't killed him so far was his generous monetary donations to the Vampire Court. She wasn't sure any of her other subjects were capable of running a software company, so she needed him to do it. Besides, as she had pointed out numerous times, she enjoyed having him in her bed. Famous for her insatiable sexual appetite, Cole wasn't surprised she kept him alive and on a short leash.

* * *

COLE PARKED his car in front of his building and headed toward the entrance. Even before he opened the door, he detected the presence of vampiric energy and halted, thousands of possible scenarios originating in his brain in a split second. With his mind on high alert, he pushed the door open and walked inside.

As soon as he crossed the threshold, his executive assistant Mackenzie met him, her eyes wide.

"Mr. Adams," she said, sounding out of breath. "You have a visitor, and I had to escort her into your office. I'm sorry, but she wouldn't take no for an answer. She said she was your... um... benefactor?"

Cole nodded. "It's okay, Mackenzie. Don't worry about it."

He didn't need to ask who the visitor was. He knew who was waiting for him. What he didn't know was why she was here. *Benefactor my ass,* he thought grumpily as he made his way between cubicles toward his office, answering the greetings of his employees on autopilot.

He halted in front of the entrance into his office, his hand lingering over the door handle. With a deep sigh, he walked inside and closed the door behind himself softly, locking it. As soon as he crossed the threshold, the sweet scent of Roxana's perfume assailed his senses, and he grunted, tugging down at his tie as if it were suffocating him.

The Queen sat on a small leather sofa positioned to the left of his desk. Leaning back, she looked as charming and beautiful as ever. Even though she was dressed in a business pantsuit appropriate for an office environment, her entire appearance exuded sensuality beyond that of a normal human woman.

Roxana tilted her head slightly. As she took in Cole's appearance, her velvety brown eyes widened a little, and her full lips parted in a smile, showing her paper-white teeth. She lifted her hand, palm up, and bent her fingers, gesturing for him to approach. Cole glanced around to make sure the blinds over the windows in his office were tightly closed. Stifling a sigh and the desire to kill, he approached her. Lowering down to one knee, he held out his hand to her and bowed his head.

"Your Majesty," he whispered, his voice a low, seductive purr.

Taking her hand, he kissed it, touching her skin with the tip of his tongue while doing it. She gasped and leaned forward. Her fingers found their way into the mass of his hair, and she held his head down for a few seconds before letting go. Remaining in a kneeling position, Cole lifted his face and met her eyes, dark and foggy with desire.

"My Queen," he whispered, "to what do I owe the honor of your visit?"

She patted his cheek and tucked his blond hair behind his ear. "I missed you, my Russian warrior," she said, leaning back on the sofa, gazing down at him from beneath her long black eyelashes.

"I was at your service less than two days ago, my lady," he said, making an attempt to rise, but she held him down. "All you had to do was summon me. You didn't need to trouble yourself with traveling here."

"Stay down, Cole," she said, suddenly all business. "You're too tall, and I don't like to feel as if you are staring down at me."

"Never, Your Majesty." He averted his gaze, his mind racing to find an explanation of what was going on.

She pursed her lips, wringing a strand of his hair around her index finger. "It's been two days, Cole, and I still have nothing from you about the Shadow Slayer and his intentions."

"That's because I have nothing to tell, my lady," replied Cole, sounding calm while his nerves were stretched to the limit. "All I know is that he didn't move here with any particular goal in mind. He said he wanted a clean slate." He shrugged. "To leave his past in the past, so to speak."

"And you believed him?" she grumbled and jerked his hair, eliciting a hiss of pain out of him.

"I had no reason to question his sincerity," said Cole, gently untangling her fingers out of his hair. "I've been with you for a few centuries, my Queen. You know I have a gift when it comes to detecting lies, and I assure you, the Shadow Slayer has no interest in our Court. All he wants is to be left alone."

"He's using you, idiot," hissed Roxana, her black eyes burning with hatred. "He's using you to get close to me."

"No, my lady," Cole objected gently. "It appears, I'm using him, while he's absolutely truthful with me."

"Did you say *no* to me!" She rose slowly, but as much as she was trying to project her royal displeasure, something else was coming through—something that felt more like fear than anger.

"My lady, I wouldn't dare," he said, gazing up at her. "I swear, I'm telling you the truth. He's not here to hunt you or your subjects, if we leave him alone."

"What is he doing in Paradise Manor?" she growled. "Why did you take him to the desert? Are you lying to me? Are you protecting the Shadow Slayer? Why do I have this unpleasant feeling you're hiding something from me, lover?"

"No, my Queen, please—"

With lightning speed, she lifted her foot, planting her high-heeled shoe into his side. He lost his balance, falling back, and before he could react, she bent forward and seized his tie. Wringing it around her hand, she pulled him closer, her blazing eyes inches away from his.

"You have forty-eight hours, Cole Adams," she said. "I'll summon you in two days and you better be ready to report. Glamor him if you have to, but I must know who he is and what he is doing here. If you can't get the information out of him, I want you to subdue him and deliver him to my dungeons. If he's just a slayer or hunter, you should have no problem doing it."

"Your Majesty—"

"It's his life or yours, Cole," she said icily, straightening. "Choose wisely."

She pivoted on her heels and stormed out of the office, leaving him on his knees.

"Fire and ice. What am I supposed to tell her in two days?" muttered Cole. "Thank God Damian is leaving tonight for at least three days. Whatever she plans, I'm not going to give up without a fight."

He folded his arms on top of the sofa and lowered his head atop his folded arms, his mind working on overdrive. The Queen knew every step he took. She even knew he took a trip to the desert with Damian.

Ace... A thought flashed through Cole's mind, and cold perspiration covered his forehead. Damian was right. By bringing her into it, he put her life in danger. *Idiot...*

"Mr. Adams! Cole!"

A girlish voice filled with worry sounded behind him, and he jumped to his feet, turning around. Ace stood in front of him, her eyes wide with concern.

"I'm okay, Ace," he said, forcing a smile. He fell silent, trying to gather his scattered thoughts. "Listen, I know we have a Sprint Retrospective meeting scheduled, and I was looking forward to it, but something came up. Do you mind giving the team my apologies? There is something I must do, and it can't wait."

"Can I do anything to help?" she asked in a soft whisper, her fingers brushing his hand gently.

He pulled his hand away, crossing his arms behind his back. "Thank you, Ace," he replied not without kindness in his voice. "I appreciate it. And yes, you can go to the meeting and do what you do best—be my most awesome developer."

She smiled, but the sadness never left her eyes. "I'll record the meeting for you, so you can watch it when you have time."

"That would be great," replied Cole, gesturing at the exit.

Following Ace, he quickly crossed the company floor and walked out the door.

CHAPTER 22

~ COLE ADAMS ~

Cole drove his car across Phoenix, completely ignoring the speed limit. With the Queen watching his every move, he knew the clock was ticking, and even though she had given him forty-eight hours, he had no illusions. If Roxana found out where he was going now, his days—or hours—were numbered.

He parked his car in a small plaza on the outskirts of Scottsdale and walked out. Wincing at the brightness of the sun, he readjusted his dark sunglasses. The stories about vampires' intolerance to sunlight were greatly exaggerated, but they held some truth. Vampires didn't spontaneously combust from the touch of the first ray of the rising sun, but they had hypersensitivity to the sunlight, and spending time outside during the day wasn't something they enjoyed.

After locking the car, he put the keys in his pocket and headed toward a small bookstore at the end of the plaza. The store was a front for one of the magical organizations—the Wardens Order. Just like the Guardians Order, they were regulated by the Destiny Council, but their purpose was completely different. Established thousands of years ago, the Wardens Order gathered and guarded the knowledge and wisdom of different generations and realms, supernatural as well as mundane.

Most of the Wardens were ancient warriors and skilled wizards, but on a rare occasion, they had humans who were exposed to the World of Magic working for them. The small bookstore was owned by Aaron Cooper—an older gentleman with no magical gift of his own, who had learned about the existence of the supernatural in his late teens when a rogue werewolf eradicated his entire family.

It was a miracle he'd survived the attack, and when a local Warden arrived at the scene of the crime to prevent possible exposure, he took the young man to the Arizona main location of the Wardens Order where the Master Warden was supposed to decide what to do with him next.

Clever and resourceful, Aaron found his way into the heart of the Master Warden, and the old man had allowed him to stay and learn. Hungry for knowledge and understanding of the new world he had been exposed to, Aaron spent years studying anything he could find about the World of Magic and its ways, and the Wardens' archives truly had no limits to knowledge. When he got older, the Master Warden relocated him back to Scottsdale and trusted him with supporting the local Wardens organization.

Cole halted in front of the store with a bright neon 'open' sign on its door. Sharpening his senses, he turned around, searching the plaza for any presence of vampiric energy. Since he couldn't sense it, he decided that either the Queen didn't bother following him here or whoever she sent after him was human. In either case, to help Damian, he needed to speak with a Warden, so he didn't have a choice.

Turning back toward the store, he put his hand on the doorknob, but as soon as his skin got in contact with it, a sharp pain surged through him. He jerked his hand back, a low hiss escaping his lips.

Silver... Oh well, information always comes at a price...

Ignoring the pain, he seized the doorknob again and turned it, leaving some of his skin on it. With a groan, he pushed the door open and walked inside. As soon as he crossed the threshold, a low buzzing noise invaded his ears, and belatedly, he realized that he just triggered some kinds of protection spells or wards. He moved to back away from the store, but something clicked, and a large net made of thin silver chains fell on top of him.

Cole cried out and dropped to his knees, fighting against his silver prison. The chains were too thin, and he had no doubt he could have ripped them off, even though silver weakened him significantly. However, he wasn't here to fight, so he pretended to give up and stilled.

Feeling a sharp pain on the side of his neck, he raised his face. A tall, wiry man in his late sixties stood next to him, holding a large machete against his throat. Despite the heat outside, he wore a thick cardigan over his plain T-shirt. His pants were wrinkled and glossy on the knees, and a pair of bifocal glasses rested on the bridge of his nose. A thick mop of silvery hair fell over his forehead in uneven strands, and he threw it off with his free hand.

"What are you doing in my shop, vamp?" he asked, his voice a little too high-pitched for his height. He glowered down at Cole, applying some pressure on the blade. "We don't serve your kind."

"I mean no harm, sir." Cole raised his arms up and winced as the silver wrapped tighter around his exposed hands. "I'm here because I need your help... I'm looking for Master Warden Luc de la Crosse."

Taken aback, the old man narrowed his eyes and recognition dawned on his face. "Son of a bitch," he exhaled but didn't lower his machete. "You're Cole Adams, aren't you? Or should I call you Nikolai Chernov?"

Cole flinched at the sound of his real name, but quickly realized that since he was one of the older vampires that had taken up residence in Arizona, his past had most likely been researched all the way to the moment of his birth and recorded by the local Wardens Order.

"Cole Adams would be fine, Mr. Cooper," replied Cole calmly, lowering his arms. "Please, remove the silver. I just want to talk."

"Come here, boys." Aaron Cooper looked back and whistled.

Two large Doberman pinschers rushed to his call from behind the counter. They approached Cole and snarled, showing off their dangerous fangs.

"Keep an eye on him, boys," murmured Aaron, petting the dog closest to him. Then he turned to Cole and smirked. "Don't go anywhere, would yah?"

Cole sighed and lowered his head. Aaron walked toward the counter and leaned over it. He came back a moment later with a cellphone in his hand. Quickly dialing the number, he put it on speaker. After a single dialing tone, a man answered the call.

"Aaron," he said with a heavy French accent. "Is everything okay?"

"Everything is fine, but I have quite an interesting situation," Aaron replied, smirking.

"Oh?"

"I have a vamp in my store. I decorated him with silver like the world's best Christmas tree," continued Aaron, throwing a sarcastic glance at Cole. "The reason I called you, Master Warden, is because he's asking for your help."

"A vampire?" repeated the man on the other side of the line, disbelief clear in his voice.

"Not just any vampire, Master de la Crosse. Cole Adams."

"Cole Adams?" repeated Luc de la Crosse. "Put him on the phone, please."

Aaron shrugged and squatted in front of Cole. Bringing the phone closer to his face, he flicked his eyebrow at him. "Speak."

"Master de la Crosse," said Cole calmly. "This is Cole Adams, and I need your help. I swear I'm not here on the Queen's behalf. As a matter of fact, I risked my life by coming here, my lord."

The line went dead, and a moment later, a portal opened behind Aaron, making him flinch and stagger back, almost running into Cole. The dogs snapped around and wagged their short tails eagerly before turning back. A young man with long dark hair pulled into a low ponytail on the back of his head walked out of the portal and halted in front of Cole, crossing his arms.

"Aaron, take the net off," he ordered with a sigh. "I'm sure *Monsieur* Adams is not here for an early lunch. Otherwise, silver or no silver, you'd be dead by now."

Cole smirked and bit his lip, stifling a burst of laughter bubbling up in his chest. Rising to his feet, he ripped the net off, tearing it in a few places. The silver burned his hands, and he hissed, throwing it to the floor with disgust. The sharp move in combination with the effects of the silver, however, made him slightly dizzy, and he swayed, pinching the bridge of his nose.

"Your chains are too thin to hold an old vampire like me, Mr. Cooper. It would probably hold a newborn vamp though," he explained quietly. "Anyway, like I said earlier, I'm here because I need help." He raised his hands up and watched the burns heal on his skin without leaving a mark.

Luc de la Crosse offered his hand to him, and Cole took it, squeezing it in a handshake.

"I've heard some interesting things about you, *Monsieur* Adams," said the Master Warden, giving him a quick once-over. "Let's sit down so you can tell me how I can be of assistance."

He motioned for Cole to come with him and headed toward the backdoor. As soon as he made a move, both dogs growled, shifting closer to him, but Aaron held them back. He locked the front door and turned off the neon sign before following the Master Warden and Cole.

As they walked through the shop, Cole couldn't help but look around, admiring the collection of printed work assembled by Aaron. The scent of books, old and new, touched his nostrils, and the corners of his lips curved up in a blissful smile as he allowed himself to relax for a brief moment.

He loved books and preferred reading to spending time in front of a TV. The old Browns' mansion, which he purchased in Blue Creek recently, had enough space, and the first thing he did after moving in was converting one of the bigger rooms into a home-library.

"You like books, don't you?" muttered Aaron, observing him with interest.

Cole nodded, coming back to reality. Aaron opened the door, letting Luc de la Crosse and Cole go through first. Leaving the dogs outside, he walked in, inviting his guests to sit down.

The backroom, just like the main area of the shop, was overloaded with books. But these books weren't your modern-day novels. Ancient grimoires and books of shadows in thick leather bounds, endless tomes of spells, collections of scrolls, demonology books and works of ancient witches and wizards were preserved behind thick glass or in air-tight compartments.

A scent of vanilla and an almond-like odor lingered in the air, and the soft blue light shone dimly, bouncing off the glass cases. Everything looked peaceful enough, but with his sharp vampiric senses, Cole detected a barely noticeable odor of some protection magic and the presence of silver all around.

"Stay away from the walls, Mr. Adams, and you'll be all right." Luc de la Crosse approached a small table, pulled one of the chairs out and sat down.

Cole took a chair across from him and settled down, folding

his arms on top of the table. The Warden tilted his head slightly, his bright hazel eyes drilling into Cole as if he were trying to read his mind.

"So, what brought a vampire to the Wardens Order?" he asked after a moment. "Speak freely, *Monsieur* Adams. Why are you here?"

"The Lady of the Mirror and Paradise Manor," replied Cole, meeting Luc's attentive gaze without blinking.

"Oh?" Luc de la Crosse frowned, his wide shoulders rising slightly as he leaned forward. "I wouldn't take you for the type to believe in urban legends."

"No, I don't believe in urban legends," agreed Cole. "I also don't believe the Lady of the Mirror is a ghost. However, I believe River Evans is in danger, and the Lady of the Mirror is trying to warn her."

Luc de la Crosse and Aaron exchanged a quick look. "And since when does the Arizona Vampire Court care about what happens to a single human?" huffed Aaron.

"I already said I'm not here on behalf of the Queen or the Court," said Cole quietly, throwing a reproachful gaze at Aaron. "I'm here because I want to save River Evans."

"I hope you understand our unease, *Monsieur* Adams," interjected Luc, raising his hand to stop Aaron. "Unless River Evans is your human... um... donor—which I have a hard time believing that—everything you say sounds too farfetched. An ancient vampire who is willing to take a chance with his freedom or life to help a single human? I'm sorry, but you have to give us a better explanation."

"Okay..." Cole closed his eyes, trying to gather his thoughts. "You know about all the mysteries surrounding Paradise Manor? The three founding families were practically wiped out of existence since they built Blue Creek."

Luc inclined his head. "Yes, I know all that."

"River Evans is the last surviving member of the founding

families, and whatever killed the other family members is now after her," continued Cole. "My old friend was hired to protect River. Unless he finds a way to communicate with the spirit of the mirror, he'll fail. River will die." He raised his hand, a bitter smirk appearing on his lips before he could stop it. "I know I'm a vampire—you don't need to remind me. But I do care. I care for my friend and for River, otherwise I wouldn't be here, would I?"

A pregnant pause hung in the room as Cole awaited the Master Warden's response.

"Who is your friend?" asked Luc after a while. "Are you sure he is your friend? Sending a vampire to meet with a representative of the Destiny Council?" Luc chuckled humorlessly. "The only reason you're still alive is because of what we've heard about you. Your reputation precedes you, *Monsieur* Adams."

Cole didn't move, didn't blink an eye, staring straight into the Warden's eyes. "I am *sure* he's my friend, and he would do nothing to endanger me." He looked to the side, breaking their eye contact. "He doesn't know I'm here. He would never let me..." His voice trailed off, and he got up, moving slowly and heavily as if he were drained. "If you allow me, my lord, I would like to leave."

"Cole, wait. Please..." Luc rose and reached to take his arm but changed his mind half-way and lowered his hand. "I want to help you, but can you at least give me the name of your friend? I have to know with whom I'm dealing, especially since he's obviously touched by the World of Magic. Don't you think?"

Forgive me, brother...

"Damian Blake," said Cole, turning to face the Warden. "He works for River's father, and that's how he got involved in the mess surrounding Paradise Manor."

"Damian Blake." Luc furrowed his brow, his gaze going out of focus for a moment. "I don't think I've ever heard of him. What is he?"

"He's nobody special, my lord," replied Cole, wondering how it was possible that the Wardens Order didn't have any records of Damian's existence. "Just a hunter. Recently, he relocated to Blue Creek from Florida."

Aaron got up, a thoughtful expression suffusing his features. "Is he—," he mumbled, scratching his head. "Whatchamacallit... I think the local vamps call him the Shadow Slayer. Is that your friend?"

Cole smirked, suppressing the desire to roll his eyes. "Slayer he is not," he replied. "He's a hunter. He hunts anything supernatural that kills humans. In your books, he should be marked as a good guy."

Leaning forward, Luc planted his fist against the table and his eyes turned white, the magical energy field spiking around him. In a few seconds, he straightened and blinked a few times, his eyes returning to their normal hazel color.

"That's strange," he muttered, confusion reflected on his face. "I couldn't find any record of a hunter with the name Damian Blake or the Shadow Slayer in the Wardens records." He glanced at Cole, shaking his head. "You're giving me a migraine, *mon ami*. You are an ancient vampire who lives among humans, leading a nearly human existence. Your friend is a slayer or a hunter who's not registered with the Destiny Council. How the hell is it possible?" He chuckled softly and gestured for Cole to sit down. "So, what kind of information do you and your friend require. I'll help you."

Cole sat down, stifling a sigh of relief. "I believe the Lady of the Mirror is not a ghost but a spirit. What I don't know is how to communicate with her."

"There are hundreds of different spirits that possess mirrors," said Aaron, wrapping his cardigan tighter around himself as if he were cold. "Do you know which one you're dealing with?"

"I can't be a hundred percent sure, but since this spirit

refused to show my reflection, I believe I'm dealing with a Zerkalitsa," said Cole.

"You're Eastern Slav, aren't you, Cole?" asked Luc. Cole nodded, and the Master Warden continued, "Aaron is right, there are many spirits that live in mirrors, but we should start somewhere, and Zerkalitsa sounds like a good place to start." He got up, a soft smile touching his lips. "Come here tomorrow at around eleven-ish in the morning. I should have an answer for you by that time."

"Thank you, my lord." Cole bowed slightly. "I'll see you tomorrow."

Luc de la Crosse nodded and arched his brow at Aaron. "Please escort our guest out," he said, humorous twinkles dancing in his eyes. As Aaron turned around to leave, he added, "And please try not to embellish him with any silver décor on his way out, Aaron."

Aaron grunted, a blush creeping up to his cheeks, but didn't say anything and opened the door for Cole.

CHAPTER 23

~ DAMIAN BLAKE ~

The walk back to Paradise Manor seemed endless. It wasn't only the sun in zenith blasting mercilessly from the unblemished blue sky that bothered him. In his mind, Damian kept going over everything he knew, wondering if there was anything he could do to avoid the trip and the meeting with the Guardians, but couldn't come up with anything that would make sense.

By the time he reached the mansion, he was drenched with sweat, breathing hard as if he had just finished a marathon. The house was blissfully empty, so he went to his room, quickly took all his clothes off and hopped into the shower without waiting for the water to warm up.

After the shower, he got dressed and made his way to River's bedroom. Even though he knew Cole was going to be keeping an eye on her, a nagging feeling of dread wouldn't leave him, constantly throbbing somewhere in his chest.

Channeling his magic, he cast a few protection spells, placing them over River's entire bedroom. Interweaving his magical energy with the elemental power of Earth, he drew a few runes at each corner of her door, creating additional wards.

He made sure that his wards wouldn't react to Cole, River, and Sam. However, he wasn't positive that they were strong enough to withhold a prolonged attack by any powerful being of magic, and that just added to his overall feeling of unease. After all, whoever this winter-monster was, it wasn't lacking in the power department.

Gypsy trotted slowly through the hallway and halted next to him, rubbing against his legs. He picked her up, scratching her head between her ears. The cat stretched and yawned, purring loudly.

"Gypsy," he said softly, walking to his bedroom, "I'll be gone for a few days, hopefully not more than three. I'm leaving you in charge. Take care of River and Cole for me, would you?"

"*You're leaving?*" The cat looked up, her green eyes staring at him without blinking. "*Not the smartest idea on your part...*" She stretched again, pushing the tips of her claws into his forearm. "*But no one ever blamed you for being smart, anyway.*"

"Thanks, darling." He laughed, dropping the cat on his bed. She snickered and sat down on her butt, hanging her hind legs off the edge and crossing them. Damian threw his hands up. "You can't even sit like a normal cat."

"*Being normal is highly overrated and extremely boring,*" murmured Gypsy. "*Frankly, you're not a poster child for normal either, as far as I can see. That's why I like you—you're anything but boring.*"

"Thank you, I guess?" Damian sat down next to her, sobering up. "Listen, Gypsy. While I'm gone, Cole is going to stay in my room. He's a lot more sensitive to the fluctuations in the magical energy field than I am, but still... You may notice something before him. So, if it happens, wake him up."

Gypsy measured him with her emerald eyes, and he could swear the cat was snickering inwardly.

"*No problem, I'll keep an eye on your cute vamp, but you have to pay for it. I don't offer my services for free.*" She winked at him in that cat-like manner, closing one eye, while keeping the other one wide open.

"Fine. What do you want?"

"A trip to the desert." Gypsy jumped off the bed and hopped on top of the bedstand, staring out the window. *"You see that purple rock formation out there?"* She pointed with her paw. *"I have always wanted to see it."*

"Not funny, Gypsy," Damian replied and lay down, folding his arms under his head. "You're a house kitty. River will kick my ass if I take you outside."

"Not the sharpest tool, are you?" asked the cat snidely. *"If I ride on your shoulder, I don't even have to touch the ground with my paws. As far as I'm concerned, that preserves my status of a house kitty."* She rolled her giant eyes and gave a few licks to her paw for good measure. *"Sasquatch."*

"You got yourself a deal…" He took a deep breath and closed his eyes. Gypsy was still talking, but he couldn't hear her anymore as his mind sank into blissful oblivion.

* * *

HE WOKE up at around five o'clock, and since neither Cole nor River was home yet, he walked around the house, quickly surveying every corner. Everything was quiet and peaceful enough to relax, but just as he was going to go back to his room, he heard a soft knock on the front door.

A light wave of vampiric energy touched his senses, and he wrinkled his nose, smirking. Cole was projecting his presence from a mile away. But to be fair, unlike wizards or Children of the Elements, there wasn't much vampires could do to conceal their energy from those who knew how to detect it.

Damian opened the door and observed his brother with interest. On top of his usual business suit, he wore a dark trench coat. It wasn't thick, but it still looked strange considering it was five o'clock in the middle of an Arizona summer, and the temperature outside was pushing a hundred degrees. Besides, vampires weren't sensitive to cold temperatures.

"Getting cold outside?" asked Damian, amused.

Cole snorted. "Did you want me to walk around with a sword in my hand?" he asked, pulling his trench coat open. A short sword was sheathed beneath his coat in a beautifully crafted leather scabbard.

"Can I see?" asked Damian, reaching for the weapon, but Cole pulled away, a mischievous grin splitting his face.

"I'm sure you have a blade, too. I'll show you mine if you show me yours." He winked, wrinkling his nose a little.

Damian threw a reproachful glance at him and waved for him to follow. "I see that in a thousand years you didn't grow up much, did you?"

"Why should I? Adulting is no fun."

They walked through the dark hallway of the right wing into Damian's room and then out into the swimming pool area. There was enough space there to move, and Damian wasn't worried that someone would walk into the foyer and see them armed with medieval style weaponry.

He extended his arms, and his daggers materialized in his hands. He spun them around, listening to the sound of the blades cutting through the air with a soft whistle, but made sure not to channel his magic through them.

As he stopped, Cole approached him and moved his fingers over the blades without touching them. "Beautiful daggers," he whispered. He rubbed his forehand, a frown shadowing his features for a brief moment. "I have a feeling I've seen daggers like this before, but for the life of me I can't remember where."

Damian pulled away gently. "Be careful, Cole. These daggers are built to kill anything un—" He cut himself off, wincing inwardly at what he almost said.

"It's okay. You can say it," he said, unsheathing his sword.

"Your daggers are built to destroy anything unholy. Like me." Cole shrugged and offered Damian his sword. "It's pretty old, and its blade has inclusions of *Ardenium* steel, but it's still just a sword."

Damian put his daggers on a small lounge chair and took Cole's weapon. Shaped like a gladius, the sword was definitely ancient, yet its blade was well preserved and polished. Its hilt was skillfully crafted, and a bright red stone that looked like a drop of blood was embedded into its pommel. He touched it and jerked his hand away as a soft wave of magical energy rushed through his hand.

"Very special weapon," he murmured, giving it back to his brother. "How did you come in possession of it? It seems to be older than both of us."

"It probably is," replied Cole, executing a perfect figure eight technique. "A gift from my maker. He was…er…is—I hope—one of the ancient ones. Even I don't know how old he is. Roxana can't stand him, but my guess is she's afraid of him and his influence over me."

Cole stopped rotating his sword and assumed a guarding stance, bringing his weapon to his shoulder. He flicked his wrist, gesturing for Damian to come closer.

Damian folded his arms and tilted his head, staring at his brother with unconcealed sarcasm. "You want to spar, little boy?"

One second Cole was standing in front of him and the next, he vanished. Before Damian realized what was going on, he felt a muscled arm wrap around his neck, holding the blade under his chin but slightly away from him so he wouldn't get hurt.

"Who are you calling a little boy, high-rise?" Cole chuckled softly.

Before his brother could react, Damian seized his sword hand with both hands, directing the blade away from his body and easily spun under his arm, breaking his grip. He didn't attempt to disarm Cole or lock his arm and laughed, releasing him instead.

"For me, you are always a little boy. Deal with it." He glanced at his brother with warmth. "You want to spar? I'm game. No vampire speed and strength?"

"No earthquakes and magic?" retorted Cole. He shrugged his trench coat off. Then he took his jacket, tie and shirt off, throwing everything on the lounge chair. "I'm ready. We fight like a man."

"Like a man?" Damian laughed, throwing his head back. "Do you even remember what it means?"

"Let's find out," replied Cole, raising his sword to his shoulder. "*En garde*, big bro."

Damian snapped his fingers, and his daggers vanished from the chair, reappearing in his hands. Cole attacked almost immediately, his blade meeting Damian's daggers with a loud clang, sending a few sparks in the air. Even without utilizing his full speed and strength, he was fast and forceful. Quickly exchanging fierce attacks with skillful feints, he moved swiftly and soundlessly like the night predator he was, and Damian had to utilize everything he had to deflect his vigorous attacks. A short while later, he was drenched in sweat again, and his black hair plastered over his face as they circled each other.

The sound of a constrained gasp made Damian stop and spin around. River stood in the doorway, watching them with her mouth open. Cole picked up his shirt but didn't make a move to get dressed and just stood there with his sword in one hand and his shirt in the other. River's eyes darted from Damian to Cole and then back to Damian as a soft blush colored her cheeks. Cole's smile grew wider.

"Stop grinning like Ivan the Simpleton and get dressed," whispered Damian.

"Wow..." River exhaled, shaking her head. "I must say..." She moved her hand in a circular motion. "You don't see something like this every day."

"Hello, detective," said Cole. "It's nice to see you again."

River nodded to him and turned to Damian. "I had no idea you and Cole Adams knew each other before that day when you saved him. Judging by the way you two behave, I would say you've been acquainted for quite some time."

"We know each other longer than we'd like to admit," said Cole, as calm and charming as always. "Unfortunately, for the last few years, we've lost contact. So, when Damian saved me, it was a double-nice surprise."

"I see," muttered River, but Damian could see she didn't buy anything Cole said. She approached Damian and tilted her head a little, narrowing her eyes at him. "Now, the truth, please. Damian, unlike you, Mr. Adams has a silver tongue. So, I have no choice but to ask you, despite your strange intolerance to anything that ends with a question mark. I assure you, whatever your history with Mr. Adams is, I'll keep it between us."

Damian exchanged a quick glance with Cole, and he gave him a short nod.

"Considering everything we need to talk to you about, I think it's a good idea for you to know the truth," he said softly. "Cole is my younger brother, ma'am. Like he said, we were separated for a few years and lost contact. I had no idea he was in Arizona until I found him in that hotel." He moved his hand through his matted hair, and added, "And that's the truth."

"Brothers?" she mumbled, her eyes flashing between Cole and Damian. "I see no family resemblance. You're opposite to each other in everything. Cole is a rich entrepreneur, and you're traveling across the country on foot with a single backpack. Everything that is dark about you is light in him. It's like you are the darkness, and he's the light."

Cole laughed, putting his shirt on without buttoning it up.

He grabbed the rest of his clothes and approached Damian, halting by his side.

"You got it all wrong, detective," he said gently. "He's the light, and I'm the darkness. And as far as the family resemblance, he was adopted. I guess he was so huge when he was born that his birth parents didn't want him." Damian gave him a scorching stare, poking him in his ribs, and Cole laughed, hopping a step to the side. "Just kidding. Damian looks like our father, and I'm a carbon copy of our dear mom."

"Your last names are different," said River dryly, folding her arms.

"When I joined—" Damian grunted, cutting himself off. "I changed my name years ago." He approached River and smiled. "River, we *are* brothers. You can run a DNA test if you want. But there is a reason we don't advertise it. Anyway, we need to talk." He wiped the sweat off his face, and a guilty smile crossed his face. "Would you please give me a few minutes to clean up and change?"

River approached Cole and ran her finger over his unclothed chest. "Isn't it amazing," she murmured with a hefty layer of sarcasm, rubbing her index finger against her thumb. "I was watching your swordplay for a few minutes before you noticed me. You, Damian, flushed and sweating the storm while your brother didn't even break a sweat, and his skin is as cold as snow. How do you explain that?"

She has to be a great detective. Damian sighed but had nothing to say to that. Instead, he headed toward the door to his room. "I'll see you both in a few minutes. In the meantime, River, you can torment Cole with your questions."

"Well, that would be a waste of breath. I think he can sell a cape to Superman." Damian heard River's grumpy remark and chuckled, crossing into his room.

* * *

DAMIAN FOUND River and Cole in the living room. They were talking softly, and River seemed to be at ease with his brother, which made Damian feel a lot better about everything he was going to tell her. He sat down on a large armchair, facing both of them.

"River," he said, carefully observing her reaction. "I need to leave for a few days."

"Okay," she said, straightening. "Why?"

Damian nibbled on his lip, thinking about how to give her the news without exposing her to the World of Magic. In his mind, he had gone over this conversation a few times, but now that he was face to face with her, everything he had prepared evaporated, and he was lost for words.

"That night when I almost froze to death, I realized that to deal with whatever is going on here, I need more information," he started awkwardly. "I can't get it in Blue Creek, but I know people in Chicago who can help me."

"More information?" she asked, her voice firm and stone-cold as she obviously switched to her detective mode. "What kind of information?"

Damian grunted, throwing a veiled glanced at Cole, asking for help.

"The kind of information that would help us figure out what's going on in Paradise Manor, Detective," said the vampire, his voice getting deeper and somehow softer.

"River, you were right," Damian took over, hoping that he sounded sincere enough not to trigger unwanted questions. "Your husband didn't commit suicide, but it wasn't a ghost or the Lady of the Mirror that killed him. I did all the research I could do here, in Blue Creek, but I still need to know more. To protect you, I must know more."

"I knew he didn't..." Her trembling voice melted into silence, and she averted her eyes, staring at her tightly clenched hands. "So, to get this... information, you must leave for a few days.

And of course, I can't ask any questions because if I do, you're going to get up and walk out on me, right?"

"No, River," Damian objected softly. "No matter what you do or ask, I would never leave you unprotected. But please, do me a favor and just trust that I will do everything I can to keep you safe."

She swallowed hard, her eyebrows snapping together as she bit her lip. "Thank you," she whispered, her voice hoarse. Then she took a deep breath and forced a smile that left her blue eyes sad. "Does it mean I can ask more questions?"

"Sure, you can," agreed Damian with a half-shrug. "Doesn't mean I'll answer."

"You're an ass," muttered River, but her smile became easier.

"I'm an ass who is going to keep you alive." Damian winked at her.

"From almost two thousand miles away?" huffed River.

"This is why I'm here," chimed in Cole. "If you will allow me, I'll stay with you while my brother is gone."

"You? A rich tech geek?" asked River, her copper eyebrows climbing up. But her shock was short-lived. As her eyes fell on Cole's sword lying on top of his trench coat next to him, she cut herself off and turned to Damian. "Damian, is your brother as *'open-minded'* as you and my father are?"

"Probably even more so," said Damian, throwing a warning glance at Cole as the vampire pressed his hand over his mouth to stop himself from laughing.

"Fine." River shifted in her seat, her eyes darting between Cole and Damian. "Do you want Cole to stay in your room while you're gone, Damian? There are enough rooms here. I can prepare a separate one for him."

"Whatever is easier for you, River," replied Damian, and Cole waved his hand, dismissing the matter.

Feeling a vibration in his pocket, Damian pulled his cellphone out and peered at the screen. Reading Jamie's name on the collar ID, he answered the call. A moment later, he hung up the phone and got up, shifting from foot to foot, unease coiling in the pit of his stomach.

"My ride is here. I have to go." He turned to Cole. "Keep me updated. And if you find anything new, call me right away."

"Will do." Cole got up, readjusting his shirt.

"Damian—," started River, but he interrupted her.

"River, if God forbid something goes wrong, and for whatever reason Cole is not here," he said, touching her shoulder lightly, "I need you to know that your bedroom is the safest place in this entire building. Go there, lock the door, and don't let anyone in except for Cole, your father or me. You will be safe there. Don't leave no matter what you hear or see. Do you understand me?" He sent a heavy glance to his brother over River's head, and Cole nodded.

Blood drained from River's face, making her pale complexion of a redhead almost translucent, but she squared her shoulders and nodded. "I understand," she replied calmly, her voice hollow but even. "I'll do as you say. Or as Cole says." She glanced at Cole, and a tiny smile touched her lips. "I'm sorry. I didn't even thank you for interrupting all your personal plans and moving in here just to protect me."

"All good," replied Cole with his usual lighthearted smile. Switching his attention to Damian, he offered his hand. "Watch your back, big bro, and stay in touch—that's what those cellphones are for." He jerked his thumb at the phone Damian held in his hand. "Don't make me fly to Chicago just to kick your antisocial ass."

Damian shook his brother's hand, nodded one more time to River, and walked out the door.

CHAPTER 24

~ DAMIAN BLAKE ~

The trip to Chicago was uneventful. Jamie had rented a Ford Expedition, and even though Damian was never comfortable inside any car, he felt more or less at ease in this giant vehicle. Despite his dislike of modern transportation, Damian had years of experience driving and was a skilled driver. They drove the entire trip, replacing each other behind the wheel every few hours and stopping only to get a bite to eat and fill up the tank.

It was past midnight when Jamie drove through the dark byroad surrounded by a thick canopy of trees and stopped in front of a tall iron gate. The sky, obscured by a shifty veil of clouds, barely produced any light, and the night seemed to be darker than ever. A single streetlight towered next to the gate, throwing a weak, glowing yellow circle at the small security monitor. A cool breeze blew through the trees, playing with their heavy branches, creating a continuous rustling noise interrupted only by the screeches of night birds.

Jamie stepped out of the car, letting the fresh night air filled with the scent of greenery and wet dirt inside. Reaching under his shirt, he pulled out a silver chain with a small round pendant attached to it. Damian looked at the pendant and stiffened, shivers running down his back.

"Guardians," he muttered under his breath, keeping his eyes on the young man. "After hundreds of years, they still keep all their members on a short chain."

Jamie moved his pendant over the security monitor and glanced up, showing his face to the camera. Something clicked, and the monitor lit up with a dim blue light.

"If it ain't James Coldwell," said a deep male voice with a southern drawl. "Whatcha doin' here, man? I thought you called it quits."

"I did," replied Jamie, chuckling. "But I have an urgent business matter with Archmage Allerton, Jack."

"Look at the time, man," rumbled Jack. "The Archmage is long asleep. You don't want me to wake him up, do yah?"

"Actually, I do," replied Jamie calmly. "Can you please tell him I am here, and I need to speak with him as soon as possible?"

Something clicked and shuffled on the other side before Jack answered. "Who's your friend, Jamie?" he asked, back to the official mode. "What's your business with Archmage Allerton?"

Jamie glanced at Damian over his shoulder, a question in his light eyes. Damian stepped out of the car and approached the security system. He looked up but made sure that his hair obscured most of the left side of his face.

"My name is Damian Blake," he said calmly, listening to his voice echoing in the speakers. "I'm here to see the Archmage. My business is private, and I can discuss it only with him. Sorry. But as Jamie said—it's urgent."

Something clicked again, and Jack asked, "Jamie, are you willing to vouch for Mr. Blake?"

"Yes. While we're within the property lines of the Guardians HQ, Damian Blake is my responsibility, and I vouch for him," replied Jamie without skipping a beat.

Jack didn't say anything else, but the screen shut down, and with a mournful noise, the gates started to move aside. Damian sat in the passenger seat of the SUV and watched as Jamie drove the car through the gateway. The metallic clang of gates closing behind them made his blood run cold, and his skin crawled as a feeling of someone watching him overwhelmed him.

"Are they watching us?" he asked, his mind on high alert.

Jamie threw a glance at him and shrugged. "You're in the Guardians HQ. I'm a guard who quit a while ago, and you're a little black horse no one knows anything about. Of course, they're watching us."

He drove the car through the shadowy night park and stopped it in a circular driveway in front of a giant mansion. Shutting down the engine, he turned to the right slightly and looked at Damian.

"Are you ready?" the young man asked, his nervousness making his voice raspier than normal. "This is the point of no return."

"I know. I'm as ready as I can be." Damian pushed the door open and stepped out of the vehicle. As soon as his feet touched the ground, the energy of Earth rushed through him, and he grunted, suppressing it completely and shadowing his magic.

Following Jamie, he walked up the steps and halted by the entrance. The tall double door was made of solid redwood, reinforced with cold iron strips and decorated with silver ornaments. Perhaps, just like iron, silver wasn't a pure décor but rather a defense mechanism against certain types of supernatural beings. Between the stones polished by time and elements, and the vines weaving their way up the tall walls, the entire building gave a vibe of agedness.

Jamie raised his hand to knock, but before he could do it, the door opened, showing a dark lobby behind it. He lowered his hand, and his eyes widened a little, a shadow of fear crossing his face. Damian frowned, a multitude of questions speeding through his mind as he noticed Jamie's reaction.

"Jamie, if you don't want to go inside, you can wait for me in the car," he offered, turning to him. "You got me in. I can handle the rest."

A soft smile touched the young man's lips, and his eyes fogged with sadness. "I'm not going to leave you here alone," he said reproachfully, shaking his head. "It's just..." He didn't finish his statement, pressing his lips in a firm line. Then he threw another glance at the dark lobby and nudged Damian forward gently. "It's just some bad memories I have. Nothing to worry about. We have a good reason to be here, so let's do what we came here to do."

The spacious lobby was empty, barely illuminated by the light of a few magical orbs lingering under its tall ceiling. A man, in his late forties by the looks of him, waited for them inside. He was dressed in a black uniform, his left hand resting on the pommel of a sword at his hip. He observed Damian with open suspicion but said nothing. As his gray eyes halted on Jamie, a warm smile lit up his features.

"Please follow me. Archmage Allerton will receive you in his office," he said coldly without formally introducing himself, but judging by his southern accent, it was the same guard who had greeted them at the gates.

Damian walked through a chain of dark corridors, following Jack and Jamie. They spoke in hushed tones, but he didn't try to listen to them. A big part of his long life he spent doing everything he could to stay away from any representatives of the Destiny Council, and now, for the first time in years, he willingly walked into the lion's den. His nerves were on edge, and even with his limited abilities, he could detect the presence of the Guardians' magic all around him.

Jack halted in front of a tall doorway leading into another lobby and gestured for them to move forward. As soon as

THE SHADOW ENFORCER

Damian passed the threshold, both he and Jamie were surrounded by at least ten guards with their swords unsheathed.

"Whoa, guys, what's going on?" Jamie raised his hands, looking around at the men who used to be his teammates. "We are unarmed, and I thought the Archmage agreed to see us."

"He did, Jamie," replied Jack icily, "but there is a problem, and I hope you understand since you used to be one of us." He pointed at Damian. "Your friend is not registered either in the Guardians' or in the Wardens' books. Unless he's human—which I sincerely doubt—we need to know who and what he is. Without identifying that, we're not going to let him pass. So, you need to stay back and let us do our job."

Jamie took a step forward, positioning himself between Jack and Damian, but Damian put his hand on his shoulder, stopping him. "It's okay, Jamie. Let them do what they need to do." He raised his arms, turning to Jack. "Please, go ahead and check me. I'm not going to resist."

Jack approached him carefully and placed his hand on his chest. Damian closed his eyes and focused on shadowing his energy signature. Sensing a weak wave of magical energy originating under the guard's hand, the corners of his lips quirked up in a barely noticeable smirk.

"I can't sense any magic in him," said Jack a moment later, confusion layering his voice.

Damian cocked his head, staring down at him. "Can we see the Archmage now?" he asked peacefully. "We drove almost thirty hours straight. We are exhausted, and after the talk with the Archmage, we have to drive back. So, please..." He sighed without finishing his statement and lowered his arms.

"Keep your arms up. No one said you're free to go." Another guard approached him. In his hands, he held a small box that looked like an ammeter but had five small lightbulbs at the top. He gestured for all the guards including Jamie to move behind him, and once they were out of his way, he pointed the box at Damian and turned it on.

Damian sighed but raised his arms again and let the guard check him. The arrow on the display of the strange device jerked limply and then fell back to the left, remaining there until the guard shut down the device.

"He's clear," announced the guard. "Not an ounce of magic—"

He didn't finish his statement when a door at the far end of the lobby opened, and a tall man appeared in the doorway. He folded his arms over his chest and leaned his shoulder against the doorframe, observing Damian with curiosity. After a moment, he raked his fingers through the unruly mass of his salt-and-pepper hair and waved his hand, gesturing for the guards to stand down.

"He has magic," said the man with a tired smirk. "He's just so skilled at concealing it that even our magic detectors are unable to detect it. You can stand down. I believe if he wanted to kill me, you wouldn't be able to stop him, anyway."

The guards backed away and took one knee, bowing their heads before the Archmage. Jamie lowered to one knee, giving Damian a pointed stare.

"Sorry," said Damian dryly, meeting the Archmage's steady gaze. "I don't bow. And I definitely don't kneel."

The Archmage chuckled, the sound of his soft laughter unexpectedly contagious. He walked among his guards, tapping on their shoulders to rise. Halting in front of Damian, he extended his hand.

"How about a simple handshake?" he asked, arching his brow. "Just a modern day greeting between two men who have no harmful intentions toward each other."

Damian took his hand, but as soon as Allerton's fingers touched his, a powerful wave of magical energy rushed through him, and he couldn't help but hold his breath. Archmage Allerton's smile grew wider.

"Please follow me, Mr. Blake," he said, heading toward his office. Passing by Jamie, he tapped his arm. "Do you need a special invitation, too, Jamie?"

As soon as they crossed into the office, the Archmage closed the door and motioned for them to sit down. He walked around the desk and lowered himself on an office chair heavily. Leaning forward, he propped his elbows on the top of the desk and rubbed his red-rimmed eyes.

"So, what are you, Mr. Blake?" he asked once Damian and Jamie sat down.

"I'm no one," replied Damian, leaning back in his chair. "But at the moment, I'm a man who needs your help."

"No one?" echoed the Archmage, the color draining from his face. "Perhaps, you are... This would explain why you're not registered in our books..." His voice melted into a heavy silence. He picked up a pencil, tapping the desk with it nervously. "So, how long have you been *no one*?"

"With all due respect, Archmage Allerton," said Damian, his voice void of emotions, "if you know what *no one* means, you should also know I can't answer that question."

"Right, sorry. I don't meet people with this status often," mumbled the Archmage. Leaning farther forward, he made a steeple out of his fingers and gave Damian an arched stare. "What can I do for you, Damian? May I call you Damian?"

"Yes, sir." Damian averted his eyes, his hand raking through his hair of its own accord. "Recently, I moved to Blue Creek, Arizona and got a job working for Detective River Evans, widow of Nicolas Lee Evans. By marriage, she's the last living descendant of the three founding families."

Damian stopped talking and looked up at the Archmage to see if the name sparked any recognition in him. But the expression on the man's face remained attentive yet emotionless, and he just twirled his wrist, encouraging him to proceed.

"Since I started to work as her personal bodyguard, Paradise Manor has been attacked by unknown supernatural forces a few times," continued Damian. "I don't know who attacked the house or what they wanted. While doing some research, I discovered a few unusual things about the building, including a heavily warded room in the left wing of the house. When I managed to pass the wards and get inside the room, among all the craziness there, I noticed a rune..." He leaned forward slightly, his hands clasping the armrests of the chair. "This rune was a signature rune of the Guardians Order. This is why I'm here."

The Archmage's eyes widened in unmistakable shock, and his mouth opened up as he stared at Damian.

"Are you sure it was a Guardians' signature rune?" he asked after a moment.

"I have no doubt, sir," confirmed Damian.

The Archmage's eyes darted to Jamie, but he just shrugged, opening his arms. "Sorry, my lord. I can't confirm it since I haven't seen it myself, but I trust Damian."

Archmage Allerton got up, unease visible in his every move. He whispered something, drawing some complicated design in the air with his fingers, and a chain of glowing white runes materialized before him. He moved his index finger over it, and it lit up brighter, forcing Damian to raise his arm to shield his eyes.

When the light dwindled down, Damian lowered his arm, blinking the dancing red spots away from his vision. The Archmage sat in his chair, a large book in a heavy leather cover lying in front of him on the desk. He opened the book at a random page and placed his hand over it without touching its surface. A soft glimmer of his magic surrounded his hand, and the pages of the books started to turn. Slow in the beginning, they moved faster and faster until they turned into a glowing blur. He let go a few minutes later and stared down at the blank page of the book in confusion.

"I don't understand," he muttered, rubbing the thick stubble on his chin. Then he raised his eyes at Damian, and a chain of emotions exchanged on his face. "Damian, if you don't mind... I understand your status of *no one* and the limitations that come with it, but as the Archmage of the Guardians Order, I also know you have magic even though it's not detectable. Please channel some of your magic through the book while asking whatever you need to know about Paradise Manor." He threw his hands up, a guilty look on his face almost comical. "I think this is the only way we can learn anything about it."

If the Archmage of the Order can't get me any information... Dammit... How am I supposed to protect River if I don't even know who I'm protecting her from and why?

With his chest tightened with worry, Damian got up and held his hands over the book. He channeled his magic and directed it through the book, asking only one question in his mind—what's hidden in Paradise Manor. To his surprise, the book responded to his magic, but not in the same way it did to Allerton's magic. It snapped shut under his hands and then immediately reopened at a blank page. As he kept channeling his magic through it, asking the same question over and over, writing materialized on the page.

"Six—two hundred seventy-three," read Damian, turning to the Archmage. "Does it mean anything to you?"

Allerton stared at the page, his lips moving as if he was repeating the numbers over and over. "Yes," he murmured at length. "I know what this means, and I haven't seen anything like this for quite some time." He scratched the back of his head and then glanced at his wristwatch. "This is a number signifying a location in the Destiny Council general archives. I can access it from here, but it will take me a couple of hours."

"Damn, more time," Damian exhaled, rubbing the edge of his bracelet absentmindedly.

"It's three in the morning," said Allerton. "I heard you drove here from Arizona without stop. So, why don't you two get some shut-eye while I try to retrieve the information you need from the archives." He turned to Jamie and a smile, kind and slightly wistful, appeared on his face. "Jamie, your room is still free, and there're two beds there. I hope you remember how to get there?"

"Yes, my lord," Jamie replied with a light bow.

"Great." The Archmage gestured at the door. "Off you go. Get some rest. I'll wake you up myself as soon as I get the information you need."

* * *

FOLLOWING JAMIE, Damian barely noticed where they were going, processing the conversation with Allerton in his mind. When Jamie stopped in front of a low door deeply embedded into the rough stonework of the wall, he almost ran into him.

Jamie opened the door, and Damian had to bend down to walk in. The room was a tiny stone-box, and he could almost feel his usual claustrophobia gripping at his chest and clouding his mind, but at least it was on the ground floor.

"Wow," whispered Jamie, looking around. He sat down on one of the beds, brushing the plain cover with his hand. "Everything looks just the same as I left it."

"Something tells me Archmage Allerton likes you and wants you back," murmured Damian, lowering on the second bed. The springs moaned under his weight, and the mattress bent down. Carefully, he lay down and stretched his legs, his eyelids too heavy to keep them opened.

"Damian," called Jamie.

"Huh?"

"No one. Is it actually a *thing*? What does it mean?" asked the young man. "All this time I thought you literally meant that you're nobody."

"I *am* nobody," murmured Damian, turning his back toward Jamie. "But *no one*, as you probably figured out by now, is my magical status. Sometimes it does feel like a terminal condition though. And one of the parts of being *no one* is that I can't tell you anything about it, or about my past for that matter."

"Dang it," murmured Jamie, sarcasm ringing in his voice. "And here I was going to ask you all these questions. Bummer."

"I'm not much into pillow talk." Damian sighed and pulled his pillow lower, hugging it. "Get some sleep while you can."

He closed his eyes and a few seconds later was fast asleep.

CHAPTER 25

~ DAMIAN BLAKE ~

As soon as Archmage Allerton touched the door handle, Damian was awake. Soundlessly, he slipped off the bed and turned toward the entrance ready to summon his daggers at the first sign of trouble. Jamie was fast asleep, oblivious to anything going on around him. The door cracked opened with a light squeak, but no one entered.

"Damian?" The familiar voice sounded from outside the door. "This is Archmage Allerton. Please, relax. I'm unarmed and alone."

"Come in," said Damian, dropping his tense shoulders.

The Head of the Guardians Order walked in, and as his attentive eyes took in Damian's appearance, he smiled. "I knew you'd be up as soon as I approached the door. Despite your *no one* status, you have pretty sharp senses. You'd make a wonderful guard." He arched his eyebrows and shoved his hands into his pockets, rocking slightly on his feet. "What would you say if I offered you a job at the Guardians HQ?"

"I would say thank you, but no, thank you," replied Damian. "I haven't been suffering my *status*"—he applied some pressure on the word 'status', placing a hefty load of sarcasm into it

—"just to willingly subjugate myself to the Destiny Council. I love my freedom."

"As you wish. If you ask me, freedom is overrated." The Archmage shrugged and approached Jamie, gently shaking him awake.

"What time is it?" Jamie sat up, rubbing his face with his hands.

"Five o'clock," replied Allerton, heading toward the door. "Follow me to my office, please. I'm not sure I found all the information you need, but I do have something that may give you food for thought."

They walked through the dark, silent hallways of the Guardians HQ. It was too early and except for a few guards on duty, everyone else—wizards and witches, mages and apprentices who were here to learn how to control and use their magic—were fast asleep.

Jack stood by the door into the office, leaning his back against the wall. As soon as he saw Allerton approaching, he pushed away from the wall and bowed, his eyes burning Damian with unconcealed threat. The loyalty of this man to the Head of the Guardians Order was beyond reproach. The Archmage opened the door, inviting Jamie and Damian to come in, and then turned to the guard.

"Jack, please ask someone to bring breakfast for Damian and Jamie, and coffee for me, and then stay outside," he said, patting the man on his shoulder. "I don't want to be bothered by anyone while I'm working."

Jack bowed and left. He came back a few minutes later, sporting a tray with three cups of coffee, freshly toasted bagels and a few small packets of cream cheese.

"I hope this is enough, my lord," he said apologetically. "I didn't want to wake up the cook, so I made it myself."

"It's perfect. Thank you, Jack." The Archmage waited until the guard left and closed the door. Then he lowered himself onto his chair and took one of the cups with steaming coffee. "Eat, don't be shy." He moved the tray toward Damian and Jamie. "You have a long drive back ahead of you."

Damian took one of the cups and a bagel but didn't bother with the cream cheese. He inhaled the bitter scent of the coffee and then took a careful gulp, feeling the hot liquid rushing down his throat, energizing him. They ate quickly, and once they were done, Allerton got up and snapped his fingers, the energy of his magic spiking around him.

A large rectangle of light materialized on the wall. He waved his hand and the rectangle was replaced by an image of an old photo that looked like it was taken some time in the eighteenth century. Six people—three men and three women—stood in the photo surrounded by the endless desert scenery. With bright smiles on their faces, they looked young and happy.

"These people," said Allerton, pointing at the photo, "are the Blue Creek original founding families—Richard and Helen Evans, George and Edith Brown, and Ralph and Lillie Anderson."

"I've seen this photo before in my father's research folder," muttered Jamie.

"I'm not surprised," replied Allerton. "This photo is not a secret. It should be available in Blue Creek's historical archives as well. However"—he raised his finger—"there is something about these three families no one knows. At least, no one in the realm of humans. To be honest, I had a hard time finding anything about them even in the Guardians' and Wardens' archives." He shrugged, rubbing the back of his neck. "Quite unusual, I must say."

"What did you find out?" asked Damian.

"First of all, every single member of the three families and their descendants were active members of the Guardians Order." The Archmage moved his finger as if he was swiping the screen of a digital tablet, and the photo was replaced by another one with different people on it. He kept swiping his hand, replacing the pictures until a photo of three people—a man, a woman and a teenage boy—showed up on the wall.

"The last three of the Evans family," whispered Jamie, rising. "I grew up with Nick." His voice shook with sadness. "So, I was right."

"About what?" asked Archmage, gazing at him with curiosity.

"Rumors, you know?" The young man shrugged apologetically. "You can't stop people from wagging their tongues, especially in a small town like Blue Creek. They used to say that the original three families used to inbreed, and I always argued with them. These people were too smart, educated, and powerful to do something as stupid as inbreeding."

Allerton chuckled, shaking his head, almost rolling his eyes. "People... No, they weren't inbreeding. At least not in the traditional sense of this word. But they chose their spouses strictly within the Guardians Order, and from what I understand, only the members of the three original families had access to their homes."

"Why?" asked Damian. "And how did it happen that Nick Evans, initiated Guardian wizard, went against his parents' wishes and married a woman who not only wasn't a part of the Order but was mundane?"

"River Rose Vetrov?" asked the Archmage. "Well, this is a topic for a separate discussion, my friend. The young man followed his heart... In a way, I respect that. Besides, there is possibly more to River Evans than meets the eye. Do you know anything about her parents?"

"Yes," replied Damian. "Her father is an old hunter. Her mother was a witch with air magic."

"Precisely. We don't know if River is touched by the World of Magic."

"Not as far as I know, and her father is hell-bent on keeping it that way," objected Damian. "Anyway, why did the Guardians

Order send their people to the Arizona desert to dig for nonexistent gold and keep them there all those years? What were they guarding?"

The Archmage sighed, unease shadowing his face. "This is the part I couldn't get a clear reading on." He waved his hand, and the photo of the Evans family disappeared, replaced by the topographic map of the area around Blue Creek. "There is something interesting that I found in the archives, but I'm afraid it would only add more mystery to the situation."

He moved his fingers, panning the image. "Look here." He pointed at the map, channeling his magic. Without touching the map, he drew three glowing circles. "These circles are the three buildings the founding families built after the pandemic was over. The one in the center is Paradise Manor. These are the houses of the Browns and Andersons."

"I believe both buildings have been rebuilt and moved off their original locations by the new owners," pointed out Damian, his thoughts darting to his brother for a brief moment.

"It's a big problem." The Archmage sighed. "I believe this is the reason supernatural activity around Paradise Manor spiked up in the last few years." He raised his hand, asking for a moment. Channeling his magic, he drew two more circles across from the location of the buildings. "These two circles are the main entrance into the gold mines and the small backdoor that leads into the underground passages." He turned back to Damian and Jamie. "What do you see?"

"I'll be damned," whispered Damian, cold perspiration beading his forehead.

"Isn't it..." Jamie swallowed, his face ashen. "A pentagram?"

The Archmage moved his finger over the map, connecting the five circles with glowing white lines made of his magical energy. "Exactly. It's a pentagram. A giant one. I'm sure the underground passages connect all five locations. It's extremely powerful protective magic, and it requires an unbelievable amount of power and skill to cover such a large area with protective magic."

He shoved his hand in his pocket, stroking his thick stubble with his other hand, and his bushy eyebrows knitted over his glowing eyes in a deep frown.

"Why didn't I detect it?" mumbled Damian, staring at the shimmering star. "This entire area should be emitting magical energy for miles around."

"I didn't sense anything," said Jamie. "And I grew up in Blue Creek."

Allerton sighed. "Jamie, your magic is too weak, and you didn't put any effort into developing it. You wouldn't notice anything if it stared you in the face. I offered you a place in the Guardians Academy, but you refused it. If you change your mind, my offer still stands. You can return here as a guard or as an apprentice. I would love to have you back in any capacity."

He turned to Damian, and pity in his eyes made Damian cringe inwardly.

"As far as you, Damian..." He shrugged and lowered down to his chair. "Do I have to rub it in and remind you of your status?"

Damian dropped his head, his hands clenching into tight fists.

"I'm sure when you accepted your status, some of your powers and magic were stripped," continued Allerton. "So, I'm not surprised you didn't detect it. You must be extremely powerful and skilled to detect the protective and concealing spells cast by the members of the Guardians Order."

"What you're saying is..." Damian smirked faintly, his heart giving a painful jolt. "If I keep my status, I can't fight whatever is attacking Paradise Manor. I'm not powerful enough."

"No, you're not," objected the Archmage flatly. "I'm not sure even in your full power you have what it takes to protect River Evans. Six extremely powerful and skilled Guardians Mages were sent to this place to shadow and guard whatever is hidden there, and now, they are all dead. Every single one of them. Including River's husband who went through vigorous training in my Academy. Poor boy... I wish I knew what we were getting him ready for, but we had an order not to—" His voice broke off, and he glanced at Damian, sympathy in his eyes. "Tell me, Damian, if you were in your full power, do you think you would be more powerful than six experienced Guardians Mages?"

Damian swallowed hard, goosebumps rising on his skin. "Yes," he said, his voice a cracked, painful whisper.

"Heaven and Earth," breathed out Allerton, his eyes widening. "Who the hell are you, Damian Blake." He pressed his hands over his mouth, staring at him in shock.

"I am—," Damian started, but cut himself off and lowered his head. "No one." A heavy silence engulfed the room as Damian dropped powerlessly in his chair. "I can't change my status. It would cost me my freedom, who I am, everything..." His hand went up to his throat of its own accord, and he jerked it back down. "Never again."

"Freedom?" asked Archmage Allerton, his eyebrows rising, but as understanding dawned on him, he added, "You keep saying that... You have to be extremely old, Damian. Can you tell me how old you are?"

"Over a thousand years old," replied Damian at length.

"Holy shit!" yelped Jamie, eliciting a snort out of the Archmage.

"Things have changed since then," said the Archmage with a nonchalant shrug. "If you choose to forfeit your status, it's not going to be as bad as it used to be, and hopefully with your full power, you can save River Evans and protect whatever is hidden within this pentagram."

Damian leaned back in his chair, folding his arms over his chest. "Since Paradise Manor has been shadowed by Guardians for years, why did you stop now?" he asked dryly. "Why don't you send a few of your overqualified Mages with Jamie and me back to Blue Creek and let them do their job?"

"I wish I could," replied Allerton, throwing his hands up. "It seems that Paradise Manor and its secrets are no longer under the Guardians Order protection. Not since Nick Evans married River Vetrov." He picked up a pencil, twirling it between his fingers nervously. "I have no idea why, but all the files related to that were archived and most of the documents were so heavily redacted, I could barely extract any information. The paths of the Board of Destiny—"

"Screw the Board of Destiny," growled Damian, rising, and the walls trembled despite his efforts to control his power.

"Whoa... What was that?" Allerton jumped to his feet, pinning Damian with his heavy gaze. "Are you a Child of Earth?"

Instead of answering, Damian turned to Jamie. "Let's go, Jamie," he said through gritted teeth. "We're wasting our time here. I'm on my own. When it comes to the Destiny Council, some things never change."

"But Damian—," started Jamie, rising.

"I'll just have to do whatever I can with my limited power," replied Damian, interrupting him. "It's okay. Won't be the first time."

He headed toward the door, his every step making the floor shake.

"Damian, wait!" Archmage Allerton rushed after him and seized his arm. "Bend your knee before me... Pledge your fealty to the Guardians Order, and I can get your status revoked. You'll have your power restored. I swear, you will report to me only, and while serving the Order, you will never have to do anything you don't want to do. You're not going to lose your freedom. You'll be free—"

"Free?" asked Damian, prying Allerton's fingers off his arm. "Define your understanding of freedom, Archmage! I'll be a branded slave on a short leash. Been there, done that. Never again!" He raised the left sleeve on his shirt and moved his fingers over his upper arm, making the rune appear on his skin. Then he let go of the sleeve and leaned down slightly. "Never again. You hear me? You want to help me because you know it's the right thing to do, send a few of your Mages with me." He took a deep breath and pushed the door open. "Thank you for your help, Archmage, but I kneel before no one."

He walked out the door and halted, waiting for Jamie, focusing on controlling his elemental power.

"Damian, it looks like you've been dealt a bad hand in the past. Since I took over the Guardians Order a few years ago, I changed a lot of the old and antiquated practices," started the Archmage, sounding sincerely crestfallen. "This brand on your arm... I can remove it. Please think about it. If you were working for me, I would have more freedom to help you..." He shrugged, his eyes almost pleading. "Besides, there is no such thing as complete freedom. Absolute freedom means absolute loneliness..."

Damian laughed bitterly, anger slowly simmering down in him. "Bad hand?" he repeated. "You have no idea. Anyway, thank you, Archmage, but I work alone."

He touched his chest over his heart and extended his arm to Allerton in a gesture of gratitude, but his move was filled with too much sarcasm for the Head of the Guardians not to notice it.

Allerton sighed, pursing his lips. "If you change your mind, Damian, you know what to do."

"I couldn't have said it better myself," murmured Damian. "If you decide to do the right thing, Archmage, you know what to do."

He turned around and walked away, followed by Jamie.

CHAPTER 26

~ COLE ADAMS ~

At precisely eleven in the morning, Cole knocked on the door of the bookstore. Even though the 'Open' sign was turned off, he was positive Aaron was inside, waiting for him by the door. He could hear his elevated heartbeat and had to wonder if the human Warden was scared of him or excited about something.

Aaron Cooper opened the door for him, excitement alight in his eyes. Even his spectacles seemed to be shining, but most likely it was just a reflection of the morning sun. He gestured for Cole to come in and locked the door behind him.

"Master de la Crosse is waiting for you," he said, pointing at the backroom.

Cole made his way between the bookshelves. Even though Aaron was glowing with glee, he didn't allow himself to get excited. Over the years of his long life, he had learned that high expectations usually led to bitter disappointments. So, he preferred to keep his expectations low and enjoy a nice surprise later, if it happened. Nevertheless, for the first time in many years, he felt jittery.

He walked into the room and halted. If he had been a human, his heart would be jumping out of his chest. Instead, he froze with his eyes wide open as he watched Luc de la Crosse get up and turn to face him.

"Master Warden." Getting in control of his nerves, Cole bowed to him, his moves stiff and unusually awkward.

"Good morning, Cole," replied Luc, pointing at a chair across from him. "Sit down. Let's have a talk. I do have the information you need." He thought for a brief moment and shrugged. "Most of it, at least."

Cole sat down, opening the bottom button of his suit jacket. "I'm listening, my lord," he said softly, squeezing his hands tightly together.

Luc de la Crosse glanced at Cole and touched his clasped hands. "Relax, *mon ami*," he said with a one-sided smirk. "It's nothing bad, just a little... how do I say it? Peculiar?"

"Peculiar?" repeated Cole, lowering his hands to his lap. "Please tell me if you find anything about Paradise Manor that's not peculiar." He chuckled, shaking his head.

"That's true." Luc's smile dwindled down. "First of all, I think you were probably right. The spirit possessing the silver mirror in Paradise Manor is a Zerkalitsa. This mirror was installed there by the first owners of the mansion—Richard and Helen Evans."

"Probably?" asked Cole.

"Yes, probably," repeated the Warden. "Here is where the peculiar part comes. Neither the Wardens' nor Guardians' books contain any information about Paradise Manor. I actually had to travel to Paris to speak with the Grand Master of the Wardens Order. Between the two of us, we were able to figure out that at some point, Paradise Manor was under the protection of the Guardians Order. However, a few years ago, all information related to Paradise Manor was archived by the

Destiny Council, and to retrieve it..." He raised his arms apologetically. "It's above my status. Even the Grand Master would have to submit a special request to make this information available to us. I think Archmage Allerton of the Guardians Order has a better chance."

Cole nodded. "I forgot about all the bureaucracy the Destiny Council surrounds themselves with."

"For good reason, *mon ami*, for good reason," mumbled Luc. "We don't always understand why they do certain things the way they do it, but they always have a reason for their actions."

"Please tell me you can help me communicate with the Zerkalitsa," said Cole.

"That I can." A wide grin crossed Luc's face, making his hazel eyes twinkle brighter. "All you have to do is make a girl happy." He winked slyly. "I'm sure you have some experience in that department."

"Excuse me?" Cole's jaw dropped as he stared at the Master Warden in shock, but as he caught the humor reflected in Luc's eyes, his shock morphed into reproach. "Luc?"

"I've heard you're a silver-tongued devil... um... vampire," he said. "You should be able to talk the Zerkalitsa into telling you the truth. After all, she's nothing more than a woman locked inside a mirror. All you have to do is make her happy."

"How?"

Luc de la Cross rose slightly and leaned across the table. In a soft whisper, he gave all the instructions to Cole, and then added louder, "Good luck, my friend. I hope after you're done, you'll come back here and tell me what happened." His smile grew wider and warmer. "What can I tell you? I am a sucker for a good story."

On the surface, it seemed as if the Master Warden was joking, but Cole knew it was an order—soft and friendly, but still an order.

"Yes, my lord," replied Cole with a slight bow. "As you wish."

"And maybe, at the same time, you could introduce me to the mysterious Damian Blake?" he asked, all humor gone from his face. "Even the Grand Master Warden couldn't find any information about your friend. If he has magic, his obscurity is quite unusual... if not impossible."

"I can't promise you that, my lord," replied Cole carefully. "But I'll do my best to introduce him to you."

"Please do," said Luc de la Crosse, rising. "If you leave now, you should be at Paradise Manor at the perfect time." He gestured at the door. "Aaron will show you out. I hope to hear from you soon, *Monsieur* Adams."

Cole inclined his head and walked out the door.

WALKING TOWARD HIS CAR, Cole pulled out his cell phone. The screen lit up, showing him the time—11:30 AM. He winced, realizing he spent more time in the store than he intended. Quickly scanning through all the messages and notifications on his phone, he didn't find anything from Damian, and his chest tightened with worry. His brother should have gotten in touch with him at least once by now.

Assuming he knows how to use his phone... Ugh... Medieval doofus. He dialed Damian's phone number, but the call was transferred straight to his voice mail. *What the hell, Dima... pick up your phone.*

He checked the time again and rubbed the nape of his neck. If he wanted to be at Paradise Manor before noon, he had to move now. And most likely, the car would only slow him down.

Goddammit!

He opened the text message window from Damian's contact and quickly typed in:

"DAMIAN. I KNOW THE NAME OF THE LADY IN

QUESTION AND HOW TO CONTACT HER. ON THE WAY THERE NOW. CALL ME ASAP." He thought for a moment, then erased the word 'ASAP', typed in 'AS SOON AS POSSIBLE', and pressed the 'send' button.

Putting his phone back in his pocket, he checked the area to make sure no one was watching and took off running. A few minutes later, he came to a screeching halt in front of the entrance to Paradise Manor. He raked his fingers through his windblown hair and readjusted his suit before dialing the security code to open the gate.

As the gate started to open, he slipped inside and jogged toward the mansion at a normal human speed. Running up the steps, he pulled on the door, but it was locked. He reached in his pocket, found the key River had given him yesterday, and unlocked it. A bright ray of the afternoon sun burst into the dark foyer but didn't reach the antique mirror.

Cole made his way through the foyer and halted in front of the mirror, smirking at the absence of his own reflection.

"It's time we had a serious talk, missy. What kind of bullshit is that? Just because I'm a vampire, you automatically assume I'm evil?" he murmured, looking behind the mirror to see how it was attached to the wall. "The stereotypes..."

He lifted the mirror slightly and carefully removed it from the hooks, feeling the rough surface of the antique frame under his fingers. With the mirror in his hands, he walked outside and placed it on the porch, leaning it against the wall. Gently moving it, he made sure the sun reflected in the mirror and playful flares of light bounced around.

"Zerkalitsa," he whispered, angling the mirror a little to create brighter flairs, "I summon thee." He waited a moment, his fingers squeezing the frame. "Please, talk to me... I swear I'm here to help. I'm not evil—"

"Says you!" A high girlish voice sounded from behind the glass.

The surface of the mirror lit up with a soft bluish glimmer, and when the light dwindled down, a young woman stood next to him. Her semi-translucent body was surrounded by a light, shimmering mist, but even through the mist, he could see a frown on her round face covered in a multitude of freckles. Her long, golden hair and silky dress flowed weightlessly even though there wasn't any wind.

"My lady," said Cole, bowing to her elegantly.

She folded her arms over her chest and turned away from him, gazing up into the perfectly blue sky. Despite the fury she was trying to project, as soon as her eyes fell on the sun, a blissful smile transformed her features, making her look like a cheerful teenager. She took a deep breath and outstretched her arms, twirling in place, her floating dress wrapping around her long legs.

Cole stood silent, allowing her to enjoy her temporary freedom for as long as she wanted. She stopped a few seconds later and turned toward him with a demonstrative sigh. Rolling her enormous pale-silver eyes that seemed to be too large for her face, she placed her hands on her hips, tapping her foot.

"So, what did you want, vamp?" she asked, tilting her head to the side slightly. "Normally, I wouldn't even talk to your kind, but since you gave me this unexpected, pleasant surprise, I feel obligated."

"Thank you, my lady," replied Cole, inclining his head to hide his laughing eyes. "I need your help." Noticing her eyebrows lowering over her eyes, he added hastily, "Not for myself. My friend and I are trying to protect Paradise Manor and River Evans, but we fight blindfolded with our hands tied."

"How so?" she asked. Taking a step closer, she reached for his hand, her translucent fingers brushing his skin, and to his surprise, he could feel her touch. "Hmm, your hands seem to be free now."

"It was just a figure of speech," he said, smiling at her. "What

I was trying to say was that without knowing whom we are fighting, we can't win this battle." He gazed down into her silvery eyes without blinking and froze, afraid to make a move. In her eyes, he could see his own reflection. "Help us. Please... I know you can."

"You know, don't you?" she grumbled, rolling her enormous eyes. She held out her hand, and he took it, gently rubbing her skin with his thumb. "I can feel your touch. So strange. Do you think it happens because you're a vampire? Your *undead* status puts you sort of between the world of the dead and the realm of the living."

"I don't know. I can feel your touch, too."

She sighed and turned away, pulling her hand out of his grip. "The giant, dark-haired man. Who is he to you?"

"Why are you asking?" Cole glanced at her with curiosity.

"Don't answer a question with a question, vampire." She pursed her lips, narrowing her eyes. "I have a reason for everything I ask. So, if you want my help, answer my questions. And keep in mind—you can't lie to me. I'm the spirit of the mirror. I can see into people's souls." She lifted her airy hand and brushed her thin fingers over his chest. "I can see your soul, too..."

"My soul?" A bitter smile appeared on his lips. "As you pointed out so many times—I'm a vampire—"

"And you still have a soul, Cole Adams." She pulled her hand back. "Please me by answering my questions with honesty, and I'll reward you by giving you the information you seek."

"The dark-haired man is my brother," replied Cole.

"I figured as much," she murmured, staring back at her mirror with sadness. "Did you know he's truly willing to die for you? It's not just words to him. Would you do the same for him?"

"The same and more," replied Cole, his voice hoarse.

"If you want to save River Evans, it may come to that, Cole," she said softly, gazing back at him. "Are you ready to do what's right?"

"Yes, my lady."

She sighed, running her fingers over the ornamental inclusions of the frame. "Both of you are in way over your heads," she whispered, sunlight reflecting in the corners of her eyes where large drops of water gathered and slowly ran down her pale cheeks. "A powerful magical artifact, well-guarded by generations of mages, lies within these walls." She waved her arm in a wide arch. "River Evans, even though she doesn't know it, is the last guardian, and as long as she's alive, the wards will hold. If she dies, nothing can stop evil from entering these walls."

"From what Damian told me, the evil has already entered the house. You were the one who helped my brother fight it," said Cole.

"No." The Lady of the Mirror shook her head. "What Damian encountered was just a powerful illusion. The astral projection of the real evil."

"Oh, God," muttered Cole, shivers running down his back. "He almost died, and it wasn't even the real enemy? With whom are we dealing? And what do they want?"

"You're dealing with gods, little vampire. Two of them... Thousands of years ago, they were cursed, and to break that curse, they need..." The sun got shadowed by light clouds, and Zerkalitsa lowered herself next to her mirror, leaning her back against the wall. "Being on this side of the mirror makes me weary. And the sun is gone..."

"What do they need? Who are these gods? Do you know their names or at least their pantheon?" Cole spoke quickly, his stomach twisting with fear.

"The lake," she whispered faintly. "They need the enchanted lake, which is guarded by the protection spell that was cast over this house. Only those who live in this house can enter the sacred grounds. So, as long as River is alive, the wards will hold.

However, if she dies before inviting someone else to move into the house... Two dark deities will walk this world again. In their wake, they'll bring the darkness, cold and lies..."

This is why the wards didn't react to Damian... River invited him to move in. He lives here. A thought sped through Cole's mind, leading to a thought that was a lot scarier. *As long as Damian lives in the house, he's also a target, just like River.*

"How do we stop them?" he asked, barely able to unclench his tightly pressed teeth.

"You cannot. Sorry." She took his hand, squeezing it with her delicate fingers. "You're an ancient vampire, and there are some perks that come with it, like your speed, strength, self-healing and possibly other talents that are unique to each one of your kind. But what you have is not enough to face two angry gods who are fighting for their future. Just keep your brother and River Evans alive. That's all you can do. Leave the rest to your brother."

Zerkalitsa jerked her chin at the mirror standing by her side, and Cole saw an image of Damian. But the man in the mirror didn't look exactly like his brother. He stood tall and proud, his muscled body clad in strange armor the likes of which he had never seen before. In his hands, he held two daggers—Damian's daggers—and they shone so brightly that Cole had to squint his eyes. His black hair fell to his shoulders, and there was no ugly scar disfiguring the left side of his face.

"Is that—," he started to ask, but she interrupted him.

"It is, but it is not," she replied, trying to get up.

"You speak in riddles, my lady..."

"When the time comes, you'll understand." She reached for him with both hands like a little girl would reach for her father asking to be picked up. Taking one knee, he lifted her gently into his arms and got up. "Now, help me. It's time for me to go back home..."

He halted in front of the mirror and saw his reflection

holding a beautiful spirit in his arms. "I can see my reflection," he whispered before he could stop himself.

She looked up, and a sad smile touched her lips. The sparkling mist around her became thicker, and she vanished just to appear in the mirror a moment later. He could see her standing by his side, her arm hooked through the crook of his elbow.

"Of course, you have a reflection," she said, caressing his arm. "When we look in the mirror, it's not our reflection we see. It's the reflection of our soul. You understand?" She looked at him through the glass separating them. "You have a soul, Cole, even though you are an old vampire. True evil doesn't reflect in my mirrors because there is nothing to reflect."

"Then why didn't I reflect in your mirror before?"

She giggled, pressing her hand to her lips, her eyes sparkling with mirth. "Oh, that? That was me trying to give you a message." She shrugged. "I bet everything on the assumption that you were smart enough to understand it. I was right." She let go of the arm of his reflection and waved her hand in a final farewell. "Take care of your brother. You both need each other more than you know..."

Her voice faded into nothingness, and she vanished. Cole lifted the mirror and headed inside the house where he carefully placed it on the wall. Readjusting its position, he made sure it was situated exactly the same as it was before and glanced into it. His lips quirked up in a tiny smile as he saw his reflection in its silvery surface.

"Thank you, my lady," he whispered. Pressing his hand over his heart, he bowed to the mirror. His reflection flickered and disappeared for a brief moment just to reappear right back, and he knew the Zerkalitsa heard him.

* * *

He locked the house and pulled his cellphone out as he headed toward the gates. Glancing at the display, he sighed. There was nothing from Damian. He dialed his number, but just like before, his call went straight to his voicemail. This time he decided to leave a message.

"Damian, I need you to call me back," said Cole, unease twisting in the pit of his stomach. "Please, brother. It's important. I talked to the Zerkalitsa. We're facing two angry deities, and everyone who lives in the house is their target because only people who live in Paradise Manor can pass through the wards. Please, brother, call me as soon as possible." He hung up the phone and put it back in his pocket. *Please, Dima... I need you to be all right...*

The gates opened with a soft noise, and Cole walked outside. Carefully checking his surroundings, he stilled as a barely noticeable wave of vampiric energy touched his senses. Positive that one of the Queen's flunkies was tailing him, he spun around but didn't notice anything alarming. Since the street was empty, he took off running and didn't stop until he reached the alley behind the shops. He halted there and quickly readjusted his suit and his hair.

He was ready to walk around the building toward the plaza where he had left his car when he detected the vampiric presence again.

"Show yourself," he growled, sharpening all his senses. "I know you're here."

A burst of soft laughter was a reply to his words. He spun in the direction of the sound, but as fast as he was, he was too slow. A strong arm wrapped around his neck, and he felt the sharp sting of a hypodermic needle penetrating his neck. As the liquid silver spread through his body, he cried out in pain, fighting against the hold of his assailant. The world tilted and shattered into thousands of pieces.

As liquid pain rushed through his veins, he collapsed,

curving in on himself. Barely realizing what was going on, he felt someone touching him, ripping his shirt off and wrapping silver chains around his unclothed body, pinning his arms to his sides. A massive fist connected with his jaw, adding to his misery, and finally, the darkness took him over.

CHAPTER 27

~ DAMIAN BLAKE ~

A few hours had passed since they left Chicago, driving without stop back to Arizona. Jamie took the first shift driving, and that gave Damian some time to process all the information he'd received from the Archmage of the Guardians Order. It wasn't much, but at least it confirmed his original suspicion that whoever he was dealing with was extremely dangerous.

The Guardians Order wouldn't shell out six high-level mages to protect something insignificant. Secretive and powerful, this supernatural Order wouldn't get involved in the affairs of the human realm unless there was a good reason for that, or unless they received direct orders from the Destiny Council. The questions still remained, though, what the Guardians Order was protecting in Paradise Manor, and why they abandoned it after Nick married River Vetrov.

Damian glanced out the window at the endless wall of greenery they were passing by. The words of the Archmage were burning a hole in his mind, and he couldn't relax. Did he have what it took to do the job of six well-trained Guardians Mages alone?

Not with my powers stripped, he admitted to himself. *I'm getting winded after a simple spell... And Cole is just a vampire. As fast and as strong as he is, he can be killed. Easily. Dammit...* He slammed his hand on the door of the car, making Jamie flinch and glance at him. Rubbing his face with his hands, he sighed. *What am I going to do?*

One thing he knew for sure—he couldn't leave River unprotected. Allerton was right about the Board of Destiny. As much as he hated to admit it, there was a reason he had met Sam Vetrov on his way to Phoenix. There were no coincidences in the World of Magic, and unfortunately, it had no sense of humor. So, if the Guardians Order sent their mages to shadow Paradise Manor for over a hundred years, whatever was hidden within those walls wasn't a joking matter.

Damian sighed and reached into his pocket. It'd been a while since he left Arizona, and he still hadn't heard anything from his brother. Unlocking his cellphone, he saw a blank screen—no messages, no notifications. His chest tightened with worry immediately, but he took a deep breath, forcing himself to relax. Cole was a big vampire-boy. He had survived without Damian taking care of him for a thousand years. He'd be all right.

He opened his short contact list and pressed the green button next to Cole's name. The phone beeped a few times and dropped the call.

"What the hell?" He tried to dial again, but with the same outcome. "Jamie, what's wrong with this thing?" he asked, showing him the phone. "Why doesn't it work?"

Jamie glanced at the screen and smirked. "You have no cell service here." He waved at the endless forest. Taking his phone out of his pocket, he quickly checked it. "My cell is also dead. We'll stop at the first gas station or a service plaza. Hopefully, we'll get some connection there. Besides, I can barely keep my eyes open. We should grab something to eat and switch for a few hours so I can get some shut-eye."

Fifteen minutes later, Jamie exited the highway and drove to a small plaza with a gas station and a fast-food restaurant. He filled up the tank and got back to the car. Starting the engine, he jerked his chin at Damian's phone that lay in the tray between seats.

"See if you have service," he suggested, directing the car toward the drive-through lane. "I still don't have any bars on my phone, but yours is newer."

Damian opened his cellphone and shook his head. "Something is not right," he muttered, shoving his phone in his pocket.

"Why?" Jamie grinned at him. "We're in the middle of God's country, surrounded by wilderness. I'm not surprised we don't have a connection here."

"And normally, I would agree with you," objected Damian firmly, "but we're dealing with the World of Magic. I'm telling you—something is not right."

"We're miles away from Arizona and Paradise Manor. What could go wrong here?" Jamie stopped the car next to a window and placed the order for himself and Damian, throwing the receipt between the seats.

"I wish you hadn't said that," murmured Damian, sharpening his senses. "Let's eat and get the hell out of here."

Jamie parked the car next to the exit out of the plaza, and they ate quickly without talking. Damian barely paid attention to what he was eating, constantly scanning the area for any supernatural presence. As soon as Jamie was done with his meal, they changed places, and Damian drove back on the highway. With his senses on overdrive, he picked up speed, trying to put as many miles between them and the gas station as he could.

Exhausted, Jamie fell asleep almost immediately, leaving Damian on his own. It was close to five in the evening, but despite the time, the highway was almost empty, only an occasional vehicle driving in the opposite direction, and that only added to his feeling of upcoming trouble.

After another hour of driving, he noticed a few vehicles approaching at a high speed in the rearview mirror. Since the road had only one lane going in each direction, he couldn't say how many cars were lined up behind him. It became darker, and Damian looked out the window, noticing gray, stormy clouds gathering over the highway.

"Perun almighty," he growled, looking over his shoulder.

The vehicles were getting closer at a considerable speed, and as the road curved to the left, he could see a chain of four large SUVs driving behind him. Damian floored the accelerator pedal, squeezing everything he could out of the heavy vehicle. The engine roared like an angry beast, but the pursuers were still getting closer.

"Jamie!" roared Damian, and the young man jolted awake, staring around wildly. "We have a problem. I need you to take over!"

"What the fuck, Damian!" Jamie yelled, his eyes wide in shock. "You're driving over a hundred miles an hour, and you want me to take the wheel without stopping?"

"Only if you want to live!" Damian pushed the driver's seat back as far as he could and shouted, "Move it!"

Jamie climbed awkwardly over to the driver's seat, exchanging places with Damian, which wasn't easy considering his height.

"If you tell anyone that I sat on your lap, I'm going to kill you," Jamie muttered, taking over the wheel. With one hand, he put his seatbelt on and leaned forward, squeezing the steering wheel until his knuckles became white.

"Now, keep your eyes on the road ahead and don't look back no matter what you hear," said Damian. "Let's survive first and then you can kill me all you want."

Damian turned in his seat and quickly assessed the situation. Unfortunately, while transferring, they had dropped some speed, and now the four massive vehicles were too close, driving almost on their tail. One of them moved to the opposite lane, picking up speed. A man in the passenger seat rolled down the window, and the dark barrel of an AR-15 stuck out as he trained it at Jamie.

"*Procedia Amnia!*" roared Damian, and a yellowish glow of his protective magic wrapped around their car just as the man pressed the trigger. The earsplitting bark of the gunshots echoed through the forest, and the bullets impacted his shield without doing them any harm. Jamie yelped, pressing the accelerator pedal down all the way.

"Shifters for hire," Damian growled, recognizing the energy signatures his pursuers emitted.

He connected with the elemental power of Earth and channeled his magic at the same time. The ground quaked, and long fractures ran across the road. Damian raised his arms, his muscles bulging with strain. The roots broke through the asphalt. Intertwining, they rose in the air, creating a thick barrier between them and the three vehicles that were still behind them.

"Damian!" shouted Jamie. "On your right!"

Damian glanced to the side just in time to see a massive black SUV take a sharp swing to the right, slamming into their car. Jamie growled as the car swayed to the side, but he managed to control it and bring it back up to the road.

"*Risurgius!*" hissed Damian, turning toward their assailants as he channeled more elemental energy into his spell.

A rock, tall and thin like an obelisk, erupted from the ground under the enemy's vehicle, impaling it and raising it high in the air. The distinct odor of gasoline invaded his nostrils.

"*Ignius*," he snarled, and the vehicle went up in flames.

Breathing hard, Damian dropped the magic, searching the area for the presence of other shifters, but it seemed like there was no one behind them on the road.

"Damian!" Jamie's voice filled with terror made him snap around.

Even though it was quite dark, he saw a woman far in the distance. Dressed in a long white dress, she stood in the middle of the highway, a light glow surrounding her body. Her long black hair lifted around her like a sinister cloud as she outstretched her arms toward them, and two powerful jets of water erupted from her open hands. The temperature dropped, and the water froze immediately, covering the road with a thick layer of ice. The woman's lips lifted in a sneer as she snapped her fingers and vanished.

"Jamie, watch out!" yelled Damian.

At full speed, the vehicle hit the ice and spun out of control. Jamie screamed, turning the steering wheel in the direction of rotation, but couldn't get control of the car. As the vehicle kept spinning, Damian noticed the same woman standing by the side of the road. Before he could do anything, she waved her hand, and a colossal wall of ice rose in front of them.

The SUV hit the wall and was thrown in the air. Jamie screamed, dropping the wheel as he lifted his arms to shield his face. The woman's diabolical laughter rolled through the frozen forest. Damian tried to connect with the energy of Earth, but he couldn't—either he was too drained from the previous use of his magic or something was blocking his connection.

The car flipped in the air and hit the ground hard, rolling off the road into a ditch.

* * *

"Wake up, boy..."

Someone slapped him on his cheek, and Damian jerked awake but couldn't get up. He struggled to inhale, gasping for air with his mouth open, his chest tight and heavy. With his vision blurry, he glanced around but could see nothing except for the bright white spots dancing before his eyes.

"Hello, Damian," a female voice purred somewhere above him.

He tried to lift his arms but couldn't—too cold, too drained.

"Relax, boy," she whispered. "I'm not here to kill you. I wish I could, but we both know you're immortal."

Something touched his eyes, and he squeezed his eyelids shut, protecting his vision.

"Open your eyes," the same voice commanded in a soft, insinuating purr. "Don't be frightened. I'm here to play."

Carefully, Damian opened his eyes and tensed. He wasn't in his car. As a matter of fact, he wasn't anywhere near the highway. Instead, he was lying at the edge of a small clearing surrounded by a dense forest, a thick canopy of branches veiling the dark sky. The place looked familiar, but he couldn't focus enough to recognize it.

The same woman he had seen on the road straddled him, sitting on his chest. She was small and delicate, but for some reason, he felt as though a polar bear was sitting on top of him. Leaning forward, she peered at him, her dark eyes glowing a deep purple just inches away from his. The long strands of her obsidian hair fell forward, brushing his face.

"Da-a-mia-a-a-n..."

Her cold breath touched Damian's face, and he turned his head to the side, positive that her icy touch left frostbite on his skin. She seized his chin, forcing him to look at her. Then she moved his hair off his face and ran her finger along the length of his scar, tracing its shape.

"Too bad," she whispered into his ear. "If not for this ugly scar, I would consider you handsome enough to screw." She straightened, laughing derisively.

He groaned, fighting nausea at the thought. "Who are you

and what do you want?" he growled, straining to get up but couldn't make a move.

"Aw, sweetie, you still didn't figure out who I am?" she sang, pouting like a kindergarten girl. "I'm wounded." She pressed heavier on his chest, her icy fingers wrapping around his throat. "Your kinsmen used to worship me not long ago. I think you still worship some gods of my pantheon."

"Mara," Damian croaked, taking short breaths through his mouth. "The Slavic goddess of Darkness and Nightmares."

"Good boy." She let go of his neck, patting his cheek. "That's right. I'm Mara. One of the most powerful goddesses of the Slavic pantheon."

He sucked in a deep breath, filling his lungs with oxygen. "Most powerful? That's a matter of opinion," he exhaled, glowering up at her. "What do you want?"

"I want you out of the game," she replied, calm and serene as if she was talking about a house poker game. "Leave Arizona and never come back. I thought the shifters I hired a while ago had given you my message already."

"They had," replied Damian dryly. "I'm not big on complying with orders I don't like."

For a heartbeat, anger turned her beautiful face into a terrifying mask with narrow, angled eyes shining with bright, purple light and skin that looked like old parchment, wrinkled and yellowish-green. Her bony hooked fingers seized his throat again, and the pressure on his chest doubled.

The gloomy surroundings became blurry, and a wave of fear engulfed him, sending his mind in a wild frenzy, making his heart beat desperately against his ribcage. He jerked, but his movements were feeble and slow, like in a nightmare. He couldn't breathe, a sickening, warm weakness overtaking his body, turning his muscles into jelly. The ground beneath him vanished, and he started to fall, his mouth opened in a silent scream of terror.

Everything went dark, and for a split second, he thought he lost his vision, but as the darkness dissipated, he found himself lying in the midst of the same forest with Mara still sitting on top of him. Her fingers squeezed his throat stronger, the long nails cutting into his skin, drawing blood. He wheezed, his eyes rolling back into his skull, and she finally let go, slapping his cheek to bring him back.

"Look around," she hissed, fury distorting her features. "Don't you recognize this place, boy? I thought it was engraved into your tiny brain forever."

She got off his chest and hauled him into a sitting position, settling down behind him for support. With his body disabled by Mara's magic, he was a helpless puppet in her hands and fighting wasn't an option. In this nightmare she created, she was the Queen, and the only thing he could do for now was to go with the flow and see what gives. Glancing around, he gave her a weak nod.

"I do," he replied, straining to sound even and indifferent. "Why are we here?"

"Because I want you to see something," she whispered into his ear, her breath touching his skin. "Just don't get all emotional on me and pay attention to the details."

Damian swallowed hard as he saw a tall man and a woman appear in the center of the tiny clearance. The shirt on the man's back and chest was ripped, and deep welts left by enormous claws were bleeding profusely. The woman's right arm hung at an awkward angle, and she held it with her other hand, her black eyes shining with desperate anger.

They both halted, looking around wildly. A deep roar rolled through the forest, echoing over and over. The ground trembled, and a terrible beast burst out of the woods, breaking the shrubbery and small trees. The man pushed the woman behind his back, and two glowing daggers materialized in his hands.

"Stop it," Damian hissed, turning his head away. He didn't

need to watch. He knew what came next as every detail of this fight was forever embedded in his mind. He lost. For the first time in years, he had lost a fight to the supernatural—the only fight that truly mattered to him.

"I want you to keep an eye on the far end of the clearing," she whispered, forcefully upturning his head. "Ignore the fight. I'm sure you know your younger self lost it." She snickered, patting his arm. "And you have all the scars on your wonderful body to remind you of that."

Damian watched himself fighting the beast, using all the magic and power he had, but even observing his fight from the sidelines, he had a feeling that something wasn't right. He was gravely wounded, and he had no time to heal himself, but that wasn't the only problem. It seemed like he wasn't only losing his blood but also hemorrhaging his magical energy—his every next strike, every energy ball he propelled at the beast, and every use of his elemental energy becoming weaker and weaker. He was surrounded by his element, yet he seemed to be blocked from connecting with it.

A loud howl shattered the silence, and a giant pack of smaller beasts resembling wolves rushed into the clearing. Larger than normal animals, with their glowing purple eyes, they were definitely not normal wolves. His younger self spun around, taking his attention off the main monster just long enough to erect protective magic around himself and his woman.

While his shield stopped the wolf-looking monsters, the giant beast slammed his terrible talons down, crushing his protective dome as if it were made of glass. The man screamed, throwing his body between the monster and the woman, spreading his arms. The claws slashed across his face, ripping it from the hairline down to the middle of his cheek. Crying out in pain, he staggered back involuntarily, clasping his hands to his bleeding face, and then fell to his knees.

"Stop! That's enough!" roared Damian, fighting the hold of the nightmare the goddess of Darkness had wrapped around him. His chest was shuddering with short breaths as he struggled to breathe in and couldn't, cold sweat running down his face and back. "I can't... I remember... God damn you!"

"Shh... It's okay... Just one more thing I need you to see. It's important," she whispered, and with shock, he heard some tones of sympathy—regret, even—in her voice. Mara wrapped her arms around him, and for a moment, everything went blurry.

When the image cleared out, the beast and the other monsters were gone. The man, drenched in blood, sat on his heels, his trembling fingers threading through the woman's hair, her head lying on his lap. She was dead. He lifted his head, and a terrible cry escaped his lips. The ground responded to his pain with a rolling earthquake, and the trees bent their crowns, reaching for him.

"Magnus!" roared younger Damian, his voice shaking with raw anguish, and the magical energy field spiked around him. "I summon thee, you son of a bitch!"

A bright white light illuminated the clearing, but Mara snapped her fingers, and everything froze.

"Look right... over... there," she murmured into his ear, pointing at the opposite end of the clearing.

Damian stared in the direction she pointed, and chills went through him. His younger self was gazing up at the bright light, so he couldn't see it. A shadow separated from the giant tree at the edge of the clearing, and for a brief moment, Damian saw a person standing there with his face upturned. With the white light blasting from the sky, he couldn't distinguish his features, but it was definitely a man.

Mara snapped her fingers again, and everything disappeared. She got up, and Damian fell on his back, still disabled by the hold of her magic. His body convulsed painfully, and he closed his eyes.

"Did you see that man?" she asked, staring down at him.

He nodded, unable to unlock his jaws.

"This is the man who's responsible for the death of the only woman you've ever loved." The softer tones were gone from her voice, and she sounded as frostily and indifferent as before. "Since this incident, you never fell in love again. You move from place to place with one purpose burning in your soul—to punish those responsible for the death of your beloved. Am I right, Damian? You slay monsters or anything supernatural that kills humans, and that pacifies your broken heart, at least for a short time. You're addicted to hunting, to hate, to pain. You can never stop. Even the message from your beloved that you received from behind the veil didn't help you move on. But I can help you." She stopped talking, staring down at him for a moment before continuing. "I can free you from this neverending pain you carry in your soul, and from your addiction."

He closed his eyes and turned away from her.

"Obey my command, and I'll give him to you on a silver platter. After all these years, you will finally be able to avenge her death. Isn't that what you want, Damian?" Her voice turned into a soft, insinuating purr as she leaned closer to him. "You kill him, and you'll be free. Truly free. What do you say, boy? Do we have a deal?"

"No deal," he exhaled, his soul bleeding.

"I'm not asking much. All I want you to do is leave Paradise Manor and Arizona unprotected, and I'll give you the name and the location of that man. We will both get what we want." She stomped her foot, placing her hands on her hips.

He laughed, a painful sound he didn't recognize as his voice. "I'm too old, Mara. I'm not gonna fall for something like this." He shrugged. "Besides, I know my place in this world, and I also know my obligations. I'm not going to make a deal with a dark Slavic deity that could potentially destroy the realm of humans."

"Aw, come on! Right now, I don't care about destroying the

human world. I just want all my powers back. I wish to be my old self again. Out of all the people, you should understand how I feel," she yelled, throwing her hands up. She lowered next to him, her eyes gleaming with a maniacal glow. "Don't you see? You and I, right here, right now... In this tiny world I created outside the human realm just to exchange a few words with you in private. It was meant to be. You and I... we're the same." She spoke fast on one breath. "We have a unique opportunity to manipulate the Board of Destiny. We can change both our futures forever. Don't be an idiot, boy! This is a onetime deal. Take it or leave it."

"Leave it," replied Damian calmly. "My answer is still no." He glanced at the dark sky, his thoughts circling back to the car accident and Jamie. He needed to get the hell out of this nightmare and see if the young man had survived the crash. "You and I are nothing alike, and I'm done talking to you, Mara. My answer is no, and you can do whatever the hell you want."

Her face transformed into a terrifying mask of fury. She placed her knee on his chest and pressed down, adding some of her magic to her weight.

"I know you lost your power, boy. I'm an ancient goddess and you"—she snickered, throwing her black hair off her face—"you are nothing. You stand no chance against me." She laughed again, her maniacal laughter echoing through the dark woods. "So, here is what your choice will lead to. You can't die, but you'll witness everyone around you perish. Your little detective will die. The old hunter will die. And that cute vamp—your brother, isn't he—will die, too. But I will still get what I want. I always do."

"If you know I lost my power and stand no chance against you, then why are you working so hard to get me out of your way?" he asked icily.

She squealed, anger modulating her voice into a high-pitched screech, but then just snapped her fingers and vanished.

The world around Damian did a sharp somersault, and when he opened his eyes, he found himself inside his car, hanging upside down, suspended by the seatbelt. The sharp odor of gasoline mixed in with the metallic smell of blood permeated the air, assaulting his senses. He glanced to the side, and his heart gave a painful jolt.

Jamie hung upside down, his arms dangling lifelessly, blood dripping from his nose and the corner of his mouth.

"Jamie!" he yelled, struggling to get himself free.

Loud laughter sounded from outside of the vehicle. Damian glanced out the broken window, and blood froze in his veins.

CHAPTER 28

~ DAMIAN BLAKE ~

A group of people stood on the side of the road, staring down at the SUV. Their eyes glowed with a hollow phosphoric light like that of wild animals, and their magical energy signature was clear enough for Damian to detect it even in his condition.

Still disoriented after the number Mara did on him, he didn't bother counting them. Judging by the size of the crowd, there were plenty of them to give him more problems than one person could handle. Besides, it seemed that all of them were armed to the teeth as if they were about to face the United States Army and not a single man who was banged up after a car accident.

Manifesting one of his daggers, Damian cut his seat belt and dropped down awkwardly, hitting the roof of the car with his head. Feeling a throbbing pain, he touched his right temple and felt the slippery wetness of blood under his fingers. His right shoulder ached with his every move, but since he was able to move his arm, he assumed it wasn't dislocated or broken.

After a short struggle, he managed to turn around. Holding Jamie with one arm, he cut his seatbelt and lowered him to the roof of the car gently. He didn't have time to check his vitals or help him because even though he didn't see movement outside the vehicle, he sensed it with his skin. His intuition sprung up, throwing one red flag after another in his mind, and he knew he had no time to waste.

All these people were supernatural swords for hire. It meant they had some kind of magic, and they were trained warriors. Attempting to fight them in a tight space where his range of movements was severely limited was suicide. He was already at a serious disadvantage—drained magically by Mara, hurt and disoriented after the car accident, and holding the low ground. He needed to get out of the vehicle before they reached him.

He made his dagger vanish and tried to open his door. Warped by the accident, it didn't budge. Leaning back as much as he could, Damian kicked it with his legs, and it flew off its hinges with a thunderous bang. He slipped out of the car and dropped to one knee, placing both palms flat on the ground. Connecting with his element, he let the energy of Earth take him over, energizing him. As the soft orange glow of his power surrounded him, he raised his head, watching the approaching enemy, anger slowly boiling up inside of him.

They halted, exchanging bewildered looks, and this momentary delay allowed Damian to get to his feet. He rolled his shoulders and touched his leather bracelet, turning it into a whip. The men exchanged a look and barked laughing.

"Remind me, guys, what do they call a man who brings a whip to a gunfight?" asked a tall man in a leather jacket who stood in front of the group. His eyes glowed brighter, and the air shimmered around him slightly, confirming Damian's original guess—all these men were shifters, swords for hire.

"They call him a dead man, commander," supplied one of the shifters, snickering, his long, greasy hair falling over his horse-like face.

"No," replied Damian snidely, a dark smirk crossing his face.

"They call him a man who is about to leave the gunfight with a few new guns."

He swung his whip, and it hissed through the air, wrapping around the neck of the man upfront. Yanking the whip back, he ripped the shifter's head off. As the corpse hit the ground, splattering everything around with bright red liquid, the copper scent of blood filled the air. The rest of the gang shouted all at once and raised their weapons, the anger around them almost palpable.

"Procedia Amnia," hissed Damian, surrounding himself with protective magic.

The short barking sounds of discharged firearms broke the silence, but that didn't slow him down. Confident that his shield was strong enough to protect him from mundane bullets, Damian spun around, allowing his whip to do its deadly job. Every swing of his glowing weapon left a dead body behind. Realizing that the guns were useless against him, the shifters stopped shooting and rushed toward him, unsheathing their swords and knives.

As anger roared through him, Damian couldn't help but laugh, and the sound of his laughter made his attackers slow down, fear reflecting in their widened eyes. He spread his arms, calling to his element. The ground opened between him and the group of shifters, swallowing a few of them. He swung his whip again, catching a few more shifters at the edge and sending them tumbling down into the trench he'd created. With one move of his arm, he made the trench close up, burying his attackers alive.

"Anyone else wants to try?" he growled, the orange light around him getting brighter.

He outstretched his arm and squeezed his fist, turning it. The ground shook, responding to his command, and the trees leaned down, smacking the shifters with their branches. The men bent down, covering their heads with their hands, yelps of fear escaping their lips. As soon as Damian let go, the shifters turned around and ran. They hopped into their SUVs and left, tires screeching on the asphalt.

Damian didn't care to pursue them. He already knew who sent them and why. The only thing he cared about was helping Jamie. Touching the cold forest floor, he gave one more command to his element, and the ground opened, swallowing the dead bodies as if they had never been there. Then he let go of the elemental power and swayed slightly, suddenly too exhausted to make another move. With a serious effort of will, he headed toward the vehicle and lowered to his knees by the driver's door.

Jamie lay in the same position he had left him in earlier, still unconscious. His pale face was covered in blood, and his left arm was turned at an unnatural angle. Placing his hand on the young man's chest, Damian didn't detect any movement and grunted, cursing quietly. He took Jamie's wrist, his fingers searching for a pulse, but since he couldn't find one, he placed two fingers under his jaw. He found the pulse right away. It was weak and uneven, but it was there.

"Jamie," he called softly, but the young man didn't respond.

Damian reached in his pocket and pulled out his cellphone. Checking the screen, he groaned, slamming his hand on the ground—still no reception. Going through everything River taught him about cellphones in his mind, he dialed nine-one-one, hoping that since he had enough battery power, the cell would connect with the emergency service.

The phone dropped the call and went dead.

"Damn you, Mara!" he shouted desperately, adding a few choice words.

"You'll witness everyone around you perish..." The words of the infuriated goddess sounded in his mind, and he shook his head resentfully. *Not if I can help it.*

Carefully, he pulled Jamie out of the vehicle and lifted him into his arms. With a strenuous grunt, he got up to his feet, his body responding with a dull ache in his shoulder and a stinging headache.

Climbing out of the ditch took more out of him than he expected, and when he finally made it to the road, he had to take one knee and give himself a few minutes of rest and catch his breath. He glanced down at Jamie's limp body, and despair washed over him as he searched the empty dark road spreading for miles in both directions. He dropped his head, and for the first time in centuries, he prayed, silently and intensely.

Perun almighty, please give me the strength to help this young man. He's just a boy... He has done nothing wrong. Don't punish him for trying to help me... Punish me, if you have to, but help me save his life...

A soft wind rushed through the forest, rustling the tops of the trees. Damian glanced at the starless sky and shook his head, a bitter smirk curving his lips. Gods had never been there when he needed them before. Some things never change.

He got up to his feet and started walking alongside the highway. He had no idea how far the nearest town was, and he didn't think anyone would stop to give him a ride at night. After all, he was covered in blood and carried an unconscious man in his arms. A few vehicles passed by, but as he expected, none of them even slowed down. After a while, he stopped trying to hitchhike and focused on moving forward as fast as he could in his condition.

He didn't know how long he'd been walking when someone flashed lights behind him, and a small pickup truck came to a sharp stop a few feet ahead of him. A man in a plaid flannel shirt, baseball cap, and old, washed-out jeans got out of the truck and ran toward him.

"Are you okay, man? What happened?" he asked, his eyes darting from Damian's blood-covered face to Jamie's limp body in his arms.

Damian stared at him, his chest shuddering with short breaths as he struggled to even his breathing. "Car accident," he managed to say finally. "My friend needs... hospital... please..."

"You look like you need a hospital yourself," muttered the man, shaking his head.

He helped him into the truck, placing Jamie across Damian's lap and took off, driving at full speed. Luckily, the highway remained empty, and the nearest town was just a few miles away. Damian barely noticed where they were driving, his mind fading on and off. The man parked the truck in front of the door into the emergency room and ran inside the building, screaming for help.

Damian opened the door and walked out of the vehicle, holding Jamie tight to his chest. He took just a few steps when a few people in disposable medical gowns ran toward him, rolling a gurney. He remembered them taking over Jamie and placing him on the gurney. Then the world spun around him and tilted. Someone's hands grabbed his shoulders and arms, holding him from falling.

"Young man! Look at me! Don't close your eyes!"

An urgent voice sounded in the back of his fading mind, and he made an effort to comply but couldn't. He moaned and let go as the darkness covered him like a heavy, suffocating blanket.

CHAPTER 29

~ DAMIAN BLAKE ~

A ray of bright light touched his eyes, and he groaned, turning his head to the side, away from the unwanted brightness. His body responded with dull aches, and that brought back the memories. Damian jolted up and looked around, searching for Jamie.

A hospital room with light beige walls and white ceiling was separated in two by a curtain, and the scent of medications and disinfectants hung in the air. His arms were attached to an IV bag and monitors that were beeping evenly, their sound jarring to his stretched senses. Even though his muscles were still sore, he didn't feel as drained as he had yesterday. Damian grabbed the IV line, about to rip it off, when a young woman in medical scrubs walked in, followed by a police officer.

"Hey, Mr. Blake, you're finally awake," she said with a kind smile, checking his monitors.

"Where is Jamie Coldwell?" asked Damian. "The man I brought in yesterday. Is he okay?"

"He's fine," replied the nurse, gesturing at the curtain separating the room. "He's still asleep, but otherwise, he's fine. A broken arm, concussion, and a few bruises. He'll be all right in no time."

"Mr. Blake," said the police officer, stepping forward, "can you tell me what happened? How did you and Mr. Coldwell sustain all these injuries?"

"A car accident," explained Damian, throwing a glance at the closed curtain. "Hit and run."

He told the police officer where the accident had happened and everything thereafter. But as he went through all the formalities, the only thing he could think about was how to get out of here and be on his way back to Arizona as soon as possible.

Jamie woke up about thirty minutes later and without thinking twice, refused to stay another night for observation, adamant about leaving with Damian. After a short but intense conversation, they both signed an against-medical-advice form and left the hospital.

It was close to noon when they finally walked out the hospital door and headed toward a car rental place. Even though Jamie kept reassuring him that he felt just fine, Damian wasn't convinced, noticing the sweat beading his young friend's face and occasional wince when he made too sharp of a move. Luckily, the car rental wasn't far away, and soon, they walked into a small, air-conditioned room.

While Jamie took care of the paperwork, Damian stepped away from the counter and reached for his phone. As the screen lit up in his hands, he saw that his cell service was restored, all four bars shining in the top right corner of the display. A multiple notification windows stacked on his lock screen, and his heart skipped a beat as he scanned through them—a few missed calls from his brother and River, a few messages and a text message from Cole.

Thousands of thoughts flashed through his mind. All this time Mara had been blocking him from the outside world. Why stop now? What had changed? With worry twisting his gut, he listened to Cole's message first.

"We're facing two angry deities, and everyone who lives in the house is their target because only people who live in Paradise Manor can pass through the wards. Please, brother, call me as soon as possible..."

"Two gods? So, Mara has a partner—" He cut himself off, cold sweat covering his forehead as a terrible suspicion originated in his mind. He dialed Cole's number, muttering under his breath, "Come on, Cole, pick up, pick up, pick up..."

"You reached Cole Adams..." His brother's even voice sounded on the other side of the line.

"Dammit, Cole!" shouted Damian, slamming his hand against the wall. Jamie spun around, and the rental rep raised his head, gaping at him with wide eyes.

Damian hung up the phone and held his hand up apologetically, giving a short nod to Jamie. Once they turned away, he redialed Cole's phone number. This time, he waited until the beep and left a message.

"Cole, call me back. I think I know who the gods are, and it isn't good news. We are dealing with Mara, Slavic goddess of Nightmares and Darkness, and Morok, Slavic god of Lies, Deceit, and Diseases. He's the dark side of Svarog and just as powerful as him. I need you..." His voice trailed off as he realized that as much as he wanted to see Cole safe, he couldn't ask his brother to leave the house. "Goddamnit... We can't leave River unprotected, and if we get her out of the house, we'll expose whatever the Guardians are shielding there! We're doomed if we do and doomed if we don't. I'm on my way home, but I still have twenty hours of driving ahead of me. Call me!"

He hung up the phone and looked at the second message. It was from River, and she had left it at around midnight last night. Expecting nothing but more trouble, Damian pressed play button.

"Damian, hi," said River, her voice unusually strained. *"I didn't want to bother you, but Cole is missing. He didn't come back home last night, and when I tried calling him, the call went straight to his voicemail."*

She fell silent for a moment, and he could hear a strange continuous noise in the background.

"Damian, something is going on," continued River, lowering her voice to a whisper. *"The house is filled with weird noises and whispers, and I can't figure out where they are coming from. I tried calling my father, but he's not answering either. I'm going to lock myself in my bedroom now. Call me when you get this message."*

The message ended, and Damian raised his eyes, staring at Jamie's back. As if feeling his stare, the young man turned around and glanced at him with a question in his eyes. Damian pointed at his cell and gave him an urgent gesture, showing him that they needed to leave promptly.

Getting back to his phone, he checked the second message from River, realizing she had left it less than an hour after the first. He pressed the play button next to it and stilled, listening to River's hoarse voice.

"Damian, something is seriously wrong." She spoke fast, and while her voice sounded urgent and strained, he could also detect a cold determination in it. *"I'm still in my bedroom, but I'm not sure I know what's real and what's not anymore. The whispers are louder and..."* Her voice broke, and she cleared her throat. *"I think I'm going crazy, Day. I can hear Nick's voice, and he's calling my name. Also, something is going on in the foyer. Someone is there... I wanted to leave the bedroom to check it out, but as soon as I came close to the door, Gypsy was ready to claw my eyes out. I can't get hold of anyone—Cole, my father, you... and I can't trust myself. I need someone with a clear mind. I'm going to call Jesse to come over. Call me when you get this message."*

Damian stared at the phone, his unbending fingers almost crushing its plastic casing. Then he dialed River's phone number and stilled, counting the beeps. Even before the call went into voicemail, he already knew she wasn't going to answer. *Dammit, what the hell is going on in Blue Creek?*

A light touch to his shoulder made him flinch and spin around.

"Let's go," Jamie said, readjusting his arm sling, giving Damian a troubled once-over. "The car is outside. Just need to check it and sign—"

"Just sign everything and let's get moving. Buy the rental insurance if it would make it faster. I'll pay for all the expenses once we get home," muttered Damian, walking out the door. "We have no time to lose."

"I figured as much," murmured Jamie. "When I caught your sight a few minutes ago, you looked like you'd seen a ghost."

"Actually, a few of them," replied Damian, staring at a car stopping in front of them. "Oh, come on, Jamie! Seriously?"

Jamie laughed, giving him a slap on the shoulder. "Well, your terrified look told me we need to... um... drive faster. So, I asked for something with extra muscle."

Damian gaped at the red Dodge Charger R/T, feeling the wave of his usual claustrophobia rising to his throat. He grunted and grabbed the key from Jamie's hand.

"Good choice," he exhaled, watching Jamie signing the screen of the tablet in the rental rep's hands. "I'm driving."

He moved the driver's seat back and got into the car, strapping his seatbelt on. Once Jamie settled in, he drove the car out of the plaza and into the first empty alley he could find. Parking it there, he made sure no one was in the area and placed his hands flat on the dashboard, channeling his magic. As he whispered a short spell, a gentle white glow surrounded the vehicle and slowly dissipated. Damian started the engine again and drove it toward the road.

"What did you do?" asked Jamie, once they entered the highway.

Damian pushed the accelerator pedal down, watching the arrow on the speedometer climbing over the hundred mark.

"A modified version of the turn-away spell," he explained, pushing the speed over the hundred-twenty mark. "You don't want cops on our tail, do you?"

"Dude!" yelped Jamie, excitement in his voice. "You have to teach me that."

Damian chuckled, thinking that his companion sounded like a teenager. "How old are you?" he asked, staring straight ahead.

"Twenty-five. Why?"

"No reason, just curious." Damian glanced at him, unable to hold a smile. "You have a lot to learn. Have you ever considered the Archmage's offer to join their academy?"

"No," replied Jamie, his expression closing up. "After being a guard at the Guardians HQ for a few years, I'm not sure I want any part of it." He thought for a moment and then added, "Although, I must admit, Quinn Allerton is the best Archmage I've seen. He's a good man, you know?"

"Maybe," said Damian softly. "But recently someone told me that in the World of Magic, there is always someone who yanks your leash. I know perfectly well who holds the Archmage's leash, and I don't want to have anything to do with them."

Jamie didn't reply, and for a while, they drove in silence, Damian focusing on the road, squeezing the maximum speed out of the powerful V-8 engine.

"Damian, would you teach me magic?" asked Jamie, fidgeting awkwardly with the Guardians pendant he wore on the long silver chain.

"You want *me* to teach you magic," repeated Damian, his eyebrows rising. "I specialize in combat magic, Jamie. I'm not sure I'm the right person to teach you."

"Combat magic is the only thing I want to learn," replied the young man, all color draining from his cheeks, making him look tired and older.

Damian glanced at him and nodded. "Let's get back to this conversation after we clear the mess in Paradise Manor."

He stopped talking, his mind returning back to the problem at hand. The short message his brother had left partially explained why Mara was trying to scare River out of her home and why all previous owners of Paradise Manor were dead. If you can't scare them away—kill 'em all. Once all the owners of the house are gone, Mara will be free to enter the building and get whatever she is after.

The last message River left for him played in his mind, and he swallowed hard—Jesse. Had she been able to reach him since everyone else was unavailable? And what kind of consequences would that have in the grand scheme of things? He wasn't sure how and why, but he was positive Jesse was playing some kind of role in this situation.

Without taking his eyes off the road, he reached for his phone and dialed River's phone number again. The call went straight to her voicemail. He tried Cole and Sam with the same result.

"Jamie," he said at length. "What do you know about Jesse Williams?"

"Jesse Williams?" Jamie turned slightly in his seat, his jaw dropped. "Why? Nothing special. Wasn't he River's late husband's partner?"

"Yes. He's River's partner now," replied Damian. "Is there anything noteworthy about him or his family?"

Jamie shrugged. "Not that I know of, but we can stop by my house and look at my father's research files. He has something on almost every family in Blue Creek." He sighed, staring out the window wistfully. "I wished I paid more attention to his research while he was alive."

"Human nature," whispered Damian more to himself than to his young friend. "We take for granted what we have until it's gone." He thought for a moment and bit his lip. "I'm not sure I'm going to have time for the research when we get home. River left a couple of troubling messages. Cole Adams and Sam Vetrov are missing. I'll drop you off at home and go straight to Paradise Manor. If you could look into Jesse's background, I would greatly appreciate it."

"Cole Adams is missing again?" he asked, but then frowned, massaging his shoulder under the sling. "No problem. I'll go through my father's records and call you as soon as I know anything."

It was close to eight the following evening when Damian drove through downtown Blue Creek and stopped the car in front of Sam's shop. Even without walking inside, he felt something wasn't right. The light scent of sulfur lingered in the air—a sure signature of a demonic presence, and the alarm system was off. Sam never left his shop without arming the alarm system first.

Damian pulled on the door handle, and the door opened up easily. He didn't walk inside. One look was enough for him to understand what had happened here. Everything inside the shop was misplaced, overturned or broken. The stench of sulfur was a lot heavier here, and the barely noticeable presence of vampiric energy completed the picture.

Vampires working with demons? Damian asked himself, backing away from the shop. *Does Sam's disappearance have anything to do with Cole missing?*

He walked around the car and dropped into the driver's seat. "Jamie, we need to move quickly. I think Sam and Cole are in serious trouble." He slammed his hand on the steering wheel. "Heaven and Earth! I can't be in two places at once."

Following Jamie's directions, he drove the car through the old-west district and parked it in front of a small, one-story house on the outskirts of town. Jamie walked out of the car but then turned back and bent down, looking at Damian with concern.

"Are you sure you don't want to stop by for a few minutes?" he asked, leaning on the car door with his healthy arm. "You drove over eighteen hours straight at a crazy speed without taking a break and barely eating anything." Jamie smiled with a guilty shrug. "Honestly, man, you look like the walking dead. I'll get you something to eat while I check my father's notes. It's not going to take long. Trust me, you need a break."

"What he needs is to put his big girl pants on and man up." A high, girlish voice sounded behind Jamie, making him jerk upright and hiss in pain.

"Who the hell are you?" yelled Jamie, massaging his shoulder.

A young woman slipped by him and dropped onto the passenger seat, completely ignoring his question. Turning to Damian, she whipped out a Desert Eagle that looked too big for her hands.

Resting the pistol against her shoulder, she said in a gruff voice, "Come with me if you want your brother to live."

CHAPTER 30

~ COLE ADAMS ~

"Rise and shine, lover."
A slap across his face brought him out of unconsciousness and submerged him under an ocean of pain as liquid silver continued to circulate through his veins. Cole moaned and cracked his eyelids open, staring at something dark and shapeless. His shoulders ached, and even without looking, he knew he was tied up to something, his arms spread wide apart. He recognized the burning touch of silver to his bare skin and shifted, pulling weakly at his restraints.

Making an effort, he lifted his head and blinked a few times, adjusting his blurred vision. As he expected, he was tied up to a tall wooden cross nailed to a wall. An area of about ten feet by ten feet was isolated by a heavy, dark curtain obscuring the rest of the room. Judging by the black marble tiles with golden inclusions, he was in the Queen's mansion in the small chamber she used for her Council meetings. A strong presence of vampiric essence drifted around him, and even though he couldn't see them, he was positive the place was full of vampires.

Roxana stood a few feet away from him with her hands

planted on her hips, her foot in a high-heeled, elegant shoe tapping the floor impatiently. She stared at him with a mix of scorn and lust in her dark eyes, and he couldn't help but wonder how this woman could experience such opposite emotions toward him at the same time.

"Roxana," he croaked, barely able to move his lips. "What did I do wrong now?"

She snickered and sauntered toward him, looking like a cat who had just found an open door into the canary cage. Her thick, long braids slithered down her shoulders, resembling two carnivorous serpents, moving and swiping with every step she took. Exotic, sensual and beautiful, she halted in front of him, her foggy eyes gliding up and down his unobstructed torso. He groaned, struggling to clear his mind affected by the silver so he could keep up with her deadly games.

"I guess we're about to find out," she whispered, running her hand through his curls. "But before we get to business, I'll give you one last chance to come clean and confess."

He smirked. "Confess? About what exactly?"

She stared at him, and if looks could kill, he would've been a pile of ash at her feet.

"I've been told there is something you're not telling me, lover," she hissed, her eyes igniting with a deep, scarlet glow. "I'm giving you the last chance to confess and beg for your life. Do what I say, and I'll let you live." She took one more step, her burning eyes only inches away from his. "Right there"—she waved at the curtain behind her without breaking eye contact —"the entire Arizona Vampire Court has assembled. Anyone who matters, at least. So, make your choice wisely, my love. You either tell me the truth now, and then I'll decide in private what to do with you, or you'll be forced to confess in front of everybody, and then you'll be executed as a traitor, anyway."

Cole searched her unblinking eyes, reading his death warrant there, or perhaps something even worse than death.

"I have nothing to confess, my Queen," he replied firmly. "Whatever you think I'm guilty of, I'm innocent. I have always been loyal to you and the Arizona Court, so if you want to kill me, I'm yours to do as you please." He smirked faintly and bowed his head to his chest.

Roxana threw her arms up, an almost desperate look crossing her features. She approached him and cupped his face with her hands.

"Look at me, my Russian warrior," she demanded, forcing his head up. "I enjoy you alive a lot more than dead. But if there is something, anything at all, you're hiding from me, now would be a good time to confess..." Her voice cut off, and she glanced over her shoulder. "Whatever will happen out there is out of my hands, and the people who are going to question you are not going to be as gentle as I am. Do you understand me?"

He nodded, jerking his face to the side and out of her grip. "Do as you wish. I have nothing to tell you."

She cursed in an old language he didn't recognize, and her fangs expanded, betraying her boiling fury.

"It's hard to find a good lover, but I have to say my position and life are a lot more important to me than your well-being." Roxana shrugged and pivoted on her heels. She approached the curtain and yanked it open on the front.

Bright lights of electric lamps hit his eyes, blinding him for a moment, and he had to drop his head and blink a few times to chase away the white spots dancing in his vision. Soft whispers and gasps invaded his ears, and he raised his face, observing a large group of vampires in front of him.

He knew them all. Most of them were the Queen's supporters and the members of her Court Council. However, there was a small group of vampires who he knew for sure belonged to her opposition, and that struck him as weird. As soon as he lifted his head, they stopped whispering and stared at him without blinking—some gloating at his desperate situation, some with regret.

An unfamiliar tall man with long, blond hair tied into a low ponytail on the back of his head approached Cole and halted a few feet away, cocking his head. A woman, small and willowy, stopped next to the man, encircling his waist with her delicate arm. He placed his hand on her shoulder possessively, pulling her closer to his side. His frosty blue eyes lingered on her for a moment, warming up slightly, before turning to Cole.

"Is that him, Mara?" he asked, his voice, deep and raspy, bouncing against the tall ceiling. The magical energy field spiked around him as he wrapped his power around Cole, and a wave of freezing air rushed through the room.

Mara? The Slavic goddess of Nightmares? Cole froze, unable to take his eyes off the small woman with long black hair. *That would make him... Morok... Damn, just like the Zerkalitsa said—two gods...* Cole swallowed hard, pressing his back against the rough surface of the wooden cross he was attached to.

Mara approached him, the weightless fabric of her dress flowing behind her in soft waves. She seized his chin with her fingers, raising his face, and peered into his eyes.

"You're not nearly as intimidating as your terrifying brother is," she murmured. Then she glanced at Roxana and smirked. "I can see why you like him, Roxana. He's cute in that"—she huffed, her lips curving in disdain, and rolled her eyes—"undead way."

"His brother?" asked the Queen, frowning. Approaching them, she pushed Mara's hand down, positioning herself between Cole and the goddess. "What are you talking about?"

"Mr. Cole Adams," purred Mara, pronouncing one word at a time as if savoring his name on her tongue, and her derisive smirk became darker and more sinister. "You naughty, naughty boy. Have you been lying to your Queen, little vampire?" She laughed out loud, glancing at Morok over her shoulder. "Would you like to tell Her Undead Majesty the truth or should I do it for you?"

Roxana turned around, her scarlet eyes bursting with undiluted fury. "What is she talking about?" she growled, her well-manicured fingers turning into claws. She seized his neck, her nails digging deep into his flesh.

Cole lifted his chin, looking down at her icily. "She's talking about my biological brother, my lady," he replied calmly, making a split-second decision to stick to the truth as close as possible. "What she forgot to mention was that I haven't seen him for over a thousand years, and until a few days ago, I had no idea he was alive. I have nothing in common with him, and I'm loyal to you only, my Queen."

Mara gave him an arched stare, and her melodious laughter rang through the room. "Are you now?" she asked, flicking her eyebrow at him. "So, why don't you tell the Queen and her councilmen your brother's name and his true nature."

"Cole," growled Roxana warningly, blood escaping from where her claws pierced his skin. "Who's your brother, and why did I know nothing about you having a brother in the first place."

Cole averted his gaze, trying to look as shameful as he could muster. "Because..." He let his voice trail off and swallowed as if fighting nausea. "My brother's name is Damian Blake, and he's a hunter."

"Not just any hunter, is he?" purred Mara. Maneuvering around Roxana, she made her way closer to Cole. She grabbed one of the silver chains and pressed it to his ribs, ripping a hiss of pain out of Cole's lips. "Don't stop now, when it's just starting to get entertaining."

"He's the one we call the Shadow Slayer," groaned Cole, shifting in his restraints to get away from Mara's touch.

A collective gasp was the response to his words. Roxana let

go of his neck and backed away from him, her lip lifting in a furious snarl.

"All this time, you lied to me?" she hissed, squeezing her hands into fists.

"No, I didn't," he replied calmly. "I did as I'd been told, my lady. I used our relation to get the information you needed. I told you the truth. The Shadow Slayer didn't move to Arizona to go after your Court. He was looking for a clean slate."

Mara made an impatient gesture, pushing Roxana away. "I don't care why he moved here," she muttered. "Damian Blake is in my way, and I'm going to do whatever it takes to get him out of the picture."

Cole stared at her for a moment and burst out laughing despite the pain surging through his body with every move he made.

"You seriously think that if you hold me hostage, Damian Blake will give in to your demands?" He shook his head, a tear of laughter running down his pale cheek. "It tells me you know nothing about my brother. He hates vampires. The only reason he lets me live is that I once was his brother. He doesn't mind me hanging around for old times' sake, but that's as far as it goes." He cut his laughter off abruptly, pulling against his silver restraints. "He is the Shadow Slayer. Killing vampires is what he does."

Mara tilted her head, a sinister smirk playing on her lips. "So, what you're saying is that you're nothing but loyal to your Queen. Is that right, Cole Adams?"

Cole turned to Roxana, gazing calmly at her. "My Queen, I swear I'm loyal to you. If you untie me, I'll bend my knee before you and swear on my sword."

Roxana and Mara exchanged a look, and the Queen flicked her wrist, gesturing for the goddess to proceed. Morok approached the curtain and yanked it to the side, exposing a tall cage.

Inside the cage, an older man was down on his knees. His arms were twisted behind his back and bound together with thick rope. A metal collar shone dimly on his neck, and a heavy chain connected it with the top of the cage. His silver-gray hair smeared with brown stains of blood fell forward, but even without seeing his face, Cole knew who he was. Despite the effort to remain calm, he froze in place, unable to take his eyes off the man in the cage.

Mara chuckled. "I see you recognized him, Cole," she purred. Approaching the cage, she pushed her hand between the bars and seized the man's hair, yanking his head up. "Great Court, allow me to make the introduction." Her black, venomous eyes slipped from one face to the next, finally halting on Cole. "This is Sam Vetrov, an old hunter who killed his fair share of vampires over the course of his short human life."

Whispers morphed into a continuous hiss, a general vibe of anger and animosity poisoning the air. Mara raised her hand, asking for silence, then she turned to Cole and a long knife shining with the reflected light of electric lamps materialized in her hand.

"Just a moment ago, Cole Adams swore his loyalty to his Queen and to this Court," she said, making a wide gesture with her hand. "Great Court, I believe it would be only fair if I asked Cole to prove his loyalty before all of you."

The vampires exchanged heavy looks but didn't say anything, staring at the Queen.

"Proceed," hissed Roxana with an indifferent flick of her wrist, but her shoulders tensed with anger.

Mara approached Cole, twirling the knife between her fingers. "Cole, I'm going to untie you in a moment," she said, scorn dripping from her every word. "All you have to do is kill the old hunter, and you're free to live your life."

Sam raised his eyes, meeting Cole's tormented gaze. "Do what you have to do, Mr. Adams," he uttered dryly. Chuckling, he tilted his head, exposing his jugular. "Damian was right—once a vamp, you're nothing more than a disgusting, bloodsucking leech."

Pain wrenched his soul, squeezing it in its iron grip, but Cole clenched his teeth and raised his head as far as the cross would allow him. He observed the Court, his eyes lingering on the members of the opposition slightly longer.

"You can consider me a traitor and execute me as such, but I will do no such thing," he said firmly. "Killing a human in our Court's headquarters is not only reckless, it's stupid. For years, the Arizona Vampire Court has lived in the shadows without attracting the attention of human authorities and staying under the radar of the Destiny Council." He jerked his chin at Sam. "I've been living among humans for a few decades without exposing the World of Magic. I know how they think and how they operate, and I assure you, killing Sam Vetrov will lead to serious consequences. He's too prominent of a figure in Blue Creek for his death or disappearance to go unnoticed."

He fell silent, observing the Court's reaction. The vampires tensed, their eyes lighting up with a hungry, scarlet glow. The members of the opposition shifted closer together, their fangs expanding, and a tiny spark of hope ignited in Cole's chest.

"It's true what your Queen said. You do have your way with words, little vamp." Mara cackled, patting Cole on his cheek. A malignant smirk lifted the corners of Morok's lips as he moved closer to Cole and halted before him, folding his massive arms over his chest. Mara turned toward the Queen. "Your Majesty, as we have agreed earlier, I delivered the proof you needed. Cole Adams refused to prove his loyalty to you. Now it's your turn to hold your side of the deal and let me proceed with my plan."

Roxana halted, her eyes darting from Cole to Mara and back. Then she huffed and waved her hand dismissively. "If his life is what you need to kill the Shadow Slayer, then he's yours. Do what you must, goddess."

"Roxana..." he called, pulling at the silver chains just to realize how truly weak he was.

The Queen stepped aside without so much as giving him a second look, and Mara and Morok took her place. Morok put his hands on his temples, staring directly into his eyes. A wave of his magic, as cold as a winter blizzard, spread through Cole, and he moaned, his body shivering uncontrollably. As a vampire, he had already forgotten how it felt to be cold, but now he was frozen to the core, his teeth chattering as a layer of frost expanded over his skin from under Morok's hands.

Morok smiled, his smile as cold as his true nature. Slapping Cole on his cheek, he reached to the side with his right hand, untying the silver chain that held Cole's arm attached to the cross.

"I'm going to remove you from the cross," he said to Cole in such a conversational tone, as if he were chatting with his best friends at a dinner party. "Don't try to run and definitely don't try to fight. Trust me, you cannot."

Supporting his body with his arm, Morok untied the remaining chains and threw Cole over his shoulder. Cole groaned, but just like the god of Lies had said, he couldn't make even the tiniest move, frozen from head to toe. Even his vocal cords refused to obey. Morok lowered him to the floor and waved at Mara to come closer.

"He's ready, darling. Do your thing." He rubbed his hands together, excitement lighting up in his icy eyes. "Let's see what's stored in that pretty head of his."

Mara stepped by his side, staring down at him, interest reflected in her gaze.

"You and your brother are nothing alike." She straddled him, shifting to his chest, and Cole groaned, feeling as if someone just threw him under an asphalt roller. "He is a beast—wild and untamed, despite the name he chose for himself. And you..." She ran her fingers over his cheek to his lips. "You're like a housebroken kitten. Pretty, but that's as far as it goes."

Cole groaned, trying to close his eyes, but even that he couldn't do. She laughed, noticing his attempt.

"Hide your little fangs, kitten. You can't use them now. You're mine." She placed her hands, palms down, against his chest. "Believe it or not, just a few hours earlier, I was just as close with your brother as I'm with you now." She channeled her magic, wrapping him into a veil of darkness. "Let's see what kind of nightmares I can find in your brain, little vamp..."

Dima... I need you to be all right... A fading thought flashed through Cole's mind as he started to fall.

CHAPTER 31

~ COLE ADAMS ~

His fall ended as abruptly as it started. He didn't feel the impact. Everything around felt soft and disgustingly mushy. He tried to get up, but his moves were torturously slow, his limbs filled with lead. Forcing his eyes open, he stared into absolute darkness.

A metallic odor of blood touched his nose, and his stomach twisted, his throat painfully dry. He grunted, shocked by the sudden assault of thirst. He hadn't felt thirst as powerful and all-consuming as this since forever. Besides the smell of blood, he detected a sickening reek of decay, sweat and human excrement.

Fighting the debilitating weakness, he rolled to his stomach and then pushed himself up on all fours. As the darkness gradually withdrew, he looked around and froze, pure terror chilling his soul.

"No," Cole moaned. "It can't be."

He sat back on his heels and raised his arms, staring at them in shock. He was dressed in ancient Russian armor, and his arms wrapped in chainmail were covered in a layer of dried out blood. Feeling a forceful call of thirst, he clutched his throat with his fingers and surveyed the area. He sat by the side of a large river, and every person next to him was either dead or dying, the moans and groans of pain tormenting his overly sensitive ears.

He remembered this moment of his life.

He could never forget it.

This was the moment when he lost everything just to gain something entirely different—the moment when his human life had ended, and his undead existence had started.

This was the event that was engraved in his memory forever—the moment he had been turned and tasted blood for the first time.

"You need to feed, child." A deep male voice sounded from behind him, and he spun around, his movements still feverishly slow and heavy. "You'll feel better after you feed."

Cole raised his eyes, recognizing the man—his maker.

"Ruslan," he whispered his name, belatedly realizing that it didn't matter what he said or did. He was reliving his hardest and most vivid memory.

Ruslan lowered to one knee next to him, and his wide smile lit up his bronze face, his velvety brown eyes crinkling at the corners.

"You fought like a lion, little one, and I could not let you die," he rumbled. "It has been centuries since I have seen a mighty warrior with a gift from the gods like you. Even though I swore I would never turn a human, you deserved immortality. I would be proud to call you my son."

"Ruslan, where are you?" whispered Cole, gazing at his maker, a terrible surge of grief overwhelming him. "I've been searching for you everywhere, Father."

His maker wasn't here—wherever this 'here' was. The man before him was nothing but a distant memory, and Cole's soul gave a painful jolt as he remembered what came next.

Ruslan walked away and came back dragging a wounded man with him. He dropped him to the ground before Cole, and the dying man stared at him, his eyes pleading silently for his life.

"If you do not feed, you will die soon, and your death is going to be torturous," said Ruslan, squatting in front of Cole. "This man will be dead in a few minutes, anyway. Give him the gift of an easy and pleasant death." He caressed Cole's pale face with the back of his hand and smiled, sadness never leaving his eyes. "Feed, my boy."

Cole looked down at the man sprawled before him, and he knew Ruslan was right—he was on the verge of crossing the veil. At the look of blood flowing from a deep laceration on his chest, Cole's thirst rose to the next level. A feral growl rumbled in his throat, and his fangs expanded for the first time. In shock, he raised his hand and touched the sharp tip of his fang with his finger.

"Feed," whispered Ruslan, pushing his head down.

With a growl, Cole sunk his fangs into the dying man's neck.

The view shook and shifted, becoming blurry. The world spun around him, and he started to fall again.

When the fall ended, he found himself standing in a dark cave. The air smelled musty and unclean, and the silence was pressing on his stretched nerves. He turned around, surveying the area, and found two men in military fatigues behind him, each holding their weapons at the ready. He remembered them. They were his friends; they used to serve together—years ago, a lifetime ago.

"Dammit," mumbled Cole, recognizing this memory. "What am I doing back in Afghanistan, Mara? What's the point of all this?"

He let the two soldiers walk past him and followed them out of the cave onto a wide mountain plateau. *What would happen if I sit down and refuse to move?* He shrugged and sat down, watching the two men heading toward their inevitable death.

"No, you don't, little vampire." Mara's voice sounded in his mind as the goddess of Nightmares cackled. "You can't fight me here. Here, I own you. You're going to go through all your worst memories until you either do what I say or become so delusional with pain that you'll beg me on your knees, willing to do whatever it takes just to stop it."

"Never," growled Cole. "I will never submit."

"I guess we shall see," replied Mara icily. "In the meantime, enjoy the trip down memory lane. Something tells me with the years of crap you carry in your head, it'll be a bumpy ride."

His vision blurred, and he wrapped his arms around his head as the world around him shifted. When he could see again, he was standing in front of a military tent. Looking back, the dark silhouette of the Hindu Kush mountain range rose against the ultramarine sky like a black wall. Cole cursed as his stomach heaved at the memory of what happened next, but now he knew that the only way out of this horrifying memory was through it.

The sound of gunshots ripped him out of his thoughts. With a heavy heart, he moved forward and walked inside the tent. The reek of death and the smell of freshly spilled blood enveloped him, spiking the thirst. Seeing all his friends lifeless, sprawled on the floor with their throats cut, brought back the anger. It wasn't just any anger. Fury, unmanageable and inextinguishable, roared through him, bringing his vampiric nature forth.

He bolted through the tent at full speed, tearing the back wall with his bare hands. It took him less than a minute to catch up with the assailants. Silent and deadly, he ripped through them, killing all of them before they realized something was up. As his fangs ripped their throats and his claws tore their still beating hearts out of their chests, he didn't blink and didn't slow down. He felt no remorse, no pity—only pain and unimaginable anger. Fresh blood rushed down his throat, catalyzing his already storming rage.

A minute later, all of them were dead. He collapsed to his knees, grief and rage combining into an explosive concoction within him. Burying his fingers into his blood-covered hair, he threw his head back and screamed, but no sound came out from his constrained throat. The world spun again, and he started to fall, dreading the next nightmare Mara had created for him.

* * *

HE DIDN'T KNOW how long Mara kept rummaging through his memories, pulling the worst moments of his life and throwing them in his face. After a while, he couldn't separate reality from the next nightmare the goddess had conjured to torment him. His soul cried bloody tears as with sudden clarity, he realized just how many people he had killed over the course of his long, undead existence.

Guilt and remorse reared their heads again, turning him into a giant ball of misery, and when the final change took place, he didn't notice. Lying sprawled on the hard, tiled floor, he curled in on himself, covering his head with his arms.

"Cole, my child, open your eyes."

He heard the deep voice of a man somewhere above him, and someone shook his shoulder gently.

"It's okay, my boy... I'm here now. You're safe," the man whispered, his strong arms turning him on his back.

Cole cracked his eyelids open but could see nothing, nightmares still flashing before his eyes like some crazy merry-go-round.

"Ruslan?" he asked, his hoarse voice barely above a whisper, his throat painfully sore. "Father?"

"Yes," replied the man, a touch too quickly.

Cole reached in the direction of his voice, blindly searching the area around him with his hand. Someone grabbed him under his arms and hauled him into a sitting position. The fuzzy silhouette of a tall man with massive shoulders broke through the never-ending chain of nightmares, and Cole moaned, reaching for him.

"Father," he moaned, "can you make it stop..." His voice shook and faded as the painful visions intensified, and he brought his hands up, pressing the heels of his palms against his eyes.

"It'll get better in a moment, my child," replied the man, his voice sounding on Cole's right. "I just need you to do something for me first. It's urgent."

"What is it?" he asked. "I can't see you..."

"I am here."

Cole felt his father's hand taking his, his strong arm supporting his back. He relaxed, leaning into him. Somewhere in the back of his mind something twitched, and a little voice screamed that something was off, but Cole was too tired and too hurt to make an effort and listen. He could no longer scream or speak. Even thinking came with an effort. He was done with fighting, struggling, surviving.

"I need you to sign something for me." His father's hand took his, placing a pen into his fingers. "Just put your signature right here."

"What am I signing?" asked Cole, touching the smooth surface of the paper with his fingertips. His vision blurred, and the nightmares intensified again, now giving a splitting headache on top of the torment of his soul. He moaned, leaning forward, blood dripping from the corners of his eyes.

His father's fingers wrapped tighter around his, supporting his hand. "Just sign right here, and I promise, I'll make it all stop. Sign, my boy, so I can help you."

Cole moved his hand weakly, scribbling his name on the paper. With his brain on fire, he couldn't think or even care about what he was signing. He just wanted everything to stop, even if it meant his true death.

His father's supportive arm disappeared, and he fell backward, hitting his head against the hard floor. For a moment, he blacked out, and when he came to, the visions stopped. He was lying on the floor of the Queen's Council chamber. Mara, Morok and Roxana stood next to him, staring down at him with mockery.

"Roxana, darling," sung Mara, a satisfied smirk distorting her lips. "Thanks for the assist. We have what we need." She glanced down and kicked Cole in his side, ripping a weak moan out of him. "He's all yours. You can do with him"—she twirled her wrist—"whatever it is you vamps do with traitors."

Mara pivoted on her heel, grabbing Morok's hand, and they headed toward the exit. Before leaving, she halted by the door and turned around, giving Cole another once-over.

"And by the way, Cole," she said, poison dripping from her every word. "Your maker? Ruslan? Was that his name?" Cole didn't reply, staring at her with murderous intent. "Well, just so you know, baby-vamp. Your maker is dead."

She cackled, and for a moment, her youthful appearance flashed to that of an old, ugly crone. Following Morok, she walked out the door.

Roxana lowered next to him and ran her finger down his cheek, wiping away a drop of blood. She stared at the dark-red spot on her fingertip and smirked. "I'll deal with you after I address my Court."

"Roxana, wait," he whispered. "Tell me what they made me sign?"

"You'll be dead in a few minutes, along with the hunter you refused to kill for me." She shrugged indifferently. "Why do you care about what you signed?"

"Humor me." Cole sighed and closed his eyes. "Like you said,

I'll be dead in a minute, so grant me my dying wish and tell me what I want to know."

"Fine," replied Roxana with an indifferent shrug. "I don't know why the two gods needed it, but you just signed the deed to your house in Blue Creek, transferring it to some human... Jesse Williams is his name, I think."

CHAPTER 32

~ DAMIAN BLAKE ~

"Who the hell are you?" yelled Jamie. He grabbed the woman's shoulder, ignoring the sizable gun in her hand, but Damian raised his hand peacefully.

"I know her, Jamie. It's okay," he said, throwing an annoyed glance in the woman's direction. "We proceed with the plan. Finish the research and call me as soon as you know anything."

Jamie nodded and backed away from the car as the woman slammed the passenger door shut. Damian bent down slightly and gave Jamie a nod before pulling the car back onto the road and starting to drive toward Paradise Manor.

"You're driving in the wrong direction," said the woman, putting her gun in the holster.

He turned to her, annoyance flaring through him. "What the hell are you doing here, Ace?" he growled. "And how did you find me?"

She pursed her lips, shaking her head with reproach. "Either I am so good, or you're really bad at magic, Damian Blake," she muttered, gesturing for him to make a U-turn at the light. "Make a U-turn here. Trust me, Cole will die if you don't listen to me."

Damian grunted and swung the car to the right, parking it at the edge of an empty plaza.

"Spill it. Who are you and what do you know about my brother?" he asked through clenched teeth, leaning toward her with unmasked threat. "And don't tell me you're his programmer."

She rolled her eyes and snapped her fingers. A powerful wave of her magic washed over him, and he gasped, pulling back.

"I *am* his programmer. Anyway, it doesn't matter who I am or how I found you," Ace said quietly. Then she frowned, looking as troubled as it got. "Listen, Damian, can you just take my word for it? We're losing valuable time—Cole's lifetime. Turn around and start driving toward Paradise Valley. Queen Roxana holds him in her mansion."

Damian put his hand on the stick shift but then took it off. "I can't," he whispered, staring out the window over Ace's head. "River Evans is in danger, and it's my obligation to protect her. Cole is an old vampire. He can stand his own—"

"Not this time, you ignorant oaf!" Ace yelled, tears gathering in her eyes. She grunted, drying her eyes with the heel of her palm angrily. Turning in her seat slightly, she put her hand on his arm. "Damian, I'm sorry. I shouldn't have said that. Here is the deal. If you don't save your brother, you stand no chance of saving River. You can't do it alone."

"And how do you know that?"

"I just do," she said, desperate tones ringing in her voice. "I have my sources. Can you just trust me?" She bit her lip, frowning, and whispered, "I guess I'm on my own?"

Damian pulled his cellphone out and dialed River's phone number. As he expected, she didn't answer his call. He threw the phone into the tray between seats and slammed his hands against the steering wheel, barely keeping control of his power. *An impossible choice...*

Ace sighed. "Start driving, Damian," she said softly, taking his hand and placing it on the stick shift. "I promise, I'll tell you everything I can on the way."

Without saying anything else, he put the car into drive and took it back to the street, driving in the direction of Paradise Valley at full speed. "Start talking," he growled. "Who are you and what do you know about all this?"

She leaned back in her seat, staring straight at the dark road ahead. "I'm not supposed to expose my true identity to anyone, but I believe the situation calls for it," she started.

As a terrible suspicion started in his mind, Damian glanced at the young woman, swallowing hard. "Please tell me, you are not a Guardians Witch."

"No, I'm not." She smiled weakly. "I'm a Destiny Enforcer—"

The tires screeched, and the car drifted to the side as Damian slammed the brake pedal. Leaning across Ace, he opened the passenger door, unlocked her seatbelt and pushed the young woman out, fury surging through him. She fell on the asphalt, but quickly recovered and jumped to her feet.

Taking a few deep breaths, Damian growled, spitting one word at a time, "I. Hate. The Destiny Council!"

"In training!" she yelled, desperation making her magical energy spike around her. "I'm not a certified Destiny Enforcer yet. Just learning."

"Oh, that makes everything so much better," shouted Damian, slamming his hand on the steering wheel. "So, you're not a certified asshole yet. You're just learning how to be one. Forgive me! What the hell are you doing here? Did they send you to spy on me?"

She stomped her foot, putting her hands on her hips. "Self-absorbed much?" she yelled, stepping closer to the car and leaning down to see him. "When you decide to pull your oversized head out of your skinny arse, you'll realize the sun doesn't revolve around you, jerk! I was sent here to keep an eye on your brother and protect him! And right now, you're standing in the way of completing my mission!"

"Since when does the Destiny Council protect vampires?" growled Damian, his anger slowly simmering down.

"Since I have no idea!" grumbled Ace, folding her arms. "I don't question their orders. I follow them."

"That's the problem with all of you—the Destiny Council's flunkies. You just follow orders," he muttered, gesturing for her to get back in the car. "Get in and start talking. How long have you been serving as the Destiny Enforcer and who's your commander?"

"Just a couple of years or so," she mumbled, buckling up. "Under Commander Moore."

Damian shuddered at the sound of the name. "Aren't you the lucky one, serving under that oversized douchebag."

"Coming from an oversized douchebag, it's priceless," replied Ace snidely. "How do you know him, anyway?"

Damian didn't reply, staring straight ahead. "At least that explains why I couldn't detect any magic in you. You're a friggin' Destiny Enforcer. The first thing you learn is how to shadow your magical energy."

"How about you not being able to detect my magic because you're magically challenged," retorted Ace, sarcasm overflowing. "You're nothing like your brother. Nothing! He's everything you're not. He's kind, smart, strong—"

"And for the last thousand years, he has been on a liquid diet of human blood." Damian shook his head, throwing a glance at Ace, wondering how long she'd had a crush on Cole. "Anyway, don't you know Destiny Enforcers can't get emotionally involved with their targets or charges? You're magical law enforcement with the license to... do anything you must to complete your assignment." He chuckled bitterly and added, "No remorse, no mercy, no exceptions, no doubts."

"You're wrong," she said quietly.

"About you being sweet on my brother or about the Destiny Enforcers?"

"Both," she said, looking out the window. "And how do you know so much about the Destiny Enforcers, anyway? It is one of the most secretive organizations in the World of Magic. To know anything about them, you must be—" She cut herself off and stared at him, shock in her wide eyes. "Are you—"

"No," he interrupted her. "I knew someone who knew someone." He took an exit from the highway toward Paradise Valley. "We're almost there. You better start talking."

"Take this road," said Ace, pointing to a narrow private path on the left. Damian made a sharp turn, and she continued, "The Queen has been following Cole for the last few weeks or so. He knew it, yet he still did something extremely stupid. I'm wondering what drove him to do something so reckless."

"What did he do?" asked Damian, shivers spreading through him as if the temperature suddenly dropped.

"He met with the Arizona Master Warden," replied Ace, throwing her hands up. "He did it even though he knew he was being followed. So, the next day Roxana showed up at his company, and they had an unpleasant conversation behind locked doors. I have no idea what she told him, but she left him on his knees in his office, and he didn't look happy. A few hours later, he was gone." She reached into her pocket and pulled out a cellphone—Cole's cellphone. "I found it behind the Warden's bookshop. The last phone call he made was to you. Care to share with the class what that call was all about?"

"Heaven and Earth, Cole. Why would you make such a dangerous move?" whispered Damian, tightening his hands around the steering wheel. "This is exactly the reason I didn't want him involved in all this mess with Paradise Manor. He has no fear, and it makes him reckless."

"Did you ask him to visit the Wardens?" asked Ace, carefully shifting as far away from him as the limited space would allow her.

"Of course not," replied Damian. "I would never send a vampire to see any reps of the Destiny Council. I know better than that."

"Do you now?" murmured Ace, aggravation making her cheeks flush hot red. "Before you showed up here, Cole was doing perfectly well. Another month or two, and the opposition would overrun the Queen's rule, and I'm sure they would select Cole as their new leader."

"This could be the true reason why the Queen abducted Cole," suggested Damian quietly. "She found out about the gathered uprising."

"Could be. Doubt it. Cole was never leading the opposition. They were looking up to him and the way he dealt with all the issues vampires have while living among humans." She pointed at a small alley branching off the road. "Park it here. We'll walk the rest of the way."

Damian turned off the road and parked the car. Opening the door, he stepped out and slammed it shut. "I still don't understand why the Destiny Council cares so deeply about the situation in the Arizona Vampire Court that they sent a Destiny Enforcer here. As important as my brother seems to be to the situation in the Court, still..." He cocked his head, staring over the top of the vehicle at Ace with a cold smirk.

"You'll understand when you grow up, sweetie," murmured Ace, checking her gun and her sword in the leather scabbard attached to her belt. "Get your weapons."

"I don't need to get anything," replied Damian dryly. "Lead the way."

"I hope you're not planning to fight the vampires with bare hands, are you?" she muttered as she headed toward the private road.

Damian didn't reply, anxiety twisting his insides as he

thought about his brother's situation, blaming himself for everything that had happened to him. *I failed to protect him in 996, and now, I put him in danger by showing up in Blue Creek...*

* * *

THEY STOPPED in front of tall, iron gates. Channeling his magic, Damian quickly checked the entrance for mundane and magical security systems. As he expected, a modern state-of-the-art home security system was installed on the Queen's property. Besides that, minor wards were placed over the gates. However, neither human nor magical protection was enough to stop him.

"Stay close to me. I'm not powerful enough to keep you hidden from a distance," he whispered to Ace as he cast a cloaking spell, concealing both of them. "Let's try not to alert the vamps before it's necessary."

She huffed, looking heavenward, but didn't object otherwise. "I'm not afraid of a few vampires."

He grunted, wondering if it would be safer for him and Cole to just leave her behind. "You should be," he whispered at length, carefully probing the wards with his magic. "Didn't Moore teach you anything? He's losing his touch."

"He's not losing his touch, alright." She shuddered. "It's not the first time I have to fight vamps. I can hold my own against them."

"Not against the Queen's Court where she assembled the most vicious, the oldest and the deadliest of them all," he objected, straightening. "Why do you think Cole was always so careful? Just do me a favor and don't go happy-go-lucky when we're there. I can't help my brother and Sam if I have to worry about you."

"Sam? As in Sam Vetrov? Why in—"

"Shut up and let me work," growled Damian. Focusing on his

magic, he placed his hands on the gates and whispered, *"Rilekti Amnia."*

A soft, golden glow expanded from under his hands, surrounding the gates with a shimmering, yellow mist. Damian lowered his arms, observing the effect of his magic, and then moved his hand through the gate. His hand went through unobstructed as if the iron bars were no longer there.

"Go," he whispered, glancing back at Ace, who stared at him in awe, and added, unable to conceal his sarcasm. "What? Moore didn't teach you the basic spells?"

She muttered something incoherent that sounded an awful lot like 'self-centered jackass' and walked through the gate. As soon as Damian crossed into the Queen's property, his training kicked in. He sharpened his senses and moved forward, stepping softly on the sandy ground. Most likely, Ace noticed the change in him because she slowed down and fell in step behind him.

As they approached the stairs leading toward the main entrance, Damian stilled, holding his arm back to stop Ace. The front lights were off, but two brawny figures towering on either side of a tall, glass door were throwing deeper shadows on the wall of the building. A scent of demonic essence enveloped him, and he frowned. Demons weren't known to favor vampires, thinking of them as a lower species, so the presence of two demonic mercenaries at the entrance into the Queen's residence set his nerves on edge.

He was positive the demons could detect him through the basic cloaking spell. Even though he could completely suppress his magical energy signature, his heartbeat would betray his location to vampires, and his body heat would show his position to demons.

"Stay back," he mouthed, turning to Ace. She frowned, folding her arms over her chest resentfully, but catching his furious gaze, she raised her hands up and halted.

In one fluid motion, Damian manifested his dagger and crossed the distance between him and the demons, running up the stairs. As he expected, the demonic guards detected his presence immediately and twirled around, unsheathing their swords. Infusing the blade with his magic, Damian thrust it through the nearest demon's chest, and the purifying energy of Creation rushed through it, obliterating the host body before the demon could shimmer out of it.

His cloaking spell dropped, but at this point, he couldn't care less. Without slowing down, Damian spun around, meeting the sword of the other demon with his dagger. As the demon pressed down on the blade, his eyes burning with hatred, Damian manifested his second dagger and pushed it into the demon's stomach. The monster cried out and tried to back away, dropping his sword.

"*Illucious*," growled Damian, and a blinding light burst out from his blade, evaporating the demon.

Glancing back at Ace, he jerked his chin at the entrance, gesturing for her to follow. She stood dumbstruck, staring at the blazing weapons in his hands, seemingly too shocked to make a move. He frowned at her and carefully pushed the door handle down. The door opened silently, exposing a dark, spacious lobby. He slipped inside and stilled, straining all his senses.

Cold air touched his skin, and a wave of shivers ran down his back, raising goosebumps all over his arms. It seemed to be a lot colder than it would be from an air conditioner, but since vampires weren't sensitive to a change of temperatures, he didn't think the Queen would run her thermostat at such low settings. Clenching his teeth, he gestured for Ace to stay behind him and crossed the lobby, moving into a side hallway.

As soon as he stepped into the corridor, the scent of pumpkin spice invaded his nostrils, suppressing all other smells, and he halted, pressing the back of his hand to his nose. Without his second sight, in complete darkness, and with his sense of smell killed by the excessive use of air fresheners, he felt defenseless and exposed. Closing his eyes, he strained his hearing. He could hear Ace's breathing behind him, and he isolated this barely noticeable sound, focusing on everything else.

A soft movement from above alerted him that he was no longer alone. Ace gasped, but he didn't turn to look at her. Holding one of his daggers up, he channeled his magic through it, and it lit up with a bright white light. Loud hisses responded to the light, and a few shadows slid away, hiding in the remaining shreds of darkness.

"Vampires," whispered Ace, but to his overly stretched hearing, her soft voice sounded like thunder. He looked back at her, pressing his finger to his lips.

Before he could take another step, a man landed on his shoulders, appearing out of nowhere. Damian fell forward, pressed to the floor by the weight of his attacker's massive body, and his fingers unlocked, dropping the dagger. As the darkness enveloped the hallway once again, the vampire wrapped his arm around his throat, forcing his head to the side. Damian groaned with strain, struggling to free himself.

Somewhere behind him, Ace yelped, and the sound of clashing metal told him she was fighting, too. He seized his attacker's shoulders and then pushed himself to the side, smashing the vamp against the wall. A strangled yelp followed his move, and the vampire's grip loosened up a bit, which was enough for Damian to get him off his shoulders.

Rising to one knee, he punched the monster, crushing his jaw, and extended his arm, calling to his dagger. The weapon reappeared in his hand, and he swung the blade, slashing it across the vampire's neck. Dark vampire blood gushed from the wound, drenching his face and chest, but he ignored it and swung his dagger again, decapitating the monster.

Jumping to his feet, he saw Ace engaged in a fight with

another vamp. He thrust his blade into the vampire's back and hissed, "*Illucious.*" As the purifying light of Creation obliterated the vampire, he spun around. A few more figures separated from the shadows and then vanished, moving at a blinding speed.

"They're coming," he yelled, spreading his arms to keep Ace behind him. "Hold on to something."

He connected with the elemental power of Earth, and the entire house rattled like a flimsy house of cards. As he moved forward, stepping heavily and slowly on the thick carpet, the walls and floors shook and fluctuated, unbalancing and disorienting the approaching adversaries. They slowed down, but he still couldn't count how many of them were there.

Speeding up, Damian summoned his second dagger and cut into the mass of monsters, slashing and stabbing without looking where his blades were landing. The vampires screamed, their claws and fangs shredding his flesh, but he didn't feel the pain, his mind focused on getting Ace and himself out of this mess alive. Leaving behind piles of steaming ash, he made his way through the hallway and into an empty lobby. Quickly surveying it, he saw four closed doors and halted, wondering where to go next.

A whistle of a blade cutting through the air made him flinch and spin around, his daggers blazing in his hands. Ace stood behind him, her chest shuddering with laborious breaths. She pointed at a vampire's body turning into ash before his eyes.

"He came from above," she managed to say.

She was covered in ash and drenched with blood, some of which was undoubtedly hers, and he cringed inwardly, blaming himself for her getting hurt.

I should have left her behind. She is still in training. Not ready for fights of this magnitude... Who knows what is behind the next door... His fingers clenched the grips of his daggers, a muscle twitching in his jaw.

"Second door on the left," she whispered, her eyes sparkling with excitement. "Cole is there. I can sense him."

"You can? I sense nothing with all the blood, ash and pumpkin spice." He wrinkled his nose, wiping his forehead with the back of his hand.

She chuckled. "You wrinkle your nose just like Cole." Then she gazed heavenward and added, "Of course I can sense him. I can see him with my other sight, too. I told you—you're magically challenged."

He sighed. "What do you see there besides Cole?"

"A large group of vamps. Around twenty, but I can't be sure. One human," she replied softly, tiptoeing her way toward the door. "Two demons on either side of the door."

Damian caught up to her and placed his hand on her shoulder, stopping her. "We'll make a memorable entrance," he whispered into her ear, leaning down to her level. "Stay back."

Channeling his magic, he felt exhaustion settling in his shoulders but ignored it. With Cole's and Sam's lives on the line, he didn't have the luxury of falling apart. *The excessive use of magic and power drains me too fast... and after all this is over, I still have to return to Paradise Manor and see what's going on with River.* A thought sped through his mind, but he pushed it away. *I'll cross that bridge...*

"*Exitius!*" he roared, and the door exploded into a cloud of splinters.

Making the floor quake and the walls tremble, Damian crossed the threshold and immediately spun around, pinning both demons to the walls with his daggers.

"*Illucious,*" he shouted, and the blinding light emitted by his blades flooded the room, evaporating the demons.

Without any rush, his movements almost leisurely, he turned around, holding his daggers down. A group of vampires—all dressed in expensive modern clothes—shifted away from him, cowering in the corners. He had no doubt all these vampires were old and strong enough to give him a run for his money. However, for whatever reason, they decided to stay back and see what gives instead of fighting, and that worked perfectly well for Damian.

He glanced straight forward and everything inside him twisted with anger and fear. Queen Roxana stood next to a tall cage, holding Cole in front of herself, using his body as a shield. Sam was restrained inside the cage, but as his eyes fell on Damian, a semblance of hope changed his tense features.

Cole hung limply in Roxana's arms, and it was obvious that if she let go, he would've collapsed to the floor. As his haunted eyes met Damian's, a cold smile spread over his face, exposing his fangs.

"Hello, brother," he croaked in a raspy voice. "You sure know how to make an entrance."

"Shadow Slayer," whispered the Queen, her arms wrapping tighter around Cole's neck and chest.

"At your service," replied Damian, bowing, his bow filled with mockery. "But please, Your Majesty, don't belittle me. I'm not a slayer. I'm a hunter. I don't discriminate against any type of supernatural monsters. They're all equal in my eyes."

"All equal?" asked Roxana, her fingers seizing Cole's chin as she yanked his head up. "Does it mean you will hunt and kill your own brother?"

"What can I say? You got me there. I guess I do make some exceptions to that rule." Damian laughed icily. "Let Cole and Sam go, and I'll consider leaving you undead."

She cackled, twisting Cole's head to the side at a painful angle to force a scream out of him. "Take one step forward, and I'll rip your brother's head off his shoulders, and then I'll kill the old hunter." She glowered at him with narrowed eyes, her lips distorted by silent fury. "If you truly are the one called Shadow Slayer, then you know I can do all that faster than you can say 'slayer.'"

"Oh, I know that," replied Damian calmly. "But it's not going to help you." For a moment, his eyes locked with Cole's, and the corners of his mouth quirked up just a little.

Damian dropped his daggers. Before the blades hit the floor, he touched his bracelet, and the silvery whip materialized in his hand. Moving at a speed he didn't expect he could draw out of his exhausted body, he swung it, channeling all the magic he could gather through it to speed up its motion.

Roxana screeched something incoherent and applied pressure on Cole's head. The whip's thong hissed through the air, and the silver blades attached to its end reached Roxana, partially cutting her neck as the thong wrapped tightly around it. She yelped, her eyes bulging with fear. Her arms unlocked, and Cole collapsed at her feet.

Damian yanked the whip, and the Queen's head rolled off her shoulders, drenching Cole in her dark blood. For a split second, her body remained standing before slowly disintegrating into a pile of ashes.

Damian exhaled, just now realizing that all this time he had been holding his breath. Pulling the whip back, he wrapped it around his wrist, turning it into the bracelet. Then he crossed the room in a few long strides and lifted Cole to his feet, supporting him with his shoulder. The vampires, who gathered at the opposite wall, stood as still as statues, their glowing eyes staring at him and Cole without blinking.

"The Queen is dead," Damian roared, his chest rising and falling with heavy breaths.

A tall vampire with long black hair separated from the crowd. Approaching Damian and Cole, he took one knee and unsheathed his sword. Placing the tip of the blade to the floor, he folded his hands on the pommel.

"Long live the King," he yelled, bowing to Cole, and the rest of the Arizona Vampire Court followed his example.

CHAPTER 33

~ DAMIAN BLAKE ~

Every muscle in Cole's body tensed as he observed the Arizona Court kneeling before him, pledging their fealty, and for a heartbeat, Damian felt as if he was holding a marble statue in his arms. Then he lowered his head and whispered so softly that even surrounded by ancient vampires, only his brother could hear him, "Do your thing, brother. I'm with you all the way."

Cole's hand squeezed his shoulder ever so slightly as he acknowledged his brother's words. He straightened as much as he could in his condition and raised his hand.

"Please rise," he said softly. "I appreciate all of your support more than I can express at this moment." A soft rustling noise filled the small room as every vampire rose to their feet, sheathing their swords and daggers. "I need a little time to recover. In the meantime, we should start getting ready for the official coronation ceremony as soon as possible." He glanced at the dark-haired vampire and gestured for him to approach. "Luciano, we need other demonic rulers to witness the ceremony to make it official. Can you please contact Akira Ida, the

Queen of Florida, and Santiago del Castillo, the King of Nevada?"

"Yes, Your Majesty," replied Luciano with a bow. "I'll get in touch with them immediately."

Cole smiled, leaning heavier on Damian's shoulder. "Wonderful," he said, inclining his head. "You may go and let's reassemble here tomorrow at ten in the evening. We need to discuss a plan of action, and we need to move fast. As you know, a change of power never goes smoothly, and we don't want any unrest in our domain associated with it."

With respectful bows, the vampires left the Council chamber. Luciano, however, halted by the door and turned around, staring at Damian with interest in his slightly downward-tilted eyes.

"Shadow Slayer, my lord," he said, his voice calm and unemotional. "My King needs blood." His dark gaze darted to Cole, and for a brief moment, warmth suffused his angled features. "He's been poisoned with silver. He needs to feed to recover."

"Thank you, sir," replied Damian, slightly inclining his head. "My blood is always available to my brother if he needs it."

As Luciano left the room, Damian lowered Cole to the floor and sat behind him for support. Feeling his brother's body going limp against his chest, he only then realized how hard it was for Cole to stand on his feet all this time.

"What's Ace doing here?" whispered Cole, staring at her in shock as she used her magic to open the cage and set Sam free. "She has magic."

Damian chuckled, manifesting one of his daggers. "Long story. I'll tell you later. But you may want to know that if it wasn't for her, I would probably never have found you. At least not in time."

He brought the dagger to his wrist, ready to cut it open, but Ace stopped him. "Not you, Damian," she objected firmly, lowering to her knees next to Cole. "You must go back to Paradise Manor. You need your strength. It was my job to keep your brother safe."

Cole's eyebrows climbed up, but he didn't say anything.

"What about Paradise Manor?" asked Sam, his face losing all color. Massaging his shoulders, he approached Damian and halted, staring heavily at him.

"I don't know, Sam," replied Damian, helping Cole to readjust his position so he could take Ace's arm. "River left me a couple of messages while I was gone. I was on my way there when Ace intercepted me to help Cole."

"Goddammit, Damian!" Sam yelled, desperation and worry in his voice. "It was *your* job to protect her. What are you doing sitting on your ass? Go there. Now!"

Damian stiffened and winced as if Sam had just slapped him across his face, guilt flooding over him. "And I will, Sam, but I can't do it alone. I need help, and Cole is too weak to fight at the moment," he said quietly. "As soon as he's back on his feet, we're driving straight there."

"I'm coming with you," grumbled Sam. "Obviously, I can't trust you with my daughter's life."

"That wasn't fair, Mr. Vetrov," said Ace quietly, shaking her head. "Damian is a jackass, but he didn't deserve that."

Sam rubbed the back of his neck. "You're right. It wasn't fair. But what is?" He looked at the door, a pained expression in his blue eyes. "River's my little girl. She's my entire world."

"I can't even imagine how you feel, sir," continued Ace, "but I suggest you stay back and let Damian and Cole do their job. Even though you're a hunter, you're still human. In a fight against dangerous opponents, you'll be nothing but a liability."

Sam sighed and turned to Damian. With his shoulders hunched, he looked like he aged twenty years in one minute. "She's right. I probably should let you and Cole handle it on your own."

"Ace is going to take you home, sir," said Damian, looking at the old hunter with remorse. "I swear I will do everything in my power to make sure River is safe."

"You better, kid." Sam nodded and lowered to the floor with a strained groan, rubbing his knee.

"Ace, you should sit this one out, too. Please," said Cole, giving her a pleading stare.

She opened her mouth to say something, but then changed her mind and just nodded. Cole took Ace's hand into his, running his finger over the blue veins bulging under her skin. His eyes lit up with a hungry glow, but he halted, sending her a veiled gaze.

"Just do it already, would yah?" she grumbled, looking away, her face turning a sickening green. "Don't ask me if I'm sure or if I'm ready. I feel as if I'm some virgin you're trying to seduce while pretending to be a real gentleman."

"What?" asked Cole, sounding genially shocked. "You're not a virgin? Sorry, I can't have your blood then. I drink only the blood of virgins."

"Dumbass," muttered Ace, but a tiny smile touched her lips as she glanced at him.

"That would be Mr. Dumbass to you. Or actually, Your Majesty, King Dumbass," he murmured and then snickered as Damian slapped him on the back of his head. "Jokes aside... Thank you, Ace. For everything." He lowered his face to her wrist, touching it with his lips gently. "I'll make it painless."

As his fangs pierced her skin, Ace moaned softly and closed her eyes. Her features relaxed, her lips parted slightly, and her breathing quickened. Damian observed her reaction, thinking that her feelings for Cole were making the "pleasure" effect of the vampire bite so much stronger. But right now, it wasn't a good time to get into it.

A few seconds later, Cole let go and touched the tip of his fang with his finger, puncturing it. As a single drop of blood gathered on his fingertip, he brushed it over the wounds on Ace's wrist, healing them instantly. After that, he leaned back into Damian's chest and relaxed, closing his eyes.

"I'm sorry," he whispered. "I know we must rush, but I need just a few more minutes."

Feeling a persistent vibration in his pocket, Damian pulled out his phone and read Jamie's name and number on the screen. He answered the call, his chest tightening up with the expectation of troubling news.

"Damian?" asked Jamie, his voice coming edgy even across the phone line. "You were right."

"About?"

"Jesse Williams," replied Jamie. "He does have a connection with Paradise Manor and the founding families. I don't know how much time it took for my father to dig out this information, but it's all here. His birth certificate, the adoption papers... Everything."

Damian swallowed hard, a sense of dark and gloomy foreboding spreading through him. "Who is he?"

"He's the last living descendent of the Brown family," said Jamie. "The illegitimate son of Jonathan Brown."

"Son of a bitch," whispered Damian. "The power of the Brown's bloodline would make the Guardians' pentagram spell accept him as one of their own. All he needs is the ownership of his family estate."

"That's right," agreed Jamie. "All he needs is the ownership of the house or an invitation from River Evans to move in to Paradise Manor. But wait. It gets worse." He fell silent, a vibe of discomfort prominent even through a phone call, and then added, "Listen, Damian, I was trying to call you earlier, but since you didn't answer, I called Quinn Allerton without your permission. I hope you're not gonna skin me alive for doing that."

"What did he say?" asked Damian, chills surging through his spine.

"He said that the way the Guardians protective magic was set up, if Jesse gets the ownership of the Brown's estate or River's invitation, it would allow him not only to bypass the Guardians wards and protective spell work but also disable them if he wishes to do so."

Damian pressed his hand over his mouth, thousands of thoughts rushing through his mind. "That's really bad news... I think River has already invited him in, but I'm not sure she invited him to stay in Paradise Manor, or to—" He stopped talking halfway through the sentence, thinking back to the last message River left for him.

"Then you better rush. Let me know if there is anything else I can do to help," replied Jamie.

"Thank you, Jamie. I'll keep you posted," said Damian and hung up the phone, putting it back in his pocket.

"Who are you talking about?" Cole got up and swayed slightly as he turned around to face Damian. "Who needs the ownership of the old Brown's estate?"

"Jesse Williams. Why?" Damian rose to his feet, meeting Cole's widened eyes.

"Oh, God," whispered Cole, pinching the bridge of his nose. "I've made a terrible mistake..."

Sam's eyes darted between Cole and Damian, and a wild, hysterical laughter burst out of his lips. "Damian, your brother signed the deed, transferring ownership of the Brown's estate to Jesse Williams less than an hour ago," he managed to say through the outbursts of uncontrollable laugher.

"Dima." Cole threw his hands up, a desperate look on his face. "I was under the control of—"

"It wasn't your fault," Sam interrupted him, finally getting his nerves under control. "Damian, they tortured him until he didn't know the difference between illusion and reality. Two crazy Slavic gods, if you can believe that the ancient Pagan gods are real and walking among us, that is."

"Everything is real," muttered Damian. "After Mara attacked me on the way back here, I expected them to act." In a few words, he told everything that happened on his way from Chicago and everything Archmage Allerton had told him. "Cole, if you feel strong enough, we should get going." He glanced at his watch. "If Jesse is working with them, Paradise Manor could be under attack as we speak. We should get going." His voice trailed off, and he exhaled, turning to Ace. "Cole and I will take my car. Call a cab for yourself and Sam."

"You mean Uber," murmured Ace, reaching for her phone.

"Whatever you kids call it nowadays," Damian muttered over his shoulder, heading toward the exit.

* * *

DAMIAN DROVE TO PARADISE MANOR, flooring the accelerator pedal. Cole sat in the passenger seat with his eyes closed. He seemed relaxed, but a muscle working in his jaw betrayed his true state of mind.

"Dima, you're drained. I could feel your arms shaking while you were supporting me," Cole murmured once they exited the freeway and took the road leading toward Blue Creek. "How are you planning to stop two gods?"

"I don't know," replied Damian at length.

"We're flying blind, you know."

"But we're still flying."

Damian drove through downtown Blue Creek without slowing down, but once he took the path toward Paradise Manor, something changed. He couldn't say what it was, but he could feel the fluctuations of the magical energy field with his skin, and that made his hair stand on end. He had no illusions about his magical abilities—his powers were extremely limited, and he was drained after the fight with the Queen. So whatever magical mayhem unfolded over this area, it had to be so powerful that even he could detect it.

He glanced at Cole, and his jaw dropped. His brother leaned forward in his seat, bracing his hands against the dashboard, his unclad torso ripped with tensed muscles. His fingers turned into terrifying claws as sharp and lethal as any dagger. His eyes burned with a bright, scarlet light, and his mouth was opened slightly, displaying a set of fangs more spine-chilling than his claws.

All in all, the vampire looked ghastly enough to give a human a heart attack, but the only thing Damian could think of was that his brother was about to jump into a deadly fight not only without any armor but half-naked.

"Dima, can you sense it?" asked Cole, his voice a low hiss.

Damian nodded. The night became darker even though the sky was absolutely clear, and the temperature dropped significantly. He glanced at the dashboard and gasped. The outside temperature reading was showing twenty-nine degrees. The speedometer arrow crossed the hundred-fifty mark, but to him, it seemed like the car slowed down, barely moving.

The darkness became heavier, and he could feel its touch to his face and to the exposed skin of his neck and arms as if it was something tangible. It wrapped around his throat, making it hard to breathe. He squeezed the steering wheel, leaning forward, his moves torturously slow. All sounds dimmed down. He could still hear the roar of the engine and the sound of the air outside rushing by the speeding vehicle, but everything was coming like through a thick wall.

The surroundings fluctuated and shifted, coming in and out of focus, and he wasn't sure where he was or if he was still driving in the right direction. Cold sweat covered his forehead, running into his eyes, but he couldn't unlock his fingers to wipe it. The darkness spun around the car, pressing on his feverish mind. He opened his eyes wide but could see absolutely nothing.

"Dima, watch out!"

Cole's desperate scream ripped him out of his dazed existence, and for a split second, he saw the road and the wall surrounding Paradise Manor covered in a thick layer of ice and snow. In one swift motion, Cole kicked the door opened, wrapped his arms around Damian, and jumped out of the moving vehicle, covering Damian with his body.

CHAPTER 34

~ DAMIAN BLAKE ~

Cold seeped into his bones, making his entire body ache and shiver. Damian moaned and attempted to sit up, but just sank deeper into a snowbank. After a few attempts, he managed to scramble into a sitting position and then up to his feet. Turning around, his heart slipped down to his knees. Cole lay sprawled, partially covered by snow, a dark red splatter spreading beneath his body.

"Nikolai!" Damian wasn't sure if he screamed his brother's name or just thought it. Dropping back to his knees, he scooped the snow off the vampire just in time to see a few terrible wounds healing, the edges of cuts and deep gashes on his chest and stomach closing before his eyes. The corners of Cole's lips lifted just a little, and he opened his eyes, staring at his brother.

"Are you okay, big bro?" he asked, pushing himself up with his arms. "Do you need me to heal you?" His eyes lit up with the red glow of thirst, and he grunted, averting his gaze, pressing his hand over his mouth and nose.

Damian glanced down, just now noticing a few lacerations on his arms and chest below the torn shirt. "I'm fine," he replied.

Rising to his feet, he surveyed the area. The car had impacted the ice wall just a few feet away from where they were, doing it no damage whatsoever. Crushed into a useless hunk of metal, it sat deep in the snow.

"Damn," he muttered, rubbing the back of his neck. "Second rental car in two days. Jamie is going to kill me."

"I'll take care of the cost." Cole got up, shaking the snow and icicles off his hair. "We have a much bigger problem on our hands." He waved his hand in a wide arch. "The gates are there, but how are we going to get in?"

The entire property of Paradise Manor was encapsulated in a massive dome of ice. Running along the perimeter of the wall, it glistened dimly with the ultramarine colors of the night. Through the thick layer of ice, Damian noticed the outline of the building in the distance, and as far as he could see, it was still standing in one piece.

Placing his hands on the bone-chilling surface of the ice dome, Damian leaned forward and channeled his magic, carefully exploring and probing it.

"I can try to break it," suggested Cole.

Damian pulled away and shook his head, looking at Cole over his shoulder. "Even you are not strong enough to do that. This monstrosity is at least three feet thick." He moved his finger over the surface of the ice, drawing a glowing, orange outline of a door on it, using his elemental energy. "But between the two of us, we can do it, I think."

Focusing all the magic he could gather in his hands, he placed them on the ice dome again and murmured, *"Calidarius."*

A powerful wave of heat expanded around his hands, but he carefully controlled its spread, concentrating it within the outlines of the door he drew earlier. The ice started to melt, quickly giving up its stronghold to the assault of Damian's magic. Freezing rivulets of water ran down the wall, but a few seconds later, Damian started to shiver violently, the wintry cold chilling him through.

"That's enough." Cole touched his shoulder, making him flinch and let go. The vampire ran his hand across the area of ice partially melted by Damian's magic, and a cold smirk crossed his face. "I can take it from here."

Damian staggered back, holding his unbending hands up, giving Cole some space to work. The vampire approached the ice and gave it a quick once-over. Pulling his leg back, he applied a mighty push kick to the part of the wall weakened by Damian's magic. With a thunderous bang, the ice exploded inward, creating an opening big enough for them to walk through.

Following his brother, Damian crossed through the icy dome and halted before the locked gates. The security system was down, the monitor was dark, and the remote key he had didn't work either.

Another spell, Damian thought as he channeled his magic again, shaking his head at the effort it cost him. He touched the gates and whispered, *"Recludius."*

The lock clicked, but the gate didn't open, frozen solid. Cole pushed it with his shoulder, and something cracked, sending a cloud of snow-dust in the air. He applied more pressure, his biceps working under his sun-deprived skin. With a loud screech, the gate moved to the side, allowing both of them to pass through.

As soon as Damian crossed the threshold, he halted, staring around in horror. The entire space between the gates and the house was submerged under a constantly moving, shifting and shimmering cloud of black dust. The particles buzzed softly, emitting an overwhelming amount of dark magical energy. He clasped his hand to his throat and leaned forward slightly, struggling to breathe.

"Holy shit," murmured Cole. He didn't appear to be affected by the dark energy, but as soon as he took a step forward, the particles stilled for a heartbeat and then started moving in a counterclockwise motion, speeding their rotation with each passing second. The buzzing noise increased, filling the air with an even vibration, and the amount of dark energy they emitted tripled. A small cloud of darkness separated from the mass, lowering down. In a split second, they charged at Cole and surrounded him like an angry swarm of wasps, biting into his unclad chest and shoulders. He cried out and jumped back, wrapping his arms around his head.

The swarm pulled back, leaving bright red spots and blisters in places where they touched his skin. Even though the wounds healed almost instantly, Damian wasn't sure his brother could make it all the way to the house. Besides, he had no idea what kind of effect this dark magic would have on him.

Glancing forward at the dark shape of Paradise Manor, he exhaled, biting his lip. It was a bit of a walk, and he had no illusions—if he had to wield even the most basic protective magic all the way through, by the time he reached the house, he would be on his knees.

As if hearing his thoughts, Cole approached him, touching his elbow. "Dima, don't even think about it. It'll drain you."

"I have no choice. Just stay close." Instead of casting a protection spell, he channeled the energy of Earth, wrapping it around himself and his brother as tightly as he could. "Let's go."

Once he took his first step, the dark magical energy assailed him, pounding mercilessly at the shield he'd created. He groaned with the strain but kept moving forward, the ground responding with soft tremors to every step he took. Keeping the connection with his element through the thick layer of ice and snow was harder than he expected, and halfway through, he had to stop to take a short break.

By the time they reached the front entrance, sweat was running down his face and back as if the temperature outside wasn't dropping lower and lower. He halted in front of the door and pushed down on the door handle. It was locked and of course, the key couldn't unlock it.

"What the hell!" He braced himself against the door and dropped his head, taking short, uneven breaths. "I need to use more magic," he groaned.

"They knew we were coming. So, they did everything they could to drain you before they had to face you," said Cole quietly. Then he chuckled and added, "It seems to me, the two Slavic gods are afraid of you, brother. Care to tell me why that is?"

"No."

"Oh, well." Cole halted by the door, carefully probing it with his fingers. "Let's see if we can get in the old-fashioned way, without magic."

Before Damian could stop him, Cole threw a chambered punch, slamming his fist into the door. The wood cracked, breaking, and the door flew off its hinges, sliding over the floor with a thunderous bang. A wide grin split his face as he brought his massive fist to his lips and blew at it as if it were a smoking gun.

"Sometimes brute force is the best kind of magic, bro." He winked and crossed the threshold.

Damian followed him, all his senses stretched to the maximum. The frozen lobby was dark, a thin layer of ice glistening on the floor, and the barely noticeable odor of dark magical energy lingered in the air. The silver mirror hung on the wall, cracked and slightly askew. The plywood lay on the floor, broken into a few pieces, and the rune was destroyed, leaving the entrance into the left wing of the house unprotected.

The foyer table was crushed into a pile of wood and splinters, and a small, furry body lay sprawled by the wall, partially covered by all the debris.

"Gypsy," exhaled Damian. He crossed the foyer and dropped to his knees, lifting the cat's limp body. "Oh, no..." Gypsy's long black fur felt wet under his fingers, and when he brought his hand up, his fingers were coated in a thin layer of blood.

"She's alive," said Cole, touching Damian's shoulder softly. "I can hear her heartbeat. It's strong. She'll be fine."

Damian lowered the cat to the floor gently and got up, squaring his shoulders.

"Let's go," he hissed through clenched teeth, and anger boiled up in him, bringing some energy into his exhausted body. Without waiting for Cole's response, he headed into the dark hallway. He didn't run, his every step heavy and measured, but it took him less than a minute to cross the entire hallway. He stopped in front of the tall, double door and whispered the revealment spell, keeping it up no more than a second.

"Dammit," he muttered, shaking his head. "The wards are broken."

Cole exchanged a look with Damian, and a feral growl rumbled in his chest as he kicked the door open.

* * *

THE ILLUSION previously concealing the room was gone, but the set of glowing runes and sigils covering the walls and the ceiling were still there. They shone brightly and evenly, and Damian didn't need to cast a spell to see them. Glancing to the side, he recognized the Guardians' signature rune. It was still shining as brightly as ever, and that told him that the protective magic of this room was still intact.

Mara and Morok stood across the room next to the shimmering outline of a door. With their hands placed on either side of it, they were chanting in hushed voices. Jesse Williams was on his knees next to their feet. In his arms, he held River. Her face was relaxed, and her eyes were tightly shut, her long eyelashes casting dark shadows on her colorless cheeks. The waterfall of her copper hair cascaded down to the floor, sparkling with the reflected light of the glowing runes. Her chest was rising and falling evenly, and that told him she was alive. At least for now.

Damian's heart skipped a beat as he observed River's limp form, and his hands clenched into fists, pain coiling within him.

Both gods stopped chanting and turned around, a crooked smirk crossing Morok's face. Jesse raised his eyes, looking first at Damian and then at Cole, and a tiny spark of hope lit up his ashen face as he silently pleaded for help, his trembling fingers threading through River's hair.

"Well, hello, boys," purred Mara, her eyes lighting up with the purple glow of her power. "We were beginning to worry you wouldn't make it." She cackled and seized Jesse's neck, yanking him to his feet. "But you're perfectly on time."

River fell to the floor, her body hitting the tiles with a dull thud, and Jesse moaned, his face twisting as if he were in physical pain.

"Please, don't hurt her," he pleaded, his haunted eyes darting from Mara to Morok and back. "You promised that if I did everything you said, you wouldn't hurt River."

Morok glanced at Mara and let out a loud guffaw, slapping his giant hands on his thighs. He bent his knees slightly, lowering his head to Jesse's level.

"Do you know who I am, tiny human?" he asked, his deep voice bouncing off the tall ceiling. Jesse shook his head, mortified. "I'm the Slavic god of Lies and Deception." He smirked icily. "I lied. That's what I do."

Damian made a move to approach them, but Mara cackled and wagged her finger at him. Morok snapped his fingers, and a thick layer of frost rose from the floor, wrapping around his legs. His limbs became heavy, and he came to a sharp halt, unable to take another step, barely able to breathe. In his peripheral vision, he saw Cole, his face strained as he tried to break through the spell holding them in place.

The room around him darkened, and a chilly wave spread through his already frozen body, making his teeth chatter.

"Mara," Damian growled, barely able to unclench his jaws. "Let the humans and my brother go. Let's settle this between the three of us."

The goddess sauntered toward him, her melodious laughter ringing painfully in his ears. She approached him and ran her fingers over the scar on his cheek.

"Sure thing, babe. As soon as we get what we came for"—she waved her hand back at the glowing outline of the door—"I promise, I'll take you to my bed, and we'll settle it there whichever way you want for as long as you can perform." She laughed again, slapping his cheek slightly. "In the meantime, just stay here and enjoy the show until we're ready for you."

She grabbed Cole by his shoulder and propelled him across the room as though a two-hundred-pound vampire weighed nothing. Cole hit the wall with the back of his head and grunted, pain distorting his features. Morok moved his hand, and both Cole and River rose off the floor, sprawled in midair helplessly. He snapped his fingers, and two blades materialized at their necks, slightly cutting into their skin, just enough to produce a few drops of blood. Then he arched his eyebrow at Mara and gave her a curt nod.

Mara seized Jesse's arm and pulled him toward the Guardians' signature rune. She moved her fingers, and a dagger surrounded by a soft wispy smoke materialized in the palm of her hand. Offering it to Jesse, she pointed at the rune.

"Now, be a sweetheart, Detective Williams." She smirked, and her eyes lit up with a carnivorous glow. "Cut your palm with this dagger and then press it to the rune. That's all you have to do. A little painful but easy."

"Jesse, no!" yelled Damian, fighting against the restraints of the dark magic, his frozen body refusing to obey the command of his mind.

Jesse looked back at Morok, but the god of Lies just shrugged his shoulders indifferently, pointing at River. "Disobey, and the woman you love is dead."

"Jesse, if you do what they ask, you will kill us all, and possibly throw this entire world back to the stone age," growled Damian, trying to channel his power. A faint wave of elemental energy traveled through him, warming him up slightly, but it wasn't enough to break the dark spell.

Morok flicked his fingers leisurely, and the blade under River's chin dug deeper, a thin rivulet of blood spilling from under it. Jesse turned to Damian, guilt and torment reflected in his dark eyes.

"I'm sorry, Damian," he whispered, his lips barely moving. "I can't let them kill River. I love her. Her life is the only thing that matters to me... above this world, even above my own."

Goddammit... I was right the first time. He's nothing more than a man in love... Oh, this fucking idiot... Damian dropped his head, powerless to do anything to stop him.

Jesse took the dagger out of the goddess' hand and carefully cut his palm, sucking in a sharp breath at the touch of the blade to his skin. Throwing one more glance at River, he pressed his bleeding hand against the Guardians' rune.

The blood spread through the rune, coloring it a deep scarlet. The entire house swayed, and an ear-splitting noise rattled the walls, seemingly coming from every direction. Jesse dropped to his knees and screamed, pressing his hands to his ears. The rest of the runes and sigils shone brighter. They separated from the wall, and for a few short seconds, levitated in the air, glowing brighter and brighter. A blinding white light flooded the room, and Damian had to close his eyes to protect his vision.

The tremors slowly dwindled down, and when the light subsided, Damian opened his eyes again. All the protective magic was gone. In the place where the glowing outline of the door had been, a portal shimmering with bright blue sparkles rotated slowly in a clockwise motion.

Morok roared in delight, and the poisonous miasmas of his dark magical energy spread through the room. He turned around, his sinister eyes halting on Damian.

"Now, you, Child of Earth," he said, impatience and eagerness underlying his every word. "You must complete the enchantment."

"Me?" asked Damian, genuinely shocked. "First, what does any of it have to do with me? I'm not a Guardian. Second, why would I do anything to help you?"

"Oh, sweetie, I had no idea you were so thick." Mara chuckled. "But that's okay. I'll walk you through it."

Approaching him, she ran her fingers over his arm, and there was something so hungry and carnivorous in her simple gesture that it made Damian shudder inwardly.

"Do you see this portal?" She headed to the swirling cerulean mass and knocked on it. A hollow sound echoed through the room, as if the surface of the portal was solid, and she turned around to face him. "You didn't think Guardians would make it so easy without leaving a nasty surprise behind, did you? The portal is locked, but I do know how to unlock it. Do you, boy?"

Damian cocked his head, and a tiny lopsided smile appeared on his face before he could stop it as understanding dawned on him.

"I see," she said dryly and nodded to Morok. "Plan B it is."

Damian stiffened, his eyes darting from his brother to River and then to Jesse. Fighting the resistance of Mara's spell, he folded his arms over his chest, planting his legs firmly on the floor.

"You're not going to blackmail me, Mara," he said icily. "You're also not going to pull a trick on me like you pulled on Cole. You can torture me all you want. Neither physical nor mental pain will force me to submit to you."

"Sweetie, you're drained. I made sure that you'd use every scrap of your limited magic just to get here. You can't fight us. You can't resist our magic." She waved her hand to Morok. "You're talking the talk, but let's see if you can walk the walk."

The god of Lies seized Cole's neck and threw him to the floor, eliciting a furious hiss out of him. Holding his head down, he snatched the blade from the air and raised it, positioning it above Cole's neck.

"Are you ready to lose your bother?" asked Morok icily, and a wave of a winter breeze rushed through the room, ruffling Cole's blond curls. "Keep in mind, once I kill him, your charge"—he waved at River, a vibe of aggravation lingering over him—"will be next." He threw an arrogant stare at Jesse, his lips curling in distaste. "And this worthless worm will follow soon after."

"Damian, please," moaned Jesse, "do what they want. I don't care about myself. Do it to save River."

Cole looked up, and a dark smile split his face, exposing his fangs. He gave Damian a tiny nod and said just two words, "Brother mine."

Unimaginable pain twisted everything inside him as Damian understood his brother's message. Cole gave him permission to kill him or do whatever needed to be done. Making a split-second decision, he gathered every scrap of magical energy he had in his drained body and slammed his hand over the Guardians rune embedded into his shoulder, sending some of his magic through it.

"Magnus!" he roared, hopelessness and finality of his decision tightening his throat. "I summon thee, and if I've ever needed you to answer my summons, it's today, you heartless son of a bitch!"

A brilliant, white light engulfed the room, and thunder rumbled somewhere in the distance. A tight hold of magical energy, stronger than the energy of the dark deities, surrounded him, lifting him off the floor, and everything disappeared into blinding whiteness.

CHAPTER 35

~ DAMIAN BLAKE ~

"Hello, my child." A deep male voice rumbled over his head, sounding almost as chilly as Morok's winter magic.

Damian opened his eyes and saw a pair of perfectly polished white shoes next to his face. With a low groan, he scrambled to his feet and straightened his shoulders, gazing down at a man in a long, white robe standing in front of him. A tired smile crossed the man's face, and his unnerving silvery-white eyes slipped up and down Damian's body as if sizing him up.

"Magnus," said Damian with forced calm, locking and unlocking his fingers.

"Dmitri Chernov. Pray tell you had a good reason to summon me," said Magnus, separating his robe on the front to shove his hands into the pockets of his pants. "Or should I call you Damian Blake, by the way? I believe that's the name you're going by nowadays?"

"Call me whatever you want," said Damian, looking to the side to avoid Magnus' blazing eyes. "Just help me to..." His voice trailed off, and he swallowed, a painful wrinkle materializing between his eyebrows.

"Oh?" Magnus rose on his tiptoes slightly. "Now, you want *my* help?"

"Yes," replied Damian through gritted teeth, every word coming to him with an effort. He averted his gaze, staring down at his hands with skinned knuckles. "My lord."

"Oh, wow, Dmitri." Magnus narrowed his eyes, shaking his head. "You must be truly desperate since you called me *'my lord'.*"

"Magnus, please," whispered Damian, lowering his head. "After all this is over, you can summon me here and kill me with your never-dying sarcasm all you want. But time is of the essence now—"

"Here, time means nothing. When I brought you here, I stopped the flow of time in the realm of humans," said Magnus, "so we could talk uninterrupted and without hurry." He shoved his hands back in the pockets of his pants, rocking back and forth on his feet slightly. "Centuries ago, you fought to be released, and I've given you the freedom you desired so deeply, even though demands like that had never been granted before. What do you want from me now?"

"I need my power back. My full power." Damian raised his eyes, meeting Magnus' steady gaze.

"Why?" asked Magnus dryly. "To save that brother of yours who killed more people than you can count?"

"You mean my brother who has a Destiny Enforcer in training shadowing him? Your Destiny Enforcer?" retorted Damian, unable to contain his sarcasm. But then he raised his hands peacefully. "I would love to save my brother, Magnus, but he's not the reason I'm here now. Two dark Slavic deities are trying to access something that's hidden under Paradise Manor —the location once protected by the Guardians Order. Without my full power, I stand no chance of stopping them. I'm sure whatever the Guardians have been protecting there for a few generations has some kind of importance to the Destiny Council?"

"The enchanted lake." Magnus nodded, rubbing his chin. "Oh yes, my child. It's very important. All they have to do is walk into this lake to break all the curses and ascend to their full power." He smiled calmly, cocking his head. "But I still have to ask you, what are you willing to give up in order to get what you need to stop them."

Damian smirked, fighting a losing war with resentment. An image of Cole with a blade at his neck and River unconscious on the floor flashed in his mind, and he took a deep breath, suppressing his anger.

"Everything," he said quietly. "What I don't understand is why you're demanding a sacrifice from me when it's in your interests to stop Morok and Mara from ascending."

"When the time comes, you'll understand."

I hate the Destiny Council...

"Oh, I know that. You hate the Destiny Council, Dmitri." Magnus chuckled bitterly, shaking his head. "Anyway, let's get to business. Holding time still is not easy, even for me. I need you to prove your willingness."

"How?"

"You know how," Magnus said and raised his hand to stop Damian from talking. "I know—you don't bow, and you kneel before no one. This is why I want to see you do that."

Damian clenched his hands into fists, staring at the white ceiling, his chest rising and falling with strenuous breaths. Then he bowed his head and slowly lowered to one knee, pressing his fist over his heart.

"My lord," he said, his voice a hoarse whisper, his insides burning with indignation. "I'm yours to command."

Magnus approached Damian and gently brushed his hair off his face, exposing the scar.

"Hmm," he murmured, lifting his face. "I think after all is

said and done, I'll leave this scar and the ones on your back, too. I want you to have this constant reminder of all your failures, Dmitri." He stepped away, smirking, but his smirk wasn't sarcastic or arrogant—only sadness reflected his silvery eyes. "Yeah, I know everything you've been through after you gave up your power and assumed the *no one* status."

"You're not supposed to be watching me, Magnus," growled Damian, raking his fingers over his hair to bring it down. "That's the point of the *no one* status—the Destiny Council and their agencies are not supposed to have any records of my existence."

"Oh, they don't." Magnus waved his hand dismissively. "It was me personally. Sorry, Dmitri. You're right. I wasn't supposed to follow you, but I couldn't help it. I wanted to make sure—" He cut himself off and raised his hand, ready to snap his fingers. "Stay down. I'll be right back."

He vanished, leaving Damian on his knees. A few minutes later, a hidden door at the opposite end of the room opened up, and a tall man dressed in a dark tactical uniform walked in. He halted for a moment, his face alight with happiness. Then he crossed the room in a few strides and dropped to his knees in front of Damian.

"Dima," he muttered, stretching his hand to him. "You're alive. You're back. I thought I'd never—" His voice broke off, and his black eyebrows pulled down over his striking blue eyes.

"Cossack," Damian whispered, staring at his old friend in shock. "But how? Why are you here?"

His friend's real name was Adrian, but since by birth he was a Zaporozhian Cossack, Damian had called him that since the first time Adrian arrived at the Destiny Council training facility, and somehow, the nickname stuck.

"Magnus sent me," Cossack replied, his raspy voice hoarser than usual. "He said he wanted me to get you ready for the ascension. Is that true, Dima? Are you coming back?"

Damian nodded. "I have to. I have no choice."

"I'm sorry, my friend, but I'm just happy to see you." Cossack got up and jerked his hand through his black, curly hair uncomfortably. "You know what I have to do, right?"

"I know. Do it." Damian spread his arms wide, his fingers clenched into tight fists.

Cossack whispered a quick spell, touching his hands, and heavy manacles materialized on Damian's wrists, thick iron chains restraining him between two walls. Damian grunted, unlocking his fingers. Then in one move, Cossack ripped his half-torn shirt off, throwing it to the floor next to him.

"I'll be with you all the way to the end, my friend," promised Cossack, his fingers squeezing Damian's arm.

He stepped back and drew a rune in the air, using his magical energy. Pressing his palm against it, he whispered a summoning spell. Before he finished his summons, Magnus materialized next to him. He approached Damian and touched his shoulder.

"Are you ready, my child?" he asked, a hint of a smile in his pale eyes.

"Yes, my lord," replied Damian, bracing for pain.

Magnus closed his eyes and raised his arms, wielding his power. His entire body lit up with a brilliant, white light. Damian groaned, dropping his head, and immediately felt a gentle touch on his shoulder.

"Dima, it's about to start." He heard Cossack's words and nodded, taking short, uneven breaths.

The words of Magnus' enchantment became louder, and his light turned so bright that Damian could barely tolerate it even with his eyes shut. A powerful wave of heat surged through his body, settling somewhere in his chest, burning him from the inside. A growl rumbled in his throat, and tears escaped from under his eyelids. The burning in his chest became stronger, and soon he could no longer endure the pain.

Throwing his head back, he screamed, and every muscle in his body strained to the point he was afraid his bones would snap. He pulled against his restraints as the pain intensified. The walls shook, and thick cracks ran away from the brackets holding the chains.

"Dima, almost over, hang in there..."

Cossack's voice sounded somewhere on the outskirts of his mind, frazzled by the liquid torment flowing through his body, gathering somewhere in his spine. He screamed again, leaning back as far as the chains would allow him, feeling as if the muscles and the bones in his back were shifting and rearranging themselves.

The relief came suddenly, leaving him hanging limply in his restraints, sweat dripping off his face, running down his back.

"Adrian, remove the chains," Magnus shouted the command somewhere above Damian's head. "Dmitri, open your eyes, my boy."

Magnus lifted Damian's face, gently slapping his cheek. The pressure of the chains disappeared, and he was finally able to lower his arms. He opened his eyes and blinked a few times, everything around him blurry.

Magnus exhaled, relief suffusing his features. He placed his hand on top of Damian's head, channeling his magic through him. "Rise, Commander Damian Blake."

As the powerful magical energy of the Head of the Destiny Council surged through him, Damian got up to his feet and opened his arms wide, enjoying the sensation of his full power soaring through his body. Two giant black wings expanded behind his back, lifting him off the ground slightly. He threw his head back and screamed in joy, a brilliant white light almost as bright as that of Magnus himself exploding around him.

A second later, Damian lowered to the floor, getting his power under control. His wings folded and disappeared, and he kneeled before Magnus, pressing his hand to his chest.

"My lord," he whispered, his vocal cords painfully sore. "I'm yours to command, but please let me finish my work at Paradise Manor first. Mara and Morok must be stopped."

"Of course, my boy," mumbled Magnus, pulling him up. "Once you're done, though, I expect you to come back here. We must have a serious conversation."

"As you wish, my lord," replied Damian, his stomach twisting at the salutation he hated so much.

"Dima, if you need my help, you know how to summon me," said Cossack, a wide smile gracing his features, framing his eyes in a set of crow's feet.

Magnus waved his hand, and a portal shimmering with rotating blue sparkles opened up next to Damian. "Go do your job, Commander," he said calmly. "I expect to see you back with a report soon. Godspeed."

Damian nodded and walked through the portal.

CHAPTER 36

~ DAMIAN BLAKE ~

As soon as Damian stepped through the portal, time resumed its flow at full speed, but to him, it felt like it was moving a lot faster than normal. Disoriented by the blinding light Magnus' spell had produced when Damian summoned him, both Morok and Mara had lost their concentration. This short moment had been enough for Cole to break through the hold of their spell.

With blinding speed, the vampire twisted out of Morok's hold and disarmed him. With a sword in his hand, he moved into a full-frontal attack, positioning himself between the god and River. Morok roared, fury distorting his face. The dark fumes of his power rose around him, and the entire building shook slightly, responding to the god's anger. He met Cole's sword with his blade, sparks flying as metal hit metal.

Morok pushed up and forward, endeavoring to disarm Cole, but the vampire stood his ground, his feet planted firmly against the floor. For a moment, they both stilled, neither of them able to move their opponent, their glowing eyes burning each other with hatred.

Mara screeched furiously, rising a few feet in the air, and

moved her arms up, channeling her powers. A dark mist gathered between her arms. With diabolical laughter, she started to spin it. Faster and faster, it rotated, spreading the suffocating miasmas of dark magical energy. Jesse, who was still kneeling at Mara's feet, screamed, his face a mask of terror, his dark eyes overflowing with fear staring blindly into nowhere. She cackled, and thick tentacles sprouted out of the dark cloud she was wielding, wrapping around Jesse. He stopped screaming and dropped his arms, hanging lifelessly within the hold of Mara's spell.

Morok roared, increasing his pressure on Cole's sword, now pushing the vampire back. Cole responded with a terrifying growl as he placed all the strength he had into holding his position. Suddenly, Morok let go and pulled back, making Cole stagger forward. He didn't fall, but Morok threw his hand forward, striking him with a burst of dark energy. A howl of pain erupted from Cole's lips as he collapsed, pressing his hand to his stomach, dark blood spilling between his fingers.

River regained consciousness while no one was paying attention to her and jolted to her feet, staring around wildly. Noticing Morok reaching for Cole, she drew her gun faster than any quick draw cowboy in a western movie would, emptying the entire magazine of her Glock into Morok's head. An ear-splitting sound of gunshots broke through the pandemonium. The reek of gunpowder mixed in with the metallic odor of blood permeated the air. The god collapsed flat on his back, his body hitting the floor with a heavy thud, but his wounds started to heal immediately, pushing the bullets out of his skull.

All these events took no longer than a few seconds as Damian watched in shock the battle unfolding in the secret room of Paradise Manor. The sound of gunshots ripped him out of a momentary stupor. Channeling his full power, he stepped forward, and the ground trembled with the terrible power he was wielding. His wings unfolded to their full extent, and his eyes lit up with a blinding orange light.

He summoned his daggers and infused them with the light of Creation. As the weapons lit up in his hands, he brought his arm to his shoulder and propelled one of the daggers at Mara. The blade pierced her shoulder, pinning her to the wall.

The goddess howled, anger and pain combined with her power swirling around her like a purple, stormy cloud. She seized the dagger, but as its magic burned her skin, she screeched louder and let go, struggling to set herself free, but to no avail. Damian approached her and seized her chin, his fingers crushing her face.

"What are you?" she moaned, the purple light in her eyes dwindling down.

"I am..." He laughed, throwing his head back, the sound of his laughter terrifying even to his own ears, as for the first time in years he realized he could answer this question. "I am your worst nightmare... No pun intended."

He smashed her head against the wall, crushing her skull. Brain matter and blood splattered the wall, but he didn't even flinch, anger sweeping over him.

"Don't go anywhere," he growled, observing Mara's limp form with a dark smirk. He knew the goddess would heal in a few minutes, but it gave him a few minutes in which he didn't need to worry about her.

Turning around, he walked back to Morok, fury fueling his adrenalin and his power. The god rose to his feet, wiping blood off his eyes with his hand. As Damian approached him, his eyes swept over Damian's wings and his glowing dagger, and he stepped backward, his shoulders stiff with rage. Moving as fast as his brother, Damian threw a short jab, infusing his hand with his power. His massive fist connecting with Morok's chin, and the god staggered backward, barely able to keep his balance.

Damian closed the distance between them and punched him again and again without giving him a chance to regroup. Morok yelped, pressing his hands to his face, blood running from under his fingers. Damian swung his arm, placing the entire weight of his body behind a mighty hook. The god fell backward, hitting his head against the wall, and then slowly slid down, blacking out.

For a moment, Damian stood over him, glowering down at the deity sprawled at his feet, his chest shuddering with laborious breaths. Even though they were gods, both Mara and Morok were bleeding, and that told him Mara hadn't lied to him. They weren't in their full power. Nevertheless, he knew they would heal soon, and he had only a few minutes to disable them while they were down.

Feeling a soft touch to his shoulder, he growled and spun around.

"Whoa, brother, relax." Cole raised his bloodied hands, smirking. "It's over."

"It's not over," exhaled Damian, rage slowly abandoning his body, leaving him calm and collected. He extended his arm, whispering a quick spell, and a pair of handcuffs glowing with a dim, white light materialized in the palm of his hand. He kneeled next to Morok and restrained him, using the handcuffs. The god cried out, and his eyes flew open, the glow of his power slowly abandoning them.

"Are those the Destiny Cuffs?" whispered Cole, cowering away from him, his eyes wide with shock.

"Cole, I can—," started Damian, turning to his brother, but didn't finish what he was trying to say. Archmage Allerton, accompanied by Ace, Sam, and two unfamiliar women walked through the doorway, his attentive eyes staring directly at Damian.

A smile touched the Archmage's lips as he approached him. "I guess you're no longer *no one*, are you, Mr. Blake?"

"No, sir," replied Damian. He let go of his power and his wings disappeared.

"Commander," Ace whispered, looking just as shocked as Cole. She pressed her fist to her chest, kneeling before him.

"Holy shit, kid," mumbled Sam, staring at him in awe. "You cleaned up nicely."

Damian sighed, all this unwanted attention making his skin crawl. "Get up, Ace," he said quietly. "I'm not a Commander—"

"Yes, you are, my lord. Your wings are black," she pointed out, rising to her feet. Her eyes darted to Cole, and she pressed her hand to her chest, noticing his blood-covered body.

"My lord," Cole snorted, earning himself Damian's stern stare.

Allerton approached Damian, craning his head back slightly to look into his eyes. "Commander Blake, my mages and I will restore the wards and protection spells in this area if we could have this room for a few hours." He glanced down at Morok and smirked. "We can take care of him, too. Unless you want to deliver him to the Destiny Council holding facility yourself."

Damian shuddered, his eyes widening for a heartbeat. "I would greatly appreciate it if you could take care of them for me."

"Them?" Allerton's eyebrows shot up.

Damian glanced at the wall where he had left Mara pinned with his dagger and cursed, his anger igniting his orange eyes with a furious glow. The bloodied dagger with a piece of flesh dangling from it was still in the wall, but the goddess of Nightmares was gone.

"Goddamnit!" he yelled, punching the air. "How is that possible?" He rubbed his forehead with his hand, dropping his head. "I failed again."

Allerton pursed his lips, shoving his hands in his pockets. "Please define the word 'failed' for me, Commander, because surely we are not on the same page here." He waved his hand around. "Between the two of you, you and your brother managed to protect the most powerful and dangerous magical artifact. You stopped two gods who were a lot more powerful than a vampire and a man with the *'no one'* status combined. You saved the lives of two people and possibly the entire realm of humans, and you captured a dark deity." He took a short pause and sighed. "So, please, define the word 'failed' for me, Commander."

Damian smirked, exhaustion settling in his shoulders. "Magnus is not going to see it this way. The only thing he is going to see is that I let a dangerous deity escape back into the realm of humans."

"Magnus?" asked Allerton, tilting his head a little. "You mean Lord Magnus, the Head of the Destiny Council?" He chuckled, shaking his head. "Oh, Damian..." He gave him a quick tap on his shoulder. "Now that your records are no longer sealed, I know who you are. Please trust the old man when I tell you, Magnus will be happy to see you when you return with your report."

"Yeah, I still have to do that." Damian sighed. "But that can wait a few hours. There is someone I need to take care of first." He bent down and lifted an unconscious Jesse, draping his body over his shoulder, and then nodded to the Archmage. "We'll leave you to it, sir."

He waved for Cole, River, Sam and Ace to follow him and headed out of the room.

CHAPTER 37

~ DAMIAN BLAKE ~

Walking through the dark hallway of the left wing of the house, Damian whispered a short spell, conjuring a few light orbs. They rose in the air, illuminating the area with a shimmering blue light. The lobby stood dark and empty. The ice was gone, and a few large puddles spread over the floor, glistening with the reflected bluish light of the magical orbs.

He halted in front of the mirror and turned to his brother. "Cole," he said, taking Jesse's body off his shoulder, "can you hold on to him? There is something I want to take care of right away."

Cole grabbed Jesse and threw him over his shoulder, as if the man were no more than a sack of potatoes. Sam snorted, his entire demeanor showing just how little he cared about his daughter's partner and received a glaring stare from his daughter. Damian bent down and found Gypsy. Carefully lifting her in his arms, he opened his other sight and quickly examined the cat. Her body was still emitting a soft white glow. It was weak and interrupted by dark patches in places, but he knew she was alive.

"Damian... is she..." River approached him and raised her arm to touch the cat but then pulled it back, tears glistening in her eyes.

"No," he said tiredly, cradling Gypsy in his left arm. "I think I can manage a little bit of magic for you." Catching a scorching stare from Sam, he cocked his head, sending a reproachful gaze to him. "It's too late for that, Sam. Like it or not, both River and Jesse have been exposed to the World of Magic. There is no way back now."

"I don't give a damn about him." Sam shrugged, jerking his chin at Jesse. "But I wish River didn't have to know all this. The World of Magic brings nothing but pain and suffering."

Damian frowned, unease spreading through him as his eyes halted on Jesse's limp body. "I know you don't favor him, Sam, but I think he's mostly a victim in all this." He thought for a moment. "Actually, his only fault is that he is—" He cut himself off and smirked. "It's not my place to tell. I guess we'll find out in a few minutes."

He placed his hand over Gypsy's body and channeled the elemental power of Earth, gently circulating the healing energy through the cat. As a soft, orange light erupted from his hand, the cat stirred and meowed, opening her bright green eyes.

"What took you so long to get here, Sasquatch?" she asked, twisting in his arms.

He chuckled, shaking his head. "Traffic."

River yelped, her face lighting up with joy as she reached for Gypsy. Damian passed the cat to her and smiled, watching River squeezing her kitty in a tight hug.

"I'll forgive you just this one time," purred Gypsy. *"And only because you healed me."* She stretched under River's fingers. *"I must admit, as a Child of Earth, you're not that bad after all."*

Damian straightened and stretched his shoulders, just now realizing how truly exhausted he was. He headed toward the living room, motioning for Cole, Sam and Ace to follow him.

Once inside, he lowered himself on the couch and leaned forward slightly, rubbing his face with his hands.

"I have to leave in a few minutes," he said, watching Cole unload Jesse on one of the armchairs. "I think before I leave, it would be nice to get some questions answered."

He got up with a groan and approached Jesse. Placing his hand on his forehead, he channeled some of the healing energy of Earth through him. Jesse's eyeballs rolled under his tightly shut eyelids, and his eyelashes fluttered as he opened his eyes. For a brief moment, he looked confused and disoriented, but as his gaze settled on River, a mix of emotions crossed his features, starting with happiness and then slowly morphing into deep remorse.

"Jesse," said Damian, sitting down on the couch across from him. "Is there anything you wish to tell us?"

Jesse pinched the bridge of his nose, frowning, deep wrinkles crossing his forehead, and Damian noticed a wide streak of gray hair running across his right temple that hadn't been there before.

"It was true then?" Jesse asked at length, dropping his hand in his lap. "These two... people. They were..."

"Ancient Slavic gods," confirmed Cole, folding his arms. "Would you like to explain how you got involved with them?"

"I wasn't involved with them, Mr. Adams." Jesse's eyes widened, unmistakable fear distorting his face. He dropped his head into his hands, his shoulders hunched. "It started a long time ago," he continued after a pause. "Before Nick's death."

"What do you know about Nick's death?" hissed River, scooting to the edge of her seat, her hand moving toward the gun holster. "Please tell me you had nothing to do with that! You were his best friend! I trusted you!"

"No, River! Of course not!" he gasped, raising his hand. "I swear, I had nothing to do with that. All I was trying to do was protect you!"

"How is that?" she yelled, pain and anger ringing in her voice. "By opening my house to some ancient monsters? Or by watching Nick and his entire family die?"

"No, please!" he pleaded, leaning forward to touch her hand, but she pulled away as if his touch burned her. "River... I'm begging you..."

"Did they blackmail you?" asked Damian, seizing River's elbow and moving her hand away from the gun. "What did they hold over you?"

"They did," whispered Jesse. His words were barely audible, but in the heavy silence engulfing the room, they sounded loud and clear. "They held River's life over my head. There was nothing else in this world that would have forced me to do what I did." He raised his red-rimmed eyes, his lips quivering slightly.

"Speak," said River, her voice icy cold.

Jesse cleared his throat, his eyes sliding over the faces of the people gathered around him, finding no support in their frosty, reproachful gazes.

"The first time, they approached me a few days before Nick's death, but I refused to cooperate with them, ignoring their warnings and threats. So, they cornered me right after Nick's funeral," he started, staring down at his trembling hands. "They told me River would be next if I didn't force her to move out of her house. At that point, I knew these weren't empty threats. So, I tried my best to talk River into moving out of the house, but she wouldn't listen."

River leaned back on the couch, pressing her hands to her face, a soft groan of disbelief escaping her lips. Jesse sighed and bit his lip, clenching his trembling hands in his lap.

"Then Mr. Vetrov returned and brought"—he threw a quick glance at Damian—"him. And that made everything so much worse. I don't know why his presence spooked the..." His voice trailed off as if he had a hard time pronouncing the word that was supposed to follow. "I don't know why, but it seemed like the gods were afraid of him or worried about his presence. Since he seemed to lead a normal life, they ordered me to get him out of the way in a legal manner and sent some woman—Roxana, I think that was her name—to help me set him up for a double homicide and a kidnapping."

He glanced at Cole, but catching the murderous intent in his glowing eyes, he quickly averted his gaze. He reached into his pocket and produced the deed to Cole's house. Leaning forward, he placed it on the coffee table.

"Mr. Adams, I'll talk to a real estate attorney tomorrow and find out what I need to do to return your property to you," he said, barely meeting Cole's eyes. "I swear, it wasn't my idea to kick you out of your home."

Cole glanced at him with interest. "Did you know that the Brown's estate used to belong to your biological father?" he asked. "It's actually your ancestral home."

Jesse smirked, lifting his shoulders in a tired shrug. "Of course, I knew that," he replied quietly with a half-shrug. "I'm a detective. Did you seriously think I didn't research my origin? Anyway, I never wanted any part of it. My father gave me up at birth, and I wanted to have nothing to do with that family." He rubbed his chin, throwing a veiled glance at River. "I don't want their money, and I definitely don't want their home. The only reason I signed the papers was because of River. I would do anything to keep her safe."

He got up and swayed slightly on his feet. Approaching Damian, he halted and stared directly into his eyes. "Damian, I'm sorry for what I put you through." He frowned, a muscle working in his jaw. "I know it's a poor excuse, but I was scared." He looked to the side, pure anguish in the set of his tense shoulders. "I was terrified of losing River, and I didn't... I couldn't think of anything past that." He smirked bitterly. "I hated you because of all the complications that came with your arrival, but now..." He swallowed hard. "Thank you."

Damian nodded and leaned forward slightly, looking up at Jesse from under his hair. "Is there anything else you want to tell River?" he asked softly.

Jesse's mouth dropped, and his eyes widened, but he didn't say anything and turned to River.

"Yes, there is," he said, clutching his throat with his fingers as if he had a hard time speaking. "River, all the whispers you've heard in your house... and Nick's voice..."

"Yes," she croaked, rising slowly, her movements stiff.

"I did it to you. I'm sorry," he whispered, dropping his head.

River swayed, all color draining from her face, giving her a ghostly appearance. She opened her mouth, but couldn't say anything, her breath coming out in short gasps.

"What you did to my daughter," growled Sam, stepping closer to Jesse, his jaw set with fury. "I'm going to—"

"Sam, I can only imagine how you feel right now, but let him speak," said Damian, putting his hand on the old hunter's shoulder, giving it a gentle squeeze. "Just let him finish."

"I'll deal with him later," Sam grumbled but stepped back.

"When Nick was alive," continued Jesse, his normally bronze face sickly yellow, "he showed me something unusual about this building. The way this house is built creates strange acoustic effects. There is one place in the attic..." He pointed up. "I have no idea how to explain it. Nick didn't know either. Anything you say there carries through the entire building. A while ago, Nick left his keys in the office. He passed away shortly after, and I never got a chance to give them back to him, so I used his keys to get inside the house without River noticing me." He reached into his pocket and produced his cellphone. "On my phone, there are a few messages Nick had left before he died. I used his voice—"

He didn't finish his statement when River swung her hand and slapped him across his face. His head jerked to the side, and he pressed his hand to his cheek.

"I deserve more than that," he said, lowering his hand, River's handprint blazing on his cheek. "But I did it under duress. If I didn't obey them, they would kill you. So, yes, I'll take this slap and a lot worse just to see you alive, River." He turned around and headed toward the exit. At the door, he halted, and a pained expression shadowed his features. "I love you, River. I always have and I always will." He threw a haunted gaze at Sam, and an uneven smile twisted his mouth. "I would die for your daughter, Mr. Vetrov."

He turned around and walked out the door.

Sam cursed under his breath, and for a few long minutes, everyone remained silent, processing everything Jesse had told them. After a while, Sam glanced at his watch and shook his head.

"I don't know about you, kids, but I need my beauty sleep." He approached River and pulled her into a tight embrace, kissing the top of her head. "I'll see you later on today, daughter. Your front door is broken again, so I need to do some fixing. Besides, I want to see what's going on in that cursed left wing and if anything needs to be fixed there." He pulled away and offered his hand to Damian. "Now that you're an angel almighty with a wingspan wider than this room, are you still willing to guard my daughter and help me around the shop?"

"My status in the realm of humans has changed, Sam, so I have no idea what is going to happen in the next few hours. But assuming everything goes well, you got yourself a supernatural handyman." Damian smiled, shaking his hand.

"Angel my ass." Cole snorted. "He's a glorified supernatural jail guard. Ouch!" He hopped aside, snickering as Ace poked him in his ribs.

"At least I'm not on a liquid diet," retorted Damian snidely. "Oversized leech."

"Doofus," murmured Cole through laughter.

Sam and River exchanged a look, and a weak smile touched her lips for the first time that night.

"I have an angel and a demon in my living room, and they're bickering like two oversized teenage siblings," she said, her eyes sliding from Cole to Damian.

"Cole's not a demon, River," said Damian in full seriousness, arching his eyebrow at his brother. "He's a vampire. Demons would get offended if they heard you say that."

"And Damian is not an angel," said Ace, stepping closer to Cole. "He's a Destiny Enforcer. Not just any. He's a Commander." She kneeled, pressing her fist to her chest. "If you would allow me, Commander Blake, I should get going, too. I must report to Commander Moore in the morning."

Damian sighed. "Please don't kneel on my account, Ace," he said, gesturing for her to rise. "I don't kneel, and I don't expect anyone to do it either. You're free to go."

She got up and took Cole's elbow. Her other hand landed on his stomach, her fingers tracing the shape of his abs absentmindedly. Damian watched as his brother's muscles contracted, reacting to her touch, and a lopsided grin curved his lips for a brief moment.

Cole scratched the back of his head and turned to River, a guilty smile crossing his face. "River, I'm really sorry, but I have to ask you for a favor. I'm too tired to go all the way to Phoenix, and I can't go back to my home," he said, placing his hand on Ace's fingers to stop her from moving them. "Since Jesse is the official owner of the Brown's estate, I can't cross the threshold of my own house without his invitation. At least not until he transfers the ownership back to me. Would you mind giving me shelter for tonight?"

"It'll take some time to get used to all this magic stuff," mumbled River, staring at him in awe. "Vampires are actually real." She shook her head as if trying to chase some troublesome thoughts away. "Yes, of course, Cole. Stay for as long as you need."

"I have to go back to the Destiny Council," Damian said, addressing Cole. "I have no idea how long they're going to hold me there, but I'll try to return as soon as possible. In the meantime, why don't you take my room."

"Watch your back, Dima," Cole muttered, all humor gone from his eyes. "See me as soon as you come back. Any time, day or night." He wished a good night to River and followed Sam and Ace out of the living room.

CHAPTER 38

~ DAMIAN BLAKE ~

After everyone had left, River made her way closer to Damian. She halted in front of him, her gaze traveling up his body, not quite reaching his eyes. He stood silently, giving her a chance to speak first.

"Dima?" she asked softly, finally meeting his eyes. "Is that your real name?"

He smiled down at her. "My childhood nickname," he explained. "My real name is Dmitri, but you probably know how Slavic names are." He shrugged almost apologetically. "Every name has one hundred and one nicknames and endearments."

"I like it," she said, averting her gaze. "Can I call you that?"

"You like it better than Day?" he asked, referring to the nickname she had given him, a thin layer of sarcasm prominent in his voice despite his effort to hide it.

"Uh-huh." Her pale cheeks turned slightly pinker, making her blue eyes shine as she nodded.

Damian glanced at Gypsy, and a wild thought crossed his mind. "I know it's around five in the morning, but... are you up for a little adventure?"

"A little adventure? I think after everything that has happened here in the last few weeks I'm adventured-out. But what do you have in mind?" She glanced at him, her face lighting up with excitement, and for a heartbeat, she reminded him of a child waiting for a Christmas miracle.

"You heard me talking to Cole," he said, his chest growing tighter at the thought of returning to the Destiny Council. "I have to leave, and it could be a while before I come back."

"How long?"

"I don't know," he replied honestly. "Could be a few hours or a few months. I truly have no idea. So, before I leave, I wanted to fulfill a promise I made to our mutual friend, and I was wondering if you'd like to accompany us." He pointed at Gypsy, making River burst out laughing.

"You promised something to a cat," she said through fits of laughter. He nodded, and she stopped laughing, staring at him, flabbergasted. "Oh... You really *can* talk to cats." It wasn't a question. She just stated the fact. "I would love to go with the two of you. Where are we going?"

Gypsy perked up her ears and tilted her head, staring at Damian without blinking. *"Finally,"* she purred. *"Get moving, peasant. Chop-chop. We Queens don't like to wait."*

Damian smiled and tapped his shoulder. "Gypsy, up," he said. "And this time, do try not to scratch me."

"Hehehe. We'll see how you behave, Sasquatch." Gypsy gathered her body into a tight ball of muscles and leaped up from the couch, landing softly on his shoulder. *"Now, let's go. Mush!"*

"I'm going to kill this cat," he murmured, laughter bubbling up in his chest.

"Not if you want to wake up the next morning with all your body parts attached," supplied River, staring up at Gypsy towering on Damian's shoulder with a smug look. "Let's go then?"

He smirked. "We're not walking. Hold on to me tight."

"Huh? You know you're covered in blood and God knows what else." She gaped at him for a moment, but then waved her hand dismissively. "Are we flying? You have those giant wings..."

He shuddered. "Perun almighty, no. I hate those things."

"You're so backward, Dima. People dream about having wings, of flying." She laughed, her eyes twinkling with curiosity.

"Not this person. The farther I am from Earth, the weaker I am. The wings are a part of the Destiny Enforcer's benefits package, but I hardly ever use them." He shrugged.

"Can I at least see them one more time?"

He closed his eyes and channeled his power, allowing it to run freely through him. His body lit up with a soft, white glow, and two giant black wings unfolded behind his back. He brought them closer but didn't fold them completely.

She exhaled, pressing her hand to her chest. "Do you have the faintest idea of how magnificent you... um... your wings look? What if I pull a feather out?"

"Ouch. Please, don't do it. I feel my wings just like I feel any other part of my body." He glanced at her, feeling strangely vulnerable.

River made a half-circle around him, her fingers brushing over the shiny black feathers. She halted behind him and a constrained gasp followed by the soft touch of her fingers to his bare back made him flinch and spin around, forgetting about the cat on his shoulder. Gypsy hissed and expanded her claws to keep her balance, but he barely registered the pain. He let go of his power, and the wings vanished, leaving him feeling more vulnerable and self-conscious than before.

"I'm sorry. I didn't mean to..." Her voice trailed away, and she swallowed hard. "Let's get going. Gypsy is waiting." She wrapped her arms around his waist, placing her head on his chest. Her hair fell over his arm as he encircled her shoulders, holding her tight.

"Close your eyes, River," he said gently. Raising his free

hand, he snapped his fingers, and they vanished from Paradise Manor.

* * *

THEY MANIFESTED at the foot of a large rock formation a few miles away from Paradise Manor. The sky just started to lighten up, the grayish colors of the approaching sunrise breaking into the dark ultramarine shades of the night. The air, cool with the morning freshness, was infused with the sweet scent of dirt and a light fragrance of vegetation.

"Freedom!" yelled Gypsy. She leaped down from Damian's shoulder and bolted toward the mountains.

"Hey, Gypsy, don't go too far," he yelled after her. "A jackalope may get you."

"The only jackalope here is you." Gypsy snickered without slowing down. *"Use the 'alone' time creatively. It's all sooooooo disgustingly romantic."* She hopped on a rock and glanced back at him, her green eyes shining brightly in the dim light of the early morning, and he could swear the cat winked at him before disappearing from view.

Damian suppressed the desire to roll his eyes at Gypsy's silly suggestion, but all of a sudden, he became too aware of River's arms still wrapped around his bare torso. He grunted and stepped back, lowering on a large boulder. She turned to face him, her eyes searching his face as if she expected him to say something. Since he remained silent, she sat down next to him and leaned forward, propping her elbows on her knees.

"What is a Destiny Enforcer?" she asked at length without looking at him.

He glanced at her sideways, wondering how to explain it to her. "Something I've never wanted to be." He rubbed his cheeks with his hand, feeling his overgrown stubble under his fingers. "You're too new to magic and everything surrounding it, and it's practically impossible to explain, but for the lack of a better word, I'm a supernatural cop, enforcing the laws of the World of Magic."

She nodded, turning in his direction slightly. "So, we're in the same line of business then. Sort of."

"Yeah, sort of," he agreed.

"Dima, why do you have to leave?" she asked, a shy smile gracing her face. "Sorry, I sound like a child."

He didn't reply right away, staring at the horizon where the first rays of sunrise colored the sky in pink and yellow shades.

"River, I know it's hard to believe, but I'm over a thousand years old. My connection with the elemental energy of Earth makes me immortal," he said after a while, giving her a tentative look from under the long strands of his hair. To his surprise, she didn't react with shock or fear, instead gazing at him attentively, and he continued, "As a human, I died in the year of nine hundred ninety-six. After my death, I was brought back by the Destiny Council to serve as a Destiny Enforcer."

He fell silent, rubbing the back of his neck. She placed her hand on his shoulder, caressing him slightly, and everything inside him flipped upside down. He already forgot the last time when someone had shown him any kind of support and affection, and to him, this simple friendly gesture seemed almost jarring.

"After a few centuries, I asked to be discharged," he continued, his vocal cords barely functioning.

"But why?" she asked, genuinely shocked.

His fingers found his bracelet, rubbing its edge nervously. "Doesn't matter," he replied. "I asked to leave, and they granted my request, but at a high price. I had to give up most of my powers and assume the *no one* status. It's like a non-disclosure agreement on steroids. Because of it, I was forced to lead... er... a certain lifestyle. To be honest, it wasn't easy, but at the time, I just didn't want to have anything to do with the Destiny Council, and I gladly paid the price they demanded." He raked his fingers through his hair and lowered his hand, rubbing his knuckles with his thumb. "Until yesterday, that is. So, now I'm back with the Destiny Council, and their first demand was for me to return to their headquarters as soon as I get Mara and Morok under control. So, I have no choice. I have to go. It's similar to a military chain of command, you know?"

He got up, searching the area for the cat.

"I'm sorry," she whispered, her eyes widening. "Because of me, you had to—"

He looked down at her, shaking his head. "I always knew it would happen sooner or later, anyway," he objected. "It's not your fault." Turning toward the mountains, he called to the cat, infusing his voice with his magic. "Gypsy, come on back. It's time for us to go."

River got up and stepped on the rock they'd been sitting on a moment ago, her eyes almost on the same level with his. Gently, she brushed his hair back and pressed her lips to his unshaven cheek, holding his face in her hands. A jolt of electricity rushed through him as his body reacted more eagerly than he expected. His arms moved up slightly of their own accord, but he stopped himself from embracing her, barely breathing under her touch.

"Thank you, Damian," she said. "I don't know how I can ever repay you for everything you've done for me. My house is always open to you. I know your brother owns a giant estate just a few yards away, but if you decide to live in Blue Creek when you return, I hope you'll choose to stay in Paradise Manor."

"Thank you." He nodded, staring into the space above her head. "I will come back. Hopefully soon. But I'm no longer a free man, and I don't know what the future holds for me now. The Destiny Council used to send me all over the realm of humans and other magical worlds on their missions."

"There are more worlds than one?" asked River, but then

lifted her shoulder in a slight shrug. "Sorry, I should stop asking these kinds of questions. Like you said earlier—everything is real."

He glanced in the direction of Paradise Manor wistfully. Gypsy came trotting from behind the mountain and rubbed against his legs, her thick, black fur covered in dust and dirt.

"So?" she purred. *"Was my mistress pleased with your—"*

"Gypsy," growled Damian warningly. "It's in your best interest not to finish that statement."

"Aw... you're such a gentleman." The feline snickered and hopped on his shoulder. *"Don't worry, you'll perform—"*

"Gypsy!" he yelled.

"First time is a learning exper-r-r-ience. Third time is a char-r-r-m..."

"Heaven and Earth, Gypsy." He threw his hands up. "You are supposed to be a house kitty. Wash your mouth out with some serious soap!"

River laughed, watching him talk to the cat. "I don't even want to ask what she said to you."

"I think it would be better if you didn't." Damian offered her a hand and when she took it, he pulled her closer. "Hold on tight."

She encircled his waist and placed her head on his chest, her warm breath caressing his skin. He took a deep breath and snapped his fingers, teleporting them back into the living room of Paradise Manor.

From his shoulder, Gypsy hopped onto the couch and curled up into a furry ball embellished by dust, hiding her nose under her bushy tail. To his relief, she was either too tired or decided to keep her smart-ass remarks for the next occasion.

For a few seconds, River didn't move, keeping her tight embrace, and he wasn't sure if he should pull away or say something to her. The sun was up, beating happily through the wide window, and with deep regret, he knew it was time for him to leave. In reality, he should have left as soon as Archmage Allerton had arrived, and he had no doubt Magnus would have something to say about it.

A heavy sigh escaped his lips, and as his chest moved under River's cheek, she raised her head, gazing up into his eyes.

"Damian, I know you have to go," she said, pulling away finally. "But before you go, there is something I wanted to tell you." She stilled, looking slightly troubled and lost. "If you repeat my words to anyone, I'll get Gypsy to deal with you." She chuckled, but the sadness never left her blue eyes.

"Your secrets are safe with me, my lady," he replied with a tiny bow.

She rolled her eyes, whispering something that sounded like *'archaic jackass'*. Her hand went up to his chest, but she didn't actually touch him, holding her fingers close enough for him to feel the heat emanating from her palm.

"Since Nick's death, I've been living in some perpetual nightmare," she said quietly, her full lips quivering slightly. "I felt like I was in some sort of dark void, and I kept falling and falling, unable to think, to stop the fall, to live. I went to work, came back home, took care of Gypsy—everything like on autopilot."

She fell silent and a deep wrinkle appeared between her copper eyebrows. Damian took her hand and squeezed slightly.

"You probably did live in a nightmare, River," he said gently. "After all, the Slavic goddess of Darkness and Nightmares was after you. I'm sure the way you felt was induced by her magic. You should feel better now that she's gone."

"Maybe," she agreed after a moment, but her eyes spoke otherwise. "The first moment you arrived at Paradise Manor, everything changed. That night when you guarded me, falling asleep on the floor by my door..." Her voice disappeared into silence, her gaze becoming distant as she traveled back in her memory. "For the first time since my husband's death, I felt safe.

I felt like that nightmarish infinite loop was broken, and I was no longer falling."

Shifting from foot to foot slightly, he had no idea what to tell her. As the pause grew longer, she smiled, taking her hand out of his grip.

"You don't need to say anything, Damian," she continued. "I just wanted you to know…" She swallowed hard, looking out the window at the view of the morning desert, and added sounding firm, "Wherever you're going now, I want you to know that if you want it, you have a home, and one person and a cat who're waiting for your return."

"Yeah, what she said," murmured Gypsy, lifting her head. *"She can definitely use you when she needs to move a couch or change a light bulb."* She yawned, showing her fangs, and then settled back to sleep, a blissful feline smirk on her face.

"Thank you," he said to River, his throat constricted, pain and warmth fusing somewhere in his chest.

He took her hand and bent down to it, kissing her knuckles gently. He straightened and let go of her. With one wave of his hand, he opened a portal and smiled at her.

"I don't know when, but I will return, River. That, I promise."

Turning around, he walked through the portal.

One day.

EPILOGUE

* * *

~ Damian Blake ~
The Destiny Council Realm

As soon as Damian walked out of the portal, he was met by one of the Junior Enforcers. It was a young man, no more than twenty by the looks of him, but Damian knew better—looks in the World of Magic could be deceiving. However, since he still wore the gray uniform of a Junior Enforcer, it meant he hadn't completed his initial training. The young man stared at Damian in awe for a brief moment but then gathered his wits and bent down in a low bow.

"Lord Commander, please allow me to show you to your chambers."

"Thank you," replied Damian, wincing at the salutation.

As the Junior Enforcer led him through a chain of brightly lit hallways with identical white doors lined up on each side, the only thing he could think of was that a few centuries later, nothing had changed here. The hairs on the back of his neck stood on end as the old memories he worked so hard to keep down flooded his mind.

The young man stopped in front of a door and bowed again. "Commander Blake," he said, pointing at the door. "Your room is all set for you. In your closet, you'll find your uniform, armor, and a few sets of civilian clothes." He took in Damian's state of undress, and a bright grin split his face. "Lord Magnus said you'd need a shower and fresh set of clothes." Since Damian didn't smile back, he sobered up and added, "As soon as you're ready, please summon me, so I can escort you to see him. He's expecting you."

Shivers ran down Damian's back, but he just smiled and nodded. "Thank you, but I still remember my way around the facility. I know where Lord Magnus' office is. I'll see him as soon as I'm ready."

He waited until the young man turned the corner, disappearing from view, and then pushed the door open. The bitter odor of Turkish tobacco hit his nose as soon as he crossed the threshold, and the corners of his mouth twitched in a smile.

Cossack lay on his bed, his feet up on the small table positioned next to it. His black shirt was unbuttoned on his chest, and with a smoking pipe in his hand, he looked relaxed, at ease. Glancing at Damian, a smile hid in his thick, black mustache.

Damian crossed the room and sat down on a chair across the table, waving his hand through the air to dispel the smoke.

"I can't believe you still smoke," he said, wrinkling his nose. "A filthy habit, my friend."

Cossack put the pipe away, slowly exhaling a cloud of smoke. "Being an immortal Destiny Enforcer has some perks." He smirked, but there was some bitterness in the set of his lips. "I don't have to worry about lung cancer."

Damian inclined his head. "That's true."

Cossack sat up and propped his elbows on the table, leaning forward slightly. "Dima," he said softly. "I know, it probably wasn't an easy decision for you to come back, but for what it's worth, I'm happy to see you, old friend."

"Me too," muttered Damian, exploring the room.

With satisfaction, he noticed that it was set up in exactly the same way as his former room was, including a small wine cabinet. For a moment, he considered opening a bottle of whatever the strongest alcohol was available, but then changed his mind, choosing to have a clear mind for the conversation with Magnus.

"First things first." He slapped his hands on his lap, straightening up. "I need to clean up and report to Magnus. Let me get the unpleasantries out of the way, and then we can get together and catch up."

Cossack put the pipe in the corner of his mouth and inhaled, sly twinkles dancing in his blue eyes. "Unpleasantries, eh?"

"I'm sorry if I don't have warm fuzzies toward him after what he's done to me," muttered Damian.

"Are you sure it was him, Dima?" asked Cossack, blowing out another thick cloud of smoke.

"Who else? After they stripped my powers, I was weaker than a baby, and they threw me back into the human realm in the same place and time where she..." His voice cut off, and he grunted, staring at the door. "Her body was gone, but all the monsters were still there." He laughed without mirth. "They did a number on me, and I didn't have the power to heal myself. Self-healing was the first power they took from me."

He got up and turned around, showing his scarred back to his friend.

"Let me ask you again, Dima," repeated Cossack calmly once Damian sat back down. "Are you sure it was Magnus who threw you to the monsters while you were weak and helpless?"

"Who else? He was the Master Commander of the Destiny Enforcers Division at the time." Damian leaned forward, narrowing his eyes at his friend. "What do you know, Cossack? Spit it out."

"I can't be a hundred percent positive, of course," Cossack started, his fingers fidgeting with the pipe, "but one thing I know for sure. Magnus fought for you, even though he was just some minor member of the Destiny Council at the time, my friend. While he realized the limitations of the status you agreed to, he tried to get the Council to preserve most of your powers. Needless to say, he lost the battle, but he's never abandoned you."

"What do you mean?" asked Damian, unease coiling in the pit of his stomach.

"You do still have your Enforcer's daggers, don't you?" Cossack cocked his eyebrows. "How do you think that happened? If they stripped all your privileges and most of your powers, turning you into nothing more than a human hunter, why would they leave such deadly and powerful weapons in your possession?"

Damian froze in place, thousands of thoughts crowding his mind. Over the centuries, he had gotten used to his daggers. They were practically a part of him, obeying his every mental command. He'd never asked this question or considered a possibility that they could have been taken away.

"Dammit," he whispered, feeling lost.

"I thought as much." Cossack shook his head. "There is one more thing you should know. Magnus summoned me right after they stripped your powers. He made me swear that no one at any level of the Destiny Council would ever find out about that. Before the Council sealed all your records and severed all connections with you, he sent me after you, my friend. To protect you. How did you think you survived all those monsters when you couldn't even walk?"

"I can't die? Immortal and all."

"Yeah, that you are, and all those years of your long life

didn't make you any smarter, did they?" replied Cossack snidely. "You *can* die a human death, dumbass, and your death at the claws of those monsters would have been pure torture. The elemental Earth would bring you back to life. I don't argue with that. But if you think your back looks terrifying now, imagine how you would have looked if the monsters finished their job. Without your self-healing power, you'd look like a monster yourself." He fell silent, his jaw clenched. "Anyway, I went after you. I was alone, but I did what I could to protect you. Once it was over, I made sure someone found you and took care of you until you were back on your feet."

"Thank you," whispered Damian, unable to speak louder than a hoarse whisper.

"Don't thank me, my friend." Cossack got up heavily and headed toward the door but halted there with his hand on the door handle. "When you see Magnus, don't jump in his face the way you usually do. He's not your enemy." He opened the door and flicked his wrist instead of goodbye. "I hope to see you soon."

For a few seconds, Damian sat silently, staring at the closed white door. Then he got up with a groan and headed toward the bathroom.

* * *

THIRTY MINUTES LATER, he stood in front of a door with Magnus' name on it. He raised his hand to knock, but never ended up doing it. He didn't know how long he just stood there, trying to organize the disarray of thoughts in his mind. He tugged at the collar of his black uniform, moving his head from left to right as if it were suffocating him, and then finally raised his hand again, ready to knock this time.

"Commander Blake, come in already!" Magnus' deep voice shouted from behind the closed door. "I promise, I won't bite."

Damian winced at the sound of the familiar voice but pushed the door open and walked into a spacious white room, halting by the doorway. Magnus sat behind a large glass desk, leaning back in a tall office armchair, his arms resting on the soft, leather armrests. With the pure-white walls and the white leather furniture, his white robes blended in perfectly with the surroundings.

"Magnus," said Damian instead of a greeting.

Magnus' lips stretched into a one-sided smirk as he all but rolled his eyes at Damian's stubborn disregard of rules. "Dmitri," he replied, gesturing for him to take a seat. "I see some things never change."

Damian crossed the room and pulled out an office chair, lowering himself down. "I don't have a written report, sir," he said calmly. "But if you take a verbal—"

Magnus waved his hand dismissively. "I don't need your report," he said softly. He didn't sound angry or upset, just tired. "Archmage Allerton was here about an hour ago. He gave me a complete report. It's good enough for me."

Damian nodded, not sure what to say next.

"The Guardians restored all the wards and protection spells over Paradise Manor," continued Magnus. "You don't need to worry about River Evans anymore. Even though Mara is still at large"—he threw a pointed stare at Damian—"she's not my main concern at the moment."

"I'm sorry, sir," said Damian, shifting to the edge of his chair, ready to be reprimanded for his failure. "I pinned her with the dagger. I have no idea how she managed to wiggle her way out."

Magnus gave him a barely visible shake of his head, leaning forward to rest his arm on the desk. "Like I said—not my main concern now, Commander."

"What is then?" Damian swallowed hard, goosebumps rising on his arms. If a dark deity on the run wasn't Magnus' main concern, what could be more important.

"A few things. Your brother for one," he replied, pinning Damian with a heavy gaze.

"My brother? What about him?" His fingers squeezed the armrests, almost breaking them.

"He's the King now as you're well aware," replied Magnus, humorous twinkles igniting in his eyes. "I can probably call you the Kingmaker now. You pretty much placed a crown on his head by killing Roxana, Shadow Slayer."

Damian growled, eliciting soft laughter out of the Head of the Destiny Council.

"Yeah, I know about all of your shenanigans, Dmitri. I know every step you took since you became *no one*." He raised his hands in a placating manner, leaning back in his chair. "Relax. I'm not after your brother. Actually, it's the opposite. The Destiny Council and I want to support him."

"You could have fooled me," said Damian, his voice harsher than he intended. "For a thousand years, you made me believe my brother was dead. How could you?"

"He *is* dead, Dmitri—"

"He's *undead*!" yelled Damian, leaning forward, his power spiking around him. "And I could have been there for him to help him with the transition! You made me betray my only brother!"

Ignoring Damian's anger, Magnus took a deep breath and waved his hand, whispering a cloaking spell. As the yellowish glow of his spell filled the room, he straightened, breathing hard. He waved his hand again and muttered a couple of other cloaking spells. Once satisfied, he walked around the desk. Separating the front of his robe, he sat down on the edge of the desk, facing Damian.

"Look at me, my child," he said, a semblance of reproach in his soft voice.

Damian raised his head, meeting Magnus' blazing eyes.

"I did what I had to do to save you," the Head of the Destiny

Council continued. "I've been doing it through the centuries, my boy, even if I had to break a few rules in the process."

Damian averted his gaze, Cossack's words sounding in his mind. "Why?" he croaked. "Why me? I'm just another ancient warrior who died on a distant battlefield and was turned into a Destiny Enforcer."

"The paths of the Board of Destiny—," started Magnus, but Damian waved his hand impatiently, interrupting him.

"Give this crap to someone else, Magnus," he growled. "You all manipulate the Board to your advantage all the time."

"That's not true," objected Magnus quietly, sadness fogging his eyes. "As you know, manipulating the Board of Destiny is the greatest offense one can commit. The former member of the Head Council, Aramir, is imprisoned for doing that."

Damian pressed his lips into a stubborn line, leaning back in his chair.

"But I did that," whispered Magnus, his voice breaking. "I manipulated the Board of Destiny for you, Dmitri."

Damian's jaw dropped. "For me? But why?"

"To make sure that your crazy, entangled path would cross its way with your brother's, my boy," he replied. "To make sure that you both survived and met when the time was right. I know you were in pain and mad with grief when you agreed to the *no one* status, and I had to do whatever was necessary to keep you safe."

"I don't understand... Why—"

"Dmitri, I need you to support your brother's reign," said Magnus, slightly raising his voice. "I'm sorry, there are things I can't explain to you, but I'm begging you to trust me. I just admitted the most horrible crime I committed for you and your brother. I hope that deserves some level of trust between us?"

"Yes, my lord," replied Damian, not even realizing that he used the proper title addressing the Head of the Destiny Council.

"I'm sorry, my boy," continued Magnus. "I know I caused you a lot of pain through the years, and one day, I promise I'll explain why I did what I did. I ordered the Guardians Order to withdraw their support of Paradise Manor after Nicholas Evans had married River Vetrov. Then I had to manipulate the Board of Destiny to make sure you would move out from Florida and chose Arizona as your destination, and that you would cross your paths with Sam Vetrov. I led you..."

He stopped talking, a deep frown on his face showing his internal turmoil.

"What did you do, Magnus?" whispered Damian, barely able to breathe.

"I forced you into a situation where you had no choice but to drop the *no one* status," answered Magnus. "I'm deeply sorry for manipulating you, and for putting your brother in danger. It wasn't my intention, but when you started on your way to Arizona, it was Mara who convinced Roxana to abduct Cole. Even though the goddess of Nightmares didn't tell the Queen about your connection and the true reason behind her request, she hoped to use your brother as leverage against you later."

"But why did you do all that, Magnus?" asked Damian, throwing his hands up. "I understand you can't explain everything but give me at least something. You had to have a reason for all this madness."

"Something? Yeah, there is something..." Magnus rubbed his forehead, absentmindedly. "Your adventures with Mara and Morok was just the beginning, and it's nothing compared to what's coming. Is that enough for you?"

"Perun almighty," exhaled Damian, staring at him in shock. "Anything else you can tell me?"

"Yes," said Magnus. "I need Cole's Court to take the same direction as the Florida Vampire Court, or at least as the Nevada Vampire Court. I can't stress enough the importance of that."

"I'm sure that was his idea," replied Damian. "Cole summoned Akira Ida and Santiago del Castillo to witness his coronation proceeding. I guess that would confirm the direction he chose."

Magnus nodded, his gaze foggy and distant. "Only if you and your brother work together can you stop..." His voice trailed off, and he turned away, staring at an unblemished white wall, and Damian knew Magnus was at the point where he could say nothing more. The Head of the Destiny Council pressed his hand to his mouth and remained silent for a few long seconds, a vibe of unease lingering around him.

"What do you need me to do, my lord?" asked Damian. "I'm yours to command."

Magnus flinched slightly, as if Damian's voice woke him up from a terrible nightmare. "I want you to return to Paradise Manor and stay with River Evans," he said. "I hope you don't object to that?"

"No, I don't," replied Damian.

"I need you to support your brother and the local Wardens," he continued. "Are you fine with working with the Wardens Order?"

"Who's the Master Warden of Arizona?" asked Damian.

"Brother Luc de la Crosse. If it would make any difference to you, he helped Cole to communicate with the Zerkalitsa," replied Magnus, raising his eyebrows.

"I was just curious. Luc de la Crosse has a good reputation in the supernatural circles," said Damian. "But yes, I will do as you command. When do you want me to go back?"

"Now," replied Magnus, sadness shadowing his features. "You can spend a few hours with Adrian. I'm sure you two have a few things to talk about. But once you're done, I want you back in Paradise Manor as soon as possible."

Magnus got up and walked around the desk. Leaning down, he murmured something, drawing a rune on its surface. A clear box filled with a shimmering white light materialized in front of him.

Damian stared at the box, and his heart pounded, alarm ringing in his mind.

"Magnus, why?" he whispered, barely moving his lips. He remembered this box. This was the magical artifact they used to strip his powers. After everything Magnus just told him, it made no sense.

The Head of the Destiny Council raised his face and gave him a quick shake no, walking briskly around the table.

"It's not what you think, my boy," he said with a slight smile.

He leaned across the desk and touched the glowing contents of the box. As his fingers lit up with the strange energy, he turned back to Damian, pulled his shirt off his shoulder and drew a glowing rune on his upper arm. The rune slowly dissipated, and Damian sucked in a sharp breath as a powerful magical energy rushed through him.

"This is your new status," said Magnus, placing his hand on Damian's shoulder. "Effective immediately, you're my personal *Shadow Enforcer*. Since the supernatural community branded you with the word 'Shadow' anyway, may as well make it official." He smirked not without warmth, but quickly returned to the serious tone. "You know what it means, right?"

"Yes, my lord," Damian replied, rising. "It means I take orders directly from the Head of the Destiny Council, bypassing the entire chain of command, including the Destiny Keeper. For everyone else in the Destiny Enforcers organization, I don't exist. I have no team and I work alone."

"That's right. You're the second Commander who has ever been granted this status, Damian Blake," said Magnus, looking up at him. "You're free to go. Make me proud, son."

Still not quite sure what just happened, Damian inclined his head and walked out the door.

The paths of the Board of Destiny are truly unpredictable...

* * *

Blue Creek, Arizona

It was late evening when Damian materialized in front of the gates into the Brown's Estate. The sky was a velvety dark, and the thin sickle of the moon, surrounded by myriads of stars, shone brightly. The air was crisp with that jarring coolness that usually blanketed the desert in the evening as soon as the sun was gone.

Opening his second sight, he quickly scanned the property, searching for his brother. He detected him right away and was a little surprised to see Cole back in his house. The only thing he could think of was that Jesse either invited him in or did the deed transfer right away.

Staring at the crimson glow of Cole's vampiric energy on the roof of the building, Damian shuddered, cursing quietly. Shadow Enforcer or not, he was still a Child of Earth, and the farther he was from the ground, the weaker he felt. With a deep sigh, he snapped his fingers and teleported to the entrance of the house.

He pressed the doorbell button, and the door swung open right away. Ace glanced at him, her eyes widened, and she dropped to one knee.

"Commander Blake," she said, inclining her head.

"Would you cut that out?" grumbled Damian, yanking her to her feet. He walked inside, searching for the way to the roof. "I need to see Cole. How do I get to the rooftop?" He pointed up. "What's he doing there, anyway?"

"You'll see," said Ace with a mysterious smile. "There is more to your brother than meets the eye." She gestured for him to follow her upstairs.

That's what I'm afraid of...

As he stepped on the dark roof, the warm, low-pitched

sound of a cello enveloped him, and he stilled, staring at his brother in awe. Barefooted and with his shirt unbuttoned, Cole sat on a chair, slowly moving the bow over the strings, his soft, curly hair falling over his face. A sad sound of Albinoni's Adagio flowed through the air, the strings under his brother's fingers sounding like a human voice filled with despair.

He tiptoed his way to Cole and lowered himself to the floor. As quietly as he moved, Cole's vampiric senses detected his presence, and his lips curved up into a feline-like smile.

"Hello, brother," he said, lifting his face. "You're back. Should I be worried, my lord Enforcer?"

"The only thing you should worry about is me putting you on a timeout, little boy." Damian smirked. "I had no idea you played the cello."

"I play a few instruments," replied Cole, putting the cello away. "You know how it is—long life with nothing but time on your hands."

"Yeah, I have no idea," muttered Damian, rubbing the back of his neck. "The only thing I had time for was fighting and running—" He cut himself off, rising.

Cole got up to his feet, too. All cheerfulness left his sparkling eyes, and his features hardened.

"Dima, not everyone is on board with my agenda. Roxana's old supporters are not going to give up without a fight. Akira and Santiago are arriving tomorrow to assist me, and I must get ready. The war is coming, and I have to make sure it's not going to spill into the world of humans."

"Then we fight." A dark smile crossed Damian's features as he stepped closer, offering him his hand. "Do your thing, brother. I'm with you all the way. No matter what—"

"—We stand together." Cole squeezed his hand in a firm handshake, a furious scarlet glow igniting in his eyes. *"Brat moi..."*

Brother mine...

EXCERPT

*Read on for an excerpt from
N.M. Thorn's new book
The Shadow Enforcer Book 2:*

~ Damian Blake ~

**Somewhere on the outskirts of Phoenix, Arizona
Halloween night**

A giant orange moon hung low over the horizon. Its bright light made its way between the dusty window shutters, reflecting in the faded mirror above the bar counter, throwing playful flares at the multicolored liquor bottles.

The bar was relatively dark, illuminated only by the LED strip lights installed around the perimeter of the room and an old neon sign above the mirror with the name of the establishment—*The Midnight Shift*. A curtain of cigarette smoke flowed under the low ceiling, and its smell mixed in with the pungent odor of different liquors seemed to be permanently etched into everything around.

EXCERPT

Fake spider webs hung in every corner, spangled with plastic spiders and other creepy crawlers. A plastic pumpkin with a wide smile shining with electric light stood at the side of the counter, completing the Halloween decor.

Owned by one of the Phoenix packs, *The Midnight Shift* had recently been declared a sanctuary, allowing all local representatives of the supernatural community to relax and have a drink or two without being concerned for their lives and safety. A powerful turn-away spell placed on the building kept all mundanes untouched by the World of Magic away, and the local human hunters who were well aware of the bar's status normally avoided it. Despite his "professional" status, Damian liked this place and allowed himself to spend a few hours here once in a great while.

Damian twirled an empty shot glass between his fingers, a muscle twitching in his tightly pressed jaws. He reached for his phone just to see the dark screen without any new notifications.

"Come on, Cole," he murmured under his breath. "What's taking you so long?"

He put the phone back into the pocket of his light leather jacket, nibbling on his lip.

"One more?"

Damian glanced at the bartender and nodded, placing the shot glass back on the counter. The man was dressed in an orange, Halloween-themed shirt with a black cat that looked too cute for a person of his size and shape to wear in public. Damian lowered his eyes, the corners of his lips quirking up in a tiny smile. It wasn't only that the bartender was almost as tall as him, but he was also a werewolf, and a picture of a kitty in a pointy witch hat stretched across his overly muscled chest just didn't fit the bill.

The bartender filled another glass with vodka and placed it in front of him. Damian took it, rolling it between his thumb and middle finger.

"Thanks, Kaleb," he said to the werewolf. "Something tells me I may need another one later."

Kaleb flicked his eyebrow at him, and his one-sided smirk exposed a set of sharp, paper-white teeth shining with bluish shades of the LED lights.

"Hey, Damian, slow down." Jamie pushed him on his shoulder slightly to attract his attention. "Are you sure drinking is a good idea?"

"It takes a lot more for me to get drunk, Jamie," he muttered, emptying the contents of the shot glass into his mouth. "A lot more than a bottle of vodka, let alone two small shot glasses. I may as well be drinking water."

He glanced sideways at the young wizard and smirked. Nervousness was shining through Jamie's blue eyes, his fingers folding and unfolding a napkin.

"Listen, Jamie." Damian straightened, turning toward him slightly. "No offense, but you're not ready, man. I've been training you less than three months which is nothing when it comes to the World of Magic. It takes years to muster your spell casting and even longer to control your magic. Fire magic is supposed to be your strength, but you can barely light a candle."

"Oh, yeah?" said Jamie, his lips forming a stubborn straight line. "And Ace is ready? Your brother has no problem with her following him everywhere."

Damian drew in a long breath and knocked on the counter with an empty shot glass to attract Kaleb's attention. Normally, he didn't mind Ace tagging along with Cole. During the day, she worked at his company, and at nights, she attended all his royal meetings and Court gatherings. Even though she was very young as a person and had barely taken off her training wheels as a Destiny Enforcer, the Destiny Council considered her fit to shadow the King of Arizona, so he wasn't going to argue. Besides, protecting his brother had always been *his* job, so he didn't count on any outside help.

EXCERPT

Today, however, his nerves were on edge, and the presence of two young people who barely had any experience with real combat situations just added to his feeling of unease. Cole was in a meeting with the leaders of the largest opposing group of vampires, hoping to find common ground and convince them to join his Court. Knowing this particular faction, Damian had been against this meeting from the get-go, considering it to be as dangerous as it was useless. However, his brother had disagreed, trying to use diplomatic methods first before plunging the state into open warfare.

Kaleb filled another glass with vodka, moving it closer to him. Damian brought it up, inhaling the burning scent of the alcohol, and then downed it in one shot. Letting out a harsh breath, he turned back to Jamie.

"I'm not my brother," he said quietly, "and Ace is not my responsibility. But it's my responsibility to support Cole's position in the Vampire Court and make sure the war between different vampire factions is not going to affect the realm of humans. And that's exactly what I'm planning to do. If something goes wrong—"

His cellphone vibrated in his pocket, and he cut himself off, rising. He pulled the phone out and quickly read Cole's message on the screen.

"NO DICE 911"

Turning toward Jamie, he looked down at him and frowned. He wished the young wizard would change his mind and stay back, but there was no power in this world that would have talked him out of going.

"Last chance, Jamie," he said softly, his voice almost pleading. "Please, stay behind, my friend. You still have a lot to learn."

"Theory without practice is useless. Practice makes perfect," retorted Jamie, sounding like a high school student reporting in front of the class. He got up and adjusted his light jacket, checking his pockets.

"And don't forget the most famous one—buy low, sell high," muttered Damian snidely. "Any other quotes you'd like to share?" He reached into his pocket, pulled out his wallet, and threw a few bills on the counter. Stifling a sigh, he headed out of the bar, motioning for Jamie to follow him.

As soon as they stepped out the door, the cool evening air enveloped him, but Damian ignored the cold, his mind set on getting to his brother as soon as possible. Quickly surveying the area, he grunted. It was Halloween evening and despite the late hour, kids dressed like assorted monsters and superheroes promenaded the street accompanied by their parents. Laughing, chatting and having fun, they were none the wiser of the terrible territorial war unfolding in the shadows behind the well illuminated and decorated main street.

He turned the corner, leaving the main street behind. Hiding in the shadows, he made sure there was no one watching them. Then he placed his hand on Jamie's shoulder and snapped his fingers, teleporting them closer to the location of the meeting. Since he didn't know what kind of security measures the leaders of the opposing faction had taken, he teleported to a secluded location he'd selected ahead of time—a tiny dark alley located away from any major streets and a safe distance from their final destination.

As soon as they manifested in the alley, he switched to a light run, throwing an occasional glance over his shoulder to make sure Jamie was keeping up with him. Soon, the tiny suburban street turned into a narrow two-lane asphalt road. Curving its way around a few sandy hills, it left the peaceful suburbia on his right side.

The farther they moved, the colder and darker it became, and Damian had no doubt it wasn't just the night desert temperatures that sent shivers down his back. Sharpening his senses, the putrid stench of demonic essence assailed him, but besides the reek of sulfur, he could detect some other presence he couldn't identify. Dark and elusive, it seemed vaguely familiar, yet he couldn't put his finger on it.

Damian pressed the back of his hand to his nose and mouth, slowing down to allow Jamie to catch up with him. The young man halted by his side and leaned forward, bracing his arms against his lap to catch his breath.

"For an old man, you sure know how to run," he said, panting. Looking up, he shook his head and straightened, wiping sweat off his forehead. "Why are we here, anyway? Farther, just around this hill..." He waved to the left at the dark silhouette of a mountain, still breathing hard. "It's Camelback mountain... Expensive homes... in the millions..."

"I figured as much. Old vamps and their money," murmured Damian. "This entire area emanates hostility and dark magical energy." He thought for a moment, staring at his young companion, and added, "Be careful. Chances are, once we breach the perimeter, I may not be able to protect you."

Quickly crossing the road, Damian switched to a light jog, following the road circling the hill. A view of a beautiful, contemporary estate perched on a hillside unfolded before him, and he halted again, quickly scanning it with his second sight. It was surrounded by black wrought iron fencing but only from three sides as the back of it was blocked by the hill. Tall double gates were locked, but as far as he could see, no one was guarding the entry and that just threw a countless number of red flags in his mind.

A thick layer of protective magic lingered around the perimeter of the property, and runes glowing with a deep purple light were inscribed on the fence and the gates, indicating the presence of powerful wards.

I can't break through these wards without triggering some kind of reaction and an alarm. Damian explored the fence as far as he could see but didn't find even one weak point. He looked up just to realize that he couldn't go over the fence either—a thin net of glowing lines encapsulated the entire estate, crisscrossing and shimmering with purple light like some freakishly large spider web.

"Jamie..." He glanced to the side where Jamie was supposed to be, but he wasn't there. Damian twirled around and found him by the gates. "Jamie, no!" he yelled, but it was too late.

The young wizard reached forward and touched the gates. The wards lit up brighter, responding with a soft, barely noticeable vibration. Seemingly, nothing changed, but Damian knew better. In one swift motion, he grabbed Jamie, pulled him away from the gates and turned him around, shielding him with his body.

"Procedia Amnia!" he shouted the basic protection spell, channeling the elemental energy into his magic to reinforce it. Just as the shield glowing with a dim yellow light surrounded them, a powerful surge of dark magical energy exploded outward from somewhere within the property lines. It traveled as fast as a blast wave, lifting clouds of sand and tiny pebbles into the air. Damian growled as the dark energy impacted his shield, his arms shaking with tremendous strain. Jamie bent down, wrapping his arms around his head.

The wave moved a few feet farther and dissipated on its own. Without removing the protective shield, Damian turned around in place, staring at the wards in shock. The lines in the sky and runes over the gates and fences shone brighter than before, the air around them vibrating with a low buzz.

"What the hell was that?" mumbled Jamie, straightening.

"Wards," replied Damian, breathing hard. "You activated the wards that were placed on this property."

"Sorry," whispered the young man, looking as guilty as a dog who had stolen a piece of juicy chicken. "What now?"

"Now, since the element of surprise is no longer an option, we make an entry," replied Damian, channeling as much magic toward his hands as he could. "And we fight. No matter what we find behind this overpriced fence."

"But we don't know what—"

"I don't give a damn. My brother is in there. I'll kill anything that gets in my way." He thrust his arm forward, his body igniting with the bright orange glow of the elemental energy he was wielding, and shouted, *"Exitius!"*

The gates blew up, turning into warped chunks of metal, and the ground shook, the tremors spreading around Damian in rapid succession. He stepped heavily over the threshold created by his magic and looked up, a dark smirk curving his lips. The glowing web of wards was gone, but the cloud of gray particles was slowly rotating above the ground.

"I suggest you run," he hissed at Jamie and moved toward the entrance into the house, following the beautifully paved driveway up the hill.

Even though the driveway lights were still glowing, and the windows of the house were shining with bright, electric lights, the closer he got to the entrance, the darker it became. As the driveway started to curve sharply, multiple shady figures emerged from the night, the hostile vibes of demonic presence unmistakable around them.

Damian didn't slow down. As his daggers materialized in his hands, he cut into the first demon who was close enough for him to reach. A ray of eye-watering white light pierced the demon's body, obliterating the host and the demonic essence before the demon could shimmer out.

"Igneous," yelled Jamie, but instead of a fire blast, a tiny flickering flame ignited in the palm of his hand, making the demon he was facing bark with laugher. The monster swung his hairy arm, aiming at Jamie's face. His massive fist was met by Damian's hand. Wrapping the demon's fist with his fingers, Damian applied some pressure, making the attacker stagger backward.

"Pick someone your own size, asshole," he growled at the

demon, squeezing his fingers tighter. Then he turned to Jamie, and his lips curved into a snarl. "Let me show you how it's done, student of mine." Extending his free hand forward, he shouted, *"Ignius Orbus."*

A fireball crackling with blistering flames materialized in his palm. With lightning speed, he thrust the fireball into the demon's chest and let go. The monster screamed in pain, twirling in place, setting other demons on fire.

"Igneous Amplio!" Damian held out both his hands, and a powerful jet of physical fire erupted from his palms, spraying the remaining monsters. He turned back to Jamie, his chest shuddering with ragged breaths. "That's how it's done, boy."

Jamie nodded, his mouth half-open, his eyes glued to the screaming monsters being devoured by the hungry flames. "But you just killed a bunch of people," he exhaled. "Their souls could have still been inside their—"

"I don't have the luxury of caring about it right now," growled Damian, heading toward the entrance door, but noticing the shock on the young wizard's face, he sighed and added, "It was either them or us. Besides, I can see human souls with my second sight. They had none. Just monsters wearing dead human bodies."

He halted in front of the door and scanned the building inside with his magical sight as far as he could reach. Glancing back at his companion, his lips pulled up into a sneer before he could stop it.

"Now the real fun begins," he whispered, channeling his magic toward his hands. "Vampires. Deadly, clever, merciless. Don't get cute with them, Jamie. Stay back and let me do all the talking."

Instead of blasting the door with his spell, he placed his hand on the lock and whispered, *"Recludius."*

The lock clicked softly, leaving the entrance unprotected. As his daggers materialized in his hands, he pulled his leg back and kicked the door open. The door hit the wall with a thunderous bang and the sound carried through the enormous marble-adorned lobby, reverberating against the tall ceiling.

As soon as Damian crossed the threshold, something heavy crashed on his shoulders, and a cold, muscled arm wrapped around his neck, squeezing it with the strength of an industrial press. A strong hand forced his hand to the side, and before he could react, raiser-sharp fangs penetrated his skin.

A wild roar broke from his lips as he grabbed the unfortunate vamp's head and twisted it, ripping it off his shoulders. A shower of gray ashes fell to his feet, and he raised his glowing eyes, his second sight revealing the position of every single vampire in the room.

"Jamie, stay outside," he ordered without looking back, "it's about to get..." He laughed and moved forward, the daggers in his hands blazing.

All the vampires came into motion at the same time, assailing him from every direction. Silent and fast, Damian spun around, his daggers slicing through the vampires' bodies, severing limbs and cutting their heads off. Leaving piles of steaming ash behind, the attackers pulled back, shock in their glowing scarlet eyes.

"What happened?" Damian snickered, cocking his head slightly. "Are you done?" The vampires froze in that unnerving way only vampires could, waiting for his next move. "What? Already? No stamina, eh?" He dropped to one knee, placing his hand on the marble floor, and a wild smile crossed his face—the marble was natural. *Got to love these rich undead assholes...*

Rising, he waved his arm, the air around him vibrating with the deadly magic he was channeling. "Well, I barely warmed up, boys."

The vamps hissed, leaping into action again.

"*Risurgius!*" he yelled, moving forward. He ripped two

massive blocks of marble off the floor and blocked both doors, barricading all ways in and out of the lobby.

Damian wasn't moving as fast as the vampires, but he didn't have to. Now that the vampires had no place to hide and no way to escape, he knew he had them exactly where he wanted them. Halting in the middle of the lobby, he allowed the monsters to surround him. As they started to squeeze the circle, he spread his arms, and the floor shook violently, deep fractures marring perfectly polished marble. The vampires hissed like a bunch of wild cats, retreating again.

He clenched his hands into fists and twisted them. The fractures grew wider, spreading farther and farther, pushing the vampires toward the walls. Once they had no more space to run, Damian touched the leather bracelet with his fingers, and it turned into a silver bullwhip. He moved around with the fluidity of a dancer, the fractures closing beneath his feet and reopening once he was gone. The whip in his hand cut through the air with a soft whistle, striking vampires with deadly precision. A few seconds later, it was over, the last remains of the attackers slowly dissolving into ashes.

Damian stopped, breathing hard. With his other sight opened, he probed the area ahead but didn't find vampires or demons. He could still detect some vampiric energy in the building, but it was weak, barely detectible.

"Cole," he breathed out, a feeling of dread settling in the pit of his stomach.

Connecting with the power of Earth once again, he moved the blocks of marble out of the way, allowing Jamie to come in. The young man passed the doorway and halted, observing the lobby with the warped marble floor covered in a thick layer of ash, awe in his eyes.

"I'm afraid to ask," he mumbled. "How many?"

Damian shrugged, wrapping the whip around his wrist, turning it back into the bracelet.

EXCERPT

"Sorry. I had no time for math exercises." Motioning for Jamie to follow him, he ran through the dimly lit hallway. With all his senses focused on Cole's dimming presence, he knew exactly where he needed to go. Soon, the hallway came to a dead-end in front of a tall glass door. Without slowing down, he pushed the door open and crossed into a large living area.

Every piece of furniture in the room was either moved, turned upside down or destroyed. The floor was slippery with blood, covered in ash and dead bodies, undoubtedly demons. At the far end of the room, he saw his brother. Cole lay on the floor, his hands clutching the blade of a sword protruding from his chest. Ace lay next to him, her blood-coated sword on the floor by her side. Her eyes were closed, blood still seeping from a wound on her neck.

"No," moaned Jamie, his grief-infused voice ripping Damian out of his momentary stupor.

Damian crossed the room, dropping to his knees next to his brother. Opening his second sight, he checked Ace and exhaled with relief. She was still alive—barely, but alive. His gaze darted to Cole. He gently unlocked his bloodied fingers and explored the wound.

At his touch, Cole's eyes opened, and his lips twitched slightly, blood dripping from the corner of his mouth. Meeting Damian's gaze, he smiled weakly, his lips forming just two words, *"Brat moi..."*

Brother mine...

TEASER: THE BURNS FIRE
(THE FIRE SALAMANDER CHRONICLES BOOK 1)

~Zane Burns, a.k.a. Gunz~
Modern Day, South Florida

The restaurant was nothing special, just another tiny hole-in-the-wall located on one of the countless South Florida canals. There wasn't anything noteworthy about its limited menu either. The only thing special about this place was its relaxed atmosphere. The restaurant had an open porch with three tables facing the canal. But the regulars were never sitting on the porch. They preferred to stay inside, leaving the romantic view to tourists and lovey-dovey couples.

Gunz had discovered this place shortly after he moved to South Florida, and since then he had become one of the regulars, visiting the restaurant at least a couple of times a week. He liked the laid-back atmosphere and easy-going crowd. It was a place where he allowed himself to relax and drop his guard. To a degree.

The inside room of the restaurant wasn't big, just a few tables and a bar. A big screen TV was hanging on the wall behind the bar, next to a few shelves with liquor. The air was infused with the smell of alcohol and fried food, and a heavy curtain of cigarette smoke was hanging under the ceiling. The room was relatively dark. Out of six wall lights only three were on, but no one ever asked to turn up the light.

Gunz walked through the room, quickly surveying every corner, and sat down at the bar. Tonight, besides a few regulars, there was no one new. A pretty young woman in her mid-twenties approached him right away. Here, she was everything—the owner of the restaurant, a bartender, a waitress—all-in-one, cross-functional queen of *Missi's Kitchen*.

"Usual, Mr. Burns?" she asked, smiling at him. Her skin, the color of dark chocolate, was smooth like silk and her large gray eyes framed with thick black eyelashes looked unnaturally bright on her face. Her long black hair was braided into countless thin braids and pulled into a ponytail on the back of her head, calling attention to her elegant neck.

"Yes, Missi, thank you," said Gunz.

She put three small shot glasses on the bar table in front of him and filled them with vodka. "I'll be back with your food in a moment," she told him, heading toward the kitchen door.

"Take your time, Missi," muttered Gunz, picking up the first shot glass. "I'm not in any rush tonight." He took a deep breath and downed the vodka without flinching. Placing the empty shot glass on the table, he exhaled and closed his eyes, enjoying the feeling of the harsh burning liquid rushing down his throat.

For a few minutes, he sat quietly staring at the TV. It was set to the local news channel, but he didn't listen to the news, his thoughts far away. Then he sighed and picked up the second shot glass. He gulped the vodka and put the empty glass next to the first one.

"Hard day, Mr. Burns?" asked Missi, placing a plate with a burger and steaming pile of french fries in front of him. "You seem to look broodier than usual."

Gunz smirked. He picked up a hot french fry with his fingers and nibbled on it. "You could say so," he said finally. "Just one of those days... This day a couple of years ago, I lost... someone."

"Your friend?" asked Missi, gazing at him with sympathy in her bright eyes.

"Yeah... friend. Vladislav Kirilenko," he replied absentmindedly, taking the next burning-hot fry from his plate. "I lost him to the world of magic. He's never coming back."

"*The World of Magic*," she repeated in disbelief, her eyebrows rising. "What is that? A fantasy novel? There is no such thing as magic. You're making fun of me, Mr. Burns." She shook her head, a soft smile tugging at her full lips.

Gunz smiled tiredly and picked up the last shot glass, squeezing it in his fist. "Third one for the fallen," he murmured and drank it quickly, returning the empty glass to Missi. "You know, Missi, I've been coming to your restaurant for over a year. Don't you think it's time you stop calling me *Mr. Burns*? I don't think I'm that much older than you. You know that you can call me Zane, or even Gunz, if you prefer to use my nickname."

"I know. I don't like nicknames. You're a man, not a pet," she said lightly, taking away the empty shot glasses and wiping the tabletop with a white towel. "Zane Burns..." She pronounced his name slowly, like she was sizing it up. "Sounds good, but I prefer to call you Mr. Burns. For some reason, it seems to fit you better."

Gunz felt someone's hand on his elbow and a hardly noticeable wave of magical energy swept through him. He snapped his head to the right and found a fake blond sitting next to him. She was devouring him with her eyes, her lipstick-enhanced lips stretched in a sensual smile. Her hand unceremoniously traveled up his arm, following the shape of his biceps, and stopped at his shoulder.

"Yum," she said, gently probing him with her magic. "I'll call you anything you want, hon."

Gunz gave her a frosty once-over, turning his senses up. He had no doubt that she was something other than human. Her fingers softly massaged his shoulder, sending a stronger wave of magical energy through him. For a moment, his mind became clouded with desire and his body responded to her salacious magic with more eagerness than he expected.

Succubus, concluded Gunz, channeling the Fire, burning the poison of her magic out of his body. Her hand traveled down his arm, landing on his inner thigh. He seized her wrist, prying it off his leg and sent some fire toward his hand. Her skin blistered like from the touch of a hot stove and she yelped in pain.

"Who are you? What are you?" she whimpered, trying to free herself from his smoldering grip, but he didn't let her go.

Gunz glanced around, making sure that no one, including Missi, was watching. "I'm a man who is not looking for company," he growled, sending some fire toward his eyes. The bright flames went up in the depths of his eyes, and she gasped. "Especially not the company of your kind." He released her wrist, observing red spots of burns and blisters on her skin. "Leave this place and forget about its existence. You understand?"

She nodded, fear making her every move jerky, and rushed out of the restaurant, nursing her burnt wrist. Gunz sighed, releasing the Fire, and turned back to the bar.

"Hey, Missi," he called and waited a moment as she appeared from the kitchen. "Can I have everything to go, please? And one more before I leave." He pointed at the bottle of Russian vodka that he usually ordered.

She put a shot glass on the bar table and filled it with vodka. "That's unusual," she murmured, her hands quickly packaging the burger and fries into a take-out box. "You never drink more than three shots."

A lopsided smile crossed his face, making a single dimple

appear on one of his cheeks. "I know. Usually three shots are my limit, but today I felt like I needed more." He downed the vodka and got up, grabbing the take-out box.

Missi shook her head, checking him with concern. "Do you want me to call you a cab?"

"Thank you, Missi. I'll walk. Take care." He nodded to her and walked out of the restaurant.

Gunz walked away from the restaurant and turned into a dark alley. He stopped and rubbed his forehead tiredly. *Maybe Missi was right. I didn't need that fourth shot,* he thought, smirking. It had been a while since he felt drunk and right now the world around him seemed to be unsteady. Possibly it was a combination of vodka with the residuals of the succubus magic. He surveyed the alley carefully to make sure that no one could see him and once satisfied, he waved his hand, unfolding the fire curtain of a portal.

He walked through the fire and ended up in the backyard of his house in Coral Springs. The house wasn't really his. It belonged to his friend, but she was away and wasn't planning to come back any time soon. In the meantime, Gunz had the full use of her house. Dizziness assailed him as he took a step forward. He chuckled and sat down heavily on the steps in front of the back door.

He closed his eyes and leaned his back against the door of the house, still feeling a little buzzed. He was about to get up when he felt a soft touch to his leg. Gunz looked down and noticed a small kitten. It couldn't have been more than a month old. The kitten was trying to climb on his lap, its tiny sharp claws catching the hard fabric of his jeans.

"Oh, hello, little buddy. What are you doing here?" said Gunz. He put the take-out box on the steps and gently picked up the kitten, holding it in his hands. The kitten turned on his engine, purring loudly, and licked his hand. Gunz laughed, gently stroking the kitten's thick gray fur with his fingers. "You found the wrong man, little buddy. I'm a dog person—give me a giant German Shepherd any day. Well, occasionally, I don't mind dealing with lizards. But cats…"

The kitten ignored his statement and climbed up his shirt, settling on his shoulder. He meowed into his ear and poked his cheek with his wet nose. Gunz petted the kitten, leaving him sitting on his shoulder, and picked up the take-out box. "Well, you're taking your life in your own paws, buddy… but if you're sure that you want to adopt a man like me then let's get going." He unlocked the door and walked into the kitchen.

Inside, Gunz put the kitten on the floor and opened the refrigerator. He poured some milk in a small bowl and placed it in front of him.

"Sorry, little buddy, I don't have any cat food or litter for you"—he quickly glanced at the wall clock that was showing past one in the morning—"and it's too late for shopping. I'll buy everything you need first thing in the morning."

The kitten ignored him, preoccupied with his milk. Gunz squatted next to him and softly stroked his back. The kitten moved closer to his bowl and growled defensively. Gunz laughed, rising. "I think I'll call you Mishka in honor of my good friend. You sure remind me of him."

He left the kitten in the kitchen and walked to the living room. His body was buzzing with the exhaustion of this endless day and the incident with the succubus didn't sit well with him. Missi's restaurant was normally free of supernatural visitors. He was probably the only one. And the succubus' behavior seemed a bit odd too. Until he used his power, she didn't sense the creature of magic in him. Something didn't feel right.

His cell phone rang, making him flinch. He pulled it out and

TEASER: THE BURNS FIRE

looked at the display. Jim. *One o'clock in the morning? That can't be good.* He clicked the green button, answering the call.

"Hello, Jim," he said and fell silent for a few seconds, listening to Jim. "You want me to come over now? Can it wait till morning?"

He lowered the phone down for a moment and sighed, bringing the shouting device back to his ear.

"No, I'm not drunk. Just a little—," Jim interrupted him urgently, obviously not pleased and Gunz fell silent again, listening to his boss. "Yes, sir, I know the consequences of losing control of my power and I assure you, I'm in complete control."

Gunz lowered himself on the couch, rubbing the stubble on his chin tiredly.

"Yes, sir, I know that my job doesn't have weekends and days off," he said, hoping to calm Jim down. "I'm sorry, sir, I needed to unwind a little... I'm not drunk..."

He had been working with Agent Andrews for over a year and he had never heard him talking like this to him. Something serious was going on.

"Yes, sir, I know what Code Shadow means... I understand the urgency of the situation... No, sir. You don't need to summon me."

Jim didn't have magic and he couldn't use summoning spells, but his partner, Angelique, could. She was a witch and a seer. Gunz hated when they used summoning spells to call him. The persistent pull of the summoning spell on his mind was driving him crazy, giving him a pounding headache afterwards.

"I prefer not to drive right now, so I'll open my portal to your office right away, if you don't mind... Yes, sir, to Angelique's office... I'll see you both in a few minutes."

Gunz hung up the phone and shook his head, biting his lip. Code Shadow. It meant an abnormally high level of supernatural activity, endangering civilian lives. Since he started to work with the secret division of the FBI, dealing with supernatural occurrences, it was the first time that Code Shadow was officially issued.

"Fire Salamander—go," he muttered to himself and waved his hand, opening the fire portal into Angelique's office.

* * *

Get your copy of The Burns Fire online.

DEAR READER

Thank you so much for reading The Shadow Enforcer. I hope you enjoyed the book and will join Damian Blake's next adventure in the second book of the series.

If you would like to stay up-to-date on the latest information about new releases, special offers, and more, sign up for my mailing list and get a FREE novella—www.nmthorn.com.

For more information follow me on

Facebook (www.facebook.com/nmthornauthor)
Instagram (www.instagram.com/nmthornauthor)
Or visit my website www.nmthorn.com
Join N.M Thorn's readers group to meet other readers, discuss the novels and the characters, get updates and do anything else related to the series.
www.facebook.com/groups/authornmthorn

BEFORE YOU GO...

Your reviews mean the world to me and are greatly appreciated. If you enjoyed the Shadow Enforcer, please take a few minutes to leave a review. It doesn't have to be long. It can be just a few words or stars rating.

Please help spread the word by taking this small extra step and leave your review on Amazon and/or Goodreads.

ALSO BY N. M. THORN

The Fire Salamander Chronicles

The Burns Path (Prequel Novella Book 0 - for my subscribers)

The Burns Fire - Book 1

The Burns War - Book 2

The Burns Defiance - Book 3

The Burns Codex - Book 4

The Burns Enigma - Book 5

The Burns Destiny - Book 6

The Shadow Enforcer Series

The Shadow Enforcer - Book 1

ABOUT THE AUTHOR

N.M. Thorn currently lives in South Florida with her husband and son. Owner of a digital marketing agency by day and a writer by night, she loves spending her times creating new worlds, paranormal planes of existence and anything that could be described as supernatural.

When she is not busy working with everything digital or exploring fantasy worlds, she enjoys spending time with her family, reading, painting and practicing martial arts.

If you would like to share your thoughts, ideas or just send N.M. Thorn a message about the Fire Salamander World, feel free to contact her at: nmthornauthor@gmail.com

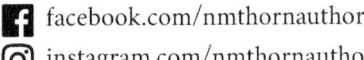

facebook.com/nmthornauthor
instagram.com/nmthornauthor

Printed in Great Britain
by Amazon